THE
TESLA
GATE

JOHN D. MIMMS

OPEN ROAD

INTEGRATED MEDIA

NEW YORK

This edition published in 2014 by Open Road Integrated Media, Inc.
345 Hudson Street
New York, NY 10014
www.openroadmedia.com

For John and Emma Lou Tyler, Darrell and Bonnie Mimms, and Sue Ann Ettman. Your love and kindness are now impalpable to the world, but will forever live in the hearts and memories of those that knew and loved you.

TABLE OF CONTENTS

CHAPTER 1: Nightmares 1

CHAPTER 2: Absent Birthday 8

CHAPTER 3: The Sign..17

CHAPTER 4: Seth 23

CHAPTER 5: Chockit Berries 34

CHAPTER 6: The Boss 42

CHAPTER 7: Boundless Limitations..50

CHAPTER 8: Rattling Bridges...60

CHAPTER 9: Father Wilson 70

CHAPTER 10: Unseen Developments......................................78

CHAPTER 11: On the Road 87

CHAPTER 12: The Birds of Fiddler Park.................................97

CHAPTER 13: Vacancy 106

CHAPTER 14: Jackson 116

CHAPTER 15: The Prodigal Guide...125

CHAPTER 16: The Search for Shasta 135

CHAPTER 17: Tears of the Recently Departed........................143

CHAPTER 18: Mother's Love 153

CHAPTER 19: The Road Less Travelled 163

CHAPTER 20: Hostage..172

CHAPTER 21: Officer Pace..181

CHAPTER 22: Lost and Found 190

CHAPTER 23: Haven 199

CHAPTER 24: Tommy and Abe...209

CHAPTER 25: Capital Secrets..217

CHAPTER 26: Historical Significance 226

CHAPTER 27: Morning Guests 235

CHAPTER 28: The Other Side 244

CHAPTER 29: Playmate..254

CHAPTER 30: Across the Mall 264

CHAPTER 31: The Plan 272

CHAPTER 32: Journey's End..282

CHAPTER 33: The Shredder 289

"Genocide is an attempt to exterminate a people, not to alter their behavior."

~ Jack Schwartz

PROLOGUE

"Though free to think and act, we are held together,
like the stars in the firmament, with ties inseparable.
These ties cannot be seen, but we can feel them."

~ Nikola Tesla

The day the storm hit, the world was changed forever.

Its severity would not be measured in property damage or loss of life, although the latter could be argued. This storm's impact turned man's beliefs completely upside down; the social upheaval would be worse than the aftermath of any storm in history.

Though this storm did not bring hurricane force winds, driving rain, cyclones or even floods, its effects would be far more subtle ... but the impact every bit as palpable. This storm had unique origins and, unlike most weather events, it was not relegated to one geographic area. Indeed it covered the entire planet; no one was left unaffected.

Living or dead.

CHAPTER I
NIGHTMARES

"Many of our daydreams would darken into nightmares,
were there a danger of their coming true!"

~Logan Pearsall Smith

I had the dream again last night. It was a recurring nightmare worse than any monster I could conjure in my sleeping brain as a child. I have been an adult now for a number of years, but time and experience don't make our nightmares any less terrifying; in some ways it makes them more real.

As the father of a mischievously precocious six-year-old boy, I share the same fear as a multitude of parents, a fear that their child may one day disappear. This worry seems more and more justified each day with another smiling angelic face on the news, snatched from their innocent existence by another real life monster. These monsters are not the ones under the bed, a product of juvenile imaginings. No, these monsters are real, and they could live next door; a fact that makes them all the more terrifying.

The dream always starts the same. I am at McCain Mall with my wife, Annabelle, and my son, Seth. The Pendleton family on another carefree family outing on a lazy Sunday afternoon. Ann is excited about looking for some new place settings and Seth is bursting at the seams to invade the toy store downstairs.

"Which color do you prefer, Thomas, blue or yellow?" Ann asks me with her usual resplendent smile.

I have no opinion on the matter and frankly I couldn't care less. I would never let her know that, though. Her thick chestnut hair bobs up and down as she bounces along with enthusiasm. She had not worn her hair that long since before Seth was born, but in the dream it did not seem unusual at all, even though her hair had only been shoulder length for years. Maybe that is just the image I hold of her in my mind: the long-haired, button-nosed, athletic beauty that I had fallen in love with in college. She is still just as attractive to me now, and even in my dream it gave me great pleasure to see her happy smile radiate her delicate features.

"Whatever you pick will be perfect, honey," I said squeezing her hand. "You are always good at that. I'm just color blind."

I really wasn't, but I might as well be when it comes to fashion and furnishings. Ann smiled proudly and gave me a quick peck on the cheek. This was not our typical family outing. Our together time, while rare, was pleasant but with less Norman Rockwell family perfection. I guess you could say we were typical.

Seth's excitement finally exploded.

"Come on, Daddy, come on!" he pleads, tugging at my arm.

"Just a minute, son," I say as a power tool display catches my eye.

I don't know why I am so drawn to it. I stare in inexplicable amazement as the powerful features of the tool are demonstrated on a small video screen. I am oblivious to anything and everything around me. The new project possibilities are endless. Nothing else matters. I guess that is why I barely noticed that Seth had quit tugging on my arm.

At what seemed to take a forceful effort, I pulled my gaze away from the display and looked down for Seth.

He was gone.

A clammy hand grasped my hammering heart as I looked about wildly for my son. He was nowhere to be seen in any direction.

"Seth!" I called as I dazedly began to walk toward the escalator to the lower level. He was at the toy store, he had to be.

I glanced at the clerk working the counter of the power tool display, it was my boss, Don Lewis, but then again, it wasn't him. It was one of those weird oddities that seem to present themselves so often in dreams. He was a no name clerk but also my boss at the same time. As creepy as that is, it wasn't nearly as troubling as the knowing grin he gave me as I walked toward the escalator. It sent a pang of terror up my spine; I knew something was wrong, something terrible … something unimaginable.

Panic filled my guts and I began to run.

I leapt down the escalator, jumping three steps at a time. I almost bounced over the side but managed to hang on and resume my mad dash to the bottom. As I sprinted toward the toy store the crowd seemed to inexplicably grow as if a thousand people had suddenly flooded into the mall at the same time. My progress was impeded causing my anxiety to rise to breathless frustration.

The bottom level of the mall was not the way I remembered it. It seemed to be completely occupied by tool stores and candy shops. When I reached the place where I knew the toy store was, there was nothing but a brick wall. A single small metal sign hung on the smooth brown surface. The message on the sign read mockingly: *Lost?*

I spun about madly looking for the store, but all I could see was a wall of people closing in, expanding, and undulating. I felt like a tired swimmer caught up in an undertow. Just when I thought I was going to be engulfed and swept away in the throng, I spotted the sign of the toy store in the distance. It was not where it was supposed to be, but it was there and there is where Seth had to be. With renewed vigor, I bolted through the crowd knocking people and my manners to the side.

After what seemed like an eternity of struggling, I finally reached the entrance to the toy store. I stopped cold at what I saw; it was as if an invisible fist had been slammed into my stomach. The metal security gate barred the entrance to the store, separating its dark interior from the brightly lit mall. A sign hung on the gate that read: *Closed for Remottling*. It seems like an odd message to have on a sign, but to me it made perfect sense; that is exactly how Seth would have pronounced *remodeling*. That misspelled sign sent a reinforcing jolt of alarm through me.

"Where the hell is my son?" I half-breathed and half-croaked as I peered into the dark cavity beyond the gate. From the ambient light of the mall I could see that the shelves were all fully stocked; it was as if the store had just been closed for the evening.

I staggered backward absently and was knocked to the marble tile floor by a passing horde of teenagers. As I pulled myself to my feet, I happened to look up the level above. My heart lifted as I saw Ann peering down at me from over the railing. I tried to call out to her but no sound would issue from my throat. It was if I had no air in my lungs to help form the words. Ann didn't say anything but looked down at me with the saddest expression I have ever seen on her face. Her sorrowful look, coupled with my sudden muteness, was nearly overwhelming as my desperation to find Seth tortured me without mercy. It has been a long-held belief that one cannot feel pain in dreams. That may be so in a physical sense but, emotionally, dreams can hurt like hell.

My torturous desperation was soon accompanied by rage as my boss, Don Lewis, aka mall clerk, walked up beside Ann and looked down at me with a damnable knowing grin. His devilish smile made my blood run cold but I did not have time to consider this; a moment later I heard Seth's faint voice.

"Daddy?" he called, sounding distant.

I froze, looking about madly. I heard the voice again, this time a little more distantly.

"Daddy?"

I'm not sure how I knew but this time I realized it was coming from somewhere deep in the toy store. I ran forward and grasped the gate, jerking up, down and side to side. It would not budge.

"Daddy?" even more faintly, like he was slowly walking away down a long tunnel.

"Seth!" I yelled as I redoubled my efforts to open the gate. I listened as I struggled but did not hear him again.

I summoned up all my strength and pushed as hard as I could while letting out one last desperate yell.

"Seth!"

With a deafening roar the gate gave way, bringing the ceiling down on top of me. I continued to wildly call Seth's name as debris rained down on my head. I was startled to feel someone take my face in her hands and kiss me on the cheek.

"Thomas, you're dreaming again … wake up."

It was Ann, and when I opened my eyes I was lying in my bed in a damp ring of sweat. As reality started to flood back over me, I turned red with embarrassment.

"Again?" I asked, sheepish.

"Yes, you were calling out for Seth again. He's all right, he's safe."

I smiled faintly and looked at my wife. Her heart-wrenching expression of sadness from my dream thankfully was not present, but her wrinkled brow clearly relayed her worry. I squeezed her hand and kissed her on the cheek.

"Okay," I said swinging my legs over the side of the bed. "I just need a drink of water."

That was not a lie. I was thirsty, but my primary intention was to check on my sleeping son. I walked across the upstairs landing to Seth's bedroom, which was directly across from ours. I gingerly opened the door and looked inside. The faint glow of the street light outside was just enough to reveal that he was sleeping peacefully; a ring of *Star Wars* action figures on his bedside table stood guard like miniature sentinels.

My first impulse, like every other time I have had this nightmare, was to enter the room and give him a kiss. But that was selfish, because I wasn't giving him comfort; I was giving it to myself. I had woken him up accidentally the first couple of times, and that never went well. He was like me; once he had been awakened, he had a hard time getting back to sleep.

I gently closed the door and carefully walked down the stairs to the kitchen. After filling a glass with ice water in the refrigerator door dispenser I sat down at the table and stared absently out the window. I couldn't help but consider the same thought that I have had so many times before.

Can dreams be prophetic?

I didn't think so. I am not a superstitious man and would have to classify myself as casually religious. I know that Joseph in the Old Testament interpreted dreams for Pharaoh, but I am no Joseph. I have no clue what the nightmare means or could mean, or if it even means anything at all. I just know that it scares the hell out of me. The one comforting thought I have is that I have had nightmares all my life in some form or fashion, but none of them have ever come to pass … thank God. I had quite an imagination as a child. Some might have even called me a bit twisted.

Whether I believed it to be a divination or not, no matter how hard I tried to bury it, the thought was still there in the back of my brain fighting for attention. I looked at the clock; it was 4:15 A.M. There was no point in going back to bed, it would take me an hour to go back to sleep and I get up at six anyway. I went back upstairs and got in the shower. I was taking Seth to school and picking him up today. I decided that once I was showered and dressed, I would make him a special breakfast of scrambled eggs and Chocolate Berry cereal, his favorite breakfast combo.

I splashed hot water on my face and stepped under the showerhead, ready to wash the monsters away. It felt good and soothing, and after a few moments I was able to relax and direct my thoughts to my plans for the coming day for a while. Shortly, my thoughts drifted back to my dream. I guess it was unavoidable but I tried to put a positive spin on it.

As the steamy water washed over my head and back, I smiled at the memory of a song my granny used to sing to me as a child when I had bad dreams.

Take a good shower every day and keep the monsters away
Eat your veggies and do what's right, and you will have no bad
dreams at night
Mind your parents and teachers, too, and sleep will be peaceful
for you

I considered the comforting words this might have to a child. All you have to do is eat right, do right, and mind your elders to ensure no monsters and peaceful sleep. What could be simpler? I considered teaching this song to Seth, but not now. He usually sleeps carefree, like a rock, but I would keep it in my mental "comforting dad queue" if needed someday. I was the one that needed comfort now. I also decided I would have the stranger danger talk with him again. The more he considered this, the safer he would be. I started to feel a little better.

Just a little.

CHAPTER 2
ABSENT BIRTHDAY

"Action expresses priorities."

~Mahatma Gandhi

That afternoon I sat outside Seth's school waiting for class to dismiss. My mind was preoccupied with a project I was working on at the office, but I also couldn't help but dwell on the nightmare. The high-pitched squeal of tires broke me out of my trance and sent my heart into my throat. As disturbing as it was, it was nothing new.

I wasn't looking in the direction of the commotion but I knew what it was; I knew it without a doubt. My son had recklessly bolted across the street without any regard to oncoming traffic. I have talked to him about this on countless occasions and he is pretty good about observing safety rules, except when he gets excited. Excitement seems to drain every bit of common sense from his otherwise intelligent brain.

I turned quickly in the direction of the noise to see him

approaching the car in a sprint, completely oblivious to his surroundings. He grinned from ear to ear with eager excitement while the drivers of the two cars looked on with what was probably extremely subdued irritation. I waved, embarrassed, and gave silent thanks for their quick reflexes.

Everyone drives cautiously around St. James School because it is a posted school zone, and let's face it: caution is not a word that is common to most primary school kids' vocabulary. Seth hit the door like a bird hitting a window and then gleefully pulled open the door to my SUV. I was just about to scold him when my phone began to ring.

"Daddy, Daddy guess what!" he blurted. I held up my finger to silence him as I answered the call. I barely noticed as his bottom lip puckered and he dejectedly dropped his *Star Wars* backpack in the floorboard.

"Thomas Pendleton, how goes it?" asked the voice on the other end of the line. It was my boss, Don Lewis. I immediately knew it was either very good or very bad news because he rarely used my last name and he usually calls me Tommy.

"Fine," I replied, cutting my eyes at Seth as he began to rummage through his backpack, "what's up?"

"I'll make this quick because time is of the essence," Don said with excitement in his voice. "We got the Memphis account!"

Don and I work for PortaPad Manufactured Homes, which is the country's largest manufacturer of mobile homes. It also is based in my hometown of Conway, Arkansas. We had been negotiating with a manufactured home retailer in Memphis for a year—a retailer which happens to manage almost 40 dealerships in Tennessee and Mississippi.

"That's great!" I exclaimed, "So when do we…"

Don cut me off before I finished my question. "We close the deal next week, but I need you in the office tonight so we can start getting everything together. We need to make sure that our *i*'s are dotted and our *t*'s are crossed."

"I'll be there!" I said and hung up the phone.

In my excitement I had almost forgotten that Seth was in the vehicle. Ann usually picked him up from school, but she had a doctor's appointment today. I had been excited about picking him up and spending some quality time together but, like on most occasions, that was not going to happen today because work always seemed to intrude. I had no sooner hung up the phone when he started in with his barrage of reporting on the day's events.

"Hey Daddy, guess what we watched today?" Before I could reply, he answered his own question. "We watched the NASA channel in science class today and guess what?"

Again he was quicker on the draw than I in answering the question. "The scientists say there is a magnetic storm heading toward Urf, and it will be here in a couple of weeks!" Seth is an intelligent six-year-old but he does have a slight speech impediment. It was cute when he was younger, and Ann and I always thought he would grow out of it, but we have recently come to recognize that he might need speech therapy. I was experienced enough with his dialect to recognize that there was a magnetic storm heading toward Earth.

"That's interesting," I said.

I had heard a snippet on the radio earlier but I hadn't really paid attention. Meteor showers, eclipses, visible planets and comets, it seems like we have some new phenomenon to observe on a weekly basis. So, I didn't believe this one would be any different, maybe some colorful lights in the sky for a night or two and even then it would probably only be visible in Nova Scotia, Oslo, Norway, or Timbuktu. Conway, Arkansas, never has anything exciting like that happen.

"We may not be able to see it but it might interfere with TV or rabio signals," he said as he pointed at the radio dial.

I barely even heard him because I noticed another kid about Seth's age dart into the street just as I was pulling away from the curb. I was reminded of Seth's earlier similar lack of caution.

"Seth, how many times have I talked to you about running into the street? I am going to have to ground you tonight to make sure you get the point. Do you understand?"

He frowned and nodded his head gloomily. After a few moments of silence, Seth replied so silently I could barely understand him.

"Okay, Daddy … could we stop at the blue store so I can get Momma a present?"

The blue store is how he referred to Walmart, one of his favorite places in the world outside of Chuck E. Cheese. He called it that because of its blue logo and saying the word Walmart played hell on his speech impediment.

I felt a knot form in my stomach and it started to work its way up my throat. Today is Ann's birthday and we were supposed to have a family dinner tonight at her favorite restaurant. I had just committed myself to go into work. I don't think I have been available for a birthday celebration in at least three years. The last birthday party I remember, including my own, was Seth's third birthday. That stands out so clearly because I was late due to a meeting at work and had to pick up the cake. My tardiness distracted me enough that I did not inspect the cake at the bakery when I picked it up. It wasn't discovered until the box was opened in the middle of the table surrounded by three-year-olds and moms that I had gotten the wrong cake. Seth frowned as I dumbly read the birthday greeting aloud: "Happy 50th Birthday, Ralph."

"I-I don't have time, buddy," I said. "I have to go to work, something really big tonight, your mother will understand."

I felt like a jerk but I justified it by believing that Ann would understand. She always did … or at least I thought she did. I believed she would appreciate the fact that my absence tonight would give her delayed gratification of her birthday wishes. The bonus I would be getting would enable us to take the dream vacation we have talked about for years but never acted on, or perhaps even enable us to move to the new affluent area of Conway known as Jefferson Place. Yes, it was for the good of the family, I rationalized. It was worth a few sacrifices.

In actuality, I don't believe Ann and Seth shared my justification.

Seth frowned and fumbled with the strap of his backpack. I saw a tear start to bead in the corner of his eye but I was distracted by another phone call from my boss. We were three-quarters of the way home when my call ended. Seth had dried his tears but still looked thoroughly disappointed. He took me completely off guard by his next question.

"Daddy, how do you commit suibside?"

I gaped at him in disbelief. My shock caused me to veer into the next lane, almost side swiping a Volkswagen Beetle.

"Suicide … where did you hear that word, son?" I stammered.

"J.C. Stensland died today; Father Wilson met with us in chapel to talk about it."

J.C. Stensland was a teen heartthrob pop star. Seth listened to Radio Disney where they usually played a lot of his music but I never thought that Seth was a fan. He usually only got excited about the show tunes from his favorite Disney movies. It seems I had heard something on the radio earlier about the music star committing suicide. The details were sketchy but it was believed that he shot himself in the head.

"What did Father Wilson say?" I asked, my jaw clenching tight. I understood the Catholic position on suicide but I hoped that the priest had not gotten too graphic with his discussion.

I still needed to have a private meeting with Father Wilson about his, in my opinion, explicit lesson about abortion. I share the same views on the subject matter as the good Father and the Church, but we have a different point of view sometimes on age appropriate discussions.

"He reminded us that suibside is a sin and anyone who does it is going to Hell. Is J.C. in Hell, Daddy?"

My jaw clenched again and my ulcer, which had not given me a problem in months, decided to rear its ugly head. It sounded as if the line had once again been crossed, but when was I going to have time to meet with the Father? My calendar is booked solid for at least a month. It is now mid-April and school will be out for summer in a couple of weeks.

"I don't know, Seth. Only God can determine that."

"Doesn't Father Wilson talk to God?" Seth asked with a frown.

I decided it was best to change the subject. "Hey, what did Mr. Lax think about your airplane project?" I asked with exaggerated enthusiasm. Seth had spent two weeks working on a project that displayed World War II airplanes.

Seth beamed with pride. "A-plus," he said with two thumbs up.

"Good job, buddy!" I reached over to ruffle his hair. His chest puffed out as he beamed from ear to ear.

"I told him we were going to see them for real at the Air and Space Moozem in Washaton as soon as school is done!" he boasted.

I had promised Seth to take him to the Air and Space Museum in Washington, D.C., as soon as school is out. However, I hadn't anticipated the big deal closing with the company in Memphis. I had a habit of breaking promises to him like that, but he had to understand that my hard work pays for his video games, toys, and everything else that is special to him. Postponing our trip would be worth it in the long run. We would take the trip later in the summer; it would be even better because we would have more money for Busch Gardens and the beach. Deep down I knew that was a load of crap but I would never admit it to myself and especially not to Seth. I was too self-absorbed to realize that what was truly special to him was time spent with his habitually absent father.

I said nothing because I knew whatever came out of my mouth would be a lie. Instead I just smiled and winked at Seth but my ulcer made me pay for my insincerity. I reached for my bottle of Zantac in the center console and popped a couple of pills, then chased them with the warm remains of my morning Mountain Dew.

Ann had not returned from the doctor when we got home. I parked in the driveway, not bothering to pull into the garage since

I would be leaving again shortly. Seth made a beeline for his room upstairs as soon as I opened the front door. He dropped his backpack on the couch as usual and bolted up the stairs.

I got another call from my boss to remind me of everything I needed to bring to the meeting tonight. I hardly noticed Seth when he came back downstairs to retrieve tape and scissors from a kitchen drawer. I was completely oblivious to his presence as I walked around with my phone on my shoulder as I made a cream cheese and cucumber sandwich. Otherwise, I would have probably scolded him as he ran up the stairs with the scissors. He was excited again.

I was still on the phone when Ann got home. She smiled and kissed me on the cheek and then excitedly hurried upstairs herself. I acknowledged her with a smile and a pat on the behind as Don rattled on about building specifications for our new line of manufactured homes. I was momentarily distracted as I watched her ascend the stairs; she was as fine walking away as walking toward me. Her silky chestnut hair, olive complexion, her long legs that went all the way up to her firm ... well, I am a lucky man to have a woman so gorgeous and understanding. But sometimes it's not enough to understand what things mean; sometimes you have to understand what things don't mean. That was Ann's gift, to appreciate and understand the present, and my curse that I did not.

It didn't occur to me at first, until a few minutes after she closed the bedroom door, what she was doing, but by then it was too late. She was dressing for our dinner out, the dinner for her birthday, the dinner I would not be attending.

I got off the phone with Don as Ann was coming back downstairs. Her black dress accentuated every perfect feature. It made it much harder to say what I was about to say. She knew me so well I could see the comprehension wash across her face like a dark cloud before I even opened my mouth.

"You have a meeting tonight?" she asked quietly.

I nodded my head and put my hand on her shoulder.

"You remember that Memphis deal? Well, it's official! Don and I have to work on it tonight."

She nodded her head and forced a smile. "That's great. When will you be home?"

"Not too late … about nine or ten." I paused and put my arms around her. "I'm sorry about tonight, but you know how important this deal is."

I felt her head nod against my shoulder. I heard a noise before she spoke; I couldn't tell if it was a sob or a quick breath.

"I'll wait up for you," she whispered.

She pulled away when we heard Seth coming down the stairs. She flashed a sad smile at me then quickly turned her attention to our charging son. He wrapped his arms around her waist and administered the biggest bear hug he could manage.

"Happy birfday, Momma!" he announced as he reached one arm up and extended a hastily wrapped package.

Judging by the snowmen, I would say he had gotten into our Christmas wrapping paper. My gut clenched when I realized I had left my present at the office. But what had Seth gotten her? A short time earlier he was asking me to take him to the blue store to get her a present.

Ann leaned down and hugged Seth's neck then kissed him on the forehead. "Thank you baby," she said. "What is it?"

"Open it!" he urged.

She gently tore back the paper to reveal more layers of snowmen. I think Seth must have used the whole roll. After several moments of peeling, Ann gently reached into the wrapping and pulled out an action figure; Seth's Princess Leia action figure to be exact. He had a large collection of *Star Wars* figures which he guarded jealously. It was indeed an esteemed honor to be presented with one of his collection.

"Princess Leia is pretty like you, Momma," Seth said, proud. Seth had always claimed that Ann resembled the galactic princess. I could see the resemblance a little, except for the hair buns over the ears.

Ann slowly turned and displayed her honored gift in my general direction. I saw a couple of tears stream down her cheeks. At the time I thought it was motherly happiness for Seth's thoughtful gift; in hindsight I'm not so sure. I think it was more a mixture of pride in her son and disappointment in me. But I was doing the right thing, wasn't I? The truth was that this had become such a common occurrence, me putting my work first, that it was a miracle Ann had any regretful tears left.

I kissed Ann and wished her what probably seemed a hollow happy birthday. I hugged Seth and told him I loved him. I had thoughtlessly left Ann's gift at the office, but promised her I would bring it home after the meeting tonight. Even though I have a lousy record with quality family time, I did put a lot of effort into gifts. Surely the diamond tennis bracelet I got her would make up for my absence.

The thing that seemed to be completely lost on me is that nothing could make up for that. I loved my family dearly, more than words could express, but actions always speak louder than words.

CHAPTER 3

THE SIGN

"When men sow the wind it is rational
to expect that they will reap the whirlwind."

~Frederick Douglass

It has been three weeks since Ann's birthday. It is truly disturbing how much things can change in such a short period of time. The deal in Memphis closed a week ago. It was a very lucrative deal, but one I would gladly undo if only I could undo what has happened. I haven't slept or eaten much since then. In fact, I have barely left the house.

As I sit and ponder what has happened, I realize that when it comes to the happiest days of my life, work never really figured into the mix. I thought it did but really it made me happy because I was making more money and a better life for the family. Yes, I was making more money, but money is a poor substitute for the priceless value of a present husband and father.

The two happiest days of my life were the day Annabelle and

I were married and the day that my premature, but miraculously healthy son, Seth, was born – thank God he got his mother's looks. Both days hold a unique place in my heart, but I never understood how large a part of my heart they occupied until I returned home from Memphis last week and realized they were gone. I had a void in my chest that far surpassed my physical dimensions; it seemed to open into a bottomless pit of despair.

I am a loyal and loving husband and father, but I guess that was hard to see considering I was never home. All I wanted was to give them everything they desired, that is why I worked long hours, traveled on weekends, and even worked when I was home. I was so busy looking to the future that I never realized the present needed me. Karma paid me a cruel visit last week, a visit that I deserved. I guess in one form or another, we always reap what we sow.

Seth is six-years-old and a very intelligent kid. He was already educating me on the solar system and universe when he was only three. Yeah, I knew all the planets in order, kind of. I always had a tendency to get Neptune and Uranus turned around in their order from the Sun, but not Seth. He could not only rattle them off in line, but could name all the moons for each planet as well. He had a steadfast belief – I have no idea where it came from – that Pluto is indeed a planet and not a dwarf planet as NASA had recently proclaimed. Well, I don't know a dwarf planet from a Disney character, so I never corrected him. Who knows? The smart little toot may have been right. Sometimes I felt like I wasn't talking to a three-year-old or a six-year-old as he got older. He is a typical kid, but don't let his speech impediment fool you; he has an intellect that would far exceed his old man's.

Ann and I were a clichéd story: nerd meets beauty, they hit it off, they get married … life is good. I wish I could say it was that easy, but it wasn't. It took a lot of persistence and diligence on my part to win her over, almost three years' worth.

Ann and I had very little in common other than the fact that we both grew up as an only child in our respective homes and we had both lost each of our parents before we were 20. We had vowed to not condemn Seth to that solitary existence; he needed family that would still be there even after Ann and I are gone. But, we had not been able to get pregnant again. I can't help but wonder if that was why Ann had gone to see her doctor, her "female" doctor on her birthday. As happy as that would have made me two weeks ago, it tears at my heart to think of that possibility now.

When I fell in love with Ann, it was one of those chick moments that guys sometimes have but never admit. I just knew I was meant to be with her. I couldn't explain it any more than I could explain the event that is presently occurring on the Earth.

I have been sitting in my easy chair for most of the last week, just as I am doing today, pondering what brought me to this point, reminiscing about the past as my guts seem to be gnawing their way out, feeding on my guilt and misery. Father Wilson had stopped by again this morning to offer support but, like I had done the past four days, I politely told him it was not a good time and sent him on his way. I had not forgotten the suicide conversation I intended to have with him, but now was not the time and I didn't think I could talk with him until that was resolved.

His visit did make me recall that Seth had told me about a phenomenon heading toward the Earth, a magnetic storm or something which they had watched in science class. I hadn't paid attention at the time because I was preoccupied with my big Memphis deal. Plus, it seems like there is always some meteor shower or eclipse to watch, a cosmic oddity and nothing more. That is why the TV suddenly caught my attention.

The news report tapped my curiosity like nothing had in the past week because I had mindlessly ignored the TV for days as it droned on not more than ten feet from my chair, it might as well have been ten miles. The broadcast from CNN said the storm had entered the Earth's atmosphere over China and would gradually spread across the entire planet. Seth had told me that the scientists said the storm might disrupt radio signals but it seemed radio was not fazed; instead television was being affected.

The reporters estimated that it would take about six hours to reach our side of the planet. But their predictions were woefully inadequate: within ten minutes my TV was reduced to nothing more than a white-noise generator. I grudgingly forced myself out of the chair and walked over to my laptop resting on the coffee table where it had sat for the past two weeks. After it booted, I clicked on my internet icon ... there was no connection. After several minutes of rebooting and troubleshooting, I saw little alternative but to go into the kitchen and turn on the radio. I absently drifted back against the wall and slid to the floor as I took in the radio report, my jaw practically resting on my chest. Yes, TV and internet were out all over the world, but that problem paled in comparison to what else was being reported. Emotional exhaustion and astonishment made it impossible to stand. What I was hearing was surely impossible.

It came from outer space.

Yes, I know that is a title to a 1950s science-fiction B-movie, but it is the most apt description I can think of for this, well ... cosmic storm. That seems to be the most agreeable buzzword for all the talking head scientists on the radio. It seems radio is it for an indefinite period of time. TV signals are blocked by this "storm." The old saying that "seeing is believing" really hits home at a time like this. I don't know what to believe about what's being reported on the radio. I can't help but think of Orson Welles' infamous broadcast of *War of the Worlds* in 1938. This can't be real, can it? No, it's not aliens. It's far more incredible.

As I said, this event, miracle, storm—or whatever you choose to call it—came from space. Ancient man believed that celestial events were omens of fate. Eclipses, comets, planetary alignments, lunar or solar cycles, and even meteor showers were believed to foretell the coming of a great prosperity or a profound cataclysm. Many still believe in the validity of these heavenly harbingers.

I have attended church with Ann and Seth more from obligation than any type of spiritual calling. I was not a deeply religious man before this event. I can say with even more conviction that I was not and still am not a superstitious man. I put no such stock in irrational, gullible thought, but it is undeniable that something has happened and is happening, something unlike anything mankind has seen before. Little did I know that I would presently be bearing witness to that as intimately as any other person on the planet.

According to the radio, which I had raptly listened to for about two hours now, a true miracle was visited upon the planet today, but was it of Heaven or Hell? Is it necessary for an event to be spawned of a loving and benevolent God to qualify as a miracle? Evil can sometimes be every bit as potent in this purview. We call horrific events disasters, but in some cases couldn't they be classified as negative miracles? Maybe this is just the last vestige of my optimism talking. Whatever the reason behind the event enveloping the planet today, mankind seemed as split about the origins as they are about religion itself. I myself am split … there are no two ways about it. I am cautiously excited, but I am also as scared as hell.

The last time I saw Ann and Seth together was the day two weeks ago before I headed for a business meeting in Memphis. Honestly, I didn't really have to go, but I have always found it difficult to delegate authority and I couldn't escape the feeling that something would go wrong if I didn't. My instincts turned out to be right, but for all the wrong reasons.

Annabelle and Seth were taking a picnic lunch to Lake Beaverfork that afternoon and they both begged me to come with them. I could have blown the meeting off and gone—a part of me wanted to, but another part won out. The selfish part, the part that knew mid-April in Arkansas was still a little too early for water activities. I hate cold water, hate it with a passion; I almost think I would rather get a root canal with no Novocain than to go swimming in a cold lake.

I wished them well, teased Seth to watch out for the toe bass that enjoyed nibbling on little boys' feet, and left without another thought for the airport. In the world of karma, that was the proverbial straw that broke the camel's back, or in this case, broke my heart. It wasn't until I returned the next morning that I realized they were gone.

As I said, my wife and son left two weeks ago. But my son returned today of all days, the day the cosmic storm entered Earth's atmosphere. The superstitious would have proclaimed the storm as a harbinger of his return, but I am not a superstitious man.

Yes, I did say that just my son returned. Where his mother is, I still am not certain. I never considered whether a human being can experience overwhelming joy and overwhelming terror at the same time, but let me tell you from personal experience … we can. It is an indescribable feeling and one I do not care to repeat. It does something to the soul, like putting it on the rack and stretching it to its limits before releasing it abruptly like a taut rubber band.

People may ask why I didn't feel pure joy for the return of my son. What is there to be terrified of?

I was terrified of the one thing that has been eating at my heart since I realized they were gone. In all of my nightmares I never considered that it does not necessarily require flesh and blood to harbor the trappings of a fiend. Fate can fit that definition just as easily.

That certainty would be the hardest lesson in my life, because two weeks ago, coming home from Lake Beaverfork, Annabelle and Seth were killed in a car accident.

CHAPTER 4
SETH

"We only part to meet again."

~John Gay

Annabelle was a diabetic and had a low blood sugar attack behind the wheel, causing her to veer off the road and hit a tree. That was what the responding officer on the scene told me, but I knew better. She was exhausted from running our household and taking care of Seth with little or no help from me. Her mild diabetes was never an issue before, and I was sure she had simply fallen asleep at the wheel. This knowledge was like pouring salt in an open wound. I was told by one of the attending EMTs in an attempt to give me some comfort that they died instantly. How can anything comfort you at a time like this? The nightmare had not happened as I had imagined, but it had happened all the same. Except it was worse; I had lost both of them.

Today when the storm hit I was downstairs in our comfortable four-bedroom home in Conway, Arkansas. "Our" is a possessive pronoun that I will have to learn to get out of the habit of saying, but it still feels right. It feels right even after the stabbing pain of recollection every time it slips out because there is no more "our," only "my."

I don't even remember what I was watching when the storm arrived, after a while it just became white noise buzzing in the background, droning away as I pondered the living nightmare in which I now found myself.

After sitting in the kitchen floor, dazedly listening to the radio for what seemed like hours, I think what finally got my attention was the light coming in through the window. It was not sunlight, although it was mid-afternoon and the sun would have been shining through the westward window I was facing. It was not lightning or car lights, although I did think it may be the taillights of a very large truck at first glance. I went to the window and looked out, almost losing all my breath in a large gasp of surprise.

The scene outside my window was surreal, like looking through a portal into another world. This was my lawn, my vehicle, my street, and my neighborhood, of this there was no doubt. But it was like the sun had been replaced by a gigantic ultraviolet light. The colors of the grass, trees, and plants were magnified tenfold, and all seemed to glow with an eerie luminescence. The blue sky had been replaced with a faint lavender hue and was speckled with yellow clouds. *Wonderland has come to Arkansas*, I thought to myself. But, I would soon find what a limited statement that was. Wonderland had come to the planet.

Like most people do when there is breaking news, out of habit I ran back to the TV to see what the alphabet networks had to say. In my distracted state of mind, I had forgotten the signal had gone out. In spite of the news reports, seeing gray static on every channel of my TV, I quickly deduced that it must be a problem with the set. After all, that particular TV was over ten-years-old and the last of the enormous cinder block televisions, so it must have just kicked the bucket.

I hurried up the stairs to tune in on the newer plasma screen in the bedroom. At the top of the stairs rested a large landing that exited to a full-size bath in front of the stairs, a single bedroom to the right, and two bedrooms to the left. The master bedroom was to the far left. Seth's bedroom was the single one to the right. The door had been closed for the past two weeks, but today it was open just a crack. I probably wouldn't even have noticed if not for the strange light outside, shining through the bedroom window and streaming out through the small crack.

I paused just as I reached the landing and looked at the door. A thin beam of purplish light flickered across the hardwood floor of the landing. I stopped and watched, mesmerized for a few moments, and then something made me jump with surprise. I saw movement in the light, as if someone inside my son's bedroom had just walked past the door.

"Hello?" I called out shakily.

How could there be anyone in there? Surely it was just a tree branch blowing outside the bedroom window, but then it dawned on me … there weren't any trees on that side of the house.Frozen, I listened and heard nothing. I was just about to move on to the TV when a faint noise met my ears. I listened curiously at first, but the longer I listened the faster my heart began to race. Was that someone crying? The more I listened, the more certain I became that a child was crying in Seth's room. Could this have been one of his friends that had snuck into his room to privately mourn? I didn't think so. Seth was only six, after all, and the nearest child his age lived about four blocks away, a far piece for a six-year-old to travel by himself. But still, I was positive about what I was hearing: it was definitely the undersized sobs of a child.

My tinge of curiosity was quickly replaced by a creepy feeling, like 100 mice were running up and down my spine. My interest about what was going on outside had been brushed aside for a new single-minded focus. Who or what was on the other side of the door?

I slowly crept toward the door, barely daring to breathe. A large vase beside the bathroom contained two large golf umbrellas. I grasped one by its protruding handle and slowly withdrew it from the vase, like a knight drawing his sword. I didn't know what the heck I was going to do with an umbrella, unless the intruder was armed with a water pistol. I guess it just gave me some sort of security as I moved to open the door, however false it may be.

I placed my left palm against the surface of the door and gently pushed as it slowly started to swing inward. I poked the tip of the umbrella into the widening crack, ready to repel any attack that came my way. The door gave one last tiny creak as it came to a stop. As I peered into the bedroom, the umbrella dropped from my hand and my heart leapt into my throat. Sitting on the bed, crying and looking sadly at his shelf of *Star Wars* toys, was Seth.

I rubbed my eyes and shook my head. Surely this was some trick of the light, some trick of this weirdness that was going on outside. No, it was definitely no trick of the light; as for a trick of the weirdness outside … that was debatable. I would soon find that this was no trick of any kind. The reports on the radio appeared to be true.

He didn't seem to notice me at first, or at least not to pay any attention as he continued to gaze longingly at his playthings. He looked the same as he had the last time I had seen him alive. His blond hair was parted neatly in the middle and he wore an orange and yellow striped shirt with khaki shorts. At the end of his skinny legs dangling over the edge of the bed, he wore a pair of faded Spider-Man tennis shoes.

As I entered further into the room, he turned his head and looked at me. It was the same Seth, but on the other hand, it was not. His whole form, flesh and clothes alike, seemed to shimmer faintly like the surface of a lake just as dawn breaks. He gave off the same ethereal glow as the mysterious light shining in from outside. Whatever this weirdness was, he seemed to be both independent and part of it at the same time.

This was the moment that I experienced the rare mix of joyous elation and profound horror. My son was back and he was sitting on his bed looking at me, which makes me happy... I should be happy but ... he's dead, for God's sake! I buried him and his mother two weeks ago! This can't be real ... it just can't!

But it was real, and that point was driven home like a bolt of lightning as Seth spoke to me.

"Daddy, you can see me?" he said in a tired and frightened voice.

It was Seth's voice all right, but a little different. It was like he was talking to me from inside a large metal drum; his voice echoed with a tin sound that sent the mice scurrying up my back again. I stood frozen, unable to muster a response through my emotional turmoil. Finally, Seth spoke again.

"Please talk to me Daddy," he said as his bottom lip puckered and silvery tears welled in his eyes.

My heart melted just enough to manage adequate lubricant to unhinge my jaws.

"Seth buddy, how did you get here?" I asked in a voice that came out squeaky, like a pubescent teen.

"I've been here a while Daddy, but you wouldn't talk to me. I slept with you every night but I guess you couldn't see me."

I walked over to take his tiny hand, which he eagerly raised for me to grasp; it felt gelatinous, like a liquid with the consistency of pudding. I felt a small electrical current run up my arm when we touched, but that was not the worst of it. His hand was frigidly cold, like he had just stuck his arm into a deep freeze. I pulled back with involuntary revulsion.

He looked at me with a hurt-filled expression, leaving me with the dilemma of whether to give him a comforting embrace or run from the room in terror. A sudden realization came from nowhere, like my brain had just snatched one of the confusing pieces of information floating in my head and enhanced it to perfect clarity.

Seth said he had been sleeping with me. Ever since the funeral, I had not slept very well, which is understandable given the circumstances, but I have also been severely chilled at night. I first thought it was the air vent above the bed, but when that was eliminated, I assumed I was coming down with something. Could it have been possible that I was feeling Seth's ... what? His ghost? Ten minutes ago I would have dismissed that speculation as inane, superstitious fantasy, but now I wasn't sure.

Seeing is believing, but how could I be sure of anything considering the bizarre phenomenon manifesting outside? I had to get my head on straight. I needed to sit down and collect my thoughts. I trudged toward an old rocking chair in the corner, but before I could sit down, Seth spoke again.

"No Daddy, that one has a broken leg ... 'member?"

Yes, I did remember. How could I forget? I broke it a month ago when I stupidly stood on the seat, trying to change a light bulb in Seth's ceiling fan. I had been too busy to get the wood glue and just fix it. If he was a figment of my imagination ... how the hell did he know that?

"Of course," I said, feeling shaky. "How silly of me."

He smiled a weepy smile. "You can sit with me, Daddy." He pointed to the other side of the bed.

I didn't want to sit on the bed, not that close. I know how crazy that sounds because this was my son. But was it really? If this were a hallucination, it is the most realistic and profound one I have ever experienced, not that I had that much experience with them. I have never done drugs. If this were a mirage, what did I have to lose? But ... if this were somehow real, then it was my son sitting there and I had been given a great miracle. Negative or positive, it was my boy, damn it!

I eased onto the far side of the bed, like I was sitting by a temperamental dog that might bite at any second. He looked at me with tearful eyes and a quivering bottom lip; I looked at him with apprehensive eyes and a trembling body. I was shaking from head to foot.

"Where's your mother?" I asked.

That was when the silvery tears hanging in the corners of his eyes let go like tiny streams of mercury. They soundlessly struck the navy blue *Toy Story* bedspread, leaving not a single mark or wet spot. It was as if they passed straight through the bed like a, well … like a ghost.

He shook his head mournfully and sobbed. "I don't know, Daddy."

My heart skipped a beat and sank into my guts simultaneously when I understood that Ann was gone, not only physically but spiritually as well. Where could she be? My son was here and he was all alone, at least he had been for the past two weeks. No wonder he seems so scared, the poor little guy. A few tears leaked from my eyes, but unlike Seth's, they made large dark blotches on the bedspread.

"Don't cry, Daddy. She was okay the last time I saw her."

"Where was that?" I asked in a hoarse whisper.

He frowned and looked back at his shelf of toys. He grabbed Anakin Skywalker and held him in his hand, rolling him over and inspecting the plastic surface like he had never seen the toy before.

"I don't know," he said. "We were picnicking and then we were in a dark place and two doors appeared. They were bright like the time we sat by the lights on top of the stadium at the Razorback game, 'member?"

I nodded my head and smiled. That was one of the few things we had done, just father and son, in his short life. I felt like crying again.

"Well, Momma smiled at me and told me it was time to go and she went through one of the doors. I haven't seen her since," he said as another stream of tears jetted down his small face, disappearing into the bedspread.

"Why didn't you go through the other door, Seth?"

He looked at me and replied as if it should have been as obvious as the nose on my face.

"We are going to the Air Space Moozem, Daddy."

29

He paused a moment, tightly shutting his right eye as if in deep thought. "The one in Washaton," he said with a sheepish smile.

My heart turned to ice and melted in the same instant. Yes, we had planned this trip to the Air and Space Museum in Washington, D.C., just me and him, father and son. We had planned many trips like this before but they never materialized; I was always too busy. I had planned this trip with the sincere promise that this time would be different, this time we would definitely go. That's what I said, but if I were truly honest with myself, this one would have probably ended up being cancelled as well. My work was always too important to miss.

Now, sitting on my son's bed contemplating what I had lost, and looking at Seth's sad and trusting face, my career seemed about as important as an amoeba in the grand scale of the universe. It's funny how kids put such trust in their parents and adults. Even though I had disappointed him a dozen times in the past, he still implicitly believed that I was taking him on his dream vacation. He trusted me so much that he refused to go … where? Was it Heaven on the other side of the door, emanating a blinding light? I don't know. As I said, I am not a religious man, but that seems as plausible an explanation as any.

My God, my son gave up Heaven to spend time with me. At that moment, I believed that more than anything, and tears began to sheet down my face. I had never felt more selfish and undeserving in my life, but I had also never loved Seth more than I did at that moment. I needed a diversion to avoid an emotional display in front of him.

"Hey Seth," I said mustering the best cheerful tone I could, "why don't we go check the TV in the bedroom and see what's going on outside."

He raised his head hopefully and looked longingly at me.

"After that you can check out Cartoon Network," I finished with a teary wink.

I looked at his happy face. His excited, childish countenance made me feel better, until I looked down. He was still clutching the

Anakin Skywalker figure in his hand, but what must be understood is that the preposition 'in' was never more appropriate than it was at that moment.

I said before that his flesh seemed to have a gelatinous consistency. Well, Anakin looked as if he had been congealed in a hand shaped Jell-O mold. Two plastic feet were sticking through Seth's thumb, a plastic right arm clutching a light saber protruded through his pinky finger. If that wasn't disturbing enough, the Jedi hero's full plastic body was visible, like looking at an object frozen beneath the ice of a lake. Seth seemed completely oblivious to the fact that his favorite toy was slowly passing through his hand like a peanut through thick maple syrup. I shuddered in spite of myself.

Thankfully, he did not notice my disconcerted expression as he happily slid to the floor. Anakin dropped with a muffled plop to the blue knit rug beside his bed. Whether he willingly opened his small fingers and released it, or the toy finally made its slow, disquieting journey through my son's hand, I do not know. I don't believe I want to know.

He followed me out the door and across the landing to the room that Ann and I shared for almost ten years. I opened the door with baited breath, half-expecting to see my lost love sitting dejectedly on her side of the bed. But, no one was there. The room was exactly as I had left it – unmade bed, dirty clothes scattered haphazardly across the floor and a half dozen dirty coffee mugs on the night stand and dresser. Ironically, one of the mugs was my collectible *Ghostbusters* mug from 1984, from which I had just drunk my initial cup of joe that morning. I say it was irony, but at that moment I still had no clue to what I was experiencing, not really. Not until I accepted that my bedroom TV didn't work either and I flipped on the clock radio on the night stand.

My radio was pre-tuned to a local talk station, which was an affiliate of one of the major national networks. As I switched on the radio and turned up the volume, the main news anchor was interviewing a scientist from NASA by the name of Dr. Smithson Turner.

"Dr. Turner," the news anchor said, "can you explain to our audience exactly what is going on?"

There was a long silence before the doctor could be heard nervously clearing his throat.

"I will do my best," he began, "which may not be sufficient considering that I don't fully understand it either."

"Are you saying that NASA, which boasts the finest and most intelligent scientists of mankind, has no idea what is happening?" the anchor said with incredulity.

There was another very long pause followed by a frustrated sigh from Dr. Turner. "The easiest way I can explain it is that a large plasma storm passed through Earth's atmosphere this morning, changing the magnetic signature of the planet."

"Does that account for the strange color of the sky, the loss of television reception and internet connectivity?" the anchor asked.

"Yes."

"Is this dangerous? Are there any health hazards associated with this … this plasma storm?" the anchor asked bluntly.

"The honest answer is … we don't know," Dr. Turner replied, and then hastily followed with, "We have no reason to believe this to be a hazard at this point in time. Our top scientists are investigating as we speak. My best advice to the public is to exercise caution and stay indoors as much as possible."

"I see, I see. When do you expect a *definitive* answer from the top scientists?" the anchor said with what was probably frustrated anxiety, but it came out sounding like sarcasm.

"Soon, soon," said Dr. Turner. "We should have a complete analysis in the next day or two."

"I see … Dr. Turner, if I may, I have one more follow-up question before we move onto the president's press conference in a few minutes."

"Of course," he replied.

The anchor gave a deep sigh followed by what almost sounded

like a muffled chuckle. "Dr. Turner," he began, stretching his words out with cautious interlude. He sounded like he gave a half-sigh and half-laugh before he continued again. "What of the unconfirmed reports coming in from around the world … the reports that seem to coincide with the plasma storm this morning?"

"I'm not sure what you mean," Dr. Turner replied indignantly.

"Come on doctor, anyone that has been listening to the radio today knows what I mean."

"I have no idea."

"Okay, Doc, I understand you not wanting to discuss it; it sounds crazy. But, I would be remiss if I did not at least mention it."

There were several moments of long silence where neither man spoke; murmuring and gasps could be heard in the background. Finally the anchor spoke, his voice sounded shaky and uneasy.

"The reports coming in from around the globe," he said then forcefully cleared his throat. "Well, they are suggesting that the recently deceased and the long dead have returned, or at least become visible, as a result of this plasma storm. Folks, I thought they were crazy rumors started by a prosaic astrological event. That is until Jake Hardee, my old producer, walked into the studio a few moments ago."

A long breath and labored exhalation followed. "Jake Hardee passed away with advanced melanoma almost ten years ago."

CHAPTER 5
CHOCKIT BERRIES

"We are what we believe we are."

~C. S. Lewis

As I sat listening to the radio reports, it was like being awakened from a dream and discovering what you believed to be a sleeping figment of the mind's eye was in fact hard and undeniable reality. But, was it like waking from a pleasant dream or a nightmare? God knows I had had enough nightmares lately.

My head rationally leaned toward the nightmare scenario, but as I looked at Seth's sweet and innocent eyes, my heart refused to go there. As terrifying as this unknown was at the present moment, Seth was a familiarity—a familiarity that made my soul flame with love, burn with grief, and, I'm sorry to say, cower in fear. This is my son, damn it, I know it … somehow I know it beyond a shadow of a doubt.

Seth waited patiently for several minutes as I listened to the eyewitness accounts coming in over the radio. The multitude of incredible stories ranged from deceased grandparents suddenly sharing domicile with their grandchildren to multiple dead celebrity sightings. There were even a few sightings of Elvis roaming around Beale St. in Memphis; every report sounded like a lead story in the *National Enquirer*.

"No cartoons, Daddy?" Seth asked, hopeful.

"No son, it looks like TV is not working right now."

He frowned with obvious disappointment then a flash of excitement washed over his face, almost like an underwater spotlight.

"Can I listen to Rabio Didney?"

Radio Disney was his program of choice when riding in the vehicle. He still had some trouble with the pronunciation, however. I had promised him, in hind sight probably falsely, that if he could pronounce it correctly, I would take the family to Disney World; or as Seth would put it, *Didney World*. I caught the little guy practicing in his room on numerous occasions, sometimes to the point of frustrated tears. I felt like the biggest and most disgusting pariah in the world; I turned my head toward the radio so he wouldn't see the tear stream down my cheek.

"Yes, that would be fine buddy. Do you need help?"

"No, I'm a big boy, I know how to work my rabio," he said, proud.

He left the room, his head held high with importance. Shortly I heard the portable radio click on in his room; this was followed by lively melody by the Jonas Brothers. It was a catchy tune, but it never made much sense to me, something about *I come from the year three thousand and everybody's great, but they live underwater*. That was an ironically fitting song, considering I felt like I was living underwater at the moment. Everything is so surreal; the world had been submerged into what the NASA scientist called a plasma storm, but this was something more than that, it seemed.

If what I was hearing on the radio was true, this event is unparalleled in recorded history. I didn't have any reason to believe it was not true. After all, I had seen Seth with my own eyes, heard his familiar voice and felt his hand with my own. But that was the rub as well. His physical features had an ethereal quality to them, his voice was the same but had an unusual echoing timbre, and his touch, well … that was the most disquieting of all.

He was dead, but he was here with me, I had to accept that fact. I had to accept it or go mad. Perhaps this was a mass hallucination triggered in our minds by this unusual energy, or perhaps not. Only time would tell, but for the moment I would have to go with what I knew – Seth and his mother are dead, but Seth's "ghost" remains here with me. I can now see him, along with possibly thousands of other loitering spirits, spirits that chose to remain here instead of going through their respective doorways – to quote Seth's terminology.

I don't know that for a fact, but it explains why Ann is not here with Seth. It sounds crazy when you say it out loud. I'll just go with the flow and continue to listen to the radio and … maybe drive around? They said to stay indoors until they had studied this phenomenon, which seems like sound advice, but I knew I just couldn't sit around much longer. I needed to go back to … to what? Work? Even now I am thinking about work again … God help me.

I focused on the radio for the next half-hour, hoping to find some reasonable answers to what was going on, but none came. The president spoke and said pretty much the same thing as the NASA scientist had, except for one intriguing point. Apparently he had just finished a one-on-one chat with President Abraham Lincoln in the Oval Office about an hour ago. I could hear the giggles and snickering emanating from the press corps, but the Commander in Chief's resolute tone quickly silenced the skeptics.

"I do not make these statements lightly," the president insisted. "After careful scrutiny, I believe it to be our 16th president. How or why I am not certain, but that is all I can say on the matter at this point."

"Can you bring him out and introduce him?" one of the reporters asked.

"I would gladly do that when the time is right," replied the president, "but I will respect his privacy for the time being. That is his wish and I shall honor it."

"Is he going to live in the Lincoln bedroom?" a female reporter asked with a very large and probably cynical smile in her voice.

The president didn't dignify her question with an answer and quickly disbanded the press conference with the promise that more information would be forthcoming when available.

I had almost completely zoned out everything else as an intense debate raged within my mind, one that was encouraged decades ago by Robert F. Ripley – "Believe it, or not." I thought my head was about to explode when I felt something cold on my arm. I jumped in surprise and looked down to see Seth's smiling face.

"Can I have some Chockit Berries?" he asked.

This had been such a common request over the past two years since he gained an appreciation of Chocolate Berries cereal, which is why his request didn't really strike me as unusual at first. It would take a few minutes for the relevance to become clear.

"Sure," I answered, still a bit distracted from his frigid touch. That was going to take a lot of getting used to.

He happily skipped from the room and bounded down the stairs. Did I just see his feet disappearing into the hardwood floor as he pranced? If not for the encounter in Seth's bedroom earlier, I would have dismissed it as a trick of the light, but after observing the tiny Jedi hero clutched in his hand, I think I might have.

I slowly got up and followed down the stairs. I had just reached the top of the landing when I heard him rummaging in the dinnerware cabinet for his favorite cereal bowl. His favorite bowl was not one that brandished children's pop culture idols, icons, or slogans on its porcelain sides. Seth's favorite bowl was a plain blue one given to him by me on my return from a business trip last year. I don't even remember where I got the damned thing, probably some airport trinket store, but it was special to him. Ann said it was a distinct favorite to Seth because I had given it to him. He had a broad collection of pop culture bowls and cups, but that didn't matter: this was the only one he used. It was an unassuming blue bowl with "#1 Son" painted on the side.

I entered the kitchen to see him staring in puzzlement at the cabinet. I was about to ask him the obvious question of how he could possibly be hungry when a sudden recollection pierced my stomach like a hot blade. I had been very stubborn about anyone touching Seth's room. In my grief clouded mind, I thought it was wrong. I wanted to keep it just the way it was. Why? Because he would be back? That pitiful hope of the bereaved now seemed ironically laughable under the circumstances.

When my friends from work came in to help me take care of such matters, I had forbid entrance to Seth's room. They spent most of their time downstairs packing away all the kid themed dinnerware, utensils and cups. I wanted to keep everything but after a lot of convincing from Don Lewis, my boss and best friend, I decided that the bedroom would suffice as an altar to my sorrow, for now, and agreed to let everything else go to Goodwill, Salvation Army or some other worthy charity. Seth's favorite cereal bowl had unfortunately been a part of that donation.

Seth turned to look at me as I entered the room. A frown and puckered bottom lip underscored sad little eyes.

"Daddy, where's my bowl?" he asked, sounding pitiful.

The red-hot blade in my gut seemed to twist and lodge in my throat as I swallowed hard and took a deep breath. I started to lie and tell him it had been sent out for special cleaning but I knew that I must be honest with him, no matter how painful it may be.

"Seth," I began, my voice hoarse, "I thought you weren't coming home, buddy. I gave it to charity so some other kid could enjoy it."

I wondered if I had made the right call when I saw the silvery tears streaming down his cheeks again. They disappeared through the beige tile floor just like his bedspread, leaving no evidence of their sorrowful existence.

He didn't say a word for several moments; he just looked at me with disappointed eyes. My heart burned with unnatural fervor, the combined emotions swirling inside felt like a tempest ready to explode. How could I reconcile my natural parental instinct with the horror of the circumstances? I decided the only thing I could do is go with what I know, go with what I have had a little over six years of experience. I would put my apprehension behind me and be what Seth required. He needed his dad.

"You can use one of my bowls buddy," I said as I opened the "adult" cabinet above the microwave. I produced my favorite bowl, a cardinal red one with a handle, giving it the appearance of an oversized coffee mug. A line of Razorback hogs formed a single ring around the outside of the bowl, completing the red and white color scheme of the University of Arkansas.

Seth smiled and said, "Woooo pig, sooieeee."

I smiled and gently placed the bowl in his small hands, bracing myself for the shattering impact on the floor when the bowl sunk through his fingers, but no crash came. He happily took the bowl and carefully placed it on the kitchen table, then moved to the cereal cabinet to retrieve the box of Chocolate Berries. Luckily I had purchased a new box shortly before Seth … well, before he left, so it was more or less a full box.

He poured his favorite cereal until about three-quarters of the bowl was full, then set the box down and went to the refrigerator to retrieve the milk. He splashed a generous portion of milk into the bowl, causing a few Chocolate Berries to lap out over the side, making dull taps like tiny marbles on the wooden table. He quickly found a spoon in the drawer beside the refrigerator and sat down, clutching the utensil hungrily in his fist. Demonstrating great enthusiasm, he plunged the spoon into the bowl with one rapid motion and then stuffed a shovelful of cereal and milk into his mouth.

I sat mesmerized by what I was witnessing. It was a sight that should have been as common to me as my own reflection; we had breakfast together several times over his short life. I guess I can take some credit that I at least made time for that. But the thing that made this situation so damned odd, the important question that had vexed me since I followed him downstairs finally came to the surface: How could he be hungry?

I watched him devour one spoonful after another, consuming half the bowl in just a few moments.

"Seth," I asked, "are you hungry?"

He stopped with a heaping spoonful halfway between the bowl and his mouth, milk slowly dripping back into the bowl. He looked at me curiously and then shrugged.

"I'm not sure," he said as if he were trying to remember something, then completed the trek of the spoon to his mouth.

"Do you feel hungry?" I interjected before he could scoop another load of chocolate goodness.

He leaned the handle of the spoon against the inside of the bowl and looked at me quizzically.

"I'm not sure I'm hungry. I just wanted some Chockit Berries."

I blurted the first question that came to my mind.

"How do they taste?"

His confused expression broke into a broad grin.

"They're 'berry' good!" he said, using his tiresome, but nonetheless cute, trademark slogan for the breakfast delicacy.

"So, they *taste* good?" I reiterated.

He shoveled another hefty spoonful into his mouth and grinned broadly at me like a chipmunk with his cereal-stuffed cheeks, slowly shaking his head in the affirmative. It was at that moment that my fascination was quelled like a block of ice sliding into my gut; it was replaced by frigid horror. As Seth sat with a stuffed, grinning mouth, I saw a few pieces of cereal ease through his cheeks and splotch with a faint smacking noise on the table top. This was followed by thin streams of milk beading down each cheek.

I tried my best to keep a placid and sane face as I smiled

stupidly at Seth. What did I expect after I saw the *Star Wars* figure ooze through his hand? I casually got to my feet and strolled to the cabinets on the other side of the table behind Seth. I didn't want to look down when I reached the other side, I didn't want to see. But why else had I made this short walk to an unfrequented row of cabinets? It ended up being a morbidly ironic stroll to the cleaning supply cabinet where my terrible suspicion was confirmed, yet I would be able to effectively deal with it ... at least physically anyway.

Seth sat in the chair, cheerfully finishing the last remnants of his Chocolate Berries and milk. He seemed completely oblivious to what was occurring beneath the view of the tabletop. The majority of the contents of his bowl were now pooled in a brown and white puddle under his chair. I had witnessed the toy pass through his hand and now the cereal through his cheeks and ... body? Is that what I should call it? I didn't know, but at the moment, that seems the most salient description. His "body" appeared unable to contain his meal as milk and cereal gradually passed through him until it reached the chair and then slowly trickled over each side, forming the chocolaty lake on the tile beneath him.

Should I bring his attention to it or should I cleverly distract him out of the room while I clean up the mess? I didn't know what the hell to do. My shock and horror intoxicated my judgment, causing me to stare stupidly at the spectacle. Seth noticed my distraction before I could pull myself together. He looked down at the mess on the floor and then looked back to me in panic-stricken horror. He squealed like a terrified rabbit and jumped across the tabletop, streaming milk and Chocolate Berries behind him.

CHAPTER 6
THE BOSS

"To be an ideal guest, stay at home."

~E. W. Howe

The icy, disquieting feeling running through me as I observed this spectacle was melted away in an instant by fatherly compassion. The terrified shrieks of my boy broke down all apprehension. I reached out and grabbed him around the waste and pulled him toward me. I fought through the initial shock of his gelatinous cold "flesh" and pulled him back as he kicked and struggled in terror. As I pulled him up and embraced him, he initially felt as if I was hugging a semi-frozen bag of ice cream, but, as I hung on, something incredible happened.

Seth embraced my torso like a small bear climbing a tree, hanging on for dear life and wailing inconsolably. The cold of his touch was almost unbearable at first then a feeling came over me that I had never experienced before, something impossible. Simultaneously, I felt the intense cold meld with an incredible feeling of warmth. As

I patted Seth's back I noticed this phenomenon more prominently as my hand went warm-cold with every pat. I slowly looked down, preparing myself for what I would see, not wanting to upset him further. What I saw didn't so much as terrify or repulse me as I couldn't escape the feeling like something inappropriately intimate was occurring. Of course there wasn't, and who is to say what is appropriate in circumstances such as these?

The areas where I felt the strange intermingling of cold and warmth were parts of Seth's body that were slowly sinking into mine. A knee, an elbow, the toes of a Spiderman tennis shoe, his chin were all protruding about an inch into my stomach, chest, hip and shoulder respectively. As I took note of this, another sensation caught my attention. I had the strange feeling of snowflakes falling on my shoulder and then turning into shooting warmth radiating from my shoulder all the way down to my feet. It took me a moment to comprehend this feeling and then it dawned on me as completely as the lavender light streaming in from the kitchen window. It was Seth's tears. They were passing through me just like I had seen them disappear into his bedspread earlier. I felt the sensation subside as Seth's crying slowed a little.

"It's okay, buddy," I said rubbing his back, feeling the strange mix of cold and warmth as my hand inadvertently penetrated his back. "I'll clean it up, it's okay."

"What's wrong with me?" he asked weakly as he pulled his head back as if to look at me, but instead buried his eyes behind his forearm to hide his sadness. I had the strange thought that considering everything I had just seen, Seth could possibly still see me through his arm. I wasn't sure and was rather doubtful; even though objects could pass through him and vice versa, I could not see through him. Well, there was the instance where the *Star Wars* figure sunk through his hand, but it was fairly close to the surface before it became visible.

"Nothing's wrong with you, buddy," I told him. "There's something wrong with the world." I pointed at the strange light out the window.

"That's what is affecting you, but I promise we'll make it all better."

He seemed to relax and even smiled a little after my promise. I'm surprised any of my promises carry any weight with him anymore. *I didn't even believe the one I had just made.* How could I? I had no idea what the hell was going on other than the reported story that the dead had become visible today, a scenario I'm not even sure I fully accept and probably would dismiss out of hand as tabloid foolery if not for the presence of my son.

I was just about to set him down on the edge of the table opposite his spilled meal when the phone rang. It startled me, causing me to flinch. I was afraid this would have an adverse effect on the mood, but it was just the opposite. Seth giggled at my reaction and commented impatiently.

"It's just the phone, Daddy."

I smiled and lovingly brushed my hand over his forehead, ignoring the cold.

He smiled. "You better get it! It might be Pubasher Kerrin House!"

Publisher's Clearing House was the running joke around our home whenever the phone rang or the mailman came – *It might be Publisher's Clearing House!* I don't think we had entered the sweepstakes in years, or at least I hadn't. Ann had a regular subscription to three different "chick magazines," so maybe we had.

I winked at Seth then walked across the kitchen to the cordless phone on the counter. I gave the caller ID a perfunctory glance and saw that it was not the Prize Committee; it was my boss, Don Lewis. Don was my boss but it was really a title he held in name only. I reported to him, but in actuality we worked as a partnership at PortaPad, Inc.; we were the two best mobile home salesmen in the state. We were also best friends. He was there for me when Ann and Seth were killed and told me to take as much time off from work as I needed. Don is a great guy, but like most of us, he has his faults. One of which happens to be letting whatever he's thinking spill out like a verbal geyser.

"Take all the time you need," he told me shortly after the funeral. "Grief is a tricky thing and can eat away at you if you don't work through it. I remembered when my dad died I locked myself in my room..." Don was cut off by his wife.

"God bless you Thomas, we are here if you need anything. Come on Don, it's time to go."

Don normally called my cell phone so this was unusual for him to call the landline. It didn't surprise me though; in fact, I was expecting it. I hadn't charged my cell phone in days and had no intention of doing so in the near future. I didn't want to talk to anyone, so I just put my ringer on silent and placed my cell in my dresser drawer to die a slow death of battery starvation. An annoying thought crossed my mind just before picking up the receiver: I should have unplugged that as well. I think the only reason I didn't is the fact that my self-imposed communication embargo would have surely brought visitors to my door, and *that* was the last thing I wanted.

"Hello," I said.

"Tommy! Can you believe this crap on the radio today? Ghosts appearing? What a hoot, eh?" Don said with the same lack of verbal filtration between his brain and his mouth. I understand his excitement, I really do.

"Have you seen any spooks on your block? I mean who you gonna call, right?" he asked with a disbelieving smile in his voice.

"What do you think, Don? I haven't listened to the radio in a little while. What is the official report?"

Don chuckled softly and took a deep breath like he was about to relay a very amusing story.

"Well..." he began, as if coming to the punch line of a joke. "They say old honest Abe is out and about in Washington, D.C., along with a few other dead presidents, and I ain't talking about cash!" He brayed with laughter at his cleverness and went on. "They also say that ghosts are showing up in people's homes and businesses, claiming they have been there all along but we just couldn't see them."

He sputtered laughter again, but this time I thought I detected something underneath his good humor and amusement. It was like hearing the faint sound of distant thunder on a gloriously sunny day; he was scared.

"Have you seen any?" I asked him.

He laughed again … there was the distant thunder, a little more prominent this time.

"It's just a big joke!" he snorted. "Dead people walking around? Please."

I know he failed to connect the dots in his head of how the event occurring today could possibly affect me considering my recent loss. I don't think he wanted to believe what he was hearing, so he was hiding under a façade of humor. I had never known Don to act this way, but then today was definitely unique circumstances.

I took a deep breath and looked up to see Seth sitting at the top of the stairs watching me. He had another toy in his hand, I couldn't tell what at this distance, and he smiled patiently at me. I was going to keep my mouth shut. I didn't want the attention and I was almost certain that any unwelcome gawkers would upset Seth immensely. I was going to remain quiet until Don spoke again, this time the fear was unmistakable.

"Gina … you know, my wife."

"Yes, I know Gina," I replied patiently.

There was a long pause and then heavy breathing, like he had just run up a few flights of stairs. He started to speak then his voice choked off like someone had just knocked the wind out of him. After another long pause I heard him swallow hard before he spoke.

"Gina called me at work about an hour ago and told me…" he took a couple of deep breaths and then changed his tone to incredulous disbelief, but the fear was still present in his voice like underlying feedback on a microphone. "I can't even believe I'm saying this!"

"It's okay, Don," I said calmly. "What are you trying to tell me?"

Nothing had ever acted as an adequate filter between Don's mind and mouth, but the fear of whatever he was trying to tell me seemed to be working like a charm.

"Gina called an hour ago … she said my dad was waiting for me in my study." His dad had passed away two years ago. I know because I was a pall bearer at the funeral, not to mention I was reminded of the fact two weeks ago when Don tried to comfort my grieving by telling the story of how he locked himself in his room after his father died. In Don terminology, his room was synonymous with his office.

"Are you going home?" I asked.

There was silence on the other end of the line.

"Don?"

There was another long silence and then Don exhaled loudly and spoke faintly.

"Would it be okay if I came and talked to you first?"

"You know I don't mind Don, but there is one thing you need to know before you do." I said.

"What?"

I closed my eyes and contemplated my response for a few moments. I had not intended to say anything on the subject but considering what Don had just told me, it might be appropriate.

"You need to know that Seth is here."

There was another long pause and then two words spoken with a hoarseness that made them barely audible.

"My … God …"

"Are you okay with that?" I asked.

"Is he, is he solid, can he walk through walls, can he fly, is he …?" Don said before I cut him off.

"He's fine, Don. Just let me do the talking when you come, okay?"

"Okay," he muttered, breathless.

I looked up and saw Seth was still sitting on the top of the stairs watching, a worried frown now creased his small face. I gave him a reassuring wink but before I could ask Don when he would be by, I saw a silvery flash outside my living room window. I looked out and saw Don's silver Camaro screeching to a halt in my driveway.

I looked back up at Seth but before I could say a word, he saw the look of exasperation on my face. He turned and retreated up the stairs, a moment later I heard the door to his room slam shut.

I met Don at the front door before he could ring the bell, knock, barge in or whatever he intended to do. His countenance did not match the jovial person I had just spoken to on the phone. My friend's fear was no longer the rumbling of a distant storm; his face was awash in a tempest of nervous excitement and terror.

"W-w-w-here is he?" Don stammered.

I was distracted momentarily by the atmosphere outside. This was the first time I had even opened a door or a window since the event began, and I quickly discovered that the mysterious lavender light was only half of the spectacle. It was hard to describe, but the air seemed to be alive; it pulsated and undulated like an electric charged breeze. It was not a visible sensation but a tactile one, felt by every square inch of my body. It was not unpleasant at all, more like being in a relaxing spa of warm electricity.

Don was about to push by me into the house when I came to my senses. I gently grabbed him by the upper arm and bade that he take a seat on the sofa. He looked at me with wild-eyed excitement, and then reluctantly sat down.

"Were you being serious with me?" he asked.

I nodded.

"Yes, but if I bring him down you have to promise me you won't say a word. You know how your mouth can outrun your brain," I said with a friendly grin.

He shook his head in the affirmative and gave me a half-smile.

"I know ... I promise."

I looked at him sternly for a few moments. He seemed to calm somewhat and then repeated his vow.

"I promise."

"Wait here," I said, then turned and slowly ascended the stairs.

I reached Seth's door and knocked lightly. No answer. I tried the knob and the door swung open effortlessly. I stepped into the room.

"Seth, buddy," I began, but then stopped in my tracks; he was nowhere to be seen.

I walked over to the closet door and called his name, no answer. I opened the door, no Seth. I turned in mounting panic, scanning the room wildly, and then my eyes fell on the bed. I walked up beside the bed, taking care not to tread on the Anakin Skywalker figure lying on the floor.

"Seth?"

No answer.

I got to my hands and knees and peered under the bed. No Seth. My heart was racing with panic now, I was frightened for the safety of my deceased son, but the irony was lost on me as I set out to inspect the rest of the upstairs rooms. After a quick and thorough search, a block of ice slid into my stomach, reminding me of the pain that was still fresh after just two weeks. Seth was gone.

CHAPTER 7
BOUNDLESS LIMITATIONS

"Only those who attempt the absurd can achieve the impossible."

~Albert Einstein

As I descended the stairs, I suspect my face looked very similar to Don's when he arrived; no … it was definitely worse. This was my child; I can't have lost him again, not this fast. I ran through the kitchen and out the door to the yard beyond Seth's window. I paid no attention to the unusual changes outside; my mind was focused on a singular purpose. My panic rose exponentially because he was nowhere to be seen in the yard.

"Seth! Seth!" I called and hopped up on the cedar picket fence surrounding our backyard. After scanning the perimeter I determined he was nowhere in sight, hopping down from the fence I was startled to see Don standing a few feet from me.

"Is everything okay?" he asked.

"Seth is gone!" I muttered breathlessly and darted past him and back into the house. I hadn't seen Seth come back downstairs, but searching the ground floor was the only option left to me. I had just searched the dining room when a shriek and a crash resounded from the kitchen. I entered the kitchen to see Don lying flat on his back and breathing heavily. He had slipped in Seth's cereal, which I had not had the opportunity to clean up yet.

"Are you all right?" I shouted.

He gave a sputtering cough and raised his thumb to indicate he was all right. Don began to slowly pull himself up using the counter and one of the kitchen chairs for leverage.

"Your housekeeping leaves a lot to be desired," he said as he plopped down in the chair, massaging his sore back and head. He pulled a couple of soggy Chocolate Berries from his sandy blond hair and flicked them onto the table with a look of distaste, like he had just removed bird poop.

"I'm sorry … Seth did that. I haven't had a chance to clean it up yet," I said as I grabbed a towel from the counter and handed it to Don. He looked at me skeptically. I could see that his belief that my dead son had returned was starting to wane quickly.

"Is he gone?" Don asked evenly as he toweled milk and Chocolate Berries off the back of his white golf shirt. There was going to be a big brown stain down his back unless he washed it soon.

"Yes," I replied between shouts for my son.

I was just about to ask Don for his help in the search when I spotted Seth through the partially opened door to the laundry room. He was hiding on the far side of the washing machine, in a three-foot space between the heavy duty Kenmore and the wall. When our eyes met, he frowned sheepishly, shook his head emphatically, and ducked back into his hidey hole. He was scared, embarrassed, and no telling what else he was feeling. I was not going to make him come out and perform like some freak for my boss's amusement.

Don always meant well, but his tact left a lot to be desired. I was just about to suggest we go search the garage so Seth could sneak back to his room when Don's phone rang.

"Hello?"

The caller ID was just visible to me as he held the phone to his ear; it was his wife.

I stood and watched his face melt into a sallow ashen mask as he listened to the one-sided dialogue on the other end of the line. At first, it was easy to tell that a woman, probably Gina, was speaking to him, in a rather scolding manner, causing a look of annoyance on his face. It was when the timbre of the voice turned to a masculine, husky drawl that all color drained from Don's face. Gina was no longer on the line, and based on what Don had told me earlier, I guessed it was his dad. I had only met the man once before he passed, so the voice was not that familiar, but Don's face was like a macabre caller ID as he listened to the deep voice he thought he would never hear again. Even at my distance several feet away, the voice was loud enough that I could hear the same tinny vibration as Seth's.

After several long moments, Don rasped a single word like it was his final death throes.

"Okay."

He dropped his arm holding the phone slowly to his side and took a deep rattling breath, then turned slowly to face me.

"I've got to go," he croaked.

"Was that your dad?" I asked.

Don didn't answer, he looked at me for several long moments with the flaccid expression of one who has just seen a ghost or, in this case perhaps, talked to one.

"I hope you find Seth," he said hoarsely as he started toward the door. The skepticism in his voice that was so prevalent a few minutes ago had been replaced by terrified sincerity.

"Thanks, I'm sure I will," I said, confident, looking over my shoulder in time to see Seth ducking back into his hidey hole.

I felt sorry for Don, I truly did. I understood the emotional turmoil and confusion he was about to endure, meeting a loved one who had just 'returned from the grave', but for him it was worse. He and his father had never had the best relationship in the world. In fact, it had been bad. From what Don had shared with me, his father was ex-military, a Marine. He was a good man but a strict disciplinarian of a father. I suspect this may have been a positive thing for Don, knowing his propensity for sloppiness, but according to Don, his father is what caused it.

He called it the "Barkley Syndrome" after former pro basketball star Charles Barkley. After years of fitness training, when Barkley finally retired he let himself go and became a rather rotund former basketball star. The logic to Don's analogy was that when he was finally out of his father's "bounce a quarter on the bed sheets, white-glove-inspected" house he let himself go out of rebellion, and quite frankly because he was tired of the stringency.

I think his real problem was the fact that he had made a number of candid and unkind remarks about his dad whenever I visited his home the last couple of years. I am certain that the negativity I heard was a small sampling of what had been discussed behind closed doors. Had his dad been there listening the last couple of years?

I guess Don was about to find that out. He had come to see me for a number of reasons – doubt, curiosity, and fear among them, but most likely he was procrastinating from facing his old man once again. It had been bad enough facing him in the flesh but now … I suspect there are a lot of people going through their own individual Hell of impromptu reunions today with the dearly departed.

"Just remember, he is still your dad," I said as I held the front door open for him. That was the best I could offer. Even though I was 95-percent sure that Seth was Seth, that 5-percent still nagged at me. I mean, how certain about anything are we really?

Don nodded imperceptibly and headed down the sidewalk like a man walking to his execution. He slumped into his Camaro and grinded the gears as he shifted into reverse and then grinded them again as he lurched forward into first gear and slowly disappeared around the corner.

Dusk was settling across the neighborhood, giving the outdoors a surreal quality. The blackness of night seemed to have been replaced by the uncanny lavender glow. It was not like the darkness was illuminated by this extra-terrestrial light, it was like it had been replaced. The air shone eerily like a large black-light painting, undulating in almost imperceptible waves.

It was late spring and an otherwise cool and pleasant evening. That's what made it so darn strange that there were no people out. No people in the yards, no kids playing, and no traffic … it was as if everyone had vanished. The only thing dispelling that perception was that most of the homes had lights on and blinds drawn; moving shadows could be seen passing about inside some of the windows. People were there, they just seemed to be heeding the warnings to stay indoors.

Turning around, I saw Seth had cautiously crept from his hiding place and was watching me hopefully from the laundry room door. I stepped back inside then firmly closed and locked the door.

"Is he gone?" Seth asked, apprehensive.

"Yes he is. Why did you do that, buddy? You had me worried sick."

"I didn't want him to see me," Seth said with a sadness that was deeper than any I had ever seen in him.

I suspected I knew the answer but I asked anyway.

"Why not?"

He pointed at the mess of cereal now smeared across the kitchen floor. A tangled knot of frustration and love formed in my gut. I loved Seth dearly and would defend him to the end of time, but I also knew he was right. The people who still occupied the world of the living would look at him as a freak, a novelty, something to ogle, but also something to fear. He would be nothing more to them than an attraction at a funhouse or a zoo.

Seth would be the amputee, the paraplegic, the burn victim, or deformed person who constantly finds himself the subject of unkind voyeurism, making him the outcast or the punch line. The world is cruel, damn cruel, to those that are different. I knew he could never live a normal life, but is that what he's doing? I buried him just two weeks ago, and now I'm talking about a normal life? How could he have any chance of normalcy if his own dad had doubts? I had to do something and do something quickly; we couldn't just sit around in the house and hope for the best.

That was not good for Seth, and as far as I knew this "storm" might pass by morning, returning things to normal, putting Seth back into his impalpable state and pouring salt on the fresh wound in my heart. Dread rose in me so quickly that my breath hitched. I could feel every blood vessel course with panic when I realized the probable truth – I could lose him again. The obvious solution popped into my head like a light flicking on, but I decided I would ease into it first with Seth, to make sure he was still comfortable with the idea and to try to get him in a little better mood. I sat down on the sofa and started the conversation by changing the subject.

"Buddy, how did you get down here without me seeing you?"

His sad expression turned to a knowing grin as he looked up and pointed his finger.

I frowned and shook my head, clearly not understanding his inference.

"Through the ceiling!" he said with his trademark mischievous grin.

I swallowed hard as understanding dawned.

"You went through the ceiling?"

He shook his head and spoke with cocky kid confidence.

"It's pretty easy. It doesn't hurt or nothing ... it kinda tickles."

"Can you go through this chair?" I asked, pointing to the La-Z-Boy in front of me.

His chest puffed up with importance and he walked to the chair.

"Okay, watch!" he beckoned like an excited kid wanting to

demonstrate his diving technique for the first time in the pool.

I stood up and crossed my arms to indicate I was paying complete attention and smiled supportively. He smiled back and positioned himself behind the chair with a look of intense concentration on his face. He swung his arms frontward and backward a couple of times and moved toward the chair. When he reached the back I didn't think he would be able to continue as he appeared to stop dead in his tracks, but then he slowly began to move forward like a person walking into a strong wind.

A few moments later he was fully submerged in the chair with only the top of his head sticking out of the back cushion. Slowly his arms emerged, then his face and torso, he was smiling triumphantly as he moved forward, still immersed from the waist down in the bottom of the recliner. He giggled as he raised his knees like he was high-stepping. His knees popping up out of the seat cushion like that reminded me of that game where gophers pop up out of holes as the player whacks them on the head with a hammer. A few moments later, he was free of the chair and grinning at me like he had just hit a home run to win the big game.

"Awesome!" I exclaimed with sincere pride. And I was proud of my boy, even if what I had just witnessed was beyond bizarre. I also felt as helpless as a man that cannot swim watching his son flounder in deep water. What could I do to help him? I did not know for sure but I suspected my idea might be a start. Now that I had gotten him in a little better spirits, no pun intended, I would lay out my plan. I knew the response it would get before I even opened my mouth. After all, it was the reason that Seth was here with me in the first place.

"Seth, buddy, how would you like to go to Washington, D.C., in the morning?"

"The Air Space Moozem in Washaton?" he beamed with excitement.

"Yes sir," I smiled and took his small hand, hardly noticing the strange sensation of cold and warmth as he squeezed my hand.

He began to hop up and down with excitement. Each time he

came down, his feet sank about three inches into the floor. Seth was positively giddy.

I didn't even think about telling Don. Honestly, I didn't really care if I told him. I was going to go regardless of what he said, and he had his own issues to handle.

"We'll leave first thing in the morning," I told him. "I'll put my bag together tonight so we can just get up and go."

I stopped and discreetly examined Seth as he continued to prance with childlike glee. Would I need to pack clothes for him? I didn't think so; his clothes and shoes seemed as much a part of him as his own skin. How was he even wearing clothes? I guess that was as much of a mystery as the very presence of him. Maybe the old expression "clothes make the man" is even more of a truism than we realize. I decided it best to let Seth take the lead; I would let him tell me what he needed.

"What would you like to pack, buddy?" I asked him. "Let's get everything you need ready tonight so we can get an early start in the morning."

He excitedly bolted up the stairs, beckoning for me to follow. I followed after retrieving his Buzz Lightyear suitcase from the hall closet. Thank God it had not been donated along with his cereal bowl.

A few moments after opening the suitcase on his bed it was filled with three *Star Wars* figures, Seth's teddy bear, Luke, and a dozen or so assorted Spider-Man and Batman comics.

"Is that all you need?" I asked with a tone urging him to think about it. "Remember, we are going to be gone several days and you want to take everything you will *need*," I added, putting special emphasis on need.

He nodded his head and then responded like he had just read my mind.

"Yep, I think so. I can't wear any of my clothes, they won't stay on me … I already tried. I guess I'll just wear this the whole trip," he said with a quick spin like he was modeling for me. He paused as a serious expression washed over his face.

"Momma wouldn't let me wear the same clothes more than once. She would tell me she ain't raising no stinky boy."

A lump welled up in my throat as I thought of Ann. I had heard her tell Seth that on more than one occasion. He had his comfortable favorites he liked to wear and wear often, but hey, don't we all? I fought back a tear as I reassured him.

"I don't think Momma would mind buddy. Besides, it's just you and me … a guy's trip," I said with a wink.

Yes indeed, it was going to be a guy's trip and like most guys, I pack light. Just the necessities. Fifteen minutes later, both of our bags were packed and stacked neatly by the door. Seth climbed in bed with me. To my surprise, he informed me that he had slept quite a bit in the past two weeks. I don't know why he has to sleep, but at least that's one more thing we have in common. I was tempted to turn on the radio and get an update but I decided against it. What were the 'experts' going to tell me? That this is going away in the morning and everything will be back the way it was? I didn't want to hear it. I would at least enjoy tonight, one quiet night with my son.

After a long period of conversation, mainly Seth telling me in great detail everything he wanted to see at the Smithsonian, he drifted off to sleep. I fought it as long as I could, fearing what the morning may bring. I wanted to relish every moment with Seth.

Rest was hard to come by as I lay awake watching him sleep. I was scared: scared to take my eyes off him, afraid that he could be gone at any moment. I was terrified of losing him again. I don't think I could take the pain.

As I considered my sleeping son, other possibilities began to float through my head. My parents had been gone now for almost 14 years. Did they stay? Did Ann's parents stay? My heart leapt with anticipation at the prospect. If they had, they were not here and their home on the other side of town was now occupied by a young family. Surely they would have called me if they had unexpected guests.

Well, unless they had fled in terror. My dad, with his gruff exterior, had that impact on people even when he was alive.

As much as I would like to see my mom and dad again, I had to focus on Seth. They were adults and, if they were still here, they could find me. I put the thought out of my head with the promise to myself that I would drive by their house on the way out of town tomorrow. Sleep finally came, but it was anything but restful.

CHAPTER 8
RATTLING BRIDGES

*"A person may cause evil to others not only
by his action but by his inaction, and in either case he is
justly accountable to them for the injury."*

~John Stuart Mill

The President of the United States got no sleep that night, as most leaders around the world didn't. He and his political and military advisors, along with scientists from NASA, MIT, Stanford, and a few other assorted government agencies spent the evening in the White House situation room monitoring developments. The scientists agreed on one thing – they had no idea what the phenomenon was or why it was disrupting television and internet but not radio. They also had no idea as to why it had suddenly unveiled the dead.

The scientists were split down the middle about whether the storm produced an unknown energy that affected the human brain, causing hallucinations, or if it really did evoke a physical manifestation of the unseen spirit world. The scientists on the hallucination side of the debate crudely referred to the visions of the deceased as "brain farts." The phrase that the scientists used describing the spirit side was one that fit perfectly and was much more refined term than its hallucinatory counterpart. It meant "not capable of being perceived by the senses." They called them "the Impalpables," or "Impals" for short.

The most important question batted about was whether or not this new form of energy caused adverse health effects. So far there was no evidence of that but it had been less than 24-hours since the storm entered Earth's atmosphere. There was no way as of yet to measure this unknown form of energy, so the only scientific method available was the tried and true technique – *just wait and see.*

There was one troubling development that had become apparent overnight, a development that the president's advisors had spent a great deal of time coaching exactly how to present to the media, a development that could easily lead to global unrest if not handled with the utmost care. Indeed it would be very important, but seemingly insignificant at first, like a single spark from a dangling tailpipe in the middle of a tender dry forest that later produced a blaze of unimaginable consequences.

Aside from the scientists, the military, and the presidential advisors, there was another present at this meeting. He was an individual who showed great distaste toward any nickname. He had seen and heard this kind of talk before, not only in his living days but in the years since as one president after another occupied the place he had called home for four years. They afforded him no more attention than they would the air in the room. But how could they? Hadn't he, by the very definition, been exactly what the despised nickname suggested? Impalpable.

Living may not be an appropriate term for the last 100 years or more, but he had existed a long time. He had existed long enough to know that he didn't care for some of the ideas and language coming from the room. He had heard it before, not only during the last great trial of his life as he struggled to keep a nation together but also since that time from the mouths and actions of a number of advisors and leaders occupying what should be an honored house.

If there was one thing he had learned the last two centuries were that the ideals that spawned and maintain America are of divine providence and should be defended to the end, but the governmental offices were rarely a reflection of these ideals. He had decided long ago that if white represents purity and virtue, the presidential residence should have been painted sack cloth black decades ago.

He had worked through the initial discomfort of the day, being ogled and stared at, because he felt like he needed to listen to what was going on as it most decidedly involved him. He had now had all he could stand after the tenth time of being asked if it hurt when he was assassinated and if he had seen John Wilkes Booth anywhere in the spirit realm. The answer to both questions was no, but that was beside the point, he felt like some freak in Ringling Brothers Circus. He had observed the spectacle when the travelling show did a special White House appearance on the front lawn for President Garfield. He found it revolting and not much more dignified than a slave auction – another place where distasteful nicknames were freely used without compassion.

After the "straw breaking the camel's back" question was asked, this time by a general, of all people, he smiled politely – if nothing else he was the consummate gentleman – and answered 'no sir' to both questions and politely excused himself from the room. While his faith in his successors may have waned over the decades, his sense of humor had not. It had been one of his strongest attributes in his political career and probably had helped him endure his life as an unseen visitor in the most important house in the world. That and the fact that he was not the only invisible resident of the nation's capital. He had made many friends over the last 100 years and he needed to talk to them now—not only for his sake, but for theirs, as well.

He had respectfully been given free rein to roam about the White House as he saw fit – respecting privacy. Of course, he had enjoyed free rein before over the last 100 years, but no one knew he was there. He edged through the doors to the rose garden under the dumbstruck and restrained stares of the Secret Service. His tall, slender, ethereal outline was barely visible until he reached the perimeter fence and then disappeared into the fading darkness.

A few minutes later, the sun's first rays began to drive back the bizarre black light nighttime, spreading fading lavender over the Washington monument as the surreal night retreated. It was like a photo negative slowly developing into a clear print. This would be the first sunrise over a new and redefined world; however, the new definition remained to be seen.

I woke up early the next morning, my heart thumping against my ribs like a caged bird. Had I been dreaming? I wasn't sure but I knew there was an underlying panic, something that I dreaded waking for. I fought hard to clear the cobwebs from my head. As my thoughts began to take cohesion, a single word came to mind ... Seth.

Remembering the past day's events and my fear of what the morning might bring, I spun in bed to verify the other side was occupied. My hopes sank like a large boulder sliding into my stomach; Seth was not there. I sprung from the bed and was halfway to the door before my sheets touched back down on my mattress.

Seth's suitcase was still there by the door but there was no sign of him. Did I have a bizarre dream and pack his suitcase and mine in my sleep? I seriously considered that possibility for a moment, but the otherworldly lavender light filtering through the drapes dispelled that thought. He had to be here somewhere; after all, the strange light was still here.

"Seth! Seth!" I called in a panic as I sprinted through my bedroom door and across the landing to Seth's room.

I was just about to fling the door open when I heard Seth's voice call from downstairs.

"Daddy? What are you doing?" he called.

"Looking for you!" I shouted back with a mixture of relief and aggravation.

I started down the stairs and saw him coming back through the door to the garage dragging a large canvas bag that I recognized as the one that stored our sleeping bags. I hadn't made it to the garage yet since the funeral, so the bag still carried all three of our sleeping bags – the down-filled plaid that was mine, the down-filled yellow that belonged to Ann, and the *Star Wars* sleeping bag.

"What are you doing Seth?" I asked, a bit perplexed. I had every intention of taking our trip but I had no intention of camping out. Motel 6 and Super 8 were my idea of roughing it.

"I almost forgot these. We may have to camp out between here and there," he said, then frowned and added, "Where's the tent?"

I had put the tent in the attic a couple of months ago. Its bulky box took up too much room in our two-car garage. It was stored against the wall in front of where I parked. I frankly had gotten tired of squeezing between the rear of my SUV and the garage door. It was not only an inconvenience but a constant reminder of my expanding waistline. With the box out of the way, I could easily walk in the three-foot area between my vehicle and the wall, no problem. Besides, it was too darned heavy to try and hoist out of the attic.

"We won't need that," I said with exaggerated excitement for his benefit. "If we have to camp, we can spread the bags out in the back of the SUV. Won't that be fun?"

He looked at me doubtfully for a few moments then shrugged and carefully placed the bags by the door.

"Okay, I'm ready!" he said as he sat down hard on the bag, his rear end noticeably sinking a couple of inches through the canvas.

"Give me a minute, buddy, and I'll be ready to rattle some bridges!"

I said before turning and heading for the bathroom where an eye opening morning shower was calling my name. I hardly noticed Seth's confusion, but he had an expression like he had come across a difficult problem on his homework. He was probably trying to figure out my expression about bridges.

Fifteen minutes later I was showered, dressed, and ready to go. Seth excitedly dragged his suitcase downstairs and through the garage door, parking it near the rear of my SUV. He then stacked the sleeping bag carrier beside it. I brought my case downstairs, locked the doors and set the security system, then closed and locked the door to the house. I hit the button opening the big garage door and helped Seth load the bags in the back. I had just one thing I needed to do before we left, I needed to call Don and let him know I would be out of town for a while. I opened the door for Seth and turned the key to accessory so he could listen to Radio Disney while I made my phone call.

I was apprehensive about making the call. Not because I was afraid he would say no and tell me to go back to work; that was immaterial. This trip is going to happen regardless. I was apprehensive because of the state Don was in when he left last night. I knew this was not going to be easy for him and I had no idea what to expect. Thankfully for me, Gina answered the phone.

"Hello?" she said, weary.

"Gina, this is Thomas. Is Don available?"

She sighed heavily.

"I'm so glad you called Thomas; it has been a rough night."

"Is everything okay?" I asked, a knot starting to form in my stomach.

"I guess as okay as can be expected, given the circumstances. Don was up until three or four this morning talking to his ... his dad. I still can't believe this is happening. It sounds so strange to talk about him again like he's still living, but I guess he is still living in a sense."

"I know exactly what you mean," I said as I looked in the window at Seth. He was sitting there, happily mouthing the words to one of his favorite Disney tunes.

"Oh ... oh, Thomas I'm sorry. How is Seth?"

"Fine," I said as I caught Seth's eye and gave him a reassuring wink. He grinned comically and winked back before resuming his radio lip sync. "That's kind of what I was calling about. I guess Don is still asleep since he was up all night?"

"Yes," she said ruefully then continued with a hopeful tone. "Do you want me to wake him?"

I suspected it was because Don's father was not asleep and she felt uncomfortable about being alone with him. She was probably looking for an excuse to wake Don. Come to think of it, I was not even sure if Seth slept or not. I fell asleep talking to him last night and he was up and about when I woke up.

"No Gina, that's okay ... can you give him a message for me?"

She sighed noticeably and I thought I detected a faint sob rattling underneath.

"All right ... what?" she said.

"Gina, is everything okay?"

I heard a faint sniffle and then she cleared her throat before speaking.

"Yes, it's just hard you know ... losing someone, making peace with the loss and then suddenly they're back." She took a deep breath and mustered a more positive tone. "I think it is going to be a good thing ultimately. As crazy as this sounds, I actually think it will help their relationship."

"That's great," I said. I could definitely relate to the losing someone and then suddenly they are back. In my case I had not made peace with it yet; it had only been a couple of weeks. Two weeks or two years, I wasn't sure with which would be the most difficult to come to terms. Maybe it was personal prejudice on my part, but I suspected that my situation had to be worse. I lost my child and that goes as much against the natural order of things as this phenomenon does. It is an abomination to nature and a terror that haunts the soul of all mothers and fathers. When I thought of it in those terms, I didn't feel so sorry for Don anymore. Empathetic? Yes. Sorry? No.

"Listen Gina, I am taking Seth out of town for a few days, maybe a couple of weeks. I wanted you to let Don know that I would be gone."

"Are you coming back?" she said in a tone that almost sounded panicked.

It never occurred to me that I would not come back, so the question took me completely off guard. It also gave me an uncomfortable moment of pause.

"Uh … yeah," I stammered. "We intend to."

I looked back in the window at Seth. He was still lip syncing and swaying his shoulders. Our eyes met and he motioned for me to come on and go already.

"Gina, I need to go. I know you and Don have my number if you need me," I said, and then told her our travel destination.

"That sounds like fun," she said. "Give Seth a hug for me."

"I will. You guys take care. Tell Don to give me a call if he needs to talk."

"I'll do that, Thomas. You are a good friend. Have a good trip and come back safely."

"We will. Goodbye, Gina."

I put the phone in my pocket, slipped into the driver's seat, and turned the volume down on the Jonas Brothers. Seth looked at me hopefully.

"Are you ready to rabble bridges?" he asked.

I chuckled when I realized he had picked up on my 'rattling bridges' expression.

"I'm ready!" I said as I turned the ignition over and fired the vehicle to life.

Seth looked at me with a puzzled frown.

"What does that mean?"

I explained to him that it was an expression I had picked up from my grandfather when I was a kid. The way he had explained it to me is that when he was young, most bridges were made of wood and they rattled when you crossed them. When you went on a trip you crossed a lot of bridges, so you were rattling bridges.

Seth looked at me with a mixture of doubt and comprehension. I suspect he comprehended the expression as well as any six-year-old could, not knowing anything of the world prior to the dawn of the 21st Century. Seth was a smart kid, though, smarter than I was at that age.

I shifted the SUV into reverse and cleared the garage door, closing it with a click of my remote. I carefully backed into the street. The neighborhood was still eerily silent and still. It was not empty, though. I noted several curious observers from a number of neighbors peering through drapes or blinds. We did live in a neighborhood with a high population of retirees and we didn't see them much. I couldn't even tell you half of my neighbors' names.

Zoning for our neighborhood dictated there be no names on the brick mailboxes, just the house number in raised brass letters. Most of my neighbors were just a number to me, I'm sad to say. I saw number 19 and 21 quickly withdraw their heads and shut the blinds as I stopped in the middle of the street and looked in their direction. They were embarrassed to be caught looking but they were frightened as well, and that I completely understood.

I was just about to shift into drive as I looked up into the lavender sky and the strange, yellow clouds. It made me think of *Alice in Wonderland* again, which made me think of Disney World, which ignited a memory, one I had not thought of in a long time. The first time I went to Disney World, the ride I was excited about the most was the Jungle Cruise. I guess maybe it was because I was a Tarzan fan as a kid. It was not just that strange sky that invoked this memory, it was also the feeling I had inside at this very moment.

When I got in the boat and took my seat in preparation for the ride, I had a nervous excitement burning within me. I was scared because I had no idea what dangers lurked ahead in the form of lions, hippos, or giant snakes, but I was excited because of the thrill of adventure and the thrill of the unknown. That was exactly how I felt now. I was scared of what was occurring and what we may encounter on our trip but I was also excited. This was definitely an unknown. I shifted the vehicle into drive and set out on a trip that would prove to be unlike any I had taken before.

CHAPTER 9
FATHER WILSON

"Preach the Gospel at all times and when necessary use words."

~Francis of Assisi

The trip was unexpectedly delayed by the flashing of headlights and honking of a horn behind me. I looked in the mirror to see Father Wilson in his small green sedan desperately trying to get my attention.

Seth looked at me with a confused frown.

I smiled sympathetically as I secretly gritted my teeth in aggravation.

"I'm sorry, buddy. I guess the trip is going to have to wait a few minutes."

His disappointed face was a direct reflection of how I felt. I was looking forward to our little adventure, I really was. I did not want to have a conversation with the Father now, I just wanted to get on the road.

"Who is it?" Seth asked, not recognizing the car.

I turned the wheel and pulled to the curb before shifting into park and stepping out.

Seth hopped out and bounded to my side.

"Is that Father Wilson, Daddy?"

"Yes," I said, but when I saw his worried look I knelt down beside him. "We won't be long; he just wants to wish us well on our trip."

"Why don't you go in the house and play while I talk to the Father."

"Can I get my toys out?" he asked.

"Of course," I said as I opened the back door.

He grabbed his duffel bag of toys and set it on the ground with one hand out.

I looked at him stupidly as he continued to hold out his hand with mounting impatience.

"Can I go inside?" he asked.

I shook my head like I was trying to sweep away the cobwebs then gently placed the keys in his palm.

"Here ya go, buddy," I said as he started for the door.

"Okey dokey," he called as he put the key in the lock and opened the door. It just occurred to me that Seth could have gotten in the house without the aid of a key. I was glad to see that we were keeping it normal. Of course, I really had no idea what was normal anymore.

Just as I watched Seth disappear into the house, a lump formed in the pit of my stomach. Father Wilson had gotten out and was walking toward me, a stern but pleasant expression on his face. I did want to talk to him about some of the discussion topics at Seth's school, but I didn't want to have that conversation now.

He was dressed as he typically is – black shirt, black pants and white priest's collar. With his gray hair and sagging jowls he has always reminded me of the old priest in *The Exorcist*. Childishly, my first impulse was to run inside and lock the door, but the time had come to speak to the man. I really didn't have any more excuses to put him off. He had been concerned for my well-being after Ann and

Seth's accident, which I appreciated. But I had blown him off because I didn't want to have that discussion with anyone especially after my friends' – primarily Gina and Don Lewis – goodhearted attempts to rid my house of all reminders of my wife and child's existence. I wasn't ready to let go, and am not sure I ever will be. I guess in my view, discussing it with a priest would put the final dagger through my heart; it would give their existence the finality that I was not prepared to acknowledge.

My issues about discussing abortion and suicide with six-year-olds seemed trivial now considering what had happened to me and what was going on in the world, but it suddenly occurred to me that he might have an interesting perspective on current events. As it turned out, he did, he had also come to discuss one of the very topics I had wanted to discuss with him.

"Good morning, Father," I said, smiling as he approached me with an apprehensive expression. I understand his wariness, since the last couple of visits from him I was less than cordial, practically slamming the door in his face.

"Good morning, Thomas," he drawled. Father Wilson had always sounded more like a stereotypical southern evangelist than a stereotypical Catholic priest. He paused momentarily, half-looking at the ground and half-looking at me before he continued.

"How are you today?" he said quietly with sincere undertones of empathy in his voice.

I extended my hand to him. "I'm fine, Father."

He looked genuinely shocked for a moment but quickly recovered and shook my hand vigorously.

"I'm glad to hear that Thomas. I just stopped by to let you know that if you ever need to talk, I am here," he said, and then paused as his face wrinkled into a more serious expression. "Especially if you would like to talk about what is going on now."

It suddenly dawned on me that he must know about Seth. Determining how he found out didn't take very long because the only people that knew Seth was back were Don and Gina Lewis. I didn't think Don had told him because he was too busy with his own issues. The question is, did Gina tell him before or after I spoke with her this morning? I guess it didn't really matter; she thought she was doing the right thing as misguided as her good intentions often were.

"We're fine," I said, watching his reaction carefully.

My suspicion was confirmed as he showed no surprise at my use of the plural pronoun.

"Glad to hear it, glad to hear it!" he said. "Is he …?"

"In the house," I finished. "I would prefer that we leave him out of our discussion."

Father Wilson nodded sheepishly.

"Of course," he said.

"And, no … his mother is not with him," I said as a breeze blew the aroma of Ann's prize rose garden past my nose. The fragrance invoked a sweet memory of my beloved wife. It took everything I had to suppress a tear.

Father Wilson did not respond but simply nodded with a sympathetic smile.

I decided not to beat around the bush.

"Can you explain what is happening, Father?" I asked.

His face lit up as brilliantly as the lavender sky.

"Oh, yes … isn't it wonderful?" he beamed.

All I could manage was an incredulous stare; the good Father had taken me completely by surprise. Before I could formulate a response, he continued.

"It proves what we have been preaching for centuries, proves it beyond a shadow of a doubt!"

"What?" I managed to utter stupidly.

He looked at me as if I was laughable.

"Why, the existence of the soul of course!" he grinned with the same overindulgence of excitement.

I have to admit that my view of the whole event had been very narrowly focused. I had not yet considered the larger implications that this incident held. Frankly, it was just not that important to me. What was important was a "who," and that "who" was in the house, and I wanted to get back to him. As anxious as I was, my curiosity kept me engaged with the Father.

"Why are they here?" I asked.

"Well from what I hear, they are here by choice," he said.

I nodded with as neutral an expression as I could manage. I had no intention of telling him anything about Seth, especially not his mention of the doors and Ann.

"That proves another point we have been preaching for centuries," Father Wilson said. "It proves that God does give us free will!"

I was starting to think that Father Wilson was sounding more like an attorney than a priest, laying out his proof to a jury of one.

"Is that what you came to tell me?" I asked, starting to get a little irritated. I really wanted to go in and check on Seth.

"No, no," he said, his jovial demeanor suddenly replaced with a look of seriousness. "I wanted to warn you."

He got my attention.

"About what?" I asked.

He blinked and fidgeted before clearing his throat and continuing with a question.

"Did you know that everyone who dies now has no choice?"

I shook my head and shrugged, clearing not grasping his meaning.

"They are stuck here whether they like it or not," Father Wilson said.

I started shaking my head, confused as to what exactly he was telling me. My shaking head slowly ceased as comprehension dawned.

"Everybody?" I asked.

The Father nodded his head curtly.

"Everybody," he said.

Grief is capable of putting all kinds of strange thoughts into a person's head. I had a thought hit me from nowhere.

If Ann and Seth had to die, why couldn't it have been a couple of weeks later?

I felt ashamed for thinking such a thing and quickly tried to shove the thought out of my head, but it refused to leave, hanging on as stubbornly as my love for my lost wife.

Father Wilson allowed me to absorb this information as he nervously pulled at his collar, trying to get cool. It was still relatively early in the morning, but the temperature was already in the mid-'80s. Sweat beaded on my lip and streamed down my back as I pondered this for several moments. Gradually my thoughts fell back to his original statement; that he had come to warn me about something.

"What did you want to warn me about?" I asked.

"Well," he began with a nervous cough. "Do you know Elbert Bachman?"

I nodded my head. I did vaguely know Elbert and his wife. They were an older couple at the church, very nice and generous, but we were not close friends. I guess that is why I was shocked last year when Elbert asked me to be a pall bearer at his wife's funeral. I agreed to the request and in the end I was honored to help lay his beloved Gertrude to rest. I guess I had something in common with Elbert now, something terrible.

"Yes," I said. "His wife died last year." I paused for a moment and asked, "Is she back?"

Father Wilson nodded his head mournfully. I didn't understand his sorrowful reaction until he answered.

"Yes and Elbert tried to be with her or be like her," he said.

"He died?" I said.

"He committed suicide," the Father said staring at the ground and slowly shaking his head.

It felt like a small tea kettle had boiled over in my stomach at this proclamation, I was suddenly reminded of the conversation I had intended to have with Father Wilson. But it was nothing compared to the volcano that was about to erupt.

"So … they are together now?" I asked.

The Father continued to shake his head sadly, keeping his eyes fixed on the ground.

"Not exactly," he said in a hushed voice.

He finally looked up at me after several silent moments and said in the same quiet voice, "It proves what we've been saying about suicide all these years."

I looked at him, feeling my cheeks start to flush with anger.

"Is he burning in Hell?" I asked, sarcasm dripping from my words.

If the Father was offended by my off handed remark, he didn't show it. His mouth was drawn in a straight line and he looked directly at me as he spoke.

"He is in a coma; well at least his spirit is any way. According to what I heard on the news this morning that seems to be what has happened to everyone who has committed that unforgiveable sin since this all started."

My curiosity dispersed my anger momentarily.

"A coma?" I repeated a bit perplexed.

"Yes, it seems the spirit left the body true enough, but then it instantly falls into a deep, catatonic sleep."

"No one has woken up?" I asked.

"Not yet, but of course it hasn't been that long yet. I think it is God's way of telling us it is wrong, and he separates these souls from the others," Father Wilson added.

I could feel my anger starting to rise again. I don't know why Father Wilson has always gotten under my skin; I generally agree with most of his beliefs. I think it is his delivery, his lack of tact, especially when it came to his non-age-appropriate discussions with the children at the school. Like Don, he never has had much of a filter between his brain and mouth. That is a dangerous condition for a priest to suffer from. Little did I know that with my next question, my inner volcano was about to blow.

"So what did you want to warn me about?" I asked, impatiently. While this information was interesting, I didn't see how any of it pertained to me.

Father Wilson looked at me with raised bushy white eyebrows and spoke in a hushed but unfiltered tone, like the answer should be as perfectly plain as the nose on my face.

"I didn't want the same thing to happen to you."

First, I was dumbstruck. The thought had never even entered my mind. That lasted only a couple of moments as the rage seemed to work its way up from my gut and spread to all of my extremities with a radiating heat, finally erupting from my mouth with a viral explosion.

"Who in the hell do you think you are? What the hell makes you think I would even consider something like that?" I hissed.

Father Wilson's mouth opened and closed wordlessly like a fish gasping for oxygen. He continued to gaze at me with eyes bulging from shock and a mouth still silently opening and closing. I walked around and opened the passenger door, pretending that I was looking for something in the glove box, hoping that he would take the hint. I am not a short-tempered individual by any stretch of the imagination, but Father Wilson was one of those few people who could push the envelope with my resolve to be civil. Thankfully, he slowly retreated to his car and drove away. Deep down I felt bad about our encounter, but on the other hand I don't think anyone has said something so offensive to me in a long time. The very idea that I might contemplate suicide to be with Seth. I would do anything for my boy, but I don't see how that could be helpful, especially now that he is back.

I went inside to check on Seth. I needed to cool off as well, between the weather and Father Wilson I felt like my head was in a crock pot. I found Seth sitting on the living room floor playing with a couple of Hot Wheels cars. He seemed as pleasant as ever, thankfully unaware of my confrontation with the good Father.

"When can we go, Daddy?" he asked.

"Now," I promised. "As soon as you gather your toys."

CHAPTER 10
UNSEEN DEVELOPMENTS

*"Travel, in the younger sort, is a part of education;
in the elder, a part of experience."*

~Francis Bacon

I managed to recapture the same sense of adventure from ten minutes earlier as we pulled away from the curb. It reminded me of my first time on the Jungle Boat Ride at Disney World. I wasn't really sure what to expect. My heart hammered in my chest like a caged bird when I remembered my promise to myself to go by my parents' old house. I exhaled and swallowed as I made a left turn at the next light and headed to the far side of town.

At first, it was nothing out of the ordinary. The streets and neighborhoods were not filled with ghosts dragging chains across the streets or odd looking specters hitchhiking, like from the

Haunted Mansion ride, which was another one of my favorite Disney attractions as a kid.

Although, I do have to admit that on my first visit, my anxiety got the best of me causing me to flee in terror through the crowd. My parents caught up to me by the Country Bear's Jamboree and after a little motherly coaxing and a Mickey Mouse ice cream bar, I was ready to brave the darkness of the old foreboding house.

The streets and neighborhoods were the same as they ever were, save the strange sky overhead. Traffic was at a minimum and the eerie lack of human activity reminded me of the sleepiness of the town at 3 A.M., not at 10 A.M. as it was now.

I didn't realize how much I wanted to see my parents until I arrived at their former abode and found it unoccupied. The family still lived there as evidenced by the furniture inside and toys in the yard but they were not home and neither were my parents. I knocked on every door until my knuckles throbbed in protest but there was no response. The Erions were our neighbors when I was a kid and they still lived next door. I started to walk over and ask questions but as I reached the property line I stopped in my tracks. Their living room curtains were open and I could see them sitting around the table and having a meal, but it was more than just Mr. and Mrs. Erion.

The ethereal glow of a person like Seth could be clearly seen through the window. Whoever it was, their back was to me. It took a few moments for recognition to sink in but when it did my stomach twisted. It was the Erions' son, Jack. He had been about ten years older than me, but he was probably the closest thing I ever had to a brother. Jack always played catch with me, took me to movies, and even bought me baseball cards. I was only nine when he was killed by an eighteen-wheeler on a snowy road just north of Conway. It broke my heart almost as much as when my parents died.

My first impulse was to run to the door and reunite with my old friend, but I had to remember why I was here. I had come to look for my parents but my first priority was Seth. Besides, as much as I was sure that Jack would like to see me again, I needed to give him and his parents some time. They needed to make the most out of their miracle as much as I needed to make the most of mine.

I cautiously stepped back and out of view then looked back at the SUV in the driveway. Seth was curiously looking at me through the window. I smiled reassuringly and waved then climbed the front steps of my former residence. I retrieved a business card and a pen from my pocket then hastily scribbled a message on the back.

Please call me if you meet Phillip or Tamara Pendleton. I am their son.

After carefully sliding the card in the door jamb where it could easily be seen, I turned and slowly walked back down the stairs and up the sidewalk to the SUV. My heart was heavy with disappointment, but it was also light with anticipation of my time with Seth. My life had become an emotional contradiction the past couple of days.

We continued to the highway looping around the south side of Conway and connecting to I-40 to the east. I tensed as we neared Oak Grove, a massive 40-acre cemetery in the southeast part of the city. I am not sure why passing the cemetery made me so nervous. Did I expect it to be one big ghost gathering of all those who were laid to rest there? If that was the reason, my fears seemed to be unfounded. No, I think the real reason for my apprehension was because Oak Grove is where Ann and Seth had been laid to rest. It looked as calm and serene as it had two weeks ago.

The monuments glistened with a bluish tint, probably a mix of sunlight and the lavender light in the sky. The lush green grass and branches from a few sporadic oak trees blew lazily in the morning breeze. It would make a lovely location for a picnic if not for the stigma all such places carried.

I could see Ann and Seth's double headstone near the east wall. It was fronted by two brown rectangles interrupting an otherwise immaculate lawn; two weeks is not enough time for grass to grow. Seth seemed unaffected as we passed; he smiled as he listened to his radio program, taking no notice of the cemetery, completely unaware of what lay beneath the ground just yards away.

I say "what" and not "who" because the "who" is sitting right here beside me. I am convinced of that. Well, at least half of the "who" in this case. A tear slid down my cheek as I thought of Ann. Her "who" had moved on, had gone through the door, had left Seth and me, leaving only the "what" – her body – behind. That thought suddenly sparked a surge of anger through my gut, considering the fact that if this storm did not happen, Seth would have been condemned to follow me around, alone and unseen for years, possibly decades.

This surge of anger frightened and disgusted me at the same time. Did she have a choice? Did she move on believing that Seth was following and he pulled back at the last minute? These were questions that I had no answer for and no comprehension of. I guess if giving someone the benefit of the doubt was in order, this was a textbook example. Ann was a good mom and would do anything for Seth, of that I had no doubt.

Passing the cemetery made me realize something. Living people would not want to hang out at a cemetery, so why should the dead be any different? The answer is that they wouldn't. Seth came home because of his love for me and that is the place where he was happy in life, which is where he belonged. Maybe there are a few people that would be completely content hanging around a cemetery for eternity, probably a very few people. Most would go where they are happy, where they feel safe, where they are familiar … for the most part they would go home.

At that moment it dawned on me just why the streets are so deserted. It has to be more than just caution, heeding the government's warnings to stay indoors, but that was only part of it. Besides, who listens to the government anyway? I suspect a lot of them had house guests, unexpected guests.

As we approached the interstate entrance ramp, I looked over at Seth and noticed his head was lolled back on the seat, the back of his head submerged about an inch into the leather, faint little snores rattled from his mouth. I guess he does sleep. It did not seem logical that a spirit, free of the limitations and weaknesses of the human body, would require sleep. It brought to mind a line from one of my favorite poems by D.H. Lawrence:

And if tonight my soul may find her peace in sleep, and sink in good oblivion, and in the morning wake like a new-opened flower then I have been dipped again in God, and new-created.

My mother used to recite that to me frequently before bed. She said that it meant sleep is just as restful to the soul as it is to the body. I don't know much about poetry and never was a big fan of it, but that passage has stuck with me all these years. Maybe it stuck with me for a reason … the truth of the verse speaks louder now than ever.

I started to wake him but then I thought better of it. I would let the little guy sleep. I reached over and gently reduced the volume on the radio, then carefully changed the station to our local ABC News affiliate; I wanted to get an update on the situation. What I heard both astounded and troubled me; it was something I had not even remotely considered.

They had the same talking heads on again, the NASA scientist Dr. Smithson Turner. He was joined by a Dr. Schoendist from the Environmental Protection Agency, the president's science advisor, Dr. Ray Winder, and a special guest that I couldn't believe. I thought it was one of those early morning drive time pranks until I was satisfied I had it on the reputable news network. There was no mistaking the unique mix of the German and Polish accent that belonged to none other than Albert Einstein.

"Mr. Einstein, can you tell us why you stayed here and what you've learned about the validity of your theories now that you have seen the universe from another perspective?"

There was a sigh followed by a deep, heavily-accented voice. There was something strange about it. Like Seth's voice, it sounded like it was softly echoing in a metal drum.

"My dear fellow, all in good time … if there is time," Einstein said with a knowing tone. In his dry sense of humor he was probably making a comical reference to one of his many theories about time. The man certainly had a sense of humor in spite of his boorish appearance and intimidating brain power, I could tell that about him very quickly. "I suggest we get to the problem at hand first, and then we can take a trip down memory lane later," he continued in a pleasant yet assertive voice.

"Very well, very well," the host said. "Would you or Dr. Turner like to bring everyone up to speed on what you believe has happened thus far, and then go into detail of the new development last night?"

"I will defer to my capable colleague, Dr. Turner," Einstein said. "He has been on top of this since it happened and was in the president's briefings all night. They just found me wandering down Nassau St. at Princeton University last night, chased me down like I was one of those musical, floppy-haired Beatles," he said with a chuckle.

"So, you have been at Princeton all this time?" the host asked.

"Please, we need to move on and use our time wisely," Einstein said, this time his voice was absent of a knowing sense of humor. His tone stressed urgency.

"Okay ..." the host continued, obviously disappointed, "Dr. Turner, what can you tell us, sir?"

Dr. Turner cleared his throat and began.

"First let me say it is an honor, being on the air with Dr. Einstein. He has inspired me and generations of scientist."

"I concur," said Dr. Ray Winder, the president's science advisor, "it is indeed an honor."

"Indeed ... a great honor!" added Dr. Schoendist from the Environmental Protection Agency.

"Thank you gentlemen, you are too kind to a lucky and fortunate patent clerk," Einstein said. "Please tell us what you know. I am interested to hear everything myself."

Dr. Turner reiterated the events that occurred the previous day. He was able to give a little greater detail today, now that the world had been able to catch its collective breath and analyze the situation.

"We have determined that the cosmic storm that passed through Earth's atmosphere yesterday has caused a significant change in the Earth's electromagnetic field, causing this phenomenon. There has been some controversy between scientists to whether this change in energy is causing one large worldwide hallucination, or whether it has actually caused the manifestation of the lingering souls for the dead."

"What is your opinion, Dr. Turner?" the host asked.

Dr. Turner cleared his throat nervously and then paused a few moments before speaking.

"I tend to subscribe to the latter theory," he said.

"Dr. Einstein, what about you?" the host interjected quickly before Dr. Turner could continue.

Einstein chuckled softly.

"My dear fellow, do you not have eyes? What are your eyes telling you? Are all you gentlemen hallucinating about the same thing? I think my very presence here today proves that Dr. Turner is correct in his thinking."

The host seemed rather taken back. He was not used to being browbeaten on his own show, especially by some of the bushiest brows in history. He decided to skip around Dr. Einstein and Turner and go directly to the president's advisor.

"Dr. Winder, we have no idea what this energy is. It is something we have never encountered before. Isn't it possible that there may be some plausibility to the hallucinatory theory? I believe some of the scientists were referring to these apparitions as 'brain farts'?"

Dr. Winder started to speak but was cut short.

"Indeed, there are possibly other theories that we may want to consider; perhaps these apparitions are extraterrestrial in origin?" the host interrupted.

There was another loud chuckle from Dr. Einstein.

"My dear man, I can assure you that I am no ... how do you say it now? Little green man?"

"But how do we know? How can we be sure? We have never encountered anything of this nature before," the host retorted.

"I can answer that," Dr. Winder said, returning the favor by cutting the host short. "I was doubtful of what was going on until the new development last night. Perhaps I should discuss that now and possibly dispel some doubt."

"Please do," the host said.

This was normally one of my favorite radio programs to listen to in the mornings. The host can be confrontational at times when he is passionate about a subject but today was an anomaly. He had three respected scientists on his program this morning and one of them was Albert Einstein for God's sake! He had a man as a guest that was one of the most important people in human history, a man that was last interviewed probably before the host was a spark in his daddy's eye, and he was being confrontational? I guess his apprehension made him passionate about this subject, the whole world is probably terrified and the host is no different. It's funny how fear works in people sometimes.

Dr. Winder took a deep breath and continued. "We have confirmed the facts with a number of hospitals, nursing homes, and even EMTs on emergency calls. It seems that this storm has done more than just cause the dead to materialize. It–" he broke off with a deep exhalation.

"It, what?" prodded the host.

"Well," began Dr. Winder. "You must understand, every soul or spirit that has remained here has done so voluntarily, of their own free will."

"Yes, that is true," Einstein added. "Every soul I have met, myself included."

"So, what are you saying doctor?" the host asked.

"The president asked me to be straightforward with people, so that is what I will do."

He cleared his throat again nervously before continuing.

"Since this phenomenon started two days ago, the persons that exercised their freewill at death reappeared, but so has everyone else."

"I don't understand, doctor," the host said. "What do you mean, *everyone else?*"

"It would seem that free will is no longer an option. You see, everyone that has died in the past two days has remained here. They have no choice."

CHAPTER 11
ON THE ROAD

*"The absence of the soul is far more terrible
in a living man than in a dead one."*

~Charles Dickens

I had to hear it repeated to understand what was said. Father Wilson
had tried to tell me the same thing earlier, but I had not been in
a listening mood. Reflecting on our conversation, I was suddenly
shaken out of my trance by an eighteen-wheeler that had just passed
at a great rate of speed. I wasn't sure, but I thought I saw someone
like Seth looking at me through the big rig's passenger window;
they appeared to have the same ethereal glow. I quickly focused my
attention back on the radio as the host dutifully asked Dr. Winder to
repeat his statement.

"Yes, everyone that has died in the past 48 hours has remained
here. There is no longer a choice, as reported by a few Impals who
I have spoken with, no great door to choose to go through or not.

They currently have no choice ... their body dies and they simply leave it and carry on, like someone parking their car and walking," Dr. Winder said in a tone reminiscent of a news correspondent reporting on some great disaster.

"Impals?" questioned the host.

"Yes ... that's the nickname some scientists came up with last night, to describe the people that have manifested as a result of this event."

"What does Impal mean?" the host asked.

"Yes, could you please elaborate on this ... this nickname?" Einstein added, a faint hint of suspicion was detectable in his tone.

"It means impalpable, which is best described as not capable of being perceived by the senses. They started calling these folks "the Impalpables" then "Impals" for short. Because before the storm they were impalpable to us," Dr. Winder said with a nervous laugh.

"I am at least glad to see that you referred to us as 'folks,'" Einstein said, his voice stern. "In my experience, nicknames for a people are never a good thing. Yes ... we are still people even though we have no physical body. I would say that we are the very essence of humanity."

"I ... I meant no disrespect, Dr. Einstein," Dr. Winder stammered. "I was just unsure of how to refer to our people who are newly visible."

"Refer to them as people," Einstein said. "Nothing more and nothing less."

I understood Einstein's concerns all too well. You never know when watching The History Channel will pay off. I found his biography fascinating. He was born in Germany and was already a world-renowned scientist before immigrating to the United States in 1933.

He made this decision due to the rise to power of the Nazis under Germany's new chancellor, Adolf Hitler. While visiting American universities in April, 1933, he learned that the new German government had passed a law barring Jews from holding any official positions, including teaching at universities. A month later, the Nazi book burnings occurred, with Einstein's works being among those burnt, and Nazi Propaganda Minister Joseph Goebbels proclaimed, "Jewish intellectualism is dead." I am sure from Einstein's point of view demographic nicknames are just the beginning to something much, much worse.

"I have heard reports of Impals being hungry and even eating," the host said. "Can you gentleman explain why this drive and function would be part of these 'people's' characteristics?"

There was a long silence before Dr. Einstein fielded the question.

"Biology is not my area of expertise so I cannot offer a valid opinion," he said with caution. "But … I can tell you from personal experience that I get hungry like before and can eat and taste to some degree just as before. I don't know why, but it is true."

"Do you … do you digest?" the host asked.

"I do not care to discuss personal matters publicly, sir," Einstein said flatly.

"Any thoughts on this, gentlemen?" the host asked addressing the other two men.

Both admitted that they were at a loss. They couldn't even begin to explain what was happening to manifest the Impals, much less explain their 'bodily' functions.

The remaining ten minutes of the program involved profuse apologies to Dr. Einstein, even though he assured them that no apology was necessary. They all confessed they had no idea what the energy from the storm is and no idea of its effects on the human body, that is to say, the corporeal body.

Dr. Einstein would be working with the scientists to find answers quickly and to alleviate fears. That was reassuring, but when you got right down to it, none of them had any more of an idea what was happening than a monkey has a concept of calculus. This was an unknown that the world would have to blunder about in for a while. I hoped for my and Seth's sakes that it would be a very long time. The program did confirm the two things that Father Wilson had told me. People who die now have no choice and apparently there had been an alarming number of suicides since the phenomenon started. The nickname bestowed on these unfortunate souls was "sleepers."

The more I thought about, in a vague way I could somewhat understand the actions of these desperate people. Not that I agreed with it, but I understood it. In the time after Ann and Seth's death, I did wish numerous times that I had died, too. The pain of losing them made death seem like an attractive alternative. It would stop the pain and I would be with them, forever. My lamenting over my mortality was more a regretful wish than a plan of action; I never thought about seriously going through with it. While I still felt Father Wilson's remarks offensive, I guess I could understand his concern. Perhaps people felt emboldened now that there was definitive proof of life after death. The mystery of mortality was now on full display.

I didn't give the new developments much more thought until we were halfway between Little Rock and Memphis. Traffic began to noticeably slow and then eventually came to a complete standstill, with everyone merging into the left lane. In a situation like this, it's either construction or a wreck. After just two miles in 30 minutes' time, I could see the ominous flashing blue and red of the police and fire department; it was a wreck, and a bad one by the looks of it. As we drew nearer, I could see an eighteen-wheeler turned on its side. It was resting on the crumpled frame of a white minivan. My stomach lurched when I saw the twisted remains; I knew no one could have survived.

Just as we passed the toppled cab of the truck, my fear was confirmed. We came upon the most bizarre sight that I have ever seen. Lying in a neat row just beyond the right shoulder were four white sheets. The length of each sheet seemed to get progressively shorter from left to right. I had the unintended and distasteful thought of that commercial showing cell phone bars. I knew it was the remains of four people, probably a family judging by the minivan, the varying sizes of the sheets covering the remains and, well … the people.

A man, woman, and two girls—the youngest of whom was probably Seth's age—stood a few feet away from the sheets, embracing each other and staring dumbly all about them. They all had the same glowing silvery shimmer like the surface of a lake on a sunny day. Their ethereal light combined with the lavender sky, giving the scene a surreal feeling, like it was some bizarre dream. But the confused and horrified faces of the officers, firemen and EMTs, who had probably seen it all at one time or another, was enough to bring the dreamlike vision into focused reality. The worst were the terrified and confused expressions of the family. They had been killed, yet they were still here – no choice.

I looked at Seth, still sleeping peacefully, his head lolling listlessly in my direction. At that moment it hit me like a slap to my face. It was easy to look at Seth as just what he appeared to be: my son. And he was, after all ... I could accept that.

No, in actuality, I welcomed that. I had him back and that was good. But when I saw the family and their bodies, the "who" with the "what," so to speak, it felt like peeking behind the scenes of a popular ride or movie; the illusion was shattered. The two faces of death were on public display by the eastbound lane of Interstate 40 today – the "who" and the "what" in full comparison and contrast. It made me pity the family and mourn Seth once again when I thought of what he suffered to reach this state. He seemed happy, but I thought I could detect a faint sadness under his boyish grin and laughter. My God, what had he seen and experienced in the last two weeks? For my own peace of mind, I wasn't sure I wanted to know.

I wanted to be sick but I held my gorge until we reached the rest area five minutes later. I had never realized what the consequences of this phenomenon could be other than my own selfish desire to have my son again. I puked until I thought my shoes were going to come up the back of my throat. I would like to say it made me feel better, but it didn't.

When I returned to the vehicle a few minutes later, I was greeted by a sleepy-eyed but smiling Seth.

"Are we at the Moozem yet?" he asked.

"No buddy, we have a ways to go," I said with a faint smile as I swallowed hard to soothe my burning throat. In kid time, we had an eternity left to go; we hadn't even left Arkansas yet.

He frowned dejectedly, and then a look of alarm washed over his face.

"I got to go tinky!" he exclaimed and hopped out the door. He was making a beeline for the restroom when I stopped him.

"Let me come with you," I said as I put a hand on his cold shoulder.

He puffed out his chest and exclaimed proudly.

"I'm a big boy!"

"Of course you are," I said as I felt the strange mixture of warmth and cold as he turned his shoulders, causing my fingers to pass through. This time it gave me the sensation of passing my fingers through a hot fudge sundae.

"I'll wait right here and watch the door," I said.

He smiled proudly and skipped off toward the men's side, drawing the looks of several rest area patrons in the process. He seemed to be the only ... what did the doctor call it? Impal? He was the only one present in the rest area, at least as far as I could see. Prudence told me that I should move a little closer to the door, just in case curious ignorance got the best of one of the bystanders. I'm sure his trip to the restroom was as much a mystery to them as it was to me, and I had seen him try to eat.

He returned a minute later with a frown on his face.

"Did everything come out all right?" I joked.

He looked at me a little confused and slightly less amused by my poor attempt at humor.

"False alarm," he said.

"Did you feel like you needed to go?" I asked.

He shrugged.

I was as flabbergasted by this as I was his attempt to eat Chockit Berries. How could he have any desire to eat or a need to use the restroom? The cereal had ended in disaster and I didn't care to think of the prospects of answering nature's call. But he said he was hungry, *and* he said the cereal tasted good even if his body couldn't contain it. Is it possible that there are some physical functions that are not solely physical? Eating can bring as much enjoyment emotionally as it can physically. Perhaps "food for the soul" has a deeper meaning than we thought. I couldn't reconcile the other bodily function, that is, until I questioned Seth further. I asked him a leading question, as is often necessary when speaking to children.

"Seth ... did you go to the restroom because you saw me go?"

He hesitated then crinkled his nose like he had just sniffed an unpleasant aroma, which was both appropriate and ironic considering the state of the lavatory. It brought a smile to my face.

"Maybe ..." he said and pursed his lips as if in deep concentration.

"You don't have to go now?"

"No."

"Did you feel the urge to p–, uh, tinky?" I asked, being careful to stay within his vocabulary.

"I don't think so," he said. "I just knew I needed to go whenever we stop, cause you don't like to have to stop too much."

I smiled and winked. "That's right, buddy. We want to get to the Museum as quick as we can, right?"

He smiled so broadly his unearthly shimmer seemed to glow more brightly.

"Let's go!" he exclaimed and sprinted back to the vehicle.

I didn't feel as sick anymore. Oh, the ghost of my nausea was still there, hiding deep inside. I knew it wouldn't take much to bring it to the surface again. I decided that I needed to refocus my attention and energy on Seth and our trip. I would focus my attention on my son, the "who" that came home, not the "what" that would forever remain under the green zoysia grass of Oak Grove. I made myself this promise with the strong hope that no more reminders presented themselves.

We started out on the road again, determined to make Memphis by noon. The remaining miles passed uneventfully. I was starting to get hungry; it had been almost five hours since breakfast, and what I did have for breakfast was left about 80 miles back. Seth claimed he was hungry, too. Maybe he was and maybe he wasn't; I was more inclined to believe the *idea* that he was hungry or that he had to tinky. Perhaps these urges were just all in his head, a latent instinct from when the "who" and the "what" were one and the same.

Of course, one of Seth's favorite restaurants was one that every kid loves and one that I absolutely despise – Martian Burger. Oh sure, when I was a kid I enjoyed it, with a high metabolism and squeaky clean arteries, but now every time I eat a French fry I feel as if I'm shoveling a little more dirt out of my grave. If I keep thinking of that analogy, I'll lose my appetite all together.

"Okay, Seth … what would you like for lunch?" I asked on his third complaint of an empty tummy.

"A Martian hambooger and grape soda!" he proclaimed.

Seth loved hamburgers, or "hamboogers," as he liked to call them. And, as suspected, it had to be the Martian joint. Whatever faint hope I had of scoring a trip to anywhere less greasy was dashed. I turned the SUV off the exit ramp and headed for the giant flying saucer burger in the sky with two animated tentacles suspended on top.

The logistics of our lunch started to weigh heavily on my mind. We couldn't eat in the vehicle, not after the cereal incident, but, that was the way I liked to travel – grab it and go and get there. I didn't like to waste the 30 minutes to an hour it would take to go in and sit down at a table like regular people.

I spotted a city park a block behind the restaurant so I told Seth that we would go through the drive-thru and then have a picnic in the park. When he saw the towering rocket slide, jungle gym and the massive A-frame of a swing set, he happily agreed. We pulled in the drive-thru, got our lunch, and then drove to the park. The streets and the Martian Burger were eerily empty. That was the first time that I can remember going to a fast food restaurant of any kind within an hour of lunchtime and not having a single car ahead of me in line.

We reached the park and pulled into the newly asphalted parking lot without seeing another vehicle or person, aside from the pimply-faced teen at the drive-thru window. It was a nice park with lush green grass, peppered with an assortment of oak and maple shade trees. A small cinder block building rested on the far side. It was obviously the restroom judging by the stick figure man and woman painted on the right and left doors, respectively. The park was centered by the play area, which had Seth enamored since he first laid eyes on it.

The perimeter of the play area was ringed with green painted picnic tables, strategically placed beneath the shading canopy of some of the larger trees. The parking lot was empty except for a single utility truck – probably a phone company vehicle – parked about a dozen yards away; a middle-aged, balding man sat behind the wheel. He was staring with a bewildered expression at something behind a large oak tree between our vehicles. My view was obstructed and I couldn't see what held his gaze until we got out and started to walk toward a picnic table directly in front of us.

A family of four was sitting around a table with their heads bowed. It looked as if they were offering a prayer over a meal of burgers and fries. A middle-aged man wearing unusual clothing administered the blessing while a red-haired, middle-aged woman with a long braid of hair hanging all the way to her posterior looked surreptitiously between us and the man in the utility truck. The children, a boy and a girl, reverently kept their eyes closed and heads bowed until the prayer was done. The man and boy had similar strange clothing, while the woman and the girl shared their own unusual fashion. They all looked as if they had just stepped out of an episode of *Little House on the Prairie*.

At first I couldn't understand why the man in the truck was staring at this unusual brood, aside from their unique clothing, but as I passed under the shade of the trees it hit me with a strong mix of shock and surprise. The entire family shared the same ethereal quality with Seth. They were all Impalpables, or what did the scientists call them again … Impals? That seemed a good enough nickname to me, but judging by the way Dr. Einstein reacted to it, I thought I would keep it to myself for a while.

The man jumped to his feet and gazed in our direction. My heart skipped a beat when I stupidly wondered if I had uttered the nickname out loud, but I quickly realized he was looking at Seth. My heart was just getting back into cadence when it was sent racing out of control again. The whole family turned and looked as the man marched purposefully in our direction.

CHAPTER 12

THE BIRDS OF FIDDLER PARK

*"Death makes angels of us all and gives us wings
where we had shoulders smooth as ravens claws."*

~*Jim Morrison*

The man approached with such tenacity and urgency that I took a defensive stance between him and Seth. He slowed a little when he saw the resolve on my face, and then smiled warmly at me. He knelt down on one knee and smiled at Seth.

"May I?" he asked, looking up at me. His voice was much smoother than Seth's but still had a faint tinge of the echoing timbre. It was a pleasant enough tone but my defenses were still on high alert.

"May you what?" I asked sharply.

I wasn't sure exactly what frightened me. Was I afraid they would take Seth away from me … take him back to where he belonged?

Perhaps. While my love for Seth had never been stronger and I knew he loved me, I also knew that our relationship now was fragile at best. I had been given a gift, regardless of how the rest of the world saw it. This storm could wear out in five minutes or five years. Seth and I were on borrowed time, there were no two ways about it.

"I…I'm sorry," said the man, "I didn't mean to frighten you. My name is Charles." He held up his hand to me. I couldn't help but think of Charles Ingalls based on the way he was dressed. It made me feel a little more at ease. After all, who doesn't like Pa?

I reached out and took his hand, bracing for the frigid cold touch of his skin. It was cold, but he grasped my hand in such a way that I felt more of the strange warmth than I did the cold.

"Nice to meet you, Charles. My name is Thomas … Thomas Pendleton."

He released my hand and smiled at Seth.

"And who might you be, young man?"

I jumped a little as I felt the cold and hot sensation inundate my right leg. I looked down and Seth was clinging to my thigh and looking distrustfully at Charles.

"This is Seth," I said, trying to step to the side, but he stuck with me like a frightened mouse clinging to a branch.

"Well howdy, Seth," he said. "I'm Mr. Fiddler."

Seth still wouldn't shake his hand, but his grip on me loosened somewhat. I could tell because it was almost all cold now on my thigh.

"Would you folks care to join us for lunch?" Charles Fiddler said, gesturing to their table. "You're welcome to some of our chicken, but it looks like you brought your own," he said, pointing to our Martian Burgers bags.

The two children waved excitedly at Seth and motioned for him to join them. Seth reluctantly let go of my leg and came forward, though he was still clutching my hand. Shortly, he released his grip, smiled sheepishly at the children and gave Mr. Fiddler a half-grin. A few moments later, we were sitting down to eat our Martian's lunch with the ghostly Fiddler family. Charles and his wife Ester, Jack, and Rebecca all gave us a warm greeting as they scooted down the bench to make room.

The man in the utility truck was still staring like he had seen a ghost. Well, I guess he had, but that is no reason to be impolite. I turned and gazed sternly in his direction until he got the hint. He quickly fired the truck to life and steered jerkily out of the parking lot and onto the street like a man who has had too much to drink. I guess there's a reason they call alcohol "spirits." They seem to have the same effect.

"Oh, such a nice man," Charles said as he waved with earnest vigor in the man's direction.

I wondered what could be so nice about an indiscreet voyeur.

As we dined on our fast food lunch, I made an observation that I found very confusing. I had expected the same result from the Fiddler family as they ate their chicken dinner that I had observed with Seth when he ate. In short, I expected chewed food to be all over the ground under our table, but it wasn't. It was as if living people were dining with us. I looked at Seth and there were already four chewed fries on the ground along with a puddle of grape soda. I didn't want to be rude, but I also needed to know, not only for my sake but Seth's as well.

"Can you tell me why that happens to Seth when he eats?" I asked Charles.

He looked down the bench at Seth and smiled broadly.

"He just doesn't know how to squench yet."

"Squench?" I repeated.

Charles chuckled and looked at his wife.

"You figured it out honey, why don't you explain it to these good folks."

She swallowed hard, having just taken a bite of a biscuit. A grimace washed over her face as she held her hand to her abdomen like she had indigestion.

"Forgot to squench, didn't ya?" Charles chuckled.

Her shimmering features seemed to glow a faint pink as she looked at her husband irritably. She smiled with ladylike modesty and looked at me.

"You must understand that we have been in this … this state a lot longer than Seth there," she said, nodding toward my son. "It was easy for us to adjust to this new status of, well, I guess you would call it existence. How long has Seth been …." her voice trailed off, unsure of how to approach this delicate question.

"Two weeks," I replied.

She nodded her head and gave me an empathetic smile.

"I'm sorry," she said in almost a whisper.

She shook her head and continued.

"Before this happened, we lived here peacefully for over 100 years," she said gesturing to the empty park encircling them. "But we never experienced hunger, not until today."

"You lived here … in the park?" I asked.

"Not exactly," Charles interjected. "To make a long and painful story short, our house rested right there," he said pointing to the play area. "It burned one night when we were all asleep."

A lump settled in my stomach like hot coals. The family had all burned to death in their sleep. I eyed the cinder block restroom across the way, thinking I might be sick again.

Charles noticed my greenish pallor and continued with strong reassurance in his voice.

"Oh, it wasn't that bad, we never even knew it was happening until we were standing in front of the bright doorways, trying to decide whether to go through or stay."

"Why did you *all* stay?" I asked with unintentional emphasis on *all*.

Charles didn't answer; instead he looked at me with deep scrutiny for several moments.

"There was someone else, wasn't there?" he asked softly.

I felt a lump start to form in my throat accompanied by welling eyes. I looked at Seth who was talking quietly to Jack and Rebecca, thankfully he was not paying attention to our conversation.

"My wife," I said, my voice hoarse, "they were killed in an accident together. Seth said she went through her doorway."

"I'm sorry," Ester said with silver tears like Seth's in her eyes. Two drops fell from her cheeks, penetrating the picnic table and disappearing without a mark into the grass beneath.

I was determined not to let my emotions get the best of me so I quickly redirected the conversation to its original path.

"So why did you stay?" I asked.

"Nathan," Ester said. "He was our oldest."

"Did he go through the door?" I asked delicately.

"I'm sure he did eventually, but not the night of the fire. He was staying in Memphis at the time working with the farmer's market." She said.

"I think we all stayed because our family wasn't together, we didn't feel ready, we felt incomplete," Charles said. He then shrugged and shook his head, "Well, that's the best way I can explain it anyway."

"So you have lived here in the park for over 100 years?" I asked, finally getting back to my original question.

"We lived in our house," Charles said with a sad smile.

"I thought you said it burned?" I asked skeptically.

"It did, *here*," he said, gently patting the surface of the table to make his point, but the house passed into where we were. Where we were before a couple of days ago, that is."

"You mean the house is a … is a…" I stammered.

"Is a spirit, a ghost, a shade, a specter?" Charles provided for me. "I don't think so. It was just a house. Besides, I think the fact that it is not with us now says that its essence is much different than our own."

"Could you see this park and the city around you?"

"Yes, we have seen a lot over the years, but yet …" he paused a moment, "from our perspective, it seems like the fire only happened a couple of months ago, or at least that is what it feels like. Time is strange in that place," he said waving his hand as if indicating something far in the distance. "I guess it helps people deal with staying behind. I never could have imagined just sitting in my house and never leaving for 100 years. But, that is what we did and did not venture out, we all knew what happened but we didn't know how to deal with the situation."

"How do you know it has been over 100 years then?" I asked.

"A couple of days ago we found ourselves sitting in the middle of this park, our house was gone. As odd as it may seem, we were all incredibly hungry. There was a family having a picnic right here at this table and when they saw us they were frightened so badly they left their food here, so … we sort of helped ourselves," he said sheepishly.

"That man that you scared off," he said pointing to where the man in the utility truck had been parked. "He came here a couple of hours ago and terrified the children with that metal contraption he was riding in. I talked to him, but he was so dumbstruck I only got him to understand a few words here and there, just enough to know that the metal contraption was called a truck and what year it is. I told him that the children were hungry. He asked if we liked chicken and he left for a few minutes and brought us these," he said, tapping his index finger on the rim of one of the chicken buckets.

Every time I thought it couldn't get any more fantastic, the bizarre factor turned itself up another notch. I felt like I was in an episode of the old *Twilight Zone*. As happened so frequently in supernatural tales of suspense, the victim would wake up only to discover that their whole experience, good or bad, had all been a dream. I won't say that the thought hadn't crossed my mind several times in the last 48 hours but the longer this continued and the longer I continued with the side effects of my physical frailties derived from my age and slightly overweight midsection … I knew it wasn't just my slumbering imaginations. Dreams don't hurt, not really; but my leg and back were throbbing like a sadistic bass drum from sitting in the vehicle so long. This was no dream, and eating greasy fast food was not going to help, either.

The Fiddlers took me a little by surprise. It was not the sad and fascinating retelling of the last 100 years of their existence, or even the fact that they were a family of Impals. No, I think what really took me by surprise was their eloquent, well-enunciated speech. It just did not jive with their stereotypical Walnut Grove appearance. The curiosity was getting the best of me and I had to ask.

"Charles, what did you do for a living?"

He smiled faintly and pointed to an open field directly across the street from the park.

"Can you see the train tracks over there?" he said.

I screwed up my eyes, trying to spy the tracks through the thick sprays of switch grass that seemed to extend for miles into the distance. As if on cue, I heard the distant wail of a train horn. A few moments later, a red and yellow Rock Island engine emerged from the tree line a half-mile to our right and slowly made its way across the field, pulling a dozen coal cars behind it.

"The railroad has run through here in one form or another since the War Between the States," he began. "I set up my practice close to the tracks. There's always folks getting hurt or sick on trains."

"You're a doctor?" I deduced with probably a little more shock in my voice than I intended.

"I was," he said.

A moment later our attention was drawn to the children as I got a full demonstration of squenching. The kids had gotten up and strolled near the play area. A flock of robins had gathered near the trash receptacle and were hungrily pecking at a half eaten box of French fries that someone had air-balled on their feeble attempt at cleanliness. Seth watched with keen interest as Jack and Rebecca Fiddler approached the birds with broad smiles on their faces.

Robins are not like pigeons. Typically they are afraid of people and will fly away when a person gets too close – not these robins.

They looked at the children with passive curiosity, but seemed to ignore them for the most part; that is until they started squenching.

Jake and Rebecca held their arms out in front of them with palms out flat. A moment later, objects started raining out of their palms like mini hailstones. I soon realized that it was not hailstones or rock or any other such thing; it was bits and pieces of their lunch. Seth giggled with amusement as the birds came forward and greedily plucked the squenched chicken dinner fragments off the ground.

"Apparently we can relish the joys of eating," Ester explained. "We can bite and chew somewhat, though it takes a lot more effort and concentration than it did when we actually had teeth. And yes, it tastes good ... in some ways even better than it did before when we actually had taste buds."

"So what the children just did is squenching ... they can control the food?" I asked pointing as more robins and even a few stray mockingbirds joined the squenching buffet.

"Yes, we just focus on it after it leaves our mouth and we can control it by sending it to our hands, feet or whatever, or ... we can hold it inside until later, like the children did, and then send it out."

I was speechless. I mean what do you say after an explanation like that? I did feel a small modicum of encouragement; I could return to my usual "run and gun" travel habits of eating while driving and just *hang it out the window* if you have to answer nature's call. Seth could possibly eat in the vehicle and squench when I stopped to, well ... squench myself. How convenient, and yet how incredibly bizarre at the same time.

"Why do you get hungry? It's not like you have a ... I stopped short before I put my foot too far in my mouth.

"A body?" Charles finished for me. "Medically-speaking, I'm not sure. I could make a guess that it is psychological, but I just don't know." He stroked his chin and frowned. "Maybe now that we are back in this existence, it is necessary." He shook his head as if warding off a pesky fly, then continued with an uneasy chuckle. "Spiritually-speaking, maybe food for the soul has a literal meaning."

"It's obvious that we really don't need it," Ester said, pointing to the children who were now surrounded by a flock of 20 to 30 birds. "At least not in the same sense as we did before."

It was an incredible sight to behold. Creatures that normally have a natural fear of man darted about in unafraid fervor, relishing what in bird terms would be considered a gourmet lunch. Seth giggled excitedly as a mockingbird snatched a squenched French fry from the palm of his hand. In just a short while, it looked like he had the basics of squenching mastered.

I smiled when he turned and looked at me proudly, like the time he had just mastered the technique of diving into the pool. Actually it had been more of a belly flop, but he had made progress and that was something to be proud of. Seth had made progress today ... no, actually I made progress. After meeting the Fiddlers, I didn't feel quite so alone in my ordeal; it was comforting to know that there were others out there. Others like Seth who could help take up the slack in the areas where my inexperience and intelligence are lacking – and those areas are great.

We left the park with me feeling a new invigoration for our father and son expedition. I was giddy with excited anticipation as I cried, "Blast off to the Air and Space Museum!" as we pulled out of the parking lot. Seth laughed and bounced excitedly. We were happy, and why shouldn't we be? We were together. There was no inkling in our minds of the tribulation that was about to be visited upon not just us, but the entire world, a tribulation that we were unknowingly headed straight into the heart of.

CHAPTER 13

VACANCY

"Until we meet again, may God bless you as he has blessed me."

~Elvis Presley

The state of Tennessee would normally take about eight hours to travel from east to west, but we spent almost a week in the Volunteer state. It all started right after our lunch with the Fiddlers. They were nice folks. We offered them a ride somewhere, but they declined, saying they were going to go to the courthouse a couple of blocks away and see if they could track down where their son, Nathan, had lived in his latter days and where he had been buried. Their hope was to reunite with him if he had chosen to stay like they had done.

After that, they would go to a homeless shelter until they could figure out what to do. I felt a stab of guilt and remorse at that prospect. I wasn't sure they needed a place to stay as shelter from the elements. I suspected it was more a matter of dignity, a proud and once successful man like Dr. Charles Fiddler wouldn't want his family living in a park regardless of the fact that their home once stood there.

It is a strange thing when your lifelong beliefs, which in my case are 30-odd years old, are taken and turned on end in just a few days. I never even considered the existence of ghosts before this event occurred, let alone their feelings and sensibilities that still make them human.

Still?

If there was one thing I was beginning to learn, it's that a flesh-and-blood existence isn't required to be human; in fact, that decrepit, meaty shell is probably much more of a hindrance than a qualifier.

When I considered the Fiddler family, a thought came to mind, one that I would never in my wildest imagination considered before. *Maybe that's why ghosts haunt houses typically.* The thought brought a waggish grin to my face, but don't they always say that humor is based on a modicum of truth? Indeed it is in most cases, but in the case of the new truth – no, that's really not accurate either; let's say new reality – the new reality was a former absurdity. This seemed to add to the amusement.

In this new reality, I actually only knew one truth – I loved Seth more than anything and I had him back, even though it may be on borrowed time. That truth would motivate me and that would keep me focused as we faced the reality that lay ahead of us.

As I said, a straight drive border to border across the great state of Tennessee usually takes about eight hours, give or take a half-hour or so for potty breaks – or squenching. I knew it was going to take longer when we hit the bridge going into Memphis, a bridge that was so choked with traffic it took two hours just to cross the Mississippi River.

My first thought was that there had been some terrible accident that was tying traffic up. My stomach knotted when I thought of the family in the minivan. I didn't want to see a scene like that again. We remained at a complete standstill on the bridge for over 30 minutes at one point and this allowed for an opportunity to converse with our fellow drivers. When I found out the real reason for the traffic jam, I was filled with a weird mixture of amusement, anger, and relief.

I was relieved of course to discover that there was no terrible accident impeding our progress, but the real reason made me angry because so many people seemed to have their priorities so far out of whack, considering what was happening in the world. At the same time I wanted to laugh at the absurdity of the situation. I guess it shouldn't have surprised me, considering that the pilgrimage every August 16th seems to get larger year after year and his record sales continue to outrank current living stars. I guess the thing that surprised me most was how close he was to his momma, and yet he was still here; he didn't move on to be with her. I guess, for all I know, she could still be here as well. Yes, Elvis Presley had been spotted near Graceland, and the word had spread on the radio. Between people looking for their long-gone relatives and celebrity hunters, it seemed like the whole world had descended on Memphis, Tennessee, to catch a glimpse of the King of Rock & Roll.

"Are they sure it's really him?" I asked an elderly man and his wife driving a silver Cadillac just outside Seth's window. "I mean, there are so many imitators and it has been rumored for years that he is not really dead."

I got out and walked around the vehicle to talk to the couple so I wouldn't have to shout across Seth, who was sleepily nodding his head while he fingered his Hot Wheels car in the palm of his hand. I got out partly to visit, partly to stretch my legs, and partly to tear my gaze away from Seth as the tiny vehicle looked like it was slowly sinking in a flesh-colored bog each time he pushed it across his hand.

"According to the radio, it was him all right," the man replied with a nasally, New England accent.

I would soon learn after they pulled forward and I got a view of his license plate that he was from Vermont.

"Heard he was spotted leaving a little deli not too far from Graceland. Said he was leaving a partially-chewed trail of fried peanut butter and banana sandwiches all the way back to the gates of his gaudy house," the man said with a shrill cackle and slap of the steering wheel.

Guess he doesn't know how to squench, I thought.

His wife smiled pleasantly but seemed to look right through me with an expression of astonishment.

"They said he had that peculiar shimmery glow about him, too," she muttered.

That was when I realized that she wasn't looking through me but rather past me, at Seth. I discreetly stepped to one side to shield him from her view. I knew she didn't mean any harm, but I still didn't like people staring, whether it was a stranger in a park or a sweet old lady. She blushed and turned her head. We made small talk for another ten minutes, but neither of them asked me about Seth. I guess it was apprehension or embarrassment, maybe a combination of the two. From my experience, northerners—or Yankees, as we call them in the South—have always been rather blunt and to the point. Tact can so often be an afterthought in a conversation. Maybe that was just my own narrow-minded view of things coming through. God knows my mind had been opened in the last few days.

Once we got around the downtown area of Memphis, it was smooth sailing. The sun was starting to set behind us, casting an odd, bruise-like color over the sky as the orange rays mixed with the lavender sky that now prevailed over the planet. When night fell, the surreal illumination returned. It was an even stranger experience driving in it than it had been walking outside in it the last couple of nights. It was like being on some high-speed funhouse ride as we streaked down the interstate at 70 miles per hour.

Jackson was about 90 miles east of Memphis, and I decided that seemed like as good a place as any to stop for the evening. Even though we hadn't made much progress mileage-wise, it had been a long and exhausting day. Unfortunately, I wouldn't be getting much sleep that evening.

The hotels in Jackson were packed. Actually, it was worse than that: the town was saturated with travelers. Possibly it was due to curious folks out and about, maximizing their experience of this historic and miraculous event, or panicked folks taking to the roadways to try and out run this anomaly, not that it was even possible to. During the daytime, aside from a lavender-colored sky, it was easy to forget what was going on, unless you ran into someone like Seth. Night was a different matter. It gave me the same feeling I had a couple of years ago when I went to Las Vegas for the first time on a business trip. I arrived in the middle of the afternoon and was mildly impressed with the mammoth hotels of the strip, but when I went back out that evening ... *wow*. Yes, those were all possible contributing factors to the vacancy problems in this small Tennessee city, but I think another plausible explanation was the excuse a tired old woman gave me working behind the desk at Motel 6.

"It's overflow from Memphis," she said, sounding like a character in a Jeff Foxworthy joke. "Isn't it funny how much attention an old dead rock star gets? There's been lots of reports on the radio, but no TV; the darn thing still won't work. Dadgum internet is out, too. Sounds kinda fishy, don't it?" she said, stifling a yawn while tapping fruitlessly on her keyboard. I had to suppress a grin as her enormous belly jiggled in unison with her hair rollers.

"What do you mean?" I asked.

"I mean that they're telling us all this mess about ghosts being visible, but the TV and internet conveniently goes out? I think the military screwed up some experiment and then cooked up this cockamamie story about a cosmic storm and spooks."

She raised one eyebrow with an exaggerated display of skepticism and gave a short bark of a laugh.

"You haven't seen any?" I asked.

"No ghosts here ... although we have had a few sheets disappear from the laundry," she snorted with a smug expression on her face. In an instant, her smugness washed from her features and was quickly replaced by confusion and then terror.

I had told Seth to remain in the vehicle, but he had gotten bored and decided to follow me inside. The silvery glow about him, like the surreal glow of the storm, was much more prevalent at night time. At night he looked much more like a ... well, like a ghost.

Her mouth gaped open comically as she pointed at Seth. He happily skipped to my side and reached out and tugged at my hand.

"Daddy, I'm tired."

"He's your ... he's your..." the woman stammered, still pointing a trembling finger at Seth.

"My son," I finished for her. "We are tired and just want a clean place to sleep."

"He sleeps??" she blurted.

I understood the woman's reaction, I truly did, but the long day coupled with the fact that it was three hours past my normal bedtime pushed my patience to the limits. Actually it was more than that. However unintentional her reaction was, she referred to Seth like he was a thing, some creature, some freak ... like some abomination of nature. Maybe this cosmic storm was an abomination, but Seth? Never. That was the proverbial straw that tripped the parental fuse in my brain. I exploded.

"Of course he does!" I snapped, grabbing Seth's frigidly cold hand and squeezing until I felt the warmth of his hand passing into mine. "He's no different than anyone else ... if anything, he's better!"

I looked down to see Seth gazing at me sleepily, confusion etched on his small face. I looked up to see the woman looking at me with a mixture of wide-eyed terror and embarrassment.

"I-I'm sorry," she stammered, barely above a whisper.

"Obviously you don't have a place for us, so we will be on our way!" I snapped as I turned toward the door. I tried to lead Seth behind me but to no avail. His hand passed through mine as he stood in place by the counter, staring at what I originally thought was the insensitive motel clerk until Seth spoke.

"Is that yours?" he said pointing at the computer monitor beside the woman.

She blinked like she had just awakened from a dream and slowly turned her head toward the area to which Seth was pointing. She stared uncomprehendingly at the computer monitor.

"Do you like *Star Wars*?" Seth asked.

Realization started to wash over the woman's features as she focused her attention on the small Darth Vader action figure sitting atop the monitor. Someone had arranged him to where he appeared to be sitting casually, dangling his black booted legs over the side.

"It belongs to the little boy I babysit" she said, her voice hoarse. "D-do you want it?"

The woman was obviously confused and terrified. I mean, it's not every day you have a conversation with someone who is like Seth. Yes, he was special, special in more ways than one, as the frightened motel clerk would soon discover.

Seth shook his head. "No, he would be sad if someone took his Darf. Here..." Seth said as he held out his hand and produced his prized Anakin Skywalker figure. "This is Darf Vader before he got his helmet and got all bad. He needs him for his collection."

My heart filled with loving pride at what happened next. Seth, with great care, set his figure on the counter next to a rack of Smoky Mountains and Grand Ole Opry travel brochures. He gave it one last loving smile, then slowly turned and walked toward the door.

My thoughts flashed instantly to an incident only last fall. Seth had just started first grade and we were about a month into the school year. For a solid week, every day after school Seth came home ravenously hungry. Upon arriving home each day, he would make a beeline to the refrigerator.

The first couple of days we thought he was just getting a harmless after-school snack, until Ann entered the kitchen on the third day to find Seth sitting cross legged in the floor and going to town on the Tupperware dish containing last night's macaroni and cheese. He had eaten half the contents when she walked in and scolded him then sent him to his room to wait for supper.

Observing this presumably gluttonous tendency over the next few days, we became worried … worried something was either physically or mentally wrong. It wasn't until I set him down a couple of days later and questioned him that we learned the true reason for his behavior.

There was a little boy in Seth's class whose name was Chad. According to Seth, Chad always came to school dirty and hungry. The church allowed him to attend school at no charge since his family had been members there for years, but that was where it seemed their charity ended.

"He said his mommy couldn't afford groceries yet this month," Seth told me with tears in his eyes. "We gots plenty of groceries so I give Chad my lunch every day. I can always eat when I get home," he implored, like he was trying to convince me that he hadn't done anything bad. I hugged him and praised him. We also made sure he had enough lunch for two every day afterwards.

Seth has always been a thoughtful child, never forgetting a birthday or Christmas gift. They were usually homemade presents because a six-year-old's allowance will only stretch so far. But aren't those the best kind? Those considerate offerings always require the most care-filled thought and, after all, it's the thought that counts.

As we walked out the door I put my arm around him and squeezed tight until I felt the odd mix of cold and warmth.

"You're a special kid, buddy," I said with a wink. "I love you."

He didn't reply, but his beaming smile was the only response I required.

"Wait!" the desk clerk shouted before we made it through the door. "Let me make a phone call."

I turned around and watched her nervously dial the phone. A few moments later, someone answered.

"Hello, Lizzie, this is Rose," she said, excited. "Can I ask you a small favor tonight?"

She paused, listening for several seconds then said, "I have a nice man and little boy that are desperate for a place to stay tonight. Your guest room still empty?"

Rose listened for several more seconds then smirked and shook her head.

"Fine, I'll make you a pot of my chili this weekend. I appreciate your *hospitality*," she said, putting sarcastic emphasis on the last word.

Rose the desk clerk hung up the phone and smiled. It was a hesitant smile as her brow wrinkled fretfully.

"You can stay in my sister's guest room tonight, as long as you keep it clean."

"Of course we will, thank you," I said, but I don't think she heard me. She was busy rummaging through her desk drawers for a pen and paper. She eventually produced a pencil that had probably made its last trip through the sharpener and a wrinkled yellow Post-It note. She pinched the stub of a pencil tightly between her pudgy thumb and middle finger, then hurriedly scribbled on the paper.

"Here is the address," she said, extending the Post-It note to me with the sticky part clinging to her index finger. "Her name is Lizzie Chenowith."

I took it from her and thanked her again. I started to leave, but Rose spoke. Not to me, to Seth.

"What's your name, young man?"

He smiled and walked back to the counter.

"Seth ... Seth Pendleton," my son said, proudly.

I could tell Rose was still apprehensive, but her sudden friendly demeanor toward Seth was genuine enough.

"Well Seth, I would like to give you something in return," she said as she reached under the counter and produced a Hershey's bar.

Seth's face beamed. Hershey's milk chocolate is his absolute favorite. When I considered the potential messy side effects of a six-year-old and a chocolate bar, I said a silent prayer to give thanks for squenching.

"Thank you." Seth rolled the chocolate bar over in his hands, anticipating the chocolaty goodness.

"You're welcome … you are a nice young man," she said.

Seth smiled and turned to follow me out the door.

"Do you need directions?" Rose called to me.

I looked down at the Post-It note and smiled.

"No, I should be able to find it with my GPS. Thank you again, Rose. I really appreciate this."

Before I could turn to leave, Rose's eyes grew as big as saucers and she shrieked. I turned back to the door just in time to see a silvery streak shoot by outside the glass, knocking Seth off of his feet and out of sight.

CHAPTER 14
JACKSON

"Nearly all men can stand adversity, but if you want to test a man's character, give him power."

~*Abraham Lincoln*

As I ran out the door, I was filled with a terror that only a parent who has lost a child can know. It was as if my nightmare had returned. What had happened to him? Had something taken him, had the phenomenon suddenly ended? That thought hung in the air like a poisonous gas as the world seemed to be moving in slow motion with the luminescent light of the phenomenon highlighting every detail of the night with eerie foreboding.

I had forgotten to breathe as I bolted through the door and rounded the far side of the car. That's why I could only rasp a one word response to the sight I beheld.

"Seth?"

Seth lay on his back giggling with joy as a small object with a similar silvery glow to Seth's hopped from his chest to his head and back to his chest again. It didn't register to me at first what I was seeing and I instinctively lunged for the object as it hopped back to Seth's chest. It turned and made a high-pitched yelp as it came toward me. I was just about to cry out with surprise when I realized what I was seeing. I stopped and dropped to my knees with amused disbelief as I felt an ice-cold tongue lapping at my hand, then glowing warmth as it penetrated through my flesh. I was briefly reminded of the phrase "warm hearts, cold noses" that was used to promote a local animal shelter back home.

Standing—no, more like bouncing—in front of me was an Impalpable, one unlike any I had seen as of yet. It was a full-grown border collie whose silvery luminescence shone as brightly as the happy dog's playful personality. It stopped licking and looked up at me hopefully. When I did nothing more than stare in disbelief, it barked twice and bounded back to Seth, planting a big doggie kiss on his cheek. He shrieked with delight and stroked the pooch's head.

"Can we keep him, Daddy?" Seth pleaded.

I absently got to my feet about the same time Rose the night clerk came through the door. I assured her everything was fine, but that didn't stop her from staring with bewilderment at Seth and his newfound friend. When I spoke again, I think it startled her, because she jumped with a start like someone had just goosed her ample fanny.

"Thank you, Rose. We're fine," I said.

She looked at me and nodded then backed through the door, keeping her eye on Seth and the dog like someone who didn't want to turn their back on a dangerous animal. The door had just swung closed when Seth asked again.

"Can we keep him, Daddy?"

It had dawned on me in the past few moments that what I was witnessing was the second most incredible thing of this whole phenomenon. Ironically enough, one of Seth's favorite movies is *All Dogs Go to Heaven*. I guess the answer to that is, indeed they do. The ones that choose to do so, anyway. This one had obviously chosen not to go through the door, or in this case, doggie door. The age-old debate of whether or not animals have a soul was just answered by a playful border collie.

"Pllleeeease, Daddy," Seth pleaded again.

Under normal circumstances, I would have said absolutely not. I am not an animal hater by any means, just not a fan of dogs. We never allowed Seth to have a dog because I had always considered them filthy creatures. Why anyone would willingly clean up the messes of a creature of lesser intelligence I would never know. Not to mention the perpetual "dog" smell that could never be fumigated no matter how many times you bathed the hairy beast. But then these were not normal circumstances, were they?

This was indeed a dog, but sans the unpleasantness of dogs. Besides, Seth needed a friend, one that was more like him. Not to compare my son to a dog, but this particular canine is more like him than I am, in the physical sense, anyway. I had just seen Seth interact with Impalpables at lunch, but there was no physical contact. It seemed as normal and as solid to them as it would for me to interact with another flesh-and-blood person. Something told me that he needed this interaction, this connection … so I agreed.

"Okay, buddy, but he is your responsibility."

The words were no sooner out of my mouth when the subject of squenching came to mind. Could a dog do it? Could they be, for lack of a better word, squench-broken? I doubted it, but I decided we would cross that bridge when we came to it.

I opened the door to our vehicle and the dog bounded inside like he belonged. He turned in the passenger seat and gave two quick barks to Seth as if to say, "*Well, are you coming?*"

Seth clambered in behind him and took his seat as the dog happily curled up in his lap.

I got in and started the vehicle then entered the address that Rose had given me into the GPS. There was a moment there that I wondered if the storm had affected my high-tech navigation system as it searched for a satellite signal, but after a few moments my course was plotted; it looked like it was going to take about 15 minutes to get there. I shifted the vehicle into reverse and glanced at Seth. He was lovingly stroking the dog's head. As I shifted into drive I said, "Well buddy, what are you going to name him?"

He closed one eye like Popeye and frowned.

"Hmmmmm … let me see," he said, then kissed the pooch between the ears. The dog happily wagged his tail and reciprocated with a lick to the end of Seth's nose.

"Rover … or Spot?" I suggested.

"That's so clickay, Daddy. Everyone names their dogs that!"

He's right, it was cliché, but that's all I could come up with at the moment. I couldn't help but smile at his use of a word that is generally above the head of a six-year-old. The pronunciation was a little off, but I give him an A for effort. Like I have always said, he is a smart little guy.

"Where are we?" Seth asked.

I squinted out the window, trying to make out the white lettering on the street sign as it reflected an ethereal glow from the phenomenon.

"Looks like Davis Street."

Seth gave a sigh of frustration.

"No, Daddy. What town are we in?"

"Jackson. Jackson, Tennessee."

He did another quick impression of Popeye and then smiled broadly.

"Jackson! How do you like that boy?" he said as he patted the dog's head.

The dog voiced its approval with a series of excited barks and another round of doggie kisses to Seth's face.

"Okay, boy," he giggled. "Jackson it is!"

The incident outside the motel changed the dynamic of our

trip, but not nearly as much as the events happening this very night, things that were very far away in both distance and concept but would soon enough be made horrifically apparent and dangerously close. It seems that the worst decisions in human history are based on ignorance and fear. Yes, the fear *du jour* is usually different—in this case it is monumentally different—but the same knee-jerk reaction is almost as constant as the sunset. Unfortunately, like the sunset, night must run its course before light can once again bring the clarity of a new sunrise.

Political posturing, manipulation, and corruption are at the very core of this issue, a fact I can speak confidently of due to the eyewitness recounting of measures taken from one of my favorite politicians, a man I had never met and never dreamed that I would, but I would soon be crossing paths with him in a most unorthodox way.

Abraham Lincoln stood in the corner of the Oval Office, staring absently at a small painting of an old wooden schooner. He was fond of the painting, though it was not one that was added during his administration but several years later by Teddy Roosevelt. The small piece of art reminded him of a simpler and happier time when he was alive, alive in the flesh-and-blood sense. It reminded him of his boat trips down the Mississippi River to New Orleans in his youth. He loved to stroll through the port in his spare time and admire the great sea vessels with masts that seemed as tall as great oak trees.

The problem with most sea ports was that one must always be on their guard. Characters from all over the world would converge there, and a person never knew if the next corner taken would put them face to face with a friendly sailor or one who would put a knife in your gut for the few pennies carried in your pocket. Or even worse, throw a hood over your head and force or sell you into servitude. Abe never had this problem, possibly because of his intimidating size and muscular frame from years of chopping wood, but he was still on his guard as he admired the ships. He was big and intimidating, but he was no fool. A strong sense of *déjà vu* descended over him as he looked at the ship in the painting and listened apprehensively to what was going on in the room.

The sitting president's staff was assembled. Most of the cabinet was present, along with two guests: the president's science advisor, Dr. Ray Winder, and the great Albert Einstein. Even Mr. Lincoln was familiar with Einstein's accomplishments; the German-born scientist had made several trips to the White House in the years preceding his death. Lincoln had observed several of these meetings, but of course he and Einstein had never really met.

Ray Winder sat on one of the blue sofas perpendicular to the president's desk. He sat quietly nursing a mug of black coffee that had just made the slow journey from lukewarm to room temperature. He had consumed copious amounts of the caffeinated beverage today, he and millions of others, so he was not in a hurry to finish this cup. He knew he needed it, though, because it was going to be another sleepless night. The stocks of Folgers and Maxwell House had probably risen ten-percent in the past few days; there weren't many people who could or wanted to sleep, not with what was currently happening. I'm reasonably sure that most of the motel rooms in Jackson were not occupied by peacefully sleeping travelers, but by people who were just tired of driving or possibly even afraid to drive any further.

Most people would have probably mistaken the sullen expression on Winder's face as that of extreme fatigue, like someone who hasn't slept in a couple of days. That much was true but Mr. Lincoln recognized this expression for what it was, God knew he had seen it dozens of times during his life. It was the sallow and haggard expression of a man under extreme stress. Abe had seen this countenance on the face of his generals shortly before they were to engage in a campaign that would undoubtedly cost dozens, if not hundreds, of young men's lives. But this unpleasant memory was not only relegated to the president's military leaders; Mr. Lincoln had seen this same look more times than he could count in the four years of his presidency, clearly reflected each time he passed one of the White House's numerous mirrors.

Something was going on, something terrible. There was little doubt left when Einstein got up and exited the room with obvious disgust. Winder sat perfectly still, staring into the dark contents of his mug as the president addressed him.

"Ray, what is your assessment? When will this get out of control?"

He paused and cleared his throat. When he spoke, his voice didn't sound like someone who had consumed large amounts of coffee but rather a person that has just spent a week in the desert.

"A week, maybe two."

"So ..." the president persisted, "you are in agreement with the military's opinion?"

A tear streaked down Winder's face and splashed into his coffee, sending a gentle halo of ripples around his mug. He did not agree, although Mr. Lincoln was not aware of that at the time; he thought the government was being hasty considering it had only been 48 hours. Yes, they were frightened, everyone was frightened, but he knew that was no excuse.

Actually ... a part of him did agree with the assessment. The facts were there; it was just a matter of simple mathematics. It was estimated that within two weeks, the US population – living and Impal – would increase by almost 300,000. That was not taking into consideration the number of Impals that were already here. The number would continue to increase the longer the phenomenon lasted.

Winder agreed with the assessment, but it was the solution that troubled his soul. He couldn't help but think of the term the Nazis used: "the final solution." Was that a fitting analogy? Perhaps not, or perhaps it was more fitting in more ways than one. He was in a precarious position as the science advisor, one that he could see no way out of for himself except death. Given the current circumstances, that was not a viable option either.

Winder did not answer aloud, but nodded his head weakly. He

excused himself to the restroom and heaved violently as if his body were trying to expel his guilt along with his stomach contents.

The president dismissed the meeting a short time afterwards while Winder was still indisposed. On the final advice of his Chairman of the Joint Chiefs of Staff, a General Ott Garrison; he gave the order to begin the "project" immediately. It was no secret to anyone in the inner circles of Washington politics that Garrison actually had more pull and influence than the Secretary of Defense, a post he would probably be appointed to in the near future. The problem was that he was still active duty in the Army, and under normal circumstances he would have to wait seven years after resigning his commission. But he was not the type of man who would let a little detail like that set him back; he was good at finding loopholes and taking advantage of opportunity, a talent that had served him well in his 30 years of service.

This would be the last night our illustrious 16th President would spend in the White House. His suspicions had been validated in his mind; he couldn't be a part of what was to come. Oh, sure, the "project" sounded innocent and helpful, but if that were the case, why were Einstein and Winder so upset? Lincoln didn't know for sure exactly what was going on, but there was one thing that 200 years of life experience had taught him: The devil's favorite disguises are always innocent and helpful.

I suppose it is a good thing that I didn't know the details of what was happening or going to happen until much later. I was already nervous about my precious time with Seth. I knew it was borrowed time, a gift that could be gone at any second. I was afraid to take my eyes off him, afraid to sleep because when I opened my eyes again he may be gone. I didn't think I could endure the pain of losing him twice.

That's why the incident outside of the Motel 6, however brief it may have been, simultaneously froze my soul and ripped my heart from my chest. Our reunion was a blessing but a very fragile one; I didn't intend to take that for granted.

A few minutes later we reached our destination. It was an old two-story house that probably had not had a coat of paint since the Lyndon Johnson administration. The yard was in severe danger of being assimilated by the nearby woods; briars, saplings, and brush covered almost every square inch of the yard, except for a narrow rock sidewalk that ran from the street to the front porch. Shutters and front porch railing sagged like old skin. A single light burned in an upstairs window, giving me a disturbing recollection of Norman Bates and his mother. The phenomenon didn't help matters either, giving everything a florescent glow reminiscent of the Bates Motel sign. As I got out of the car I looked at Seth and his newfound friend, then back at the house. I couldn't help but think this was definitely a night of clichés ... or was it irony?

CHAPTER 15
THE PRODIGAL GUIDE

> *"Nibble, nibble, little mouse,*
> *Who is nibbling at my house?*
>
> *The wind, the wind,*
> *The heavenly child."*

~ *Jacob and Wilhelm Grimm, "Hansel and Gretel"*

My apprehension was short lived. Lizzie Chenowith, the younger sister of Rose the Motel 6 clerk, proved to be a warm and inviting host. She shared the same unmarried last name with her sister, but that was where the similarities ended. Rose was short and portly. Lizzie was tall and slender, with milky skin and long, straight salt-and-pepper hair that hung just an inch above her narrow waist. Her gray blouse and black skirt were a complement to her hair. If it weren't for her rosy cheeks, she could have almost been mistaken for a character that just stepped out of a black-and-white movie.

"Please come in!" she beckoned. "I just took a batch of my famous peach muffins out of the oven."

She paused like she almost forgot something important.

"I've also got a pot of snickerdoodle coffee brewing!"

"Thank you, but we just ate not too long ago. I appreciate your gracious hospitality, but we are really tired," I said before complimenting her on her beautiful décor. I guess the doilies and Depression glass would have been in some folks' *Southern Living* best decorated homes, but to me it just reminded me of my grandmother's house. At least Granny Pendleton had a nice TV, an appliance that was noticeably absent from Miss Chenowith's home. Not that it would do any good since the phenomenon was still interfering with the signal.

She did have a nice huge antique 1930s Midwest radio. It sat in the corner of her living room belting out a steady stream of gospel music. "Dead Man Walking" crackled through the old speakers.

I was dead in my sins, just as if I had been
Buried and laid to rest.
Then the One who overcame life and death called my name.
He said, "Child, arise, and be blessed."
I was a dead man walking, but praise God I am alive.
And I can't stop talking, I've just got to testify.
Resurrected from the grave, from death's darkness I am saved.
I was a dead man walking, but praise God I am alive."

I shook my head as I listened to the lyrics. I couldn't take any more irony this evening; it had been a long day and I needed some sleep. I had a fleeting thought of wondering why there was music and not news playing. After all, every other radio station had been running nothing but news coverage ever since the phenomenon started, except for Disney radio. My fatigue forced me to file this thought away for future consideration.

"Do you have room for three?" I asked as Seth and Jackson slipped in the door.

To my surprise there was no unusual reaction to Seth and his dog. She greeted them as if they were no different from anyone else. I was very appreciative for that, she was the only person – including myself – who had treated him as normal on first meeting. I also felt a little guilty because I had wondered what kind of unusual person was still up at this late hour, fully dressed, baking muffins and brewing coffee. On first appraisal, she seemed to be a very caring and generous person, whatever her quirks may be. She was willing to open her home to strangers on such short notice. Not many people would do that.

"Would you like a muffin, young man?" she asked Seth. "Perhaps a treat for your pooch?"

Seth smiled and spoke with the good manners that made me so proud.

"No thank you ma'am. I'm just really tired."

I thought I saw a brief look of confusion pass across her features, but it passed as quickly as it had come and she continued with her same pleasant demeanor.

"Well I've got a nice snuggly warm bed for you and your dad and some big fluffy pillows for your dog ... what's his name?"

"Jackson," Seth said.

"Well, Jackson ... would you like a cookie?" she asked as she withdrew a large cookie from a red cookie jar on her kitchen cabinet.

I couldn't help but wonder how she knew that Seth and Jackson ate, but I filed the question in my exhausted brain to ask tomorrow.

Jackson happily wagged his tail and gratefully accepted the treat with one quick chomp. She then led us past the kitchen and through a wooden door at the end of a long hallway. It opened into a room that was a stark contrast to the rest of the house.

While the outside of the house had not been painted since the Lyndon Johnson administration, this room was likely added sometime during the presidency of Bill Clinton. A tall queen sized poster bed was centered between two windows covered with green drapes. The floor was covered with a fairly modern maroon carpet, the new carpet smell still hung in the air. The room probably didn't get much use. Just the occasional wayward traveler, perhaps.

She made a bed of pillows for Jackson under the window and turned down the sheets for Seth and me. She wished us a good night and closed the door. I was just about to undress and turn out the light when I got confirmation that squenching was not amongst Jackson's talents. I carefully cleaned up the pile of cookie bits by his bed and disposed of them in a tacky brass trash can. Could Jackson be squench broken? I didn't know, but one thing was certain … he wouldn't be eating any cookies in my vehicle any time soon.

Morning came quickly and we were awakened by a soft knock at the door.

"Mr. Pendleton, you up?" Lizzie called in a loud whisper.

"Yes, ma'am," I said rolling out of bed. "Is everything all right?"

"Oh yes, I was just making breakfast and I wondered how you and Seth liked your eggs."

"You don't need to go to any trouble." I slipped my pants on and Seth hopped on the floor to play with Jackson. "We can hit Martian Burger on the way out of town."

What I didn't realize is that we wouldn't be leaving town today or even tomorrow.

"Don't be silly!" she said. "It's no trouble; I almost have it ready, anyway."

I heard her shuffling away down the hall. I turned to Seth who was lying on his back in the floor. Jackson was happily licking his fingers.

"Come on, buddy. Let's go eat!"

He hopped up and started for the door.

"Don't forget your squenching," I said, like I had just reminded him to brush his teeth.

He gave me a look as if to say, *no duh, Daddy,* before opening the door and heading down the hall. Luckily I had just zipped my pants and buttoned up, because Miss Chenowith was in full view at the end of the hall. She was now wearing a generic white robe with green fuzzy slippers, much more appropriate attire for the hour of the day.

Breakfast was incredible, the best I had had since I was a young boy spending the night at my grandparents' house. Granny Pendleton was a heck of a good cook and Miss Chenowith was the first rival to her culinary skills I had ever run across.

She gave me an inquisitive look as if seeking approval before asking Seth how he liked his eggs. I nodded and gave her a reassuring smile. I truly appreciated her effort to treat Seth normally. It was a legitimate question and her discreet, wordless query again gave me a stab of guilt when I thought of my first impression of Miss Chenowith last night. What I didn't realize at the time is that what I mistook for instinctual kindness was much more akin to familiarity with the subject matter, the subject matter being Seth and Jackson. Yes, the people now known to the world as Impalpables or Impals were very familiar to Miss Chenowith, actually quite a bit more familiar than they were to me.

"Seth can sit here with me," I told her then continued with a wink, "but if you give anything to Jackson, you may want to do it outside."

She led Jackson to the back door and gave him a couple of pieces of bacon and a large biscuit. He took them eagerly and sat down to dine on his treat which would soon be scattered in bits on the ground, fodder for the birds outside our host's back door. She closed the door as Jackson ate and returned to the table, joining Seth and me in pleasant breakfast conversation. The radio played another gospel tune in the next room. I couldn't help but crack a smile when I realized the song playing was "How Great Thou Art," sung by none other than one of the most famous people, or should I say Impals, on the planet: Elvis Aaron Presley.

After I had taken my last bite of the delicious meal, I leaned back in my chair and patted my stomach.

"Miss Chenowith, that was incredible! That's the best meal I've had in years!"

She blushed modestly and gently blotted her lips with a large lacy napkin.

"Thank you," she said. "I'm sure your wife is a good cook, too."

I paused to look at Seth before answering. I had hoped that he was not paying attention, but he was. He sat back in his chair looking at me with sad, glimmering eyes. The subject of his mother had not come up since the day the phenomenon started, and I hoped it was a topic that could be avoided. I mean, what purpose would it serve? She was gone and there was nothing we could do about it. That fact only served to remind me that Seth could be gone again at any moment. A lump formed in my throat as I replied in a hoarse voice.

"She was ... she's no longer with us."

"I'm, sorry," she said as she reached over and squeezed my hand. She looked at Seth and smiled warmly. "Sweetheart, why don't you go check on your doggie? You can play awhile in the backyard if you would like."

Seth looked to me, his eyes welling with silvery tears.

"It's okay, buddy. You and Jackson go have fun. I'll be out to check on you in a minute."

He slowly got up from the table and cheerlessly walked down the hall and out the door.

"Your wife went through the door, didn't she?" Miss Chenowith asked.

I stared at her incredulously for several moments before replying. "Well, yes ... but how ... how did ...?"

"How did I know?" she finished for me.

I nodded my head. Miss Chenowith smiled and rose from her seat then beckoned me to follow her. She led me into the room with the antique radio. "He's Alive" by Dolly Parton crackled from the seventy-year-old speakers. The room looked quite a bit different now that I was standing inside of it in full daylight. The radio was the least of the curiosities contained inside the faded floral antique paper print of its walls. There must have been at least four dozen white candles arranged on small tables surrounding a large round wooden table in the center of the room. The large table sat on top of a large oval Turkish rug. The ornate design of the floor covering was not what drew my attention; it was what sat on top of the round table.

I was just about to ask about the object when Miss Chenowith spoke.

"Do you know what I do for a living, Mr. Pendleton?"

I stared at her blankly for several moments. I didn't have a clue. As it turned out, I did have an idea as I looked at the object on the table and recalled Miss Chenowith's unusual attire for the late hour we arrived last night. It all started to fall into place like tumblers in a safe, but before I could venture a guess she answered her own question.

"I'm a medium."

Well, I guess that was kind of what I was thinking. Actually another term came to mind.

"I was going to say fortune teller," I said as I pointed to the object on top of the table, which was a large crystal ball.

She put her hand over her mouth to suppress a giggle which seemed uncharacteristically girlish from a woman her age.

"No, I don't tell the future," she smiled. "I help people talk to their departed loved ones. Or should I say, helped people. There's not much call for me since all this mess started."

I looked at her skeptically. I didn't want to be rude, but I had always pictured mediums, psychics, or fortune tellers as frauds, predators preying on the grief of others. I thought it was crazy that people could be that gullible, but, due to recent events in my life, it didn't seem so crazy anymore. In fact, it almost seemed natural for people to want to reach out, to have one last conversation with their departed loved ones, to want to quell the grief that consumed every second of their lives. My God, what a true gift I have been given, however short lived it may be.

"Really?" I asked, trying to filter as much skepticism out of my voice as I could. My filter was woefully inadequate because Miss Chenowith's face washed from a pleasant smile to a look of someone who had just had their feelings brutalized.

"Yes, really," she said coldly. "I would think someone in your situation would be a little less skeptical."

I felt my face flush red. I had hurt her feelings and Lord knows the sweet lady didn't deserve it.

"I-I'm sorry," I stammered. "I guess that was me talking through my beliefs from a few days ago." I paused and said, "I have become a lot more open-minded since then."

Miss Chenowith smiled ruefully, then walked over and gently rubbed her right hand over the crystal ball. After several moments of uncomfortable silence, she sat down at the table and invited me to sit across from her. I did as I was bid and sat in the matching Queen Anne armchair opposite her.

"I have lost someone as well, Mr. Pendleton."

"Did they go through the door?" I asked.

"No," she replied glumly. "They stayed here ... in fact, they have been here for years."

"I don't understand, were they ... I mean are they an Impal?"

She looked at me blankly.

"I don't understand. What's an Impal?"

I assumed that Miss Chenowith had at least listened to *some* news the past few days. Or at the very least was psychic enough to divine the meaning of the word. Okay, I admit that was a little of my old skepticism still talking; Miss Chenowith had made it very clear that she was a medium, nothing more.

"Impals are what they have been calling people like Seth on the news. It's short for Impalpable."

"Clever name," she smirked sarcastically. "What are they calling people like me? Impal pals?"

I couldn't help but laugh.

"No, but that's not bad," I said with a broad smile, a smile she thankfully returned in kind. "I'm sorry, I assumed you had heard some news," I said pointing at her radio in the corner, which was belting out a gospel oldie that I was not familiar with.

She smiled and opened a drawer under the table then produced a small black object and pointed it at the radio. The music instantly stopped.

"I had a CD changer put in that old box years ago. I don't think the radio had picked up a broadcast since the moon landing."

"You don't have another radio?" I asked.

"No sir, I don't even own a car. And TV … forget about it."

"But, why?"

"Because the news and TV programs serve nothing more than to depress us and make mush out of our brains. I prefer to read and make up my own mind!" she proclaimed.

"I can't disagree with you there," I said, looking around at her formidable library on the shelves semi-circling the room. I gave her a brief update of everything going on in the world for the past few days.

She listened quietly, registering very little emotion except for a smile when I mentioned Albert Einstein and Abraham Lincoln.

"You said you had lost someone?" I asked when I had finished my news update.

She nodded her head.

"Yes, his name is Shasta. He was my spirit guide for years. I had never really seen him, at least in the way that I see you, that is … until a few days ago."

"When the storm started," I guessed.

"Yes, I came downstairs and saw him sitting in here on the floor by the radio," she said nodding her head at the now-silent antique. "He was tapping his foot and singing along with the music … I can't remember the song now but it did have a catchy beat. He was eating a cookie and got crumbs all over my rug."

"What happened?" I asked softly.

"He got scared," she said as tears began to streak black eyeliner down her pale cheeks. "When he realized I could see him, really see him, he ran out the door ... or maybe he thought I would be angry about the mess he had just made, but I haven't seen him since." She began to sob uncontrollably.

"What would you like me to do?" I asked with true sympathy.

She looked up at me pleadingly as tears began to stream and spoke in a quivering voice.

"Find him ... please find him."

CHAPTER 16
THE SEARCH FOR SHASTA

"People are meant to go through life two by two.
'Tain't natural to be lonesome."

~*Thornton Wilder, "Our Town"*

My initial thoughts were to thank her for her hospitality, quickly retrieve Seth and Jackson, and then, with utmost haste, resume our journey. This was not at all what I had planned for our trip, but how could I say no? All I wanted was to spend time with my son, as much time as I could for as long as I could. But how could I say no? Miss Chenowith had been very kind to us.

She was a sweet lady and she was very upset. Could this boy, Shasta, be in danger? I didn't think so, but how could I be sure? I was terrified for a few brief moments when I thought something had happened to Seth outside the motel. Unfortunately, I would soon enough discover that those instincts would prove to be correct. None of us are invulnerable.

Before I agreed to anything of the sort, I had a few questions to ask of Miss Chenowith.

"What is a spirit guide?"

She smiled and dabbed her eyes with a lacy handkerchief produced from her robe pocket.

"Well," she began. "They are most commonly thought of as an entity that remains a disincarnate spirit in order to act as a guide or protector to a living, incarnated human being." She tapped her fingers on the table and said, "In this case, the human being is me."

"I don't understand. He protected you?"

"No, at least not that I know of."

She pursed her lips into a thin line and twisted her mouth from side to side as she considered her answer. Miss Chenowith stopped and exhaled deeply before replying.

"I guess the only way to say it that makes any sense is that he was a kind of enhancer or amplifier, relaying messages back and forth between this world and the next."

I stared at her blankly, having no clue what she was talking about.

"He was always there with me, well … most of the time, anyway. He would occasionally wander off," she said with such endearment in her voice that it sounded like she was recalling the exploits of a beloved mischievous child. She shook her head and continued, "He talked to me often, told me things about himself, kept me company. He loved me …"

Tears began to stream down her cheeks again.

"You said he was an enhancer or amplifier." I tried to get her back on track. "What did you mean by that?"

She sniffled and dabbed her eyes again before blowing her nose into her handkerchief with a tuba-like report. She screwed up her tear-swollen eyes to look at me and took a deep shuttering breath before answering.

"If I ever had trouble getting through to a soul, Shasta acted like an interpreter or go-between to clear up the communication that I was having trouble picking up on."

I felt like I was trying to have a serious conversation with someone as to the exact location of Santa's workshop. Yes, I felt ridiculous, but I knew that what we were discussing was as real as the sunrise that brilliantly shone through the window behind Miss Chenowith. My mouth twisted like I had just sucked on a lemon as I forced myself to finish the conversation.

"You talked to him ... but you couldn't see him?"

She smiled and put her index finger to her forehead.

"Not like you and I, but in my mind's eye."

She tapped her finger on her brow. "It's really hard to explain if you haven't experienced it."

I knew I was getting out of my comfort zone, and this really wasn't the point anyway, was it? I had no hope of understanding what Miss Chenowith was telling me, not without a common point of reference, and I was about as psychic as a grilled cheese sandwich. She wanted help finding this boy, a boy who now had some hybrid blend of the ethereal and physical form like Seth. That was something I could comprehend, something I could wrap my mind around. I started to ask if he looked the same when she saw him as he did in her mind's eye, but again, what would be the point? I needed to keep it simple and to the point.

"What does Shasta look like?" I asked. "What can you tell me about him that might help me find him?"

I discovered that Shasta had been a slave on a plantation just a couple of miles outside of Jackson. He was about nine or ten-years-old when he died, but Miss Chenowith did not know how he died because Shasta did not know. That was a memory that was thankfully lost to Seth, as well. Hopefully that was a subject that was forgotten to all Impals, but I knew that wasn't entirely true. The Fiddlers were very much aware that they had perished when their home burned.

Perhaps that was a different circumstance because they all died together, or because their house seemed to have passed on with them even though the house didn't return when the phenomenon started. I didn't know; my head could explode just thinking about it.

"What was he wearing? What was his hair like?"

According to Miss Chenowith, Shasta wore a pair of gray trouser overalls with a white button-down undershirt. He wore no shoes and his head seemed to be shaved. A chubby face that she fondly described as "bubble gum" cheeks topped a slender body, giving his head an oversized appearance. He had an unusually dark complexion that was clearly visible under the shiny translucent sheen characteristic of all Impals.

"Any idea at all where he may have gone?"

Before she could answer, Seth and Jackson came trudging up the hallway. It startled me a little because I had not heard the door open. I guessed Seth must have taught him the trick of passing through the door like he did through the chair and the ceiling at home a couple of days ago.

"Seth, we are going to look for a little boy named Shasta. Is that okay with you?" I asked as I felt the cold and warmth of Jackson lapping at my hand.

He looked at me skeptically for several moments and then shrugged.

"I guess so ... when are we going to the moozem?"

"A couple of days," I promised. "As soon as we find Shasta, we'll be on our way."

Seth was not keen on this idea but he grudgingly went along with it. We searched the neighborhood around Miss Chenowith's house. Evidently the neighbors thought our gracious psychic host was every bit as unusual as Seth and Jackson. They gave her the same wide berth they afforded my son and his pooch. I didn't know for sure, but I guessed her neighbors probably referred to her as Dizzy Lizzie or Spooky Chenowith, the weird old woman at the end of the road.

The neighbors watched us comb the streets from behind the comfort of their drapes, autos, fences, and hedges. A light wind rustling through the leaves of the ancient sycamore and maple trees lining the sides of the street gave a comedic whispering overture to the obvious murmuring going on about our little posse. We searched the streets thoroughly, and then by late afternoon we had covered a good portion of the woods that bordered the neighborhood. As a matter of fact, Miss Chenowith's home backed right up to the woods, and we accessed her back yard via a loose board in her cedar fence.

No one was any worse for wear, except me. My neck and ears were on fire from the itch of what seemed like a thousand mosquito bites. I also suspected I might have a tick or two burrowing into an unpleasant spot on my body. I gently fingered a couple of knots on my head from running into low hanging tree limbs. I am usually not that big of a klutz but my attention was drawn to the forest floor; I am deathly afraid of snakes.

I was not surprised to find Seth or Jackson unaffected by our woodland excursion but Miss Chenowith was a surprise. She was spry for her age, not only had she kept up with us all day, I guess if I were being honest, I would have to admit to trying to keep up with her, but she seemed completely unaffected by the insect barrage that now had me in so much misery. Was she one of those rare people that seem to be invisible to mosquitoes or maybe tasted bad to the little winged blood suckers? Perhaps she just had the foresight – no pun intended – to apply insect repellent before we left.

Whatever the reason, she was more than happy to immediately start dinner for us as I bathed. She thoughtfully handed me a bottle of Calamine lotion as I made my way to the bath tub with utmost haste. I felt like I was going to skin myself if I kept up the vigorous scratching. I had never been more eager to soak in a hot tub.

I felt somewhat better after I bathed and applied generous portions of Calamine to my swollen skin; of course, when it comes to bug bites, only time can completely get rid of the incessant itching.

We had a dinner that was every bit as fabulous as breakfast. It was so good and I was so stuffed, I secretly wished that I was capable of squenching.

Seth thought it was delicious as well, and usually he is a finicky eater. I was so preoccupied with complementing our gracious host on the meal that I did not notice Seth when he excused himself to go outside and squench. I didn't notice that he had taken a couple of rolls with him, along with a hand full of casserole. If I had noticed, I might have saved us a lot of time and trouble.

We spent the following day helping Miss Chenowith in her search for Shasta. We made another pass through her neighborhood, this time in my vehicle, and then drove a couple of miles away to the location of the plantation where Shasta had lived 150 years ago. The house and out buildings were gone, the only evidence of their existence was a thin weathered stone outline of the foundations. The property was now owned by a local dairy farmer and a dozen black and white heifers grazed nearby. Miss Chenowith knew the farmer and was able to access the property by unlocking a padlock securing a large metal gate.

"Charlie told me I could come out here whenever I wanted," she said, referring to Charles Paladino, the owner of Paladino Farms.

"Did you come out here to talk to Shasta?" I asked sympathetically.

Miss Chenowith made a little barking sound as she quickly threw her hand over her mouth to suppress a laugh. When she was confident her laugh stifled, she brought her hand down, revealing a humorous grin.

"No, he hung out at my house most of the time ... why would he want to live out here by himself?"

I shrugged but before I could reply she pointed her finger at something over my shoulder.

"I liked to come out here to fish!"

I followed the direction of her finger and saw a small pond nestled amongst a group of mimosa trees. A couple of cows frolicked nosily in the shallow water near the far bank. I smiled. I loved to fish as a kid, but as I got older and my work took more and more importance in my life, that pastime was relegated to the back burner … like so many other things.

"Crappie or bass?" I asked.

She looked at me indignantly. "Catfish."

I smiled. I loved catfish. The Trotline was one of my favorite restaurants back in Conway. Their secret recipe deep-fried batter was so good I was amazed that in the 30 years they had been in business, they had never expanded or franchised. They had stayed in the same little cinder block building for years, near … well, it was near Lake Beaverfork, the place that Ann and Seth spent their last day together. A pain shot through my gut as I tried to redirect my thoughts away from that terrible spot.

"Southern fried or Cajun?" I asked.

She looked at me with the same indignant expression.

"My dear man, you are not in Louisiana, in case there was any doubt. We southern fry our chuckleheads in Tennessee. That's the way God intended it!"

No pun intended, but I couldn't help but chuckle. I had heard that term before but it was by my granddad when we would go crappie and bass fishing and he would inadvertently pull in a catfish.

"Away with you, chucklehead!" he would shout as he pitched the unwanted catch back in the lake.

Miss Chenowith looked at me suspiciously for a moment then her face split in a huge grin. She gave a tittering laugh before she suggested that we split up and meet back in the vehicle in an hour. Seth was to go with her, a prospect I was uncomfortable with but decided to allow as long as Jackson accompanied them. Besides, it's almost impossible to separate a boy and his dog. So I was on my own.

It wasn't long before my apprehension returned as I waded through the tall grass. The sky and clouds might be a different hue right now. The situation in the world currently was unprecedented, including my own personal situation. But nothing, not even a mysterious cosmic storm and return of the dead, could completely distract me from my lifelong phobia of snakes.

The hissing sound the wind made as it blew through the green wispy waves did not help matters either. My apprehension was soon relieved when I came upon an ancient, knee-high rock wall surrounding a neatly manicured burial plot. I could tell that the cemetery was old from the weathered appearance of the headstones, but the grass surrounding the 40 or so markers had been recently trimmed. As I walked around the perimeter of the little cemetery, I saw a small wooden sign posted on the outside of the south wall. It read: *Cared for by the Madison County Historic Preservation Society.*

There was nothing else posted, no indication if this little grave yard had any historic significance or whether it belonged to a particular family or to a long-forgotten community. I soon came upon a relatively smooth surface of the wall that afforded a good view of all the markers. I sat down to rest and to ponder.

CHAPTER 17

TEARS OF THE
RECENTLY DEPARTED

"There is no grief like the grief that does not speak."

~Henry Wordsworth

I sat and looked at the headstone nearest to me. It was weathered so badly that I could just make out the first letter of the last name and the date of death: August 8, 1881. The stones beside it and behind were not in much better shape; I couldn't make out any dates, but the last name was clearly visible on both. The one to the left belonged to a Nesbit and the one behind belonged to a Smith. I guess that outside of a family plot, there was probably not a single cemetery in the United States that did not have at least one Smith. I got up and strolled a little ways in. The next four stones presented different last names, which told me this probably was not a family plot but a long forgotten burial site of a town that had also slipped the recollection of the living, aside from a few caring souls in The Madison County Historical Society.

I passed two more rows of stones, all of which were so badly weathered that they could have been little more than smooth rocks protruding from the ground. As I approached the far wall of the little cemetery, I stopped in my tracks as a lump formed in my throat and my heart started to flutter. A single headstone had caught my eye, one that was probably in the best condition of any I had seen so far. It was not the condition of the stone that got my attention, it was the name on the stone: *Stan Pendleton.*

I walked up and ran my hand over the smooth surface, reading the rest of the inscription. Stan was born in July of 1842 and passed away on February 3, 1884. He was a loving father and husband. That was it, nothing more.

I, at first, felt a flash of intense grief as I was reminded of a tombstone back home in Conway with the same last name, but it memorialized two names, not just one. It also displayed two epitaphs, not just one: *Beloved wife, mother and friend*, and the other short and to the point: *Sweet angel.* A tear streamed down my cheek as I absently knelt then sat in the grass. I pinched the bridge of my nose and wept for a few moments until the realization of where I was came back to me with a jolt. I looked around at the headstones with embarrassment, like I had just been caught weeping in a crowded room. Were any of these people around now, due to the storm? I didn't know, but I did know they definitely weren't here, not in this sad and lonely place.

It suddenly dawned on me just how woefully inadequate the living are when it comes to memorializing our fallen friends, family, and fellow people. This little cemetery was a perfect example of this shortcoming. How can a life lived be reduced to a name, dates, and a clichéd sentence or two carved into a rock? A life that will gradually be forgotten as those who do remember move on to receive their own carved epitaphs, until presently there are none that remain who remember ... or care? We leave their memory to the mercy of time and the elements until nothing is left to remind us that they once lived, once laughed, and once loved, nothing but a weathered stone.

I thought of a play which I participated in high school. *Our Town* by Thornton Wilder was probably one of the most depressing stories I had ever read, but it got me an "A" in drama, which I desperately needed for my GPA. A woman named Ellen or Emily, I can't recall which, was allowed to return after her death and relive the day she had celebrated her twelfth birthday. She realizes just how much life should be valued, "every, every minute." She poignantly asks the Stage Manager whether anyone realizes life while they live it, and is told, "No. The saints and poets, maybe – they do some."

This conclusion to the famous stage play suggests that we have no value for life because we take it for granted every day, and there are only a few of us who harbor any appreciation of the gift at all. Wasn't this cemetery and thousands more around the world direct proof of that? Isn't our dealing with death a direct reflection of how we deal with life? Of course it is, both are forgotten and taken for granted.

As I leaned against the headstone behind me and rubbed my eyes, I heard Seth calling for Jackson in the distance. The unusual sound of his voice, like someone talking in a tin can, did not faze me anymore. He was my son, he was my buddy, he was my Seth ... he was my *sweet angel*. The gift I had been granted was far better than the one the woman in the play received. Or was it the gift Seth had been granted? I wasn't sure, maybe both would be accurate.

Except what would have become of Seth if this cosmic storm had never come along? Would he have been relegated to an existence of vying for the attention of a father who could not see or hear him? I shuttered and quickly tossed the thought aside. Too many questions to ponder and I didn't have the answer to any of them. We were together now and that's what mattered. We needed to make every, every minute count, as the woman in the play realized.

I wiped my eyes on the back of my hand then got up and looked around. It was truly amazing how quickly a person can get used to something; the lavender sky now seemed completely prosaic to me, like it had always been that way. I gave the headstone that had prompted this emotional distraction a perfunctory glance. It didn't even occur to me that this could possibly be some long forgotten relative of mine, perhaps even an uncle or granddad from many generations ago. I wanted to get away from it as quickly as possible. I strolled past and carefully climbed the rock wall. Seth laughed in the distance and Jackson barked, so I headed in that direction.

We had no success finding Shasta that day. We stayed another hour combing the field; miraculously I saw no snakes, not even by the pond. Miss Chenowith told me that the plantation was part of a small community called Pascoe, which disappeared over 100 years ago when the town and plantation was leveled by a massive tornado. A short time later, before the inhabitants could rebuild, the town was consumed by a terrible flood that didn't recede for almost six months.

Everyone that was left moved on to seek work in Memphis or Nashville. The cemetery was mysteriously tended periodically until the mid-1950s when the Paladino family bought the property from the county and started the dairy farm. It was assumed that some of the surviving members of Pascoe had tended the burial site and had gotten too old to continue, or gave up when the barbed wire fence was constructed for the dairy.

If Shasta had been buried there, I doubt it was in the town cemetery. According to Miss Chenowith, he had been a slave, and sadly slaves were not afforded elaborate burials and not in a white cemetery. If there was any marker for poor Shasta, it was probably made out of wood, not stone, in a place that had now been erased by time and the elements. I pictured in my mind's eye a small makeshift wooden cross, wood that had probably rotted and washed away decades ago, probably in the flood that finished the town. I had no reason to believe that Shasta had any reason to hang out in such a sad, forgotten, and empty place.

The only thing the day had given to me was a rejuvenated desire for Seth and me to resume our trip. I felt for Miss Chenowith, I truly did, but I had to remember why I was here, why I was on this trip. I was on this trip for Seth, and I had to make the most of every, every minute because I knew that Seth could be gone again. If that happened I might never get another chance. I made up my mind that we would head out first thing in the morning – Shasta or no Shasta. I would use our drive back to Miss Chenowith's home to try and decide the best way to break the news to the sweet lady. I thought I would soften the blow by treating our gracious host and cook to dinner. She proclaimed that she wasn't fit to be seen in public, so I drove through a popular local Mexican food establishment that she recommended; it turned out that Tex-Mex is her favorite cuisine. I never would have guessed that. We took our meal back to her place for eating and squenching, leaving my vehicle smelling like refried beans and hot sauce.

Miss Chenowith was very quiet on the trip home and during dinner. I think I saw a tear slip down her cheek a few times. I felt sorry for her; I knew what it was like to lose someone. Well, maybe not in the same way as she did. The person she lost was already deceased. I knew, though, that it didn't make him any less a person or make her grief any less painful than mine. He wasn't gone, he couldn't be. He had to be somewhere close, didn't he? Again, more questions that I didn't have a clue how to answer.

I told Miss Chenowith after dinner of my intentions to resume our trip in the morning. She was noticeably upset, but she said she understood.

"I know you have to cherish every, every minute," she said with a sad smile.

My heart leapt into my throat and my eyes felt like they bulged as big as saucers. "Why did you use that term?" I asked barely above a whisper. She said she was just a medium, but could she be more than that?

She looked at me, obviously a little surprised at my reaction.

"That was one of my favorite plays growing up," she said. "It really puts things in perspective."

She frowned.

"Why does that bother you?"

My heart was still racing but I felt stupid. What had I expected her to say? *I read your mind, Thomas. I know everything about you!*

"It doesn't," I said, mustering a smile. "It was one of mine, too. It really does make you think."

She smiled, patted my arm, then drew a shawl around her shoulders.

"I'm not feeling well," she said as she placed her hand over her stomach. "I think I got too much sunnin' today."

She did look a little flushed, and now that she mentioned it, I kind of felt a little weathered. It had been an unusually sunny day, very few of the yellowish clouds could be seen. Of course, any day was unusual now whether it was sunny or not; the sky is lavender, for God's sake. I may have gotten used to it, but I was still aware of it. Maybe that had an effect on us, being out in the phenomenon all day; after all, they had warned everyone over the radio to stay inside until they had more information.

I suddenly realized that it had been almost two days since I had listened to a radio. I had no idea what was going on in the world right now. That gave me a pang of panic. Could they be reporting that the phenomenon had passed in Europe and would eventually pass here just hours or minutes from now, putting everything back to normal? The bottom line is that it did me no good to worry about my weathered skin or the passing of the phenomenon. I could do nothing about either one. I tried to push it out of my mind, but the searing flame of worry in my gut kept pushing back with a vengeance. I couldn't forget, no matter how hard I tried. I suddenly had an overpowering desire to see Seth.

"Y'all make yourselves at home," she said pointing to the kitchen.

"Give Seth a kiss for me and I'll see you in the morning."

As she turned to go upstairs her tired expression and posture made her look every bit of her 70-plus years. It was the first time I had seen her like this and it took me back a little. I knew it had been a tiring day and she was stressed from the loss of Shasta. Hopefully, it was nothing a good night's sleep couldn't fix, or at least make better. I could use a good forty winks myself, especially since I planned on hitting the road early in the morning.

I said goodnight to Miss Chenowith and went out to the backyard to find Seth and Jackson. The sun was beginning to set, and the weird, luminescent light show was once again descending over our side of the world, turning the outdoors into an enormous black-light painting. I was outside for just a few moments when I thought that worrisome flame was going to erupt from stomach – Seth and Jackson were gone.

I started to call out when they emerged sheepishly from behind the storage building.

"Hey, buddy, what are y'all doing?"

Seth shrugged and patted Jackson on the head as they approached me.

"Nuffin,' we was just playin'," he said.

I was a little curious to see what they were doing, especially since Seth was acting like I had just caught him with his hand in the proverbial cookie jar. I might have pushed the matter if not for feeling the cold paws of Jackson on my thigh as he yipped for my attention. I stroked his equally frigid head and then beckoned them to follow me inside.

"We need to get some rest, buddy. We are heading out for the moozem in the morning," I said with a weak impression of Seth's pronunciation. He wasn't impressed with my jest as he gave me an annoyed smirk but his face brightened when he realized what I had just told him.

"Really?!?" he beamed.

"Yes, really," I said as he took my hand and started to pounce up and down with excitement. Jackson barked playfully and ran around Seth and me in a large circle, looking like a silver ring the faster he travelled.

"Can I see all the spaceships?" Seth asked as I led him toward the door.

"You bet!" I said, "Every one of them!"

We went in the house and Seth scored a couple of cookies from Miss Chenowith's teddy-bear-shaped cookie jar. He gave one to Jackson and trotted off happily toward the bedroom. I made a mental note to check the carpet for cookie fragments later. I didn't know if it was possible to teach an Impal dog to squench. I had seen only one, after all. But even if it was, Jackson sure didn't have the hang of it yet.

I made myself a glass of cold buttermilk. I was thirsty with an unsettled stomach, and buttermilk always seemed to do the trick. The worry that burned in the pit of my stomach, however, would have probably been best quenched with a stiff drink, but there was none to be found. Unless she had a secret cabinet somewhere, it seemed that Lizzy Chenowith was a teetotaler.

I searched for a piece of cornbread and found one wrapped up in the bread box next to the fridge. I crumbled it into my glass and swished it around until the crumbs were sufficiently saturated with fermented milk. It was a little trick I learned from my granddad. He did it every night before going to bed. He claimed that it enhanced the taste, settled his stomach faster, and helped him sleep better. I knew it settled my stomach, but I wasn't sure about the other two ... but I needed all the help I could get tonight.

I took the final swig from my glass and sat it on the table in front of me, staring at the milky film coating the inside of the glass. I could feel the flame in my gut again, trying to rebel against the lactic acid onslaught. I might save myself a lot of worry and aggravation if I could just accept and appreciate the way things are instead of constantly asking why. Maybe I am not meant to know, or maybe I am just incapable of comprehending. Maybe it's both.

I got up and washed my glass in the sink then set it out to dry. I pushed the questions and the worry to the back of my mind as best I could and focused on tomorrow. Seth and I would be resuming our trip in the morning, and that made me happy; that soothed my stomach better than anything. I got in bed and slept relatively peacefully, but I couldn't shake the feeling that something wasn't quite right. It had nothing to do with Seth, of that much I was certain, but it was something close. I awoke to the distant sound of someone sobbing. I couldn't tell if it was outside our window or somewhere in the house. I sat up and listened. I heard it again, this time I could tell it was the unhappy sobs of a woman. Could it be Miss Chenowith? I swung my legs over the side of the bed and quietly slid to the floor. I looked at Seth and Jackson. They were still resting peacefully. I silently dressed and tiptoed to the door. I listened intently, and when I heard the crying again, I could tell it was coming from just down the hall, maybe the kitchen or the crystal ball room.

I opened the door as carefully as I could; every muscle in my body was stiff with anticipation as I tried to move without being heard. Now that the door was open and I was in the hallway, the sobs were much more pronounced and I could tell they were not coming from the kitchen, but the room with the crystal ball and radio.

It dawned on me how silly I was being and I instantly felt like some kind of perverted voyeur. Why was I trying to sneak up on sweet Miss Chenowith in her own home? If she was upset I either needed to give her privacy or attempt to comfort her. I decided that since I was this far committed, I should see if I can help her. She had probably heard me opening the bedroom door, anyway.

I walked past the kitchen and entered the doorway to the room where Miss Chenowith was sitting at the table with the crystal ball, her back to the window. Her head was buried in her hands as she continued to weep copiously. As I slowly approached and my eyes became accustomed to the morning light streaming in through the window, my guts twisted like someone wringing a towel and my heart leapt into my throat. I was in complete and utter shock.

Miss Chenowith heard my clumsy footfalls and she lifted her head and looked at me. She was wearing the same clothes as yesterday and wearing the same hairstyle as always, but she was different. Her predictable clothing and pale complexion were enhanced by a silvery glow. A stream of silver tears rushed down her cheeks and disappeared through the tabletop, not leaving a spot.

"What has happened to me?" she pleaded.

I could not give her an answer, I was still paralyzed from the shock, but I knew. I knew that Miss Chenowith had passed in the night, but like every other person that had passed during the storm, she had no choice, no free will to pass on or to stay. She was stuck. Miss Chenowith was now an Impal.

CHAPTER 18
MOTHER'S LOVE

"In death - no! Even in the grave all is not lost.
Else there is no immortality for man."

~Edgar Allan Poe

It seemed like it took me an eternity to unhinge my jaws and mutter a response. My answer was as inadequate as my ability to stand up at the moment, and I grabbed the chair across from her and tumbled into it.

"My God," was the only thing I could say at the moment.

Miss Chenowith looked at me pleadingly, tears still cascading down her cheeks and passing through the tabletop like it wasn't there. After several moments of uncomfortable silence, I managed to speak, albeit stupidly.

"Are you okay?"

That idiotic question forced her head back into the palms of her hands. She moaned pathetically as her shoulders heaved up and down with uncontrollable sobbing. Of course she wasn't okay. She had died, for God's sake. She was now stuck here like everyone else who had died since this phenomenon started. I had a feeling that this made it worse, made it much more stressful on the poor people as they left their physical lives. They had no choice to move on or to stay. They were stuck here, and nothing had really changed for them other than their physical body had been discarded and they … I trailed off as another thought popped into my head like a macabre road sign. Miss Chenowith was here, but her body was where … upstairs? That seemed the most logical place, and it was something that had to be dealt with and dealt with soon, but not now. The most pressing matter was to help Miss Chenowith cope with this new development, to try and put her at ease somehow.

I quickly decided the best way to handle this is not to be apologetic or sympathetic but be upbeat. That is what I had done with Seth. Of course, Seth had chosen to stay, and he had spent a couple of weeks … where? I hadn't really thought about it before, other than imagining how hard it must have been on the little guy because he was able to see and hear me but I had no idea he was there. I guess you would call it "between." I took a deep breath and spoke softly.

"Miss Chenowith," I said, "you look very beautiful this morning."

She stopped crying abruptly and her head shot up from out of her hands like a Jack in the box. She looked at me incredulously as if I had just asked for her hand in marriage.

"What did you say?" she asked between latent sniffles.

"I said, you look beautiful. Nothing has changed for you; in fact, it may be better."

She looked at me like I had a tentacle growing out of each ear. Before she could retort, I explained how Seth could do things like push through a solid object or jump and tumble without being hurt.

"He enjoys everything he did before," I said, choosing my phrasing very carefully. I didn't want to say something stupid like before he died or before he passed on. "He still loves his favorite foods!" I interjected when I reminded her of squenching.

She paused and stared at her hands thoughtfully. Miss Chenowith reached out and touched her crystal ball. She watched with fascination as her fingers slowly penetrated the glassy surface. Without warning, she jerked her fingers back as if she had been bitten. She stretched out her hand and inspected the surface like she was admiring a new manicure, then smiled awkwardly.

"This is going to take some getting used to," she said as she carefully pushed her other hand through the top of the table. She jerked it back with the same panicked reaction, and then rubbed her hands together like someone trying to get warm or trying to determine if they were really solid.

"You know, I can sit here and not go through the chair or the floor, but if I try to push through something I can," she frowned and rubbed the last vestiges of silvery tears from her eyes. "Now that you mention it, I am kind of hungry," she said as a small trace of happiness seemed to creep across her face.

"Let me cook for you this morning," I insisted. "I'll be right back!"

She flinched as I bolted up from the table and headed for the door, but an idea had occurred to me, one that was sure to help Miss Chenowith more than I ever could. I went to wake up Seth.

Seth was already awake and playing in the floor with Jackson. I tried to explain the situation to him as delicately as I could. After all, he is only six-years-old, and I don't think he really has a full grasp of what has happened in his own situation. I basically told him that Miss Chenowith was like him now. He looked at me blankly like he didn't fully understand, then I told him that he needed to teach Miss Chenowith about squenching. His face brightened and he hopped to his feet. He was more than happy to be helpful. He trotted down the hallway to where Miss Chenowith was sitting, but not before stopping by the kitchen and grabbing a large handful of cookies. I guessed that the large quantity must be for training purposes.

Before starting breakfast, I made the phone call I was dreading. I called 911 and explained the situation. Thank God that cell phones still worked. I had expected to get hung up on or have a cop sent out to arrest me for misuse of an emergency number, but it seemed routine to the operator.

"Yes sir, we've had a few of these calls in the last few days," she said. "I'll send an ambulance out shortly to collect the body; you can make arrangements with them on where you want it taken."

I started to thank her and hang up when a thought occurred to me.

"One more thing ... could you have the ambulance driver call me before they arrive? I don't want any unpleasantness when they ... well ... take her out."

"Sure thing, hun," she said, with her professional tone giving way to one of Southern grace. "I was going to suggest that to them myself. It just seems only right." She paused and said, "I'm sorry for your change, I know that sounds strange but that's what we've been telling folks in your situation because, well, it's not really a loss is it?"

As bizarre as it sounded, that did seem like a more accurate description to me.

"Thank you," I said and hung up the phone.

I started breakfast and was just in the middle of scrambling the eggs when it occurred to me that I probably needed to call Miss Chenowith's sister, Rose from the motel. I pondered it for a moment and then decided I would let Miss Chenowith make that determination. After all, it was just a change and not a loss.

A few moments later, Seth came trotting down the hallway and headed for the back door. As he passed the door to the kitchen he looked in at me with a jubilant, toothy grin.

"Where are you going, buddy?"

He didn't break stride as he continued for the door.

"It's a s'prise!" he called, as I heard the door creak open and then shut.

I paused, a little curious, and then I figured that he was probably going out back to properly squench the cookies he had been training with. The problem was that Jackson or Miss Chenowith was not with him. I grabbed a paper towel to wipe egg white residue from my fingertips and casually peered through the door at Miss Chenowith. She was still seated at the table but had scooted her chair back slightly. Jackson was curled in her lap and his eyes closed contentedly as she stroked his head. Miss Chenowith was smiling; that was good to see.

I was just about to dish the eggs out of the pan when I heard the back door open again. Something was strange. Instead of the dull pitter-pat of Seth's feet, I heard two sets of feet coming down the hall. I turned around to see Seth beaming at me in the doorway. Someone was standing in the shadows behind him.

"Daddy, I would like you to meet my friend," he said in a hushed voice.

I knew who it was before he said anything more. I think I had suspected, at least since last night, anyway. His "friend" had been hiding in the shed, and Seth had been sneaking him food. He ran away after the storm started and he was very hungry. I didn't know whether to be angry because we had spent so much time looking for this person, not to mention Miss Chenowith being worried out of her mind, or to be proud because Seth had been kind enough to take food to this person. The hungry boy at Seth's school came to mind, causing my anger and frustration to fade away. Still, he should have told me.

"This is Shasta. He lives here with Miss Chenowith. He's been hidin' because he was scared."

A black boy, a few inches taller than Seth, stepped out of the shadows and extended his hand.

"Howdy, Mista Penalton. Seth sho' spoke awfully fine of you!"

The description provided by Miss Chenowith was dead on. Well, maybe that is a poor choice of words, but her description was very accurate. Shasta wore a pair of gray trouser overalls with a white button down undershirt. He wore no shoes and his head seemed to be shaved. A chubby face that she had fondly described as "bubble gum" cheeks topped a slender body giving his head an oversized appearance. He had an unusually dark complexion that was clearly visible under the shiny translucent sheen.

He looks like an oversized bobblehead doll, I thought but did not say. An amused grin came to my face and I did my best to channel it into a polite smile.

I extended my hand and shook his, experiencing the same cold and then warm sensation as my hand slowly sank into his.

"Thank you, Shasta," I said. "There is someone who wants to see you very much," I said as I nodded toward the door where Miss Chenowith sat.

"Yessa," he said sheepishly then looked at Seth.

Seth gave him a reassuring smile, then took him by the hand and led him down the hall. A few moments later I winced from what I thought was screaming coming from the next room but as it turned out, it was cries of pure joy coming from Miss Chenowith.

"Oh, Shasta! Thank God, thank God, thank God, thank God, thank God ..." she repeated over and over again.

The return of Shasta made things more tolerable for Miss Chenowith. In fact, it may be accurate to say it made things okay. She wouldn't let him out of her reach, let alone out of sight. She was as doting as a mother bear. I would have to say that this was the first real "mothering" that Shasta had enjoyed in well over 100 years, and the first time that Lizzie Chenowith had been a mother. That was sad, because from what I saw, she would have been a good one.

The 911 operator was as good as her word because the ambulance drivers called me ten minutes later. I served breakfast on the old wooden picnic table in Miss Chenowith's backyard while the paramedics respectfully retrieved the sweet lady's remains. No one ever knew they were there except for me.

After breakfast, which entailed some more squenching lessons from Seth, Miss Chenowith shocked me.

"You and Seth should get on the road. I don't need to hold you up any longer," she said.

"Are you sure? Will you be okay?"

She smiled reassuringly at me.

"Yes, very much so. As strange as it may seem, I can't remember the last time I was as happy as I am today."

"What about Rose, your sister?" I asked, doubtful.

She half-smiled and half-smirked.

"Oh, I can call her when I get ready," she said, pretending to punch buttons on an invisible phone. "Actually, I can't wait to see the look on her face," she said with a mischievous twinkle in her eye. "I have a few other calls to make before I trouble myself with that old biddy."

I was dumbstruck at her transformation. In an hour's time she had gone from deep despair to mischievous exhilaration. Part of me wanted to question this rapid emotional metamorphosis, but another part of me was anxious to take her at her word and set back out on our trip. The latter part won out. Miss Chenowith and I exchanged phone numbers before we departed 30 minutes later.

She winked. "Going to the Air and Space Museum, eh? I might be able to help you. Let me make a call or two."

I didn't follow up this comment because Miss Chenowith had turned her attention back to Shasta. I told her to call if she needed anything. Seth said his goodbyes to Shasta and presented him with the Hot Wheels car he had gotten in his Martian meal a few days before.

"Shasta doesn't have any toys," Seth explained as he got in his seat and shut the door.

I smiled.

"I know son. I'm proud of you, but ..." I said and paused as he looked at me like he was about to be scolded. "Promise me you won't keep any secrets from me going forward. You can tell me anything, okay, buddy?"

He nodded his head.

"Pomise," he said, dropping the 'r' as usual.

We waved goodbye and pulled away. I could see several neighbors gawking from the security of their yards. I honked and waved at them, shaming them back in their houses. Maybe that was rude of me, but I thought it was cruel spying on Miss Chenowith and Shasta. I wanted them to just leave her alone.

We had just pulled onto the entrance ramp to I-40 when I turned the radio back on. Seth pleaded for Radio Disney, but I needed to catch up on the news.

"Later," I told him. "Daddy needs to listen to some boring talking first."

He frowned and pulled out a Clone trooper action figure and began to pretend like the door was a great military fortress for the Galactic Republic. I smiled and found my favorite news station then carefully turned it up. I didn't like what I was hearing in the discussion.

"Do you believe it is constitutional, Dr. Winder?" the host asked.

It was Ray Winder again, the White House scientific advisor. Why were they asking him about legal concerns?

"We have legal experts reviewing it now, including a Federal judge. The consensus is that the current situation is appropriate justification for exercising the president's emergency powers."

"But don't these people have rights?" the host pressed.

Another voice piped in, sending chills up my spine.

"It is for their own protection," the man said. "Please keep in mind that it is yet to be decided how far constitutional rights extend. I mean, what would the Founding Fathers say about it?" The man finished with a laugh that was anything but humorous.

"For those of you just tuning in," the host said. "You just heard from General Ott Garrison, the Chairman of the Joint Chiefs of Staff. He has joined me here with the White House's scientific advisor, Dr. Ray Winder. We are discussing the Executive order coming out of Washington yesterday stating that all Impals that have passed away since the phenomenon started should be redirected to military bases until they can be acclimated into society or until the phenomenon passes, whichever comes first."

My heart sank when I thought of Miss Chenowith and Shasta. My first instinct was to call and warn them, but I decided to get more information first. The fact that General Garrison was involved with this did not make me feel any better. He had been involved in some sort of human rights or war crimes investigation about a decade ago. I couldn't remember the details because it was quickly swept under the rug like so many other transgressions by people of power and influence. I guess the world forgot it completely when he was appointed by the current administration. I'm starting to think that my vote was severely misplaced.

"General Garrison, why can't we let these people's families take care of them and help them to acclimate?"

There was that unsmiling laugh again.

"It's not that simple. It's a matter of simple mathematics. In a very short period of time, we will start to have a population problem. Death is a natural thing; it is a necessary thing to make way for new generations. This storm, phenomenon, whatever you wish to call it, has removed death from the natural equation in a sense."

"But General, people are still dying, are they not? I mean their bodies are dead." The host said.

"Yes, but the individual is not removed," Garrison said with what sounded like sterile indifference. "The storm gives their spirits, or whatever the hell you want to call them, physical substance. In my book it means they are still here. It is unnatural. It is quite frankly a little sick."

The general breathed a deep sigh and continued, "Look, let me spell it out. In the United States alone, approximately 8,000 people die each day, not to mention some 12,000 births. If you take the births out of the equation as a given, the unnatural 8,000 which stay here gives us an unnatural population increase of about 56,000 Impals per week. That's each week! That's not even taking into consideration the untold thousands—if not millions—that were already here before this storm began. It is a crisis to the natural order and business of the country, make no mistake!"

His attitude was making me sick. These were people, for God's sake. I looked at Seth as if to confirm that, and he smiled back at me with a goofy grin. My heart melted but my stomach twisted; I didn't have a good feeling about what I was hearing.

CHAPTER 19

THE ROAD LESS TRAVELLED

"So we drove on toward death through the cooling twilight."

~F. Scott Fitzgerald, *The Great Gatsby*

By the end of the interview with the two men, I felt much worse about the situation. They were going to be relocating RDIs, which was now the short term for *Recently Deceased Impals*. They were relocating them for their own safety and security to military bases around the country until they could figure out how to acclimate them. The first question I had, aside from how could this be morally acceptable, is how would they differentiate between an RDI and a PDI – what they were calling *Previous Deceased Impals*, the ones that were here before the storm. They both looked identical with their silvery sheens and physical capabilities, so who was to say whether they died today or 200 years ago?

I could tell from his tone and reactions that Dr. Winder was struggling with the decision. I think he probably felt like I did but he was stuck in his position between a rock and a hard place. General Ott Garrison, on the other hand, seemed to be relishing the decision. I don't know if he was enjoying the fact that he actually had something to do, a potential crisis to deal with, or if he got some kind of pleasure rounding up these "things," as he referred to them at one point in the interview.

I suppose his military duties had been noticeably reduced since the conflicts overseas had subsided recently, but was that any reason to be a heartless bastard? He obviously didn't see the Impals as people, just some sick nuisance that needed to be rounded up and discarded. That was a dangerous attitude for anyone to have, but even more so for a soldier. I think the most troubling statement made by the man was when he was asked a legitimate question by the host.

"General, we only have so many military bases. What happens when we run out of room on the bases?"

He gave an arrogant laugh and replied in a chilling tone, "We'll cross that bridge when we get to it."

He refused to elaborate on his response.

Did the president willingly order this? Had he been given fair and balanced advice? I did not know; I hoped he didn't know fully what he was doing because I voted for the man, for God's sake. Of course, the president makes decisions based on the best advice of those in his circle. Dr. Winder could be included in that exclusive group, but General Garrison could as well. That fact made my blood run cold.

As if on cue, when the interview was over, we were passed by a convoy of military transport trucks heading east. They were camo green with a canvas cover over the bed like a cloth camper shell. I noticed the last truck that passed; the flap on the back had become untied, affording me a glimpse of the interior as it sped past. I could make out the silvery luminescence of several Impals, but that was not what caught my attention.

A solitary Impal girl peered through the open flap at me. She smiled and raised her hands as if to wave. I had just enough time to see before the truck sped out of view that there was something blackish gray binding her wrists like shackles. She waved her right hand up and down in a friendly childlike greeting and smiled, but then the truck was gone. A sudden feeling of panic washed over me like an icy wave, forcing me to pull off on the shoulder.

I clicked on the flashers and then turned to look at Seth. He had been sleeping but my sudden stop had awakened him. He looked at me sleepily.

"What's wrong, Daddy?" he asked as he craned his neck like a turtle to look around.

I was still breathing heavily from my instant of panic and it took me a moment to compose an answer.

"Seth, buddy," I breathed. "How would you like to play in the back for the rest of the trip?"

He looked over his shoulder and then looked doubtfully back at me.

"But it isn't safe, Daddy … you says I have to buckle up."

"That's true buddy, I did say that, but I think it will be okay. We have a big safe vehicle in case anything happens. Besides," I continued as I patted him on the head, "I know it can get boring for a little guy to sit up here, and you'll have plenty of room to play back there."

He beamed excitedly.

"You mean it?"

"Absolutely."

"Can Jackson come with me?"

"You bet."

That was all the confirmation he needed. In a flash he was out of his seat belt and scurrying between the front seats and over the back seat into the cargo area. Jackson followed him over the seat like they were tethered together. We only had a couple of bags with us, so he had plenty of room to spread out and play. We had two bags plus a duffel bag full of Seth's favorite toys, of which I immediately heard the contents dumping onto the floor.

I smiled and faced forward. I could hear Seth getting thoroughly engrossed in play as his own personal playtime sound effects drifted up from the back. He was occupied and he was happy, and if he got tired he could stretch out and take a nap. As happy as he was, I had not sent him back there for his own enjoyment, but his own safety. The windows were tinted and it was impossible to see in from the outside. If we were passed by another convoy or stopped for any reason, I thought it was best if Seth were not seen.

Did I have anything to worry about? My head told me no but my gut told me a different story. My gut is seldom wrong. I knew I had just seen a convoy of trucks full of Impals being carted off to God knows where, but that wasn't the scariest part – the little girls hands had been bound with something. I would have thought that impossible if I had not seen it with my own eyes, the Impals that I had encountered could pass through anything if they desired. When I thought about it, I realized how stupid that sounded. Of all the materials on planet Earth, how many had I actually seen them pass through? It was probably one tenth of one percent, if it was even that high.

What I believed this meant is that any Impal could be bound and contained. Even if an Impal got put in a cinder block prison and under normal circumstances they could easily pass through the wall, they would be stopped like an anchor by whatever bound their wrists. I shook my head in disgust. If that weren't bad enough, they would be forced to face constant humiliation with their wrists bound in perpetuity. Maybe I was assuming too much. I mean, I had just caught a glimpse; maybe the girl was playing. I didn't think so. In any case, I wasn't taking any chances. As much as I enjoyed the little guy sitting next to me, Seth was spending the rest of the trip in the back.

We resumed our journey a few minutes later. It was hard for me to focus on the trip or our destination. I kept having a disturbing thought running through my mind: what if we got to our destination and Seth was taken into custody? I mean, we were going to Washington, D.C., just a short walk from the White House.

I had the sudden impulse to turn around and head back to Conway and our home. Seth and I could hole up in our house and no one would ever know about him. We could spend every minute together without fear. I almost got off at the next exit and reversed course when I heard a song coming from the back, one that Seth had made up to the tune of one of his favorite lullabies: *Are You Sleeping, Brother John?*

Going to the moozem, going to the moozem, gonna see airplanes, gonna see airplanes, rockets and space ships, rockets and space ships ... gonna have big fun, gonna have big fun ...

I took my finger off the blinker and hit the gas, zooming past the exit ramp. I couldn't disappoint him again. Not again, not like this. His short life had been filled with too much disappointment, and most of it was my fault.

We would be careful; we would continue on. I would keep my promise. Besides, they were just rounding up RDIs, weren't they? Seth was a PDI, even if only by a couple of weeks. He wouldn't be subject to the Executive order. I tried to tell myself that he wouldn't, but my own question kept coming back to haunt me. *How could they tell the difference?*

We drove on for the next few hours. I wanted to cover a lot of ground before we stopped to eat lunch, although Seth had asked for a Martian Burger a couple of times already. I didn't see another military convoy until we reached the other side of Nashville; this one was at a safe distance from us, way over in the westbound lane.

We stopped at a Martian Burger in Lebanon, Tennessee, per Seth's request, and then I made an executive decision of my own. I didn't feel comfortable continuing on a major thoroughfare like Interstate 40. It would take us a little longer, but I decided to take Highway 70, at least until dark. It turned out to be a mistake—a huge one.

The scenery was pretty except for the occasional redneck condo which consisted of a dilapidated mobile home with a sofa and recliner on the front porch for lawn furniture. Every state has them, it just seems that some states are more proud of them than others. Of course, the small towns had their own nostalgic charm that almost made you forget that anything strange or foreboding was going on in the world. That might have been completely possible for a while, to forget your troubles, if not for the lavender sky and yellow clouds that hovered just overhead.

It was nearing dusk when we passed a pristine little cemetery. We hadn't seen a town in a while, so it seemed as if we were in the middle of nowhere. The ancient rock wall surrounding it made me think of the one I had explored just yesterday when we were looking for Shasta. It reminded me of Miss Chenowith and Shasta. I knew I needed to call her and warn her about what was going on; after all, she has no radio. Her sister might know, but I wasn't sure if she had contacted her or not. She did not seem to be in any big hurry, but she did seem keen to experience the shock on her sister's face when she saw her.

Traffic was noticeably sparse. I don't think we had passed another vehicle in the last 15 minutes. Shortly after we passed the small graveyard, I saw a roadside park with picnic tables. There were no facilities, so thankfully nature wasn't calling me just yet, but I did need to stretch my legs and I thought this was as good a time as any to give Miss Chenowith a call. The nightly black light display was starting to creep across the sky, only tonight it was much more pronounced as it reflected off a mostly cloudy sky.

I thought about catching a few winks here because I had no intention of staying in a motel or with any relatives of motel employees again, not given the current circumstances. We had maybe eight to ten hours of driving time left, which meant we could be at the museum tomorrow. But I decided against snoozing in this little park. It was somewhat concealed from the road by a group of pine trees but it was still too close, I felt too exposed. We would find someplace more secluded; I had to keep Seth as hidden as possible.

Seth was asleep in the back with Jackson curled up beside him, so I carefully parked and got out, closing the door softly behind me. I took out my cell phone and turned it on. My heart sank for an instant when I saw no bars on my phone, but a second later, two bars grudgingly materialized. Maybe I could get a quick call off before they dropped out again. We were in a rural area, so that was probably as good as it was going to get. I removed the address and phone number from my pocket that Rose had given me at the motel on the day we arrived in Jackson. I entered the number in my phone and hit send as I leaned back against the front bumper. Much to my surprise, the phone was answered on the second ring.

"Yes," rasped a woman on the other end. It did not sound like Miss Chenowith, but it was. It was the wrong one, though.

"Rose?" I said.

"Yes," she repeated.

"This is Tommy Pendleton, from the hotel the other night. I ..."

"I know who you are Mr. Pendleton," she interrupted. I was starting to get a bad feeling. At first I thought Rose had been upset about her sister's change, but her demoralized tone seemed much worse than that.

"Well, may I please speak to Lizzie?"

There was a long pause on the other end of the line.

"She's not here," she said, this time with a strong undertone of malice. Before I could respond she cut across me scathingly. "They took her and that ... that thing away!"

My heart sank into my stomach like a block of ice. I knew who "they" were. I had seen "them" carting innocent people down the interstate today. I started to tremble with sadness and anger, the poor, sweet woman, but my thoughts turned suddenly to the other part of Rose's statement.

That thing?

I had to assume she was referring to Shasta. The anger in me started to boil over when I thought of her initial reaction to Seth. I thought she had come around after her interaction with my son, but perhaps she hadn't. I couldn't believe her fear and prejudice toward Impals would be enough to turn in her own sister.

"You ... you turned them in?" I said loud enough that I woke Seth and Jackson up. "Why?? Why the hell would you do that?"

"You wait one minute, buster!" Rose retorted. "I was not the one who called 911 and reported it this morning!"

I didn't think it was possible, but my heart sank even lower. Rose had not called and turned them in, it was me. Of course, I didn't know what was going on this morning. I hadn't heard the radio reports yet. I thought I was doing the right thing. Maybe my intentions had been honorable, but that did not make me feel any less guilty. Obviously, emergency services were under orders to advise the military of any RDIs immediately. The terrible efficiency of this Executive order was even more horrifying than I had imagined. I found it hard to speak because I felt like someone had just knocked the wind out of me. I managed to rasp six short words.

"I'm sorry, Rose. I'm terribly sorry."

There was a long silence that made me wonder if I had just uttered my apology to a disconnected line. Finally, after several long moments, I heard Rose start to cry. I waited patiently until I heard her sobs calm a little and then repeated my apology.

"I'm very sorry. Is there anything I can do?"

She took a couple of shuddering breaths before replying.

"Where did they take her?" she said, still sounding accusatory.

"I don't know, Rose," I said. "I wish I did. I thought I was doing the right thing ... I'm so sorry."

"Are you coming to the funeral?" she asked in almost a civil tone.

I hadn't even thought of a funeral; my thinking had changed so much in the past few days. Of course there would be a funeral, Miss Chenowith's remains deserved that dignity, but it was hard to think of a funeral when the person was still here. But she was gone now, for how long I do not know. She and her beloved Shasta would be held indefinitely, or at least until the phenomenon ended.

I looked up and saw Seth watching me from the back window. He smiled and waved, then fell back with a laugh as Jackson jumped on him. It may be the right thing to do, but I knew I couldn't go back. I grieved for what had happened to my friends but I couldn't turn back. My time with Seth, however much may be left, was far too precious. Guilt and sorrow twisted my guts savagely.

"I'm sorry, I won't be able to ... can you give me the name and number of the funeral home so I ..." but Rose cut me off before I could finish.

"Don't bother, I'll sign the guest book for you!" And with that wounding remark, she hung up.

I stood there feeling numb. I didn't know whether to feel guilty, angry, or just break down and cry.

I didn't have time to consider my feelings, though. I looked up at Seth. His sweet face was pressed against the window, but instead of his happy playful expression, he wore one of terror. Before this could fully register with me, I felt a white, blinding pain on the back of my head and then the world spun out of control and everything went black.

CHAPTER 20
HOSTAGE

"You're a beast and a swine and a bloody, bloody thief!"

~William Golding, "The Lord of the Flies"

I don't know how long I had been unconscious. It was still dark when I came to. A black void seemed to hover directly above me as I lay motionless on my back. It took a moment to realize I was staring at the ceiling of my SUV, the cargo area to be exact. I could tell this because the void was ringed with the crazy black light cloud coverage shining in through the windows semi-circling my head. It was somewhat obscured by the tint in the glass, but was still impressively bizarre.

My head throbbed with the worst headache I have experienced in my entire life. Something stabbed me hard in the back and when I groggily reached back to inspect the source of the pain, I retrieved a Hot Wheels car. My heart jumped as the disorientation instantly dissolved and I remembered where I was. But where was Seth?

I tried to sit up but I felt something tighten on my neck. It didn't take long to figure out that my neck and my feet had been bound, but bound to what I did not know. The prickly roughness on my neck told me that my captors had used a rope.

The vehicle was moving. I listened to the low drone of the tires on the pavement and watched the slow movement of the luminescent clouds through the windows. Who was driving and where we were headed were as much of a mystery as how I had wound up back here. I was just about to call out when I heard Jackson bark and emit a low growl. This was followed by the sound of clinking metal and a man's cruel voice.

"I told you to shut up, you damn mutt! One more peep out of you and I'll toss you out the window!"

There was a sharp clink of metal, followed by a high-pitched yip of pain from Jackson.

"Maybe I'll just tie him to the bumper like that dog in the *Vacation* movie, eh Hamm?"

Every muscle in my body tensed with the desire to break free of my bonds from what I heard next.

"Please don't hurt him!" I heard Seth plead with the man.

Another man spoke; he sounded like he was out of breath as he snorted after almost every word.

"I told both of you to shut up or I'll tie all three of you to the bumper!" the man wheezed. "Didn't I tell you not to use our real names, you idiot?"

"You're right, Ha – I mean, Butch," the other man corrected himself before he could draw the wheezy man's wrath again. His tone became noticeably more pleasant when he continued.

"Who'd a thunk we would have hit such a gold mine when we knocked that sap over the head, eh, *Butch*? This kid's gonna make us rich, I tell ya!"

The man named Butch, formerly known as Hamm, merely grunted and exhaled loudly.

Seth was okay, at least for the moment, which made me relax a little—but only a little. I didn't know whether to pretend I was still unconscious or to say something. I could picture Seth sitting up front somewhere trembling with fear. He was afraid not only for himself and Jackson but especially for me. I never thought they could hurt him physically, but after the cry of pain I just heard from Jackson, I wasn't sure. That scared the hell out of me.

I didn't think I could just lay back here and do nothing; I had to help my boy. Even if it was just giving him the comfort of knowing I was okay. I tested my bonds one more time. I might be able to work loose, especially since my hands weren't tied, but it would be a long and arduous process, one I didn't think I could carry out without drawing unwanted attention. I decided to speak. Seth needed to hear me.

"Where are we going?" I asked as calmly and loudly as I possibly could.

I saw the silhouette of a head appear over the top of the seat. The only features I could see were a long, bushy mane of hair framing a slender face. I saw a metallic flash as his arm swung out and then I felt the unmistakable death-like cold of a pistol barrel pressed under my chin.

"Well, sleeping beauty is awake!" he said.

"Put that gun away, you idiot!" the man named Butch hissed. "If that thing goes off … he's the only leverage we have with the kid!"

I felt the cold metal slowly withdraw, and then a hard smack on my cheek from the open hand of my captor.

"You keep your mouth shut, too, moron!" he sputtered with a venomous tone. "When I want you to talk, I'll tell you!"

"Daddy, are you okay?" Seth cried out.

"Yes, buddy, I'm fine!" I answered before I got another hard slap on the cheek.

"I told you to shut up!" he sputtered with such rage I thought his head might explode.

"I don't want another word out of anyone," Butch huffed like he had just run a marathon. "One more word and I'm gonna hurt your dad and your dog, do you understand?"

I could hear Seth sobbing. I could not see him, but I could picture him shakily nodding his head in understanding. I knew he was terrified. My heart burned with the desire to tear free of my bonds and use the ropes to summarily strangle the two sadistic scumbags. As crazed as I was, I finally allowed reason to win out. I laid back and shut my eyes, my heart hammering against my ribs like a frightened bird in a cage. My brain pounded against my skull with cruel intent as I thought feverishly for a way out of our predicament.

What the hell did these guys want? They mentioned using me as leverage with Seth, but I had no idea what that could mean. A few minutes later, I found out.

I felt the vehicle pull off the road and stop.

"Showtime!" The man with the gun chortled.

I looked out the back window. The faint outline of a sign could be seen towering over the vehicle. As I strained to read the sign, I turned my head just right so that the phenomenon's light reflected off the painted letters and I could read the message. It read: *Lucky's Saloon.*

"Okay, kid, I want you to go through the door, get everything out of the register, and bring it back out. Oh yeah, and get me a six-pack of Schlitz while you're at it," the man with the gun ordered with glee.

"You idiot!" Butch huffed, "I told you he can't do that! He can go in and get things but he can't bring it out if it can't pass through a wall!"

"Huh?" the man with the gun asked with such confusion and stupidity in his voice, it left me little doubt who was the brains of this duo.

Butch let out a long wheeze that sounded like air escaping from the tire of an eighteen-wheeler. When he spoke he was still agitated but he also had a measure of patience in his voice.

"My cousin in the Army told me that they found that these spooks, or whatever the hell they are, can't pass through iron. Iron affects them the same way it affects us, they can't pass through it and they can be knocked around with it. That's how they are catching all these creepy bastards, by slapping iron collars on them." He laughed cruelly but the laugh quickly turned into a hacking cigarette cough. It sounded like a lung was going to fly out of his mouth any second.

"You okay, Hamm?" the stupid pistol-wielder asked.

"I told you," Butch hacked between words, "don't call me that name!"

"Okay, Butch," he muttered. "So he can't pass through the wall if he's wearing iron collars, eh?"

The man with the pistol did not get a response until Butch's coughing fit was over.

"You idiot, just let me handle this. He's gonna go in, get the cash out of the register and pass it to us through the mail slot – in and out with no alarm." He coughed once and then started to wheeze like an asthmatic, making me think of Seth's Darth Vader figure, which was probably lying beside or under me.

"All right, kid, come on!" Butch hissed as he opened the door to get out.

The overhead light came on as the stupid sidekick opened his door to get out. He glanced back over the seat at me, displaying what he probably thought was a sufficiently intimidating and sinister smile, but he was so ridiculous looking I would have laughed if the situation had not been so serious.

The man was slender with long greasy blond locks draping razor and pimple stubble cheeks. His ridiculous smile exposed a lifetime of dental neglect. Crowning his unwashed head was a ball cap that looked like it had been buried in a pig pen for a couple of weeks. The dirt and filth almost completely shrouded the logo on the front that professed his undying devotion to his favorite NASCAR driver. The look in his eyes was not one of malice, but instead was reminiscent of that of a deer or squirrel caught in headlights. There seemed to be little going on in the man's head.

I actually felt a brief moment of sympathy for him. He was

obviously acting under the direction of his wheezing friend. He had probably never had an independent thought in his life. My sympathy quickly faded when I heard him slam the door and yell at Seth.

"Come on, you little creep!" he snapped. "Get over to the door!"

I could hear Seth crying as the two men barked orders in hushed but harsh tones.

"Shut that cryin', you freakin' creepy spook!" the man named Butch rasped before erupting into a coughing fit. As he sputtered and hacked, the stupid sidekick chimed in.

"Yeah, don't make me hurt your old man, creep! You better do what we say!"

I was livid with rage as I strained against my bonds. I didn't think these idiots could physically hurt Seth, although I wasn't sure of the full impact that iron could have on an Impal. They could definitely hurt me, but that didn't concern me at the moment; my only thoughts were for Seth. Mentally, he was very vulnerable.

I managed to work my fingers under the rope binding my neck. It was an extremely tight fit; I had been bound tightly enough that I couldn't move my head, but not so tightly that I couldn't breathe. I wondered for a brief moment which one of them had made such a precise knot when I heard footsteps approaching the vehicle. I quickly put my hands to my sides and closed my eyes a moment before the stupid sidekick shone a flashlight on me. I could see the beam through my eyelids as it panned back and forth across my face. A moment later the light went out and I heard footsteps walking away.

"He's in!" I heard Butch puff excitedly. "Turn out that light, you idiot!"

"I thought I heard something, Hamm," the stupid sidekick explained.

I heard a hard smack like skin on skin and then a pitiful yelp from the sidekick. Butch must have struck him for his trouble.

"Quit using my real name, you idiot, and turn off that damn light!"

I hadn't heard anything for several minutes when the silence was broken by enthusiastic laughter peppered with an occasional barking cough from Butch.

"You're not right about many things, Howie, but you were right when you said the kid was gonna be a gold mine!" Butch proclaimed.

"Hey ... I thought we wasn't supposed to use real names," the stupid sidekick now known as Howie said with deep puzzlement.

"Just not mine ... H-o-w-i-e," Butch said, stretching out the name sarcastically. He intermingled a belly laugh with a fit of coughs. "All right Howie, get the kid out here and let's move on to the next one!"

"Come on out, kid!" Howie barked. A few moments later I heard Seth crying again.

"I wanna see my daddy!" he pleaded.

"Show him, but put the collar back on first!" Butch barked. "Then let's get going!"

I squinted from the glare of the overhead light as the door was jerked violently open. I heard a metallic clinking noise and then a harsh command from Howie.

"Look!"

A moment later, Seth's silvery, shiny head popped over the seat to look at me. My heart leapt and sank in the same instant. I was happy to see him, but the iron collar around his neck made me burn with a parent's fury. The collar was attached to an iron link chain that stretched out of sight and into the grubby hands of Howie. He glared at me from just outside the door, holding the end of the chain up by his cheek as if he were modeling a piece of expensive jewelry. Sympathy for the stupid be damned; I would have ripped his head off if I could.

"Daddy, are you okay?" he asked over a puckered lip. I felt the cold on my skin and warmth shoot through my brain as his tears dripped onto my forehead.

"Yes, buddy, I'm fine!" I said with as much reassurance as I could summon. Truth is I wasn't fine: my back was killing me, my feet were losing feeling from the rope binding them to the spare tire well, I had a splitting headache from the blow delivered to my head, and my stomach was boiling with frustration. I felt as hopeless as a fly caught on sticky paper.

"Let my daddy go!" Seth screamed. The fear seemed to have left him, at least for the moment; he was furious.

Seth disappeared from view with a loud clank as Howie jerked him back violently. He cried out in pain before he hit the ground and then was picked up and shoved into the front passenger seat beside Butch, who had once again launched into another violent coughing fit.

Howie resumed his place in the backseat as we pulled away from Lucky's Saloon. He gave me the occasional glance over the seat as we made our way to the next "withdrawal," as Howie had put it. With each passing mile and each passing minute, my frustration grew exponentially. Under the watchful eye of my simple-minded captive, I had little hope of working free of my bonds.

They hit three more places before the sun started to rise. I could see the sign of the first location, Petersen's Git-n-Go, where Howie claimed they scored $300, but the other two I could not see and they did not mention the name, only that they hadn't quite done as well as they had at the first two "withdrawals."

As I lay there helpless and hurting, another unwelcome visitor started to creep into my gut: guilt. What the hell had I done? I had gotten Seth and myself into a terrible mess. I should have been more attentive to my surroundings. Heck, I shouldn't have pulled off at that desolate roadside park in the first place. Maybe I'm being a hypocrite by calling Howie stupid.

I guess I could try to justify it by saying I was distracted by the news of Miss Chenowith, or I was trying to keep Seth protected by bringing him to what I thought was a safe and secluded place, but those were just excuses. It was my fault and my responsibility; I would have to live with the consequences of my irresponsible decision.

I turned my head as much as I could to look out the back window of the SUV. I had never seen the odd mix of colors at daybreak as the black-light weirdness gave way to lavender skies. It was actually one of the most beautiful sights I had ever seen; I just wished I weren't watching it through tinted windows or in these circumstances. As I took at the amazing montage of colors, I noticed something else very odd. The sky seemed to be pulsating like a blue strobe light. A moment later, I realized that it was not part of the phenomenon because Butch cried out and the SUV began to accelerate.

"Hold on, Howie!" He sputtered, "It's the cops!"

CHAPTER 21
OFFICER PACE

"To Protect and to Serve"

~Police credo

The rope pulled taut against my neck as the vehicle took off at a great rate of speed. I was just moments from not being able to breathe at all when our speed evened out and the G-force pulling on my body dropped enough that the rope loosened. My first impulse was to be happy that these two scumbags were about to be caught and Seth and I would be freed, but when I considered the bigger picture it scared the hell out of me. If the 911 operator had been working in conjunction with the military, the odds were that the police would be, as well. Even if they managed to take these two degenerates safely into custody, they would probably take Seth, too. I didn't see any other way out of this. Either way, it looked bad for Seth and me.

The chase was over as soon as it began. Butch erupted into a fit of coughs that shook the vehicle violently with each sputtering heave. A few seconds later, we careened off the road, bounced twice, and came to a vicious halt. I was thrown skywards as the rope binding my neck pulled like a garrote against my Adam's apple. Before the cutting pain could register, I saw Howie fly forward, his gun careening in the air. My heart almost stopped when it flew back over the seat and landed inches from my head. Thankfully, it didn't go off.

"Let's get out of here!" Howie shrieked as he flung half of his body over the seat to retrieve his gun. I almost felt sorry for him again because he sounded like a terrified kid. His partner in crime replied with only a rasping heave and cough as he lunged out the door.

My neck was on fire from rope burns and I felt like my throat was the size of a drinking straw. I wheezed and coughed as badly as my asthmatic captor. Reaching up with the panic of a drowning man, I pulled against the rope. To my surprise, it came loose. I propped myself up on my elbows as every square inch of my neck screamed in hideous protest. I gasped and sputtered for air so desperately that I barely noticed what was happening outside.

"Freeze!" the cop shouted from behind the vehicle. I looked back to see him standing behind the open driver's side door of the patrol car with his gun drawn and pointed directly at Howie.

"Drop it, asshole!" the cop ordered as he reinforced his grip on the handgun and cocked his head to signal he was also reinforcing his aim.

Howie did the first intelligent thing I had seen him do yet: he dropped the gun like it was a hot potato. But it seemed that Howie had a daily allotment of intelligence and he had just spent it all. I did feel a little sorry for him after what happened next. He turned his head as if to seek approval from his partner. I followed his gaze even though I was still fighting for breath. Before I could take two deep breaths, I saw him take off out of the corner of my eye.

"Hamm!" he shrieked with horror.

This was followed by another forceful command from the police officer.

"Stop!" he ordered.

Howie didn't pay any attention, so what happened next was inevitable. I jumped, my breath catching in my already narrow throat, as two loud pops rang out. I knew what it was before I looked; the cop had opened fire.

I managed to pull myself up and drape my arms and upper torso over the back seat. In a desperate juggling act, I tried to get air back into my deprived lungs and see what was going on at the same time outside. I could only turn myself halfway, as my feet were still tightly bound to the spare tire well.

"Don't move!" the cop yelled as he cautiously crept around the vehicle with his gun still brandished in front of him. He disappeared behind a group of trees directly in front of us. I couldn't believe he hadn't checked the inside of the vehicle but I guess he had bigger fish to fry at the moment.

"Daddy?" A small frightened voice called in almost whisper.

"Seth?" I squeaked from my damaged gullet like someone slowly letting the air out of a balloon.

I looked up and saw him peering at me from the passenger side floor board, his knees hugged to his chest like someone in mortal terror. The damned iron collar was still around his little neck.

I took as deep a breath as I possibly could, figuring I would have one shot at this before the cop came back and inspected the vehicle.

"I need you to hide, buddy!" I said, sounding like air escaping from a punctured tire, but Seth understood. His head dipped out of view and I heard him grunting like he had the night he pushed through our living room chair. A few moments later, I saw the police officer coming back, his gaze and gun were focused on our vehicle. As he made his way toward the passenger door I intentionally lurched out with my legs causing me to roll sideways and smack hard against the side of the cargo area. It was sufficient enough that the cop turned his attention from the front of the vehicle and now focused on me.

"Come out slowly, with your hands up!" he ordered.

I took another deep and rattling breath then exhaled with all my might.

"Help."

"Who's back there?" he bellowed.

I took another deep breath.

"Hostage … hurt."

A moment later I heard the latch on the cargo door click, and then it slowly opened. The cop stood to the side with his gun trained on me. He looked at me suspiciously and then looked at the rope binding my feet.

"Anyone else?" he asked.

I couldn't muster another deep breath at the moment so I vehemently shook my head.

He gave the backseat a perfunctory glance then holstered his gun and removed a pocketknife from his belt. Moments later my legs were free.

"Can you stand?" he asked.

I shrugged and took another deep wheezing breath as I massaged my neck.

The cop removed his sunglasses and narrowed his gray eyes as he examined my neck.

"Jesus," he muttered. "What the hell did they do to you?"

I made a motion like I was tying up something and then pointed to my neck.

"How did you get loose?"

I pretended like I was steering a vehicle and then turned hard. I then made an up-and-down bouncing motion with my hand.

The cop shook his head sympathetically.

"My God, do you need an ambulance? I already called one for the other two," he said pointing to the radio mic clipped to his shoulder.

My heart jumped. More people were on their way, and it was just a matter of time before Seth was discovered. The truth is I probably did need one, or at the very least I needed to go see a doctor, but

I couldn't risk the exposure. I couldn't leave Seth or he would be discovered for sure. I animatedly shook my head.

"I'll be fine," I exhaled, sounding like Marlon Brando in *The Godfather*. My breathing was starting to get a little better, but it was a long way from normal. Why the hell that simpleton had decided to tie me like that I did not know. That made me wonder if he had been shot or possibly even be dead. .

"Holy crap!" the cop exclaimed looking over my shoulder. "It is true!"

He turned and sprinted back to his patrol car and quickly popped the trunk. He produced two large iron chains attached to what appeared to be iron handcuffs. My heart leapt into my throat, my only thought was that Seth had been discovered. An image played in my mind's eye like a cruel movie, an image of Seth being bound and transported away from me like the little girl in the truck. I would never see him again. I stumbled out the back of the SUV, my legs were as steady as a newborn giraffe's and a moment later I landed flat on my gut knocking what little wind I had left out of me.

"No!" I tried to yell but it came out sounding like "*h-h-h-h-h*".

I rolled on my side and watched as the cops shiny black shoes pounded through the dust and away from the vehicle. He was not running to snatch Seth out of the SUV or even pursue him into the woods; he was running for Howie and a large behemoth of a man that looked suspiciously like Jabba the Hutt with legs. Hamm was not too far off from my mental image I had developed listening to him cough and hack the last few hours.

He was fat, bald, and could have been the poster boy for redneck slobs of America. But that was not what I initially noticed. What I initially noticed is that there was two of each of them. One sprawled on the ground like a restful sleeper and another standing beside the sleeper, all silvery and shiny, with a look of pure horror on their faces. Judging by the blood on the back of the "sleeping" Howie, I would say he became an RDI via his stupidity – the officer had told him to stop. I saw no blood on the "sleeping" Hamm, so the only guess I could come up with is that he keeled over with a heart attack. I think that logic is sound based on his size and respiratory condition.

Neither of them put up any resistance as the officer knocked them to the ground with the iron chains with a couple of quick Indiana Jones movements. He then had their hands chained like a couple of hapless sheep being led to the slaughter. The officer herded them to the back of the patrol car and forced them in the back seat. They complied with no argument; I think these two criminals would be in shock for some time.

The officer slammed the door shut and adjusted his uniform, then wiped sweat from his brow. He then strode back to me.

"Okay, where is he?" the cop asked softly.

I blinked up at him, the sun blinding me as I tried to focus. I shook my head and shrugged.

He removed a handkerchief from his breast pocket, wiped his cheeks and mouth, then squatted down beside me.

"I know that these two stole your vehicle and had a little goblin boy sneaking into stores to steal for them. Where is he and who is he?"

I realized that playing stupid would get me nowhere. Look what it had done for Howie. From my vantage point on the ground I could see Seth's small legs protruding through the floorboard and almost touching the ground. The poor kid was trying to get as low as he could to hide, just as I had told him, but the iron collar severely limited his mobility. I could lay here and act ignorant and shrug my shoulders, but Seth would be noticed. It was only a matter of time.

I struggled to get up. The cop extended his left hand and helped me into a seated position. I took a deep breath before I replied.

"He's my son."

The officer looked at me for a long moment.

"Are you Thomas Pendleton?"

I blinked in surprise. How did he … But before I could ask the question in my head, he smiled and pointed to the radio mic clipped to his shirt.

"Called in your tags."

I nodded.

"I'm Officer Pace. Officer Clint Pace."

I raised my hand to shake his but he quickly stood up.

"Don't take this the wrong way, but I don't shake hands when I'm wearing a gun. It's not good practice."

He offered me his left hand again – not his gun hand – and helped me to my feet. Once I was upright and eye level, he asked again.

"Where is your son?"

I instinctively glanced at the SUV and Officer Pace picked up on this right away. He cautiously walked to the passenger door and opened it. In the floorboard, only visible from the chest up, was Seth. His mouth gaped in terror as the formidably-sized policeman towered over him.

"Come on, son," he said in a kind voice. "You can't stay in there; it isn't safe."

Seth looked at me for reassurance and I calmly nodded my head. I didn't know what the hell else to do. I was far from calm on the inside. I actually, for a moment, considered overpowering Officer Pace, but I knew that in my weakened state that would be a fruitless effort. It would probably make things worse.

Seth grudgingly got to his feet then pushed sideways and through the running board until he was clear of the vehicle.

"Are you okay?" he asked Seth with the same soothing voice.

I have to admit, I was a little shocked. I had expected him to treat Seth similarly to the two hoodlum Impals he had just cuffed and stuffed. Maybe not quite that viciously because Seth had been forced into his short stint of juvenile larceny, but he was still just a "goblin boy," as Officer Pace had described.

He smiled at Seth and walked back to me.

"Do you know what my orders are to do with Impals?"

I nodded my head and swallowed hard, wincing with pain as my own saliva felt like molten lava pouring down my damaged throat.

Officer Pace reached into his pocket and produced a memo pad and ink pen then handed them to me.

I took the pen and wrote: *I thought it was only for RDIs – the recently deceased.*

Officer Pace shook his head.

"Hell, it doesn't matter anymore, not that it ever did. How can you tell the difference? They all look alike."

I gulped painfully. That had been my thought exactly.

Officer Pace looked at me apologetically like he had just uttered a racial slur.

"Sorry," he muttered.

I wrote again: *I understand what you mean. Please don't take my son. He is a PDI and he's all I have. I was taking him to Washington, trying to fulfill a promise I made to him before he...*

I stopped writing as I reached up to wipe a tear that was streaming down my cheek.

Officer Pace looked at me sympathetically and put a hand on my shoulder. At that moment we heard the distant sound of several sirens approaching.

Officer Pace pulled me close as he spoke harshly into my ear.

"Let's get one thing straight. You were driving across country and these two punks travelling with an Impal kid jumped you and took your vehicle with you as a hostage. They dumped the kid out a couple of miles back when I started to chase them. They wrecked here and I had to use deadly force on one, and the other expired as a result of his own fat-laden ass. Got it?" he finished like a drill sergeant.

Officer Pace turned to Seth.

"Son, I need you to run that way," he said pointing at the distant woods. "There is a deadfall of trees a short way up there. Stay there until I or your dad come to get you. Got it?"

Seth once again looked to me for reassurance. I nodded fervently and waved my arms like I was rooting him on in a mile relay. The sirens were getting louder now, maybe just a few seconds from coming around the bend. Seth took off like a sprinter in the direction that Officer Pace had told him. He had just disappeared into the tree line when the first of three patrol cars and an ambulance skidded to a halt behind us.

CHAPTER 22
LOST AND FOUND

"No man stands so straight as when he stoops to help a boy."

~Knights of Pythagoras

The arriving officers took statements from me and Officer Pace. Due to the present condition of my throat, I provided a written statement for the patrolpersons, one of whom was a woman. Not that it matters much for my account of things, but the female cop, Officer Bargone, reminded me a great deal of Ann. She reminded me of how much I miss her.

My statement was pretty much word for word with what Officer Pace had advised me to say in his drill sergeant tirade, with some slight embellishment thrown in to add to the realism of being a firsthand witness. The paramedics tended to my neck injury and kept insisting that I go to the hospital to have it checked. I assured them I was fine and needed no medical attention, although my croaking voice espoused just the opposite.

The bodies of my two captors were bagged by the medics and placed in the back of the ambulance. It took the help of all the officers on scene to hoist Hamm's large frame onto the gurney. The former residents of the bagged corpses sat placidly in the back seat of the cruiser, not daring to look, not daring to speak. It was almost as if they were terrified that the other shoe was about to drop any minute and the slightest movement by either would bring down the proverbial footwear on their silvery-hued heads.

I thought it was an interesting observation that while Impals look like their physical selves, they don't seem to be troubled with the physical defects. I didn't take much note of that with Miss Chenowith because I was in too much shock. While Hamm still looked like a stout fellow, he wasn't quite the blubbery creep he had been in life. Also, his cough was noticeably absent. Howie didn't look much different except maybe a couple of years younger. It was hard to tell because I had never really seen him in full light. The clothes were what struck me. Hamm the Impal was wearing a nice button-down Oxford, jeans topped with an enormous silver belt buckle, and snakeskin boots. His body had on a baby blue warm up suit with sneakers that were holier than the Pope.

Howie the Impal wore a Tennessee Volunteers jersey with jeans and high tops. His body wore dirty jeans with a stained black t-shirt, complimenting his mud-covered NASCAR hat, which incidentally the ambulance drivers hadn't bothered to pick up. It set against a large pine tree like a mini-NASCAR memorial.

Of course, Miss Chenowith had a very stagnant wardrobe; I suspected she had only one color dress and a different one for every day of the week. But Seth wasn't wearing his favorite Spiderman shoes when he was killed, nor his favorite shirt and shorts, but somehow he wound up in them as an Impal. It made me scratch my head, but I had no real answer for it. Maybe we get to wear our favorite wardrobe for eternity? I just don't know.

When Officer Pace came back to talk to me, I got an amusing

surprise.

"Do you know the names of those two?" he asked jerking his thumb over his shoulder toward the cruiser.

"I think their real names were Hamm and Howie." I whispered, trying to rest my throat.

Officer Pace chuckled.

"Well that's close, get this … their real names are Hammond Bannister and Howard Longsworth. Don't exactly sound like the criminal type, eh?"

I shook my head and smiled then looked distractedly over the officer's shoulder. I could see Seth's head peeking over the top of a group of sapling pine trees. He hadn't gone as far into the woods as Officer Pace had directed. I knew he was scared and didn't want to let me out of his sight, but he was dangerously close to being visible to the other officers.

Officer Pace saw the look on my face and knew immediately what had me distracted. Maybe he was psychic or just had good old keen police instincts, but I suspected it was because he knew how I felt and could empathize with me. My good old dad instincts told me he was a father, too, and the gold band on his left ring finger solidified that belief. He smiled discreetly at me then turned to talk to the other officers. He stood so that all of their backs would be to Seth's position; just a simple distraction. Hopefully he would be able to keep it up, because if any of the cops turned to look in that direction, unless they were myopic they would see him for sure.

The ambulance left shortly, toting the mortal remains of the two partners in crime whose names sounded like they should be Ivy League school chums, but their eternal dress suggested they were a high-class honky-tonker and a seasoned tailgater. I suppose if my theory was correct regarding comfy dress for eternity, I would probably wind up in my Razorback hoodie and red sweat pants along with padded moccasin house shoes. Not exactly stylish, but if comfort were style you could call me Armani.

My heart almost slid into my shoes when Officer Bargone asked me if I would like a lift into the station so I could give my statement.

"I'll have Jimmy come out and tow in your SUV, on the county's dime of course," she said with an accent that was reminiscent of Scarlett O'Hara.

"I've got him covered," Officer Pace interjected. "He said he feels up to driving, so he's going to follow me in."

My heart retracted back into my chest.

Along with Officer Bargone, there were two other cops that had reported to the scene. I was never introduced to them, but one was big and beefy with a neatly parted haircut that was white-walled just above his ears. The other looked like a junior high kid playing a cop for Halloween. He had a buzz cut that had grown back just enough to tell he was a carrot top. I could have sworn he had a slight case of acne blemishing his pale cheeks.

"Well, we need to get back up the road and find that Impal kid they dumped," the beefy officer said.

"Why?" carrot top asked.

The beefy cop looked at him disgustedly like that was the stupidest question he had ever heard.

"Because we are under orders, too, numb nuts."

"We're under orders to turn in PDIs, not RDIs," the carrot top reminded him.

The beefy cop looked at me.

"Well, what was he, a RDI or a PDI?"

I shrugged and swallowed hard to lubricate my throat.

"I never saw him; I was in the back. I believe he was a PDI."

The beefy cop shook his head and laughed.

"Previously deceased, recently deceased, how can you tell the difference? They all look alike to me, the ones I've seen have."

He looked at Officer Bargone and carrot top with serious, narrow eyes and spoke in a low tone that sounded more sadistic than sarcastic.

"We'll question him before we chain him, all right?"

The other two officers shook their heads and turned to walk back to their cruisers. But not the beefy officer, he was looking suspiciously at me and Officer Pace.

"So what are you two looking at?"

We both shrugged, a little too simultaneously to avoid suspicion. His eyes narrowed into slits and his jaw tightened. The veins in my injured neck pulsed with cruel fervor as my heart went into overdrive. The beefy cop had turned to look in the direction of the patch of pine saplings where Seth was hiding. I could no longer see Seth's head, but the beefy officer had a much better view than I did. His eyes narrowed even further like someone trying to read small print and his hand instinctively went for the butt of his gun. He took a few steps toward the pines. Officer Pace looked at me worriedly and followed after the beefy cop. I didn't know if he planned to distract him with more conversation or smack him over the head with his billy club, but as it turned out neither one was necessary.

The two cops had barely made it ten yards when an enormous buck came bounding out of a patch of wild blackberries next to the pines. The beefy officer drew his pistol but then quickly lowered it before he aimed at the animal. He let out a booming laugh.

"You're lucky it isn't season yet, you big bastard! But I'll be back to get you then!" he taunted as he slid his pistol back into the holster. He spun and looked at me and officer Pace with the expression of a kid on Christmas morning.

"Did you see that?" He asked. "That had to be an eight-pointer, at least!"

Officer Pace agreed with the same enthusiasm. I had no idea what "an eight-pointer" even meant. Was there some kind of hunting scorekeeper and that deer was worth eight points, like a three-point shot in basketball? Officer Pace explained later that it was the number of literal points on the deer's antlers. Oh, well; I was never much of a hunter.

The encounter with the eight-pointer seemed to have satisfied the beefy cop's curiosity, and he set out back up the highway in his cruiser to catch a "spook," as he put it. As soon as he was out of sight, I quickly went to retrieve my own little spook.

Seth was sitting on a large moss-covered rock behind the pines. He was sobbing and he was terrified. I picked him up and hugged him tight, hardly noticing the weird cold and warm sensation as his arms and legs slowly sunk into me. I did notice the cold iron of the humiliating, rusty collar on his neck as it brushed against my cheek. I carefully sat him down to examine the cruel choker. Officer Pace bent down and examined it as well.

"I believe I can fix that," he said, and produced a Swiss Army knife-looking device from his utility belt. He selected a small metallic extension and pulled it up until it locked into place. He stuck it in the small keyhole on the side of Seth's collar. After a couple of quick counterclockwise motions, there was a faint click and the collar swung open and fell to the ground, bouncing off of Seth's Spiderman sneakers. He let out a small squeak of pain and instinctively jerked his foot back.

Seth frowned as he rubbed his neck.

"Does it hurt?" I asked worriedly.

His bottom lip puckered as he nodded his head.

"Feels like I got a sore throat."

Two hurt necks; weren't we the pair. Of course, I worried about Seth. I had no idea how something like that might affect him or what the long terms effects might be for an Impal. As it turned out, I was worried for nothing. Within ten minutes, Seth was good as new. Officer Pace had gone out near the road to smoke a cigarette while Seth and I sat on the back bumper of the SUV, nursing our wounds. I was fully prepared to hide Seth if a car should happen by, but thankfully we were in the sticks and there was not so much as a riding lawnmower in the vicinity. After we had sat quietly for a few minutes, Seth jumped to his feet in a panic.

"Jackson! They left Jackson behind!" he cried.

I grabbed his hand and squeezed.

"It's okay, buddy, we'll go find him."

"We have to go now, Daddy! We have to go now! They'll catch him like they did those two mean men!"

I swallowed hard and nausea started to flame in my belly. Seth had seen it all: the shooting, the capture of the Impals, everything. Kids are innocent of a lot of things in the world, but they are not stupid. They can add two and two really fast. He saw, he heard, and I was kidding myself if I thought he didn't hear the radio broadcasts I had been listening to in the vehicle. There was no point in lying to him; he needed to know the truth.

"Okay, buddy, let's go find him," I said as I got to my feet.

He paused and stared at the cargo area of the SUV.

"Is that why you made me get back there?" he asked.

"Yes, son. I will do anything to keep you and Jackson safe. Let's go find him."

Officer Pace came over and shook my hand as we started to get the vehicle ready to go again. There were a few dents and scratches in the paint, but we were blessed with the fact that all the damage seemed to be cosmetic.

"Good luck to you and Seth," he said, then gripped my hand tighter and pulled me close so he could whisper without Seth hearing. "For God's sake, keep him out of sight!"

I nodded and thanked him I started to ask him why, but he was a good cop and he anticipated the question before I could articulate it.

"They took my dad yesterday," he said, very solemn. "He's been dead almost 20 years, living in our house, watching over us. I had two days with him, two miraculous days. I made the mistake of mentioning it at the station, and, well …" his voice trailed off sadly.

"But he was a PDI, they …" Deep down, I already knew the answer.

"It doesn't make a damn bit of difference!" he snapped. "Don't you make any mistake about that!" he said nodding his head in Seth's direction. "The government sees them all as a threat!"

"A threat?" I parroted. "I thought it was just to give them a place to stay, to avoid population crowding." I winced, not from the pain in my throat but from how stupid my own words sounded to me. I knew better, I just didn't want to believe it. That was not the American way, but neither were Japanese internment camps. People can be capable of a lot of things they ordinarily would not when their back is against the wall. But why had this been done so quickly?

Officer Pace shook his head and looked at me dejectedly.

"Please tell me I haven't risked my career for someone this naïve. For your son's sake, please tell me."

"You're right," I croaked. "You are 100-percent right." I paused before asking, "Why was this ordered so quickly?"

Officer Pace shrugged. "Not sure, fear I think. Which I can understand because the first time I saw my dad it scared the hell out of me, but ..." he hesitated as his jaw stiffened. "I think it's more than that. I think that sicko General Garrison gets off on stuff like this. You remember what he was accused of in Panama several years ago?"

I suddenly recalled exactly what Garrison had been accused of. He was the head of a military drug task force charged with stopping trafficking out of Panama. After the killing of one of the soldiers under his command, he allegedly rounded up women and children in the surrounding community for interrogation. The story was that there was more torture than interrogation, that General Ott Garrison was more interested in revenge than justice. No one has ever been able to confirm the horrific stories, but there was enough smoke that he was brought back to Washington to be an "advisor" to the Pentagon for the remainder of the operation. Someone important liked him then, and our president likes him now. I voted for the current president, but I will not do it again, not after he supported someone like that.

I nodded my head grimly.

Pace studied my eyes intensely for several moments then shook and patted me on the shoulder.

"Good luck," he said.

"And to you," I said. "I'm sorry about your dad."

He smiled sadly and bowed his head.

"I think this belongs to you," he said as he retrieved something out of his pocket and offered it to me.

I looked down to see my cell phone resting in his palm.

"Where did you find it?"

He smiled and placed it in my hand.

"It fell out on the ground when I helped you out of the back earlier. I can't believe those two morons left it back there with you. Well, maybe I can. They weren't exactly Einsteins."

A thought flashed through my mind. *Had Einstein been rounded up?*

"Thanks," I said.

Officer Pace smiled then turned and walked toward his cruiser. A minute later, the engine fired to life and he pulled back onto the road, waved once, and disappeared around the bend in the road, leaving Seth and me to continue our journey.

CHAPTER 23
HAVEN

"Nibble, nibble, little mouse,
Who is nibbling at my house?

The wind, the wind,
The heavenly child."

~ Jacob and Wilhelm Grimm, "Hansel and Gretel"

I guess fate was smiling on us in more ways than one. Seth and I had escaped, relatively unscathed. However, every time I swallowed my opinion wavered. To add to our good fortune, we had driven maybe half a mile when a silver streak erupted from the bushes. I slammed on the brakes hard enough that Seth went through the backseat and landed dazedly between the two front seats. We heard a series of excited barks and the metallic clanging of a rusty iron collar knocking against the passenger door. Seth leapt forward into the passenger seat and threw the door open. A silver streak hopped on his lap and began to excitedly jump about like a canine jumping bean. I couldn't believe my eyes, but there he was: it was Jackson.

"Owww, Jackson! Down, boy!" Seth yelled as his furry companion continued to jump at his face.

I had never heard Seth complain about pain, not since the phenomenon had started anyway. It didn't take long to figure out; the iron collar still around the pooch's neck was slamming against Seth's face, arm, or torso every time the dog jumped. It appeared iron not only can bind Impals, but can hurt them as well. Maybe not permanently, but enough to cause a great deal of discomfort.

I grabbed Jackson by the collar and gently pulled him away from Seth. I soothingly prodded him to calm down and lie between Seth and me on the seat. He complied, though I don't think his tail got the message from the rest of his body. It swung back and forth like a crazed pendulum.

"Easy, boy," I said as I stroked his frigidly cold head.

Within a few minutes we had the frightened pooch calmed and ready to ride in the back with Seth. I didn't have a super-duper Batman utility belt like Officer Pace, so I had no way of removing Jackson's collar. In the long run, it would prove to be a good thing to have that restriction. He was limited and controllable over where he could go. He needed to keep his head down and stay put … he and Seth both.

Once I had Seth and Jackson secure in the back, I pulled my cell phone out of my pocket and plugged it into the car charger. It was low but not completely drained. The sound must have been turned off because it made no noise as it sprung to life, and I noticed I had about 15 missed calls along with a few voicemails. I hadn't heard the phone ring a single time. Oddly, they were all from the same number, which I did not recognize.

I decided it was best to keep moving and get out of the area as soon as possible. The SUV seemed to drive fairly well, except for a faint shimmy. Hamm's expert driving had probably knocked it out of alignment. I felt lucky that was it; if we had to put the vehicle in the shop, or worse yet, get towed, Seth would be discovered for sure. I couldn't continue to count on the good charity of our rescuers. Someone would eventually turn us in.

As we drove, I laid the phone on the console beside me, put it on speaker, and played the voicemails. Little did I know they would change the course of our trip. The first one almost made my jaw drop into my lap.

"Hello … Mr. Pendleton. I was trying to get a hold of you because, well … my good friend Lizzie Chenowith told me to. She told me your situation and said you might need some help. Please call me at 703-555-7798. Thank you. God Bless."

This was followed immediately by a second message.

"Hello, Mr. Pendleton. I don't think I told you my name before. My name is Mollie Hartje. I called Lizzie back tonight and spoke to her sister. I was so sorry to hear about Lizzie and Shasta, it's terrible, just terrible." This was followed by a couple of sniffs and a stuttering sob. "Please call me, if nothing else to let me know that you and Seth are okay. Please … 703-555-7798. Call anytime, day or night."

The third message was much shorter and to the point.

"Please call Mollie at 703-555-7798. Please, I am worried."

In spite of my desire to get down the road as soon as possible, I pulled over on the shoulder and looked at my phone like it was some strange piece of alien technology.

"Daddy, is Shasta okay?" Seth called from the back.

I jumped guiltily. That's what I get for listening to messages on speaker.

"Yes, buddy. I'm going to call and check on him right now," I said through gritted teeth. I was not much in the mood for phone conversation, I felt like I had the worst case of tonsillitis ever, but this was a call I had to make. Seth nodded, seemingly satisfied with my answer, and lay back down with Jackson. I picked up the phone and punched the number. I didn't even hear it ring before it was answered.

"Hello, this is Mollie Hartje."

I let her know upfront of my injury, then struggled and strained to get through the conversation. Thankfully, she did most of the talking. It turns out that she is a medium, as well. Mollie and Lizzie were friends and colleagues for several years in the tiny North Carolina town of Mount McColby. When I-40 was built, Mount McColby went the way of so many other small towns in America that weren't fortunate enough to have an interstate exit: it dried up. The two ladies went their separate ways, with Lizzie of course setting up shop in the interstate town of Jackson, and Mollie relocated to Landover, Maryland, just outside our nation's capital.

"I have had a bunch of high-profile government clients over the years," she told me with a confidential whisper, as if she were discussing national security matters. "But of course, I can't say who."

"Of course," I agreed, that old nasty skepticism rearing its head in my belly again. I should be over that by now, but it's hard to teach an old dog new tricks. Jackson barked playfully in the back as if to confirm the truth of that old saying.

"Lizzie's sister didn't seem too fond of you," Mollie said.

"I didn't mean for any of it to happen. I thought I was doing the right thing," I croaked.

"I know you didn't, sugar," she said. "But all the deceased have to be careful now. You watch over that young one of yours and get up here to my house."

"Your house?"

"Yes sir, Lizzie told me you were taking your boy to D.C. I can't think of a better place for you to stay and be safe. Also ..." she continued with her whisper, like she was divulging top-secret information, "I may be able to help you. I can't say how right now, but you'll see when you get here."

I thought about it for a few moments. It wasn't like I had reservations waiting on us at some nice hotel; this trip wasn't exactly planned out. Of course, Mollie was right. I had to be careful. I couldn't just march into the local Hilton with Seth and Jackson without a very good chance of being turned in. Besides, if Mollie was half as good a cook as Lizzie, how could I say no?

"Thank you Mrs. Hartje. What is your address?"

"First of all, you should call me Mollie. Can you do that?"

"Yes, ma'am."

"All right then, my address is 24 Salem Road in Landover. How long do you think it will take you to get here?"

"Just a minute," I said as I grabbed my GPS and entered the address. Just as I had completed the entry I cringed as a vehicle slowly passed. An old man wearing a fedora was behind the wheel of a muddy, ancient station wagon. He peered up at me quizzically. I smiled and waved, indicating everything was okay. He nodded and continued up the road backfiring twice and belching blue smoke.

"Are you there?" I heard Mollie ask.

"Yes," I said looking at the GPS, "it looks like it will take me about seven hours to get there."

"Listen sugar, don't follow that GSP machine to the letter," she said in a secretive tone, inadvertently mixing up the letters in the abbreviation. "You need to come in this way or you might be discovered." She gave me a more roundabout way to come in from the east. It added about an hour to our arrival time. Mollie reminded me of my mom, she always spoke with gracious Southern sweetness and she never could get an abbreviation or an acronym correct, God rest her soul. I had to assume she was resting, that she had made the choice to move on, because I hadn't seen a sign of either one of my parents at their old home and they were buried just 30 yards from Ann and Seth.

"Looks like about eight hours," I corrected.

"Great, I'll see you then! Oh, and don't eat anything, I'll have a good dinner waiting on you!"

"Thanks Mollie," I said and hung up the phone.

Another good home-cooked meal sounded terrific, but the truth is I didn't know if I would be able to swallow it. Having a safe haven right on the doorstep of the very place we had set out for seemed like a miracle. But in a sense, hadn't the last week been a miracle? There was one thing that troubled me far more than my ability to swallow a good meal; it was the prospect of an eight hour drive without being discovered; an eight hour drive right into the heart of where all this nonsense against the Impals had started. Part of me said I was being a good father, the other part said I was being a fool. I don't know, maybe I am both.

I tried to listen to the radio on our trip but I was surprised to find that the 24-hour, wall-to-wall news had been replaced with music and radio dramas. There was an occasional public service announcement about the Impal Safety and Integration Measure. Evidently, Congress had just passed this Act yesterday. The ads consisted of various dead—now Impal—celebrities, like Marilyn Monroe, Johnny Carson, and Clark Gable. They all made identical appeals to the public.

Protect our ancestors, help them find safety, let the government help them integrate. Call 800-555-IMPAL. Help them to find peace and security in their new world.

Each time one of these played, it sent an icy chill up my spine. Not because I was listening to the voices of the deceased. I was used to that. It was because of the frightening contradiction of what they were trying to make people believe and what I knew to be the real truth of the matter. They wanted them out of the way. As to why, I could only speculate. My speculation would be made crystal clear when we arrived at Mollie's.

The trip to Landover was thankfully uneventful. We met two more Army convoys travelling in the opposite direction and another passed us like the one yesterday. I told Seth to get down and keep Jackson down with him. Soldiers peered out the passenger window of a couple of the trucks. Their close scrutiny of our vehicle made my skin crawl. I nodded and waved at the men but the gesture was not returned, they just looked at me stoically before turning away. Thank God for tinted windows.

We arrived at Mollie's home around 5 P.M. It was not what I had anticipated. I had expected a modest dwelling in the suburbs of D.C., but this house was a showcase. The house sat at least 50 yards off of the road. The sweeping green yard was populated by a dozen or so huge, ancient oak trees that were probably pretty good sized when George Washington was in diapers.

As we pulled up the brick driveway leading to the house, the massive trees revealed an 18th Century Colonial-style home. If not for the modern addition of a sunroom on one side of the home and a visible air conditioning unit, I could have imagined myself arriving in a carriage 200 years ago, a beautiful debutant in a silk bustled dress with a lacy bonnet greeting me with a large fan fluttering in front of her face.

The truly strange thing is that there was a woman fitting that description watching us from the massive front porch. She smiled and waved as we pulled to a stop in front of the porch steps. Aside from her outdated wardrobe there was something else unusual about her: she was an Impal. Her silvery sheen was a bizarre complement to her natural beauty and elegant dress.

"Where's the moozem, Daddy?" Seth asked excitedly as he and Jackson peeked curiously over the back seat. I knew he had been seeing a lot of signs the last hour for Washington D.C. Each time we would pass one, his head would pop up like an excited gopher, and then just as quickly pop back down as he remembered why he was in the back. He was cute, but watching the little guy have to forcibly restrain his excitement made me angry.

"We're not there yet, buddy." I shut off the engine. "Soon, we'll be there soon."

I stepped out and walked toward the porch. Seth and Jackson half crawled over and crawled through the seats as they made their way to my open door. The woman stepped to the top of the stairs with a big beaming smile. She carried no fan, but she did have a small walkie talkie clutched tightly in her hand. I didn't think this scenario could get any stranger than a Colonial-era Impal woman talking on a walkie talkie, but I was soon to find out that I was incredibly wrong. We were just scratching the surface.

"*It's okay,*" she said into the walkie talkie before she spoke to me.

"Mr. Pendleton?" she asked.

"Yes, and this is …" I said turning to Seth and Jackson, but she cut me off.

"This must be Seth," she said bending down and smiling with a crinkled nose. "And who is this little guy?" she said, pointing at Jackson.

Seth looked up sheepishly as he clung to the back of my leg. He was being uncharacteristically bashful; he got that way sometimes when he was tired.

"Yes, this is Seth Pendleton," I said patting him on the head. "The cute little guy is Jackson."

She looked curiously at Jackson.

"I haven't seen many animals like us. There are a few, but …" she trailed off as Jackson cautiously approached her, sniffing at the hem of her dress. "Hello, fella," she said, bending down to scratch his head. Jackson happily, stretched his neck out to maximize the petable area; he was shameless that way.

"Is Mollie here?" I asked.

"Why, yes, she's been expecting you," the woman said with a peculiar accent that seemed to be a cross between Southern and British. "By the way," she said, sliding the walkie talkie into her apron pocket while delicately extending her right hand. "My name is Esther Baldwin."

I wasn't sure if she wanted me to shake her hand or kiss it so I awkwardly did both, chilling both my lips and my right hand. She smiled and led me in the large oak front door. We entered a large foyer backed by an ornate winding staircase. A woman of at least

80 years was hobbling down the stairs. I sucked in air as I watched her cling to the banister with each tottering step down. When she finally reached the bottom she straightened up as much as her stooped frame would allow and smiled a bright toothy grin, which was a stark contrast to her apple doll appearance. Maybe she wore dentures, I thought.

"Hello Thomas!" she said. "I'm Mollie!"

"Pleased to meet you Ms. Hartje ..." I started, but she held her hand up curtly.

"I told you, Thomas. It's Mollie. Is that a problem for you?" she asked firmly, but with a twinkle in her pale blue eyes.

"No, ma'am," I said, like a reprimanded school kid. "Mollie it is."

I couldn't help it. I was used to showing the appropriate respect for my elders, especially one who could pass as my great-grandmother. Lizzie, or Miss Chenowith as I called her, had been much less informal. She never insisted that I call her Lizzie but she also never corrected me for calling her Miss Chenowith.

On appearance, Miss Chenowith and Mollie could have passed for mother and daughter in spite of the fact that only five years separated the two of them. The years always seem to be kinder to some than others. Aside from youthful appearance, the most glaring contrast between the two women were their fashion choices. While Miss Chenowith looked like she could be going either to church or a funeral every day, Mollie's floral silk dress and bright red scarf in her thinning gray hair seemed to be a glaring contrast to her physical appearance but was also the perfect complement to her pleasant personality.

"This must be little Seth," she said with an adoring, ear-to-ear smile. "You are such a beautiful child. I am pleased you came to my home."

Seth's previous shyness seemed to have left as he walked past me and accepted a hug from our gracious host. She was not a tall woman and her stooped posture put her on the perfect level with Seth.

"I'm glad you brought your beautiful doggy, too," she whispered in Seth's ear. "What's his name?"

"Jackson," Seth replied proudly.

"Mighty fine, mighty fine," she said, straightening up and looking back at me. "Well, I have a lot of people for you to meet. I think you will find them very interesting."

CHAPTER 24

TOMMY AND ABE

"Caves are whimsical things, and geology
on a local scale is random and unpredictable."

~*William Stone*

Mollie stopped before she had fully turned toward the large arched doorway to our right. "I take it you have met Esther here?" she asked, pointing a bony finger toward the beautiful Impal.

I nodded my head.

"She was my spirit guide," Mollie said then paused. "I take it you met Shasta?"

"Yes, we did," I replied.

She frowned thoughtfully and nodded her head, seemingly confident that a lengthy explanation of a spirit guide was not necessary. I knew what she was talking about, but I was still curious about the origins of Esther Baldwin. Judging by her clothing, she had been around at least a couple of hundred years.

"Where are you from, Esther?" I asked.

She glanced at Mollie as if searching for approval. When Mollie nodded, she smiled and started her story.

She was born in the year 1786, the daughter of an independently wealthy ship builder from Annapolis. She had no formal education but was very well self-educated by the extensive library her father provided in their home. While she was well read, she had no ambition to be anything other than a wife and mother. In any case, it would have been difficult to have fulfilled any ambitions at that time in history for a woman. Esther died suddenly before she could marry a local attorney, whom she had been courting for a year.

"I don't remember how or why," she said, "but I was told that I passed from a case of milk fever. My mother and I both drank contaminated milk." She looked at Mollie with a sad expression. Mollie smiled reassuringly and nodded her head. Esther turned back to me and finished.

"My mother went on and I stayed," she said as silvery tears slid from her cheeks and disappeared through the shiny hardwood floor.

"I'm sorry," I said. "So, you have been by yourself all these years? That must have been very difficult."

She looked at me and shrugged.

"It has been sad without my mother but actually time was quite a bit different for me before all this."

"What do you mean?" I asked.

"Well, even though I know it has been 200 years here, for me it only seems like it has been a couple of weeks. I know that sounds strange, but I think it's a good thing. I can't imagine experiencing all that time invisible and intangible like I was."

I thought I saw an almost imperceptible shudder as she finished. What she just told me made me feel a little better about Seth. It may have been two weeks between his death and the phenomenon, but if what she experienced was true for all Impals, two weeks may have seemed like two hours to him. I hoped that was the truth for all.

We entered a large library that was at least two-stories high. A catwalk extended around the top that was accessible by a singular wrought iron spiral staircase; hundreds of leather bound volumes ringed the room. I had the fleeting thought of wondering if Esther had been able to continue her education in here, but that thought vanished after what happened next.

Mollie walked up to the bookcase on the far wall and extended her hand. I first thought she was retrieving a book until she pushed it in and there was a loud clicking noise as the bookcase started to swing inwards. A moment later, a large doorway was revealed. A faint light in the distance provided enough illumination to see a short hall leading to a stone staircase. The light was coming from the bottom of the stairs.

A secret passage … really? I guess something like that shouldn't surprise me, considering everything I had seen the past week but I just couldn't get the *Scooby Doo* theme music out of my head. Of course, Scooby and his pal Shaggy would have been terrified of Impals and would have run off to the Mystery Machine to drown their terror with a gluttonous feast. Now that I thought about it, I was kind of hungry. I had been so stressed today and afraid to stop anywhere, so Seth and I had not had anything to eat since last night.

Hopefully Mollie is as good a cook as Miss Chenowith, I thought to myself as I followed Mollie and Esther into the passage. With what seemed like psychic intuition, I felt Seth reach out and tug at my leg as we entered the semi darkness.

"Daddy, I'm hungry," he whispered.

Esther turned and smiled at Seth and me.

"Of course, we have a big dinner planned for you shortly." She looked at Seth and asked, "Do you know how to purge, sweetheart?"

Seth frowned uncomprehendingly and looked up at me. I smiled and patted him on the head.

"Yes, he does. But we call it squenching."

Esther looked at me like I just announced that I was a cannibal.

After several long moments, she blinked and gave a tittering laugh.

"Well, I guess that name is as good as any," she said with an amused smile.

"It's not original. We ran into an Impal family on our way that called it that. I guess the name stuck."

Mollie stopped and turned around so quickly I almost ran into her. She looked up at me with a kind but stern expression.

"We don't use that term around here," she said. "Impal seems too much like a racial slur."

Impal was the term I had become accustomed to. It seemed to fit, since it referred to people who had once been impalpable to us, but I guess I could see Mollie's point. That term had been created by the very people who were now rounding these people up for their own 'safety' and 'security,' our government. I had assumed that this was the name that everyone was using to refer to these people, but now that I thought about it, where had I heard that term? The answer was the radio. That question begged for a second one: who really had control of the airwaves? I had always adhered to conservative principals when it came to politics, so by nature I had a distrust of the government, a healthy one during normal times. But these were anything but normal times.

I blinked sheepishly down at Mollie. She smiled and patted me on the arm with a leathery hand.

"We refer to them as souls."

I nodded. "Sorry."

Both women smiled at me and beckoned for us to follow them down the stone stairs in front of us. The light was getting brighter and I could hear a smattering of voices. I jumped a little when the hidden door clanked shut behind us, sending a metallic echo bouncing off the stone walls. We seemed to be descending into a basement or root cellar, judging from the thin layer of moisture on the stone walls and floor. A musty, earthy smell grew stronger as we descended. When we reached the bottom, my jaw almost hit the floor.

We were in a very large room; actually, it was more of a cave. Small stalactites hung from a cathedral-like ceiling some 30 feet above us. The room was at least 50 yards across and ringed with a multitude of Coleman camping lanterns hanging from hooks embedded in the walls. I had been in much bigger caves before, so that was not what caused my awestruck reaction. It was the 100 or so Impals … I mean, *souls*, that populated the cavern.

Their combined ethereal glow, mixed with the lantern light, gave the place a surreal look, like a magical cave from a children's story. The souls were an eclectic mix of different time periods, genders, and ages. One of them caught my eye immediately, and incidentally that was the one who Mollie led me to.

The soul stood up from the wooden rocking chair he had been sitting in and met us halfway, giving Mollie a big bear hug as he bent his long and lanky frame over to embrace her. He stood up and stroked the tuft of black hair on his chin.

"Well, it looks like you have brought us more guests, Mollie," he said giving us an appraising look. "Well, hello, young fella!" the man said, waving to Seth. "That's a fine-looking pup you have there!"

Seth stepped forward with a look of wonderment on his face.

"Are you Aberham Lincoln?" he asked, his pronunciation slightly off.

The man stood up straight and grabbed the lapels of his black coat. He looked at Seth with a twinkle in his eye.

"Well, that depends, what have you heard about Abraham Lincoln, my lad?"

Seth, being the intelligent kid that he is, recited his thorough grade school understanding of our 16th President. Lincoln seemed both impressed and amused with Seth's knowledge. He shook his head and chuckled.

"Well, I was from Illinois, but I never freed any slaves or restored the Union. I was just an old country boy who had some good folks and some good generals working for him. I was a lucky man." He shook his head with a look of embarrassment on his face and waved his arm as if he were pointing at an object in the far corner of the cave. "I sure don't deserve that gaudy monument they built with me sitting in that uncomfortable-looking chair, like it was a dadgum throne."

I suppose I looked like a deer caught in headlights as I stared at my idol. Lincoln was my all-time favorite president and I had read countless books and watched numerous movies about his life and presidency. He was not only a great leader but also a very humble man, with a modesty that seemed true to form of historic accounts. He saw me gawping at him and smiled politely as he extended his right hand.

"And who might you be, good sir?"

I stood with my mouth agape, hardly hearing his question. After several long moments he raised his eyebrows and started to withdraw his hand.

"This is Thomas Pendleton," Mollie interjected. "He is Seth's father."

I quickly snapped out of my hero-induced trance. I grabbed his hand before he had completely withdrawn it and shook enthusiastically, the cold and warmth mixing vigorously as I probably grasped his hand too hard.

"Nice to meet you Mr. Pendleton. Please, call me Abe."

"Oh, I don't know if I could do that, Mr. President. It doesn't seem right."

"What doesn't seem right," Lincoln said with cautious exasperation, "is that folks should take on about me. I'm just a man, and not really that anymore." He said as he paused to look at his luminescent hands. "I haven't been involved with anything important in 150 years. I've felt useless watching the thirty administrations that followed mine; all I have been able to do is watch. I haven't even been able to compliment a president when he does well or criticize when I know he is making a boneheaded mistake." Lincoln paused with a disconcerted look on his face. He stroked his beard thoughtfully for several moments before he spoke again.

"That is, until this president. He is a good man at heart, but he really has nincompoops working for him, giving him advice. No, I think that is too inadequate, too trivial a word to describe it ... there is a lack of morality by some of his advisors. It is scary."

General Garrison immediately came to mind.

He shook his head as if to refocus his thoughts then looked at me and smiled.

"I'm sorry. I have a tendency to ramble sometimes." He winked and said, "I'll make you a deal. I'll call you Tommy if you call me Abe."

I still didn't feel comfortable addressing my hero informally, but I agreed to his proposal. The only person who had ever called me Tommy was my mom and Don Lewis. I guess I could make that exception for one of the most revered men in history. I wanted to talk with him, ask dozens of questions, but that would have to wait as Mollie announced it was time for dinner. I felt like a kid on Christmas morning who is ravenously hungry but doesn't want to tear himself away from his presents long enough to eat breakfast.

When Seth looked at me with excited anticipation over getting another home-cooked meal, I decided I could put my excitement aside long enough to have a good dinner. Besides, we were here for Seth and not my own historical curiosities.

But it's Abraham Lincoln, for God's sake, I thought to myself as we all walked to a large cedar table in the corner.

A line of souls had formed to make a plate and then seat themselves orderly at one of at least a dozen tables nearby. I had not noticed at first, but it seemed that Mollie and I were the only non-deceased, non-soul, non-Impal ... I wasn't sure what to call us. For the first time I felt like an outsider, a minority. Was that the way the people in the government felt? Part of me could see their side of the argument: the living could rapidly become a minority if this phenomenon kept up. Yes, I could understand their fear, but I couldn't condone how they were dealing with it. I wasn't sure we could do anything about it, either. I mean, the Constitution doesn't specifically guarantee rights to the deceased.

When we reached our turn in line, I didn't know whether to be disappointed or laugh. Instead of an immaculately prepared home meal, there was a platter full of hamburgers still in the wrapper. I smiled and took one, along with a handful of potato chips from a nearby ceramic bowl and a Coca-Cola from a Styrofoam cooler. I was a little disappointed, but I was also grateful for what we had. So were Seth and Jackson. Seth put his dinner on a paper plate while Jackson had his very own burger in a Styrofoam bowl. We took a seat at one of the dozen or so folding tables laid out as neatly and evenly as a school lunch room. We would have dinner and then, little did I know, I would have the conversation of my life.

CHAPTER 25

CAPITAL SECRETS

"Vision is the art of seeing what is invisible to others."

~Jonathan Swift

Dinner was greasy and good. The honorable Abraham Lincoln seemed to have a special affinity for hamburgers. I don't think they had them in his time, but if they had, I don't think he would have had such a slender frame.

Even though I did not use the term Impal publicly anymore, it was still the descriptor of choice in my head. I took notice of each and every one sitting at our table. Many were from Esther's time, I would say about 50-100 years before Lincoln. There were a few from the Civil War, as evidenced by the uniforms and clothing they still wore. Another dozen or so were probably from the early 20th Century, and then a potpourri of time periods was represented from the 1920s all the way up to present day.

A small boy, not much older than Seth, watched us with keen interest from two tables over. When he got up and walked to get a refill on chips, I could see that he was wearing a green Lego *Star Wars* t-shirt. His silvery shimmer gave the two characters on the front, R2-D2 and C-3PO, a surreal animated appearance like they were moving about, as if they were doing a droid jig. When I saw his shirt, I thought to myself how well that Seth and the boy would get along with their common interest in *Star Wars*, but to my surprise, he kept his eyes on me most of the time, hardly noticing Seth.

When dinner was over, Mollie stood up and hobbled to the center of the tables on her cane. She looked around at the room and smiled brightly at everyone.

"I would like to thank everyone for being here tonight, and I hope you enjoyed the wonderful food provided by my son from his favorite burger place."

As it turned out, Mollie's son owned a chain of the Martian joints in the Maryland and northern Virginia area. I guess it's good to have connections, especially when you have this many mouths to feed.

She proceeded to introduce Seth and me to the group. I felt like I was at an Impal Alcoholics Anonymous meeting as the unanimous response came back like it was spoken from inside a tin can.

Hi, Thomas and Seth.

"All are welcome here, souls and fleshers alike," she said, pinching the sagging age-spotted skin on her right forearm, I would guess to demonstrate her status as a flesher. "It's terrible times out there right now, terrible for us all."

There was a murmuring of agreement from the crowd.

I didn't want to offend, but I also wanted to know two things: why we were all eating burgers in a cave, and what else was going on that was more terrible than just rounding Impals up and relocating them? I slowly raised my hand.

"Yes, Mr. Pendleton," Mollie smiled.

"You have a beautiful home, ma'am, and I'm happy to be here," I said, cautiously. "But, what is this place we are in?" I asked, gazing up at a rather jagged stalactite above my head.

"Why, thank you, Mr. Pendleton!" she said, her pearly-white dentures in full display. "As to what this place is, I think Mr. Lincoln would be more qualified to give you a thorough explanation." She gave a quick cackle of a laugh and said, "I have no doubt you will find it both fascinating and useful!"

When Mollie's pep talk was over, everyone contributed in the cleanup and the Impals slowly made their way to an unassuming set of rock steps on the opposite wall of where Seth and I had entered. I tried to strike up a conversation with Lincoln again, but he politely interrupted me as he reached the base of the steps.

"Excuse me, Tommy," he said. "I have to go up and purge. Gotta keep Mollie's dogs fed and our house clean," he said with a chuckle.

"Seth, you probably ought to go up and squench," I said patting him on the head.

Lincoln emitted such a loud belly laugh, I jumped. His tinny laughter echoed through the cavern.

"Squenching … I like that!" he said in between guffaws. "Would you mind if I used that term? It sounds far less nasty than purging."

"Be my guest," I said, a little bemused. For a man that history reported to be somewhat melancholy, he sure liked to laugh.

He held out his hand for Seth and said, "My lad, would you care to join me for squenching?"

Seth couldn't help but laugh and eagerly took Lincoln's hand and followed him up the steps.

"We'll be back shortly," he promised as they rounded a bend at the top of the stairs and disappeared.

It made me nervous to let Seth out of my sight, if only for a few minutes, but my gut told me we were safe. I had no reason to believe otherwise. I turned to face the cavern in time to see the stuttering feet and cane of Mollie as she reached the top of the stairs leading to the secret passage. Shortly I heard the door in the bookshelf creak open and then clang shut a few moments later. I was alone in the cavern.

I stared around at the lanterns ringing the cave. They provided ample light by which to navigate, but they also gave the cave a mysterious aura like I was standing inside an ancient tomb that had just been lit for some sort of sacred ceremony. The only thing that dispelled that illusion were the rows of beds on the far wall. I had not noticed them at first because of the viewing angle I had when we came down the stairs and the fact that they were slightly obscured by a couple of rotund stalagmites.

I walked over and examined what I guessed must be the sleeping quarters for all the Impals that lived here. Actually, "lived" here might not be the correct word; it was more like they had taken refuge here with Mollie in her basement cave. The beds were in neat rows, much like the tables had been and were made up so tightly you couldn't see a wrinkle on any of the sheets. I had counted up to 35 beds when I heard everyone coming back down the stairs from their squenching expedition.

I quickly stepped back, as not to appear snoopy, and turned to face the stairs. A man and a woman came down first. They were dressed in garb that suggested that they might have lived during the Great Depression or slightly before. They looked at me warily, obviously aware that I had been examining their sleeping area.

"Hello," I said.

"Good evening, Mr. Pendleton," the man said with a pensive smile. The woman did not speak but nodded at me with a wistful smirk.

"Where are you from?" I asked.

"Fairfax," the man said then grabbed the woman by the hand. "Excuse us, Mr. Pendleton," he said, then led the woman over to the farthest row of beds. They took a seat facing each other on adjoining beds and engaged in muted conversation, casting me an occasional furtive glance.

They were obviously frightened of me. It bothered me, but I understood their reaction. After all, it was people like me that were causing all the problems. What did Mollie call us … fleshers? I didn't have time to consider this because I heard more people returning down the stairs. Several of them revered me the same way that the man and woman had, while some were quiet pleasant, smiling and speaking and asking how my trip was. There were none as friendly as Abe Lincoln who showed up a few minutes later with Seth in tow.

But before Seth and the president made it back, I was surprised when I felt the strange cold and warmth sensation as I had so many times when Seth took my hand. I looked down expecting to see him smiling up at me, but instead of Seth it was the little boy I had seen earlier with the green Lego *Star Wars* shirt.

"Hi," he beamed with a broad, toothy grin that stretched his freckles from ear to ear.

"Hi," I said. "What's your name?"

"Patrick," he said maintaining his goofy kid-like smile.

"Well, Patrick," I said, shaking his hand up and down. He had not released his grip. "Where are you from, young man?"

He shrugged. "Around."

"Are your parents around?" I asked.

He didn't say a word, just shook his head in the negative, his smile drooping slightly.

I didn't know what to ask him. Did your parents move on? Are they alive and moved to another part of the country? Did you run away? The book of etiquette would need to have a new chapter or two written as a result of this phenomenon. In the end, I decided not to push it.

"Well, I am glad you are here Patrick," I said. "Have you met my son, Seth?"

He frowned and shook his head. It was at that moment that I heard Seth and Lincoln coming back down the stairs. I looked up for a moment and when I looked back down, Patrick was gone. I glanced around and did not see him, but I had little time to look as Seth ran up and grabbed my leg, the sudden cold sending shivers up my spine.

"Daddy, you should see all the animals! There's horses, cows, and a whole bunch of doggies!"

Abe Lincoln walked up behind Seth with a nostalgic grin on his face.

"Yep, I haven't seen that many critters since my days on the farm when I was a lad. Of course, we only had one dog because that was all we could afford to feed." He frowned with a puzzled look on his face. "I still can't understand this eating thing, though."

"What do you mean?" I asked.

"Well, I get hungry as a horse, just like I did before, before, well …" his voice trailed off distantly.

I nodded my head in understanding.

"Well," Lincoln continued, "when I eat, I get full." He shook his head disconcertedly. "And chewing … I guess our teeth are more solid than the rest." He said this in such a tone I couldn't decide if it was a statement or a question. He chuckled loudly, drawing stares from several others in the cavern.

"And then there's squenching," he said between snorts. He leaned close to my ear and whispered confidentially, obviously not wanting Seth to overhear.

"What is squenching, anyhow? Ghost scat?"

He let loose with another echoing belly laugh. No, Mr. Lincoln was not melancholy; he was as jovial as good old St. Nick and as crass as my great uncle who had an affinity for potty humor. If my uncle had decided to remain when he passed 15 years ago, I could only imagine the field day he was having with squenching.

He furrowed his brow and frowned slightly, trying to put the humor aside, at least for a moment. He extended his index finger and made a circular motion.

"I guess it's kind of a circle of life thing. We eat the food, we purge the food, and the animals clean up. I just don't understand why we souls need to eat; we obviously don't need it, at least as nourishment, anyhow." He shook his head dismissively. "I know that's not what you want to talk about. Tommy and I could go on all night and not understand it a bit better in the morning. I guess we should just go on and accept it, cause we sho' can't change it," he said with a wink.

He pulled up a chair at one of the tables and beckoned me to sit across from him. He leaned back and crossed his hands over his slender belly. It was surreal talking to this man who was not only an American hero and my personal hero but he was also famous around the world. He was an icon to say the least, but still he was not what I expected. I expected a serious and deliberate man, someone who demanded respect and reverence, in short I expected a stiff. But his light-hearted personality took me by surprise. I was pleasantly surprised and instantly felt at ease, like I was talking to a lifelong friend. That was a good thing, but it only enhanced the fantastic nature of our conversation each time I thought about who I was actually speaking to.

"Well, Tommy, I know you want to know where we are. All you have to do is ask."

I did ask.

As it turned out, the cavern that we were in was the end of a very old tunnel system that had been started and finished prior to the Civil War and reinforced in 1862. The tunnel was around three miles long, and was designed for the sole purpose of sneaking people and supplies in and out of the city. Primarily for the safety of the president because of what happened when the British invaded the capital city in the War of 1812, and the reinforcement was done years later because of the potential threat of a Confederate invasion.

"The other end comes out in the basement of an old townhouse a few blocks from the White House. I managed to elude my pursuers the night I made the decision to leave the place I had dwelt in for the past 150 years. I got into the basement and into the passage which has been sealed for years now, probably a century. I was fortunate enough to find a kind heart like Mollie's on the other end, and the rest is history, as I believe that is the expression nowadays."

I nodded and started to stupidly ask how he made it through a sealed passage. I guess I was getting tired. I smiled when he demonstrated how this was accomplished by slowly pushing his hand through the table.

We must have talked for at least three hours, but it seemed like only ten minutes. I was fascinated to learn about his stay in the White House up until the time he left almost a week ago. It was then that he told me everything he had observed in the Oval Office since the storm arrived. He watched and observed what was transpiring and made the conscious decision to leave and get as far away as he could. Lincoln was and is an intelligent man, and he could see where circumstances were headed; he got out while he could.

"I knew they were following me every time I left," Lincoln said. "I guess they suspected I was up to no good, because I would take my walks around an older, less visited area of town. The truth is I was checking on the townhouse, and quite frankly I didn't want to be recognized and molested. Things aren't what they were in my day when I could walk to the Capitol and back without anyone hardly noticing, especially when I left my hat at home," he said pointing to the top of his head, which was completely devoid of eternal headwear.

Lincoln was relegated to his eternal existence in his classic black suit and tie, but his iconic stovepipe hat was not part of his attire. I have to admit, I found that small detail a little disappointing.

"Anyway, when I heard their plan to round up Impals," Lincoln said then stopped and held up his hand with a wry smile. "It's okay, Mollie's in bed. Besides, I don't find it offensive. Sticks and stones …" he trailed off with a wink and a grin.

"When I heard they were planning to start rounding Impals up and relocating them, that troubled me, but the reasoning scared the hell out of me." He lowered his voice and leaned toward me, "They said the Constitution didn't grant rights to the deceased, only the living. I guess their definition of living is different from mine. I feel pretty alive," he said, patting his cheeks.

That had been my thought exactly, but to now hear it confirmed I felt like a hole was torn out of my gut. I swallowed hard. My throat had started feeling better, as long as I was careful when I swallowed or didn't talk too loud or too long, but that unprepared gulp set my throat on fire again.

"They said that we would soon have an overcrowding problem and we needed to take preemptive action for the good of the living and the Impals before it got out of hand. I knew it was only a matter of time before I was included in that." He paused and placed his hands together in front of his mouth like he was in prayer. "Please understand, I didn't run because of my own cowardice, although I do admit to being afraid. I ran so I could warn as many people and Impals as I could, because I felt it was going to get much worse."

"How much worse?" I croaked, my throat still burning.

Lincoln shook his head and frowned as if he were considering the best way to couch his answer. After several long moments he spoke slowly, barely above a whisper.

"I overheard one of the president's advisors, Garrison, he was a general or something. He was telling another man, a Dr. Winder, that they had come up with a way to get rid of the Impals, to send them back where they belong."

CHAPTER 26
HISTORICAL SIGNIFICANCE

"To pity distress is but human; to relieve it is Godlike."

~Horace Mann

My heart sank into the pit of my stomach. The very thing I had been worried about, Seth and the other Impals leaving, the government was now trying to expedite.

"How?" I asked.

"I don't know," admitted Lincoln. "They had been discussing theories of how we were here. They had Einstein, trying to figure out the secret of our appearance."

"He cooperated?" I asked incredulously, I couldn't believe that to be true, not after the couple of times I had heard him on the radio; he had been clearly disturbed by developing events.

"Well at first, he had no reason not to. Everyone was curious as to what had happened, including Impals. But as time went on, his mood changed; he was less and less engaged in discussions, until eventually he stopped coming to meetings all together."

"Did they take him off for relocation with other Impals?"

Lincoln shrugged.

"I don't know, maybe, but … I hope not. I guess it's possible if he refused to cooperate," he said with a troubled frown.

I closed my eyes and focused on the background noise, the low murmur of Impals bedding down for the night, and the sometimes distant and sometimes very near drip of water echoing melodiously through the cave. It was not that melodious when you really honed in on it, it was maddening. I felt physically and spiritually ill, there was no other way to explain it. Refocusing did little to hinder my troubled thoughts. Things were much, much worse than I imagined.

After several long moments I reopened my eyes and looked at Lincoln. He was looking at me sympathetically.

"I know you're worried about Seth," he said. "I give you my word that I will do everything in my power to see that no harm comes to him."

My mind was swirling with a cesspool of terrible thoughts, try as I might I couldn't get a single positive thought to come to the surface. I looked over at Seth, who was sleeping peacefully with his head on the table. Jackson was curled up on his feet. This view of my sweet little son and his dog unhinged my mouth, and I blurted out the first thing that came to mind.

"Why am I the only flesher here?"

Lincoln looked at me surprised; a slight hint of bemusement washed across his face.

"Because we knew you could be trusted," he said.

"How?" I demanded.

He stroked his beard and smiled wanly.

"Because Mollie puts a great deal of stock in her friend Lizzie's opinion, I guess. Plus, you have a son whom you love very much who is, forgive me, part of the oppressed class."

I looked at him blankly for a long time. Deep down I knew he was right; how could you predict how anyone was going to react unless they stood to lose something, namely a dearly departed loved one? Even then, nothing was certain. This was uncharted territory in human history. I felt a bizarre mix of emotions swelling inside. I felt pride in what seemed to be acceptance from my hero and the Impal community-at-large. This mixed unnervingly with a gripping panic on the thought that my son could be taken away in any case, regardless of whether the phenomenon did or did not pass, taken away by mere human ignorance.

At that moment I heard the sound of the hidden door opening, and a minute later, the slow shuffling steps of Mollie gingerly traversing the stairs. I looked up to see her emerge from the shadows accompanied by Esther on one side and what appeared to be a family of Impals following closely behind. There were a man, woman, and a little girl who I guessed to be ten or eleven years of age. They all wore tired and frightened expressions on their silvery faces. Their clothing suggested that they were recently deceased, especially since the little girl wore Arizona jeans and a polka dot Tommy Hilfiger blouse.

"Good evening, gentlemen," Mollie said, taking special care not to wake the sleeping Seth. "This is the Lieblong family: Mark, Susan, and their daughter, Samantha."

They all nodded sheepishly, their eyes darting nervously around the cave. That is, until their gaze seemed to fall on Lincoln at the same time. Their confused expressions melded into the same bewildered countenance of unified recognition.

"Hello," Lincoln and I said together.

I'm sure Mollie saw their looks of celebrity infatuation because she quickly ushered them off toward the beds on the far wall of the cave.

"Don't go, I'll be right back," Mollie promised with a wink as she took the silvery hand of Samantha and urged her to follow. I had no idea where I would possibly go.

She showed the Lieblongs to their beds and stayed to chat with them for a few minutes. Shortly they all took seats on their respective beds and sat there with looks of utter perplexity, occasionally casting a furtive glance in our direction.

The Lieblongs were clearly out of their element; they were frightened and confused. I guessed that it had been a short time, maybe a few hours, since they were separated from their mortal tether. Something terrible had happened to this family and it had not been that long ago. I suddenly remembered the family that Seth and I had seen the day we left on our trip: the victims of a terrible car wreck. They were Impals standing next to their bodies, which were covered on the side of the road. They wore the same bewildered expressions as the Lieblongs.

Once the Lieblongs were somewhat settled in, Mollie tottered back over to Lincoln and me. Try as I might, I couldn't stifle an enormous yawn as she approached. It not only reminded me of how tired I was but also that my throat still hurt.

"I know you must be tired," she said. She looked lovingly at Seth as he peacefully stirred in his sleep. "I know that little fellow is."

"Well, this old fellow definitely is," Lincoln proclaimed, stretching his long lanky arms into the air. "I think it's time to hit the rack!" He turned and shook my hand and then delicately kissed Mollie's hand, causing her to blush noticeably in the low light. "Sleep tight, don't let the bed bugs bite!" he advised as he strolled toward the beds.

"Well, Thomas, I have a special place prepared upstairs for you and Seth," Mollie said giving Lincoln a final wave before he reached his bed.

I looked over my shoulder at the rows of Impals, some sleeping, some sitting up and a few milling about, quietly visiting with fellow Impal insomniacs. Lincoln was already stretched out on his bed, his head underneath the pillow I would guess to filter out the ambient noise in the cave, or, maybe that was just his quirk. I felt guilty.

"Why do Seth and I get to sleep upstairs when they all have to stay down here?" I asked.

Mollie smiled.

"Lizzie was right about you. You are a good man," she said patting my shoulder with a gnarled hand. She looked at Esther and nodded. Esther gently scooped Seth up, taking special care not to wake him and headed toward the stairs. Mollie gently took my hand and led me in the same direction. "Sleeping down here is not very conducive to we fleshers' good health," she said with a suppressed laugh.

"I thought *souls*," I said, taking special care to use the right word in the presence of our host, "I thought they felt much the same things we do."

"They do, they do," Mollie agreed, patting my arm. "But they are not susceptible to heat, cold, and wetness as we are. They don't have to worry about such bothersome things as colds, flu, or pneumonia," she said.

In our short walk out of the cave and to a second floor bedroom in Mollie's impressively large home, I learned a great deal about the house and history of the tunnel, getting much more detail than I did in my discussion with Lincoln.

There was a small cave discovered in the early 1800s underneath the then fledgling city of Washington, D.C. A townhouse was built by a wealthy resident over the cave, and it was used as a wine and root cellar by the owner until just a few short years after the War of 1812. The traumatic experience of the British marching into the city and burning most of the Federal buildings convinced many in the government that an escape route was needed in case anything like that ever occurred again. The cave was a few short blocks from the White House, so it would be an ideal route by which to evacuate the .president.

Construction was started sometime in 1815, funded by a secret measure passed by Congress. A newly formed coal mining company that had just started prospecting in the Appalachian Mountains was tapped to construct the tunnel. They began digging in the cave under the city, and in just a little over a year, they broke into another cavern system—the one under Mollie's house. They were pleasantly surprised that the cave under Mollie's was completely stable and had a natural exit, or entrance, depending on your perspective.

The natural opening was hidden for many years by selectively planted trees and shrubs, and a small military guard post was constructed to guard it. In 1850, the government built the existing house over the cave because some believed it would make the escape tunnel less conspicuous and give the president a temporary headquarters if needed in the event of an evacuation from the city.

The less practical proponents thought the president needed a nice place to rest and clean up after a crawl through a nasty tunnel. In truth it became a vacation home to many in the government or a retreat for Congressmen and their mistresses. I guess little has changed in the last 150 years.

The truly incredible thing about it all was that the tunnel was kept such a tight secret up until the time it was abandoned by the government in the 1880s that it has been all but forgotten by history. I certainly don't remember studying about the president's subterranean escape tunnel in school, or even seeing some obscure television program on the History Channel. No, according to Mollie, there are only a handful of people with knowledge of the tunnel.

"How did you happen on this house?" I asked.

"I married into it," she said with a modest smile.

It turned out that Mollie had married a man by the name of Shainard Hartje shortly after moving to Landover after she and Lizzie Chenowith parted ways. The house had been in the Hartje family for 100 years and they had kept the tunnel a closely guarded secret, not with the motive of protecting classified information but to keep tourists and gawkers away.

"Shay, that's what I called him, passed away almost 30 years ago," she said as we slowly ascended the ornate staircase. "He was a good man with a good heart, just not a very strong one, I'm afraid."

"I'm sorry, did he—" I broke off the question when I realized how stupid it was.

She gave me an appraising look and then smiled faintly.

"Did he stay? No, I'm sorry to say he did not, although I have talked to him a few times in the past 30 years."

"How?" I asked, forgetting some of what Miss Chenowith had told me.

Mollie gestured to Esther, whom was gently laying Seth down on a large mahogany covered bed in a room to the right of the second floor landing. It reminded me of my upstairs landing except it was much larger and much fancier.

"My spirit guide," she said. "Didn't Lizzie tell you about Shasta?"

I shrugged. It seemed like she had mentioned something about how spirit guides work but I had either forgotten it or didn't comprehend in the first place.

Mollie hobbled over to a high backed chair in the corner covered in yellow fabric festooned with tiny red roses. She plopped down alarmingly like a sack of potatoes and motioned for me to come and sit on the matching loveseat nearby. When I obliged, she leaned as far out as she could using her cane for support and spoke to me in a low voice like she didn't want anyone overhearing.

"People like Lizzie and me are called mediums, but that is actually a misnomer. Our spirit guide could be more accurately described as a medium."

I looked at her with blank incomprehension washing over my face. She continued.

"We have a strong bond to the spirit guide, and as a result of that link we are able to tap in on connections the spirit guide makes."

"Connections?" I asked.

"Yes, many spirits that have chosen to remain will speak to me freely, but many more are a little shy or just don't want to be bothered. That's where Esther comes in; she is able to be a little more persuasive than I can, since she is like them."

I looked over to see Esther watching us as she sat on the side of the bed, nervously stroking Seth's hair as he slept. She looked anxious, like she wanted us to hurry and finish our conversation. I didn't know whether it bothered her that Mollie was discussing their relationship or if she was just as tired as I was and was eager to call it a night. She returned my look with a faint smile.

"I see," I said, turning my attention back to Mollie. "So she acts like a medium between you and spirits that are shy or antisocial?" I intended that question to be sincere but with a little dry humor thrown in. I'm not sure Mollie took it that way.

"No, not antisocial, they're just people who want to be left alone even though their loved ones want to talk to them. I think it's too painful for them to focus on their past lives. It's sad, really, and this whole event, or phenomenon, or whatever you want to call it, has been the hardest on them. They no longer have a choice."

I nodded my head and offered an apologetic smile.

Mollie looked at me with a stern expression, one that made me feel as if I were being scolded by my grandmother. But she wasn't scolding; she was trying as best she could to educate an ignorant ex-skeptic like myself.

"A spirit guide is most literally a medium when they are communicating with someone who has passed on, someone who has chosen to go through the door, so to speak."

My heart skipped a beat when I thought of how Seth had told me about the doors and that his mother had chosen to go through hers. Could it be possible that I still might be able to communicate with my beloved Ann, even though she had chosen to move on?

"How is that possible?" I asked, breathless.

"I'm not really sure," Mollie admitted. "The best explanation I've heard is that the spirit guide can sometimes find a random door and just go up and knock on it and ask to speak to so and so."

"Ask who?" I said and we both turned in unison to look at Esther. She must have anticipated this, because a moment before she bent down to pet Jackson, who had taken up station beside the bed. Her back was partially turned so she didn't have to look in our direction.

"I don't know," Mollie said. "Best advice is don't ask her about it, it upsets her somethin' awful," she said in a low whisper as she nodded her head discreetly in Esther's direction.

Mollie put her cane in her left hand and stuck her right arm in the air.

"Can you please help me up, Thomas? We all need our rest tonight."

I stood up and gently took her hand. She pulled on my hand and pushed with the cane, with minimal effort she slowly rose to her feet.

"I expect we might have visitors in the morning," she said hobbling toward the door, Esther taking position at her side.

"Who?" I asked.

"The military," she said with a tone of "been there, done that."

I swallowed hard, igniting the burn in my throat again.

"The military?" I croaked, my heart beat starting to accelerate.

"Yes," she said, like she didn't have a care in the world. "They are after the Lieblongs."

CHAPTER 27
MORNING GUESTS

*"There are three things in the world that deserve
no mercy: hypocrisy, fraud, and tyranny."*

~Frederick William Robertson

Mollie left the room before I could question her further about her ominous statement. I was exhausted and laid down next to Seth in the large canopy bed. The mattress was incredibly comfortable and soft, but in spite of that I lay awake all night. Why in the hell had she been so nonchalant about a subject that was extremely important to 99-percent of the souls in the house and below in the cave? Were we going to have soldiers showing up any moment with iron cuffs and chains? While the implications of her carefree statement troubled me, I believe it was probably the secondary cause for my insomnia. I spent most of the night thinking of Ann.

I couldn't get the thought out of my head about the prospect of still being able to talk to her, to communicate, to share with one another. I missed her dearly and there was still a massive hole inside of me that could never be filled again. I had been able to cover this hole to disguise it from my feelings by focusing on my time with Seth. But it was still there, brought into full relief by the hope of talking with my wife just one more time. My hopes were darkened, however, when I considered the logic of the situation. Esther would have to go back for that to be possible. This meant that the phenomenon would have to end, which means Seth would go back, too. As much as I wanted to talk to Ann, that was a sacrifice I was unwilling to make.

I awoke with a start as I felt a cold hand on my chest.

"Wake up! Wake up! The Army is here!" Esther said as she gently shook me out of the short cat nap I had eventually fallen into.

I sat up quickly, catching Esther by surprise and causing her hand to penetrate my chest a few inches. My heart felt frozen, which was only intensified when I looked over and saw Seth was gone.

Esther quickly withdrew her hand from my chest with a look of embarrassment like she had just seen me naked. She stood up and rushed to the door.

"Where's Seth?" I asked as I stumbled out of bed rubbing my cold chest.

"He's safe," she said in a hurry. "Get dressed. I'm going to join him." She pointed to the floor, which I took to mean he was in the cave. Esther paused like she was trying to remember something, "Oh, and you're Mollie's son today!"

I stood there staring at the closed bedroom door, dumbfounded. The shock of waking up suddenly and finding Seth gone, coupled by an Impal heart massage had left my head spinning. I was rudely shaken back to comprehension when I heard shouts and slamming vehicle doors outside the window. I ran to the window and looked down to the front drive.

Three troop transport trucks accompanied by as many Humvees had pulled up in front of Mollie's home. A dozen soldiers appeared to be combing the front part of the house. They carried a mix of automatic weapons and iron chains. My cold heart seemed to drop to my shoes when I thought of Seth. I didn't know for certain where the hell he was. I hurriedly got dressed and headed down the stairs.

I reached the bottom of the stairs to find Mollie waiting patiently, leaning on her cane.

"Well, good morning, Peter! I am so glad my son has come to visit me!" she exclaimed with a wink.

Before I could reply, there was a thunderous knocking noise at the front door.

"Open up, by order of the US Army!" a deep baritone voice called from the other side.

"Just a minute, officer!" called Mollie sweetly as she slowly hobbled toward the door.

Mollie turned the handle and the large door slowly swung open to reveal a host of soldiers, some brandishing rifles and some armed with iron chains and cuffs.

"Oh my," she said. "Whatever is the problem?"

The soldiers did not readily offer an explanation; the majority entered cautiously and skirted past Mollie and me, their heads on a swivel as they looked for any sign of Impals. The large baritone-voiced soldier stepped in last and stood like a towering giant over Mollie.

"We tracked an Impal family here. Have you seen them?" he boomed authoritatively but respectfully down at Mollie.

"First of all, these people are souls, not Impals," she corrected scathingly.

The soldier, in appearance, was a stereotypical jarhead with buzz cut blond hair and a square jaw. Whether or not his personality matched his appearance remained to be seen. I could now see he had the name "Sitkowski" sewn above the breast pocket of his uniform. Sitkowski leaned low as he spoke his next question.

"Have you seen this family of *souls*, ma'am?" he asked more delicately this time, putting emphasis on the corrected terminology.

"No, sir … I have not!" she exclaimed.

"Mind if we search your house, ma'am?" he asked like he hadn't even heard her answer.

"Do you have a warrant?" I interjected.

His eyes flashed at me, seeming to bore holes through me with his laser-like stare.

"Who are you?" he asked with none of the courtesy he had afforded Mollie.

Mollie started to raise her hand, but I answered before she could speak.

"My name is Peter Hartje," I said. "Why are you inspecting my mother's house without a warrant?"

He gazed at me appraisingly for several moments before he replied. I had the strange sensation that he didn't believe my alias. I also had a feeling I wasn't going to like his answer, even though I probably already knew the answer.

"I don't need a warrant with an Executive Order, *Mr. Hartje*," he repeated. I could have sworn that the last two words sounded more like a question than a statement. "You would do well to remember that … the penalty for treason is pretty severe," he said in a matter-of-fact tone like he had just told me what he had for breakfast.

"What are you looking for?" I asked, knowing full well what they were after, but the question was drowned out by the sound of combat boots plodding up and down the stairs above us. My heart felt like it turned to ice and slipped into my stomach when I turned and saw a group of soldiers heading for the library where the secret door lead down to the cavern, down to where the Impals were hidden, down to Seth.

I turned to walk in that direction but I didn't know what I intended to do – keep an eye on the search for my own comfort, cause a distraction, or attack the soldiers myself. I didn't have time to consider my reaction, though; I had barely taken two steps when I was grasped firmly by the elbow. I was spun around abruptly and was standing nose to nose with a man about my height, wearing a black beret and green camo like the other soldiers. Unlike the other soldiers who were wearing berets, his was the only one that had stars on it—three of them, to be exact. I recognized the face, but I was in so much shock by his sudden appearance I didn't immediately put a name with it. After all, I had not seen his image lately, just heard him on the radio. So when he spoke, his identity hit me like air from an icy tomb.

"Please stay here and let the men do their work," he said with a casual coolness that made the statement sound rather creepy. "Mr. ...?"

"Hartje," I said. "Peter Hartje."

A look of bemusement washed across his face as he cut his eyes at Mollie.

"I am General Ott Garrison." He nodded toward Mollie. "Your mother?"

I nodded my head stiffly as Mollie focused her eyes on the floor.

I had seen this man on the news. He was the Chairman of the Joint Chiefs and the president's most trusted military advisor, the man who Lincoln had seen in the Oval Office, the one I had heard on the radio; he was the man who was probably most responsible for the government's treatment of the Impals. He had convinced the president they were a threat, and the Commander in Chief had naively let a terrible genie out of the bottle, one that now seemed would be extremely difficult, if not impossible, to rebottle.

"Why are you here? We've done nothing wrong!" I demanded with as much courage and authority I could manage. I'm sure the general heard the fear in my voice because of his satisfied smile. I was scared, scared as hell, but not for me. I was scared for Seth.

He strolled to the nearby window and drew the lacy curtains back just enough that I could clearly see my SUV parked in the driveway. Fear burned in my stomach like acid as I looked at the Arkansas license plate clearly displayed on the back of the vehicle. I knew what that meant. How could I have been so stupid to not hide the vehicle?

"Is that your vehicle, Mr. Hartje?" he asked, jerking his head casually toward the window.

I said nothing. I just stared as coolly as I could back at him. I had to push Seth to the back of my mind to keep the fear out of my eyes.

"It's a nice vehicle," he said, indifferent. "I used to have one myself. Pitiful gas mileage though." He looked at me with raised eyebrows. "Not very green are you, Mr. Hartje?"

I stared at him, not blinking and not moving. Nausea threatened to betray my cool exterior.

I heard books crashing to the floor in the library as soldiers carelessly tossed the shelves. It was all I could do to control my feeling of terror as the general stood there, X-raying me with his eyes. Were the soldiers about to find the latch that opens the secret door?

Mollie turned and walked toward the library. I was just turning to follow when the general spoke again.

"That SUV really gets around. I understand it was in Tennessee a couple of days ago?"

I took a deep breath; it seemed my heart was in my throat as my sore neck burned with every rapid pulse. I could feel a cold sweat beading on my brow.

"I wouldn't know."

"I see," he said. "Well, what would you know? Do you know, Mr. Thomas Pendleton?"

My heart rate went up a notch as I felt a bead of sweat cascade over my eyebrow.

The general carried on conversationally. This was worse than yelling and screaming; his tone sent chills through my body.

"It would seem that Mr. Thomas Pendleton, who happens to be the owner of the vehicle I might add, was involved in a carjacking in that very vehicle where an Impal boy was used to go in and help burglarize several establishments."

I stood motionless, trying not to react, trying not to alter my expression, but that was getting difficult. Sweat was starting to sting my eyes.

"They never found the little perversion of nature," he said.

I could feel the anger rising in me now, quickly swallowing up my fear. For Seth's sake, I couldn't let it dissuade all my fear. I needed a little to control my anger. I am not a violent person, but I could have easily punched the general square in the nose and not felt the least bit guilty about it. But that foolish and rash reaction would do Seth no good.

"That just proves my point," he said. "These Impals are nothing but perversions of nature—*arrogant* perversions, I might add. They take up our space, with more and more of them coming every second. In just a few months there is literally going to be very little elbow room left in this great country without rubbing elbows with one of them. I can't think of anything more disgusting, can you?"

I said nothing, still staring stoically at him. My inclination to punch him in the nose had just risen to ripping his throat out.

"Well," he said shaking his head like he was warding off a pesky fly. "At least we know how to deal with them." He said as he patted a coiled iron chain hanging from his belt.

I could feel the anger blooming red in my cheeks and I'm sure the general saw it as well.

"Do you know, Mr. Pendleton?" he asked pleasantly.

I shook my head.

"Pity," he said with obvious mock disappointment. "I was hoping I could clear up something with him. You see, the official report says that the delinquent little Impal was travelling with the two carjackers, but I think that must have been an error on the police report. You know what I think?"

I shook my head, fighting hard to keep control as my anger was starting to win out.

"I think the little punk was Pendleton's son, or should I say the foul remains of him. You see, he was killed in an automobile accident before the storm."

"What difference would that make?" I asked angrily.

He smiled at me humorlessly and shrugged.

"None really, one Impal is like another … arrogant, deceitful, and abusive with their abilities. Abominations that need to be eradicated. It's patriotic to take them out. It's the American way to stand up and defend our liberties!"

"What about their liberties?" I growled.

General Garrison burst into such a boisterous bout of laughter that several of his men came back to investigate. After several moments, he took a deep breath and dabbed mirthful tears from his eyes.

"What liberties?" he chortled. "The Constitution guarantees liberties to living people, not sullied freaks. They don't even have real bodies, for God's sake!"

"You're wrong!" I felt like I was back in school retorting the taunts of a bully. My disagreement would just make matters worse

"No, *Mr. Hartje*," he said. "I'll show you who is wrong."

He grabbed me by the elbow, but I pulled away.

"Please," he said, gesturing toward the library.

I reluctantly turned and walked in that direction with the general following close behind. The clattering of boots and men seemed to have quieted; in fact, it was eerily quiet in the house. That was nothing compared to what I found in the library. The soldiers were standing in a semi-circle around the room like they were waiting on something. When the general entered they all snapped to attention. The only thought running through my head was how in the hell he knew about me. They had just gotten there, for God's sake. He didn't have time to run my tags and collect that much information. They were after the Lieblongs, and running into me was purely incidental. Or was it?

Mollie was standing in the middle of the room leaning on her cane; she had a surprisingly peaceful look on her face, considering the circumstances. The general stepped in front of me and addressed

Mollie.

"You know what I miss, Mollie?"

She gave him a wry smile.

"I miss all the time I spent in this room having brandy and cigars with Shainard. He was a good friend," he said.

Mollie nodded her head.

"Well, I didn't come here to reminisce. I take it the net is pretty full?"

Mollie nodded her head sheepishly. "Are you sure I'm doing the right thing?"

"Absolutely," General Garrison said. "You are a good American and a patriot just like Shainard, who had the good sense to move on when his time was up, I might add. You're doing a great service."

As sweet as he sounded on the surface, it sounded to me like the devil trying to tempt someone. The horrifying truth was that this demonic deal had been sealed probably long before I arrived. Mollie smiled and glanced at me, then hobbled over to the bookcase. She reached her hand up on the shelf that was now void of books. A moment later there was a loud click and the secret door began to swing open.

CHAPTER 28
THE OTHER SIDE

*"Carve a tunnel of hope through
the dark mountain of disappointment."*

~*Martin Luther King, Jr.*

I don't think there has ever been a time in my life when I was filled
with such a cacophony of emotions as I was at the moment. Fear,
anger, shock, betrayal, rage, hatred, and terror had hollowed me out,
leaving only room for pure instinct to fill the void. I couldn't think,
I couldn't feel; all I could do was act. Before the secret door had
completely opened, I launched myself across the room and through
the opening before any of the astonished soldiers could react.

I skidded across the stone floor like a baseball player doing a
belly slide and then rapidly began bouncing downwards when I
reached the steps.

"Run! Tunnel! Army! Run!" I repeated over and over as the air
was hammered out of me with each tumble into the blackness.

I could hear the voice of General Ott Garrison behind me yelling orders of pursuit and curses, while in front of me I recognized the clear and decisive voice of Abraham Lincoln as he shouted instructions to his Impal counterparts.

"To the tunnel, quickly! Come now! Make haste!" his authoritative and tinny-sounding voice echoed through the cavern. This was followed by a mixture of gasps and shrieks from the subterranean refugees and then a stampeding of soft Impal footsteps.

I finally hit the cavern floor after what seemed like an eternity of falling. I quickly got to my feet, oblivious to the pains of my fall, and headed in the direction of Lincoln's voice. I had barely taken two steps when a blinding light flooded the cavern, bringing everything into full relief and causing me a moment of disorientation as I stumbled over a short stalagmite. Apparently, the Coleman lanterns ringing the walls were completely unnecessary, all a part of the ambience or very probably the ruse of a safe and secluded hiding place. The place was now lit up like the Superdome.

I looked over my shoulder to see dozens of boots descending the stairs, accompanied by the clinking and dragging of dozens of iron chains. My newly-found sixth sense drove me to my feet once again. My emotions had shut down for the moment, and fight or flight instinct had taken over. I did have enough sense to know that fighting would be foolish, so my sole thought was finding Seth and getting as far down the tunnel as we could. I looked about wildly and saw several Impals disappear into the tunnel entrance about 30 yards from me, Lincoln stood to the side, waving them through.

"Seth is here with me!" Lincoln bellowed over the shouts and iron clanks echoing deafeningly through the cavern.

I started to run in their direction when I felt something cold latch onto my leg. I whirled about to see the little boy I had met last night, Patrick, with the green Lego *Star Wars* t-shirt; he clung to my leg like a vise. His goofy kid smile had been replaced with a look of livid terror.

"Help me!" he pleaded.

Without another thought I scooped him up and headed for Lincoln, ignoring the fact that his right arm and leg were half in my torso.

"Come on!" I yelled as I reached Lincoln and scooped Seth up with my free arm.

I hesitated a moment before entering the tunnel, just a brief hesitation for a look behind me. I wish that I hadn't. There were a significant number of Impals, at least a dozen, who had been in the wrong place at the wrong time. They were caught on the far side of the cavern when the soldiers entered and had been cut off from the tunnel. Some had tried to go up the stairs leading to Mollie's yard, but soldiers were pouring down those stairs as well. Most of these poor Impals had been knocked to the ground with the heavy iron chains and were in the process of being collared or cuffed. There was no discrimination: man, woman, and child were all handled with the same brutality. They were all dirty abominations in the eyes of General Garrison. He seemed to have been successful instilling that belief in his men.

My feelings were still numb, but this sight would be one more barb of pain to add to my emotional suffering when my anesthesia of fear and adrenaline wore off. Fortunately, I didn't have a lot of time to absorb what I was seeing as Lincoln grabbed my arm and pulled me rudely into the pitch black tunnel.

We ran and stumbled through the darkness for what seemed like several minutes, Lincoln guiding me by the arm all the way. I wasn't sure if Impals had a special ability to see in complete darkness or if Lincoln was just familiar with his surroundings. The floor was surprisingly smooth. I had expected to be tripping over rocks and debris, but it was more easily navigated than the cavern had been, and without light. But as we started to catch up with some of the other Impals, I saw that there was a light.

It was very faint, just enough to see a few feet in front of me, but it was unlike any light I had ever seen. There was a faint silvery shimmer to it, kind of like the Impals. That was when I realized that it *was* the Impals, not just one or two, but when several of them were in close proximity in the dark it became very noticeable. It was more like one of Seth's glow-in-the-dark toys than a true light, but it did give me brief opportunities to take note of my surroundings as we hurried through the darkness.

I could see intermittent wood beams lining the ceiling like an old west mine shaft. Some were sagging so precariously with the weight of earth above them that I thought it a miracle they hadn't collapsed.

"Daddy, where are we?" Seth asked softly as he clung to me harder. Patrick did the same thing on my other side, seemingly in reaction to Seth's tightened grip. Patrick didn't say anything, but his little arms and legs sank deeper into my torso to the point that I thought they must be touching Seth's somewhere around my pancreas. The sensation had taken some getting used to when dealing with Seth, but now it was doubled; I had to block the weird cold and warmth inside of me and focus on getting through the tunnel. The soldiers were coming and it was only a matter of time before they caught up to us at the other end—if we even made it to the other end.

I was starting to get a stitch in my side when Lincoln stopped.

"Keep going!" He said, "I'll hold them off!"

"How?" I asked incredulously. "They are carrying iron, you'll be captured!"

"Not today!" Lincoln said as he retrieved an ancient mining pick from the shadows. "Now, run!" he yelled as he took a swing at the wooden beam overhead.

Lincoln had the reputation of being a woodsman and a rail-splitter, so when I realized what he intended to do, I had no doubt that he could and would accomplish it in short order. A beam of light appeared in the distance as the soldiers pursued. When the pick made contact with the wooden beam, there was a loud crack followed by creaks and groans of wood about to give way under extreme pressure. In spite of their noisy and hurried approach, the sound of a potential cave-in got the attention of the soldiers. The light stopped moving and the whispered conversations of the soldiers were just audible in the distance.

"Go!" Lincoln muttered in a harsh whisper as he waved me away. "Go, I'll be right behind you!"

A few choice expletives echoed down the tunnel from a couple of soldiers followed by derogatory remarks about Impals. They started to cautiously move in our direction again.

"Go, Daddy!" Seth urged.

"They're coming, Daddy!" Patrick squealed.

The kids were terrified, and Patrick had no family that I knew of, so the comment didn't sound out of place to me. He needed comfort and if I could provide it, I would. I turned and ran down the tunnel, clutching the kids tighter, just as Lincoln landed another blow on the beam. This time the ancient support gave way, releasing a thunderous crash of dirt and rock into the passage, blocking the tunnel permanently. But just a second or two before the crash I heard a noise that sent icy fingers probing my spine and stomach: I heard Jackson's barks. He was nearby, but not near enough.

I accelerated as I held my breath. A cloud of dust followed, encompassing me like a swarm of angry bees. I knew that I would suffocate if I could not out distance it soon. Just when I thought my lungs would explode, I gasped in a large lungful of air. The dust had thinned but not enough; I inhaled a good portion of earth, causing me to drop Seth and Patrick as I fell to my knees, coughing violently, expelling soil from my lungs, and fighting for clean air with each sputtering gasp. I was on the verge of blacking out when I felt two icy but strong hands grab me from behind and pull me forward.

I was pulled over wet and rocky dirt for what seemed like hours; it was difficult to tell because I kept lapsing in and out of consciousness. My oxygen-starved lungs burned like hot coals in my chest. The next thing I knew, I was being pulled up a steep embankment. My arms and shoulders felt like they were submerged in ice. I managed to open my eyes enough to see four Impal men, one of which was Lincoln, dragging me forward through the damp and the darkness. When I didn't see Seth, I snapped to as if I had been slapped from a deep sleep. I tried to speak but all I could manage was a long sputtering cough, copious amounts of dirt spewed from my mouth, letting me know that I was in bad shape and my throat still hurt, but … I was alive.

"Easy, lad," I heard an unfamiliar Impal voice whisper. "Easy, we're almost done."

I coughed and hacked until the world spun into a big black void and I passed out. I came around later blinking up into a bright ray of sunlight. I had the strange feeling like the whole thing had been one big nightmare. I sat up a little and felt a mix of cold and warmth shoot through each arm. I squinted my eyes as dirt and dust tumbled from my lashes and eyebrows. I gave my head one big dirt-clearing shake and looked down to see Seth laying on one arm and Patrick on the other. They were both sleeping soundly.

"Are you okay, Thomas?" a familiar yet unfamiliar voice asked nearby. I suddenly remembered it as the Impal's voice I had heard in the tunnel before I passed out. I turned my head in that direction and emitted a shuddering cough, causing dirt to tumble from my hair and shoot from my mouth and nose like tiny mud balls. I pulled my arm gently through Seth and wiped my mouth with the back of my hand. I winced as my throat throbbed with pain. Breathing in a wheelbarrow full of dirt and coughing profusely was the worst thing I could have done to my injury. I needed a doctor, but I knew that was not possible, not now. Not unless I wanted Seth taken away and for me to go to jail for treason.

"Do you need a doctor?" the male Impal voice asked ironically.

I shook my head and hocked an enormous dirt loogie into my palm. Ignoring all couth and manners, I wiped it on the front of my shirt. What the hell, I was already filthy. I was determined that I would let nothing separate Seth and me, not even my own poor health. As my old football coach would say about an injury: *shake it off, rub some dirt in it, and you'll be fine.* How ironic.

"No," I wheezed. I sputtered, holding back another coughing fit as I asked, "How many got away?"

The Impal stepped forward and knelt by my side. He wore clothing that reminded me of someone that might have been around to take a cruise on the Titanic. A thick handle bar moustache made his round face look like it might take flight at any moment. He was completely free of any dirt or dishevelment whatsoever. *He was an Impal, he had probably squenched it away,* I thought but did not say.

"About half of us got away," he said. "But ... only about a quarter of the children did." I saw a silvery tear streak down his cheek, snake through his moustache, and then tumble to the ground where it disappeared without a trace.

"Where's Lincoln?" I asked, and then coughed up another wad of dirt. I pulled my other arm gently through Patrick and sat up all the way.

"He's here ... let me get you a drink of water," the man said as he stood up and disappeared into the shadows behind me.

I suddenly remembered Jackson's barks in the tunnel.

"Is there an Impal dog here?" I asked.

The man slowly walked back from the shadows with a forlorn look on his face. I knew the answer to all my questions just by looking at him, but he answered anyway.

"You mean Jackson. Cute little fellow," he stopped and rubbed his head as two silver tears dripped onto his moustache. "He didn't make it through the cave-in, what with that iron collar and all ... he couldn't."

A sudden wave of nausea washed over me like a pungent wave. The soldiers had Jackson, or worse yet, he was buried under the cave-in with no way out, anchored for eternity by that stupid iron collar. I shuttered and coughed. I wasn't sure if I had just vomited or expelled another glob of mud. Either way, I was much better off than poor Jackson. What the hell was I going to tell Seth?

I turned my shirt tail inside out and rubbed my eyes as the stranger retreated into the shadows to get my water. It seemed that the inside of my clothing was the only clean spot on me. When my eyes were relatively sludge-free, I looked up into the light above and blinked. It was coming through a small rectangular window about six feet off the floor.

As I looked about at my surroundings, I could see two more identical windows about ten feet on either side of this one. All presented similar radiant beams of sunlight. I was in a cellar or basement, a very old one judging by the dirt floor and the musty, aged smell of an ancient house or building. Impals lined the brick walls around the perimeter, some standing, some sitting, and some lying down. Most looked terrified, while many wept inconsolably. Who could blame them? The atrocity we had just endured made me feel like crying. Was this America? I felt a strong rush of shame surge through me and that only reinforced my sadness. My strong patriotism for the country I have loved dearly my whole life was being called into question.

"How could this happen in America?" I unconsciously said aloud.

"It's happening all over the world, I'm afraid." The man with the handle bar moustache said behind me.

I jumped with surprise causing me to launch into another fit of coughing. He sheepishly extended his arm toward me, offering me a large glass of ice water. I took it gratefully and rinsed and gargled profusely before I took a drink. I handed the glass back to him feeling much better, albeit I still felt like a vacuum cleaner that had just been perfunctorily rinsed out.

"Thank you," I said, and then repeated his statement. "It's happening all over the world?"

He nodded.

"Yes, just heard it on the sound box upstairs. Something called the United Nations has mandated all spirits be rounded up for our own safety and for the continued order of society," he said like someone reciting a limerick they had just memorized. I couldn't believe he had never heard of the United Nations in his 100-year existence, but I guess he had been some place secluded. I wish I had never heard of the UN.

"What's your name?" I asked.

"Frederick. Frederick Sax."

"Pleased to meet you, Frederick," I said as I shook his hand. It's amazing what you can get used to. The frigid touch of an Impal almost seemed normal to me now.

"Thanks for the water," I said, and turned and walked to the window. I was partially tingling with excitement and partly with fear in anticipation of what I would see outside.

We were in the basement of a building on a city street. Numerous vehicles sped past behind several pairs of feet belonging to bustling pedestrians. I jumped back from the window in surprise as a skateboard passed precariously close to the glass.

A moment later, a large shadow blocked the sunlight and I stepped up on a pile of bricks for a better look. A large city bus had pulled up at the bus stop just to my left. An elderly couple and a couple of teenagers with their underwear hanging out of their pants got on. I was about to turn away when a familiar face caught my eye.

A large rectangular panel that ran for over half the length of the bus had an advertisement pasted on it, an advertisement that gave me a strong feeling of nostalgia while at the same time made me sick. Johnny Carson, not as I remembered him on *The Tonight Show*, but what I thought was a slightly haggard-looking Impal version of him, stared at me pleadingly from the yellow background of the advertisement. This incidentally was the same shade of yellow of the clouds hovering in the sky since the phenomenon started. His hands were open in supplication, like he was terribly desperate to relay his point. The caption read: *Help your loved ones and ancestors find peace and dignity, call 800-555-7789 for assistance.*

"Peace and dignity, indeed!" I spat. I hoped my favorite boyhood comedian had not done this willfully. For all anyone knew he had an iron rod shoved in his back or iron shackles around his feet when the picture was taken. Maybe he was begging them to let him go, not begging America to turn in Impals. That thought sent a chill up my spine.

As the bus thankfully pulled away, taking the despicable ad with it, I strained my neck and looked as far as I could to the right. A familiar sight caught my eye. Over a small building down the street, I could see the Washington Monument towering in the sky with all its majesty. It had a surreal quality as it was backdropped by the weird lavender sky and a couple of yellow cotton ball clouds. Based on my past experiences travelling to the nation's capital, I estimated we were only about a ten-minute walk from the Smithsonian or, more exactly, the Air and Space Museum.

My first impulse was to wake Seth and tell him the news, never mind I had no idea how I would get him there without being spotted. But that thought was dashed as Abraham Lincoln came down some wooden stairs directly across from me. He was followed by a strange man. In the light, I could not tell if the man was an Impal or not. The former president had a somber expression on his face.

CHAPTER 29
PLAYMATE

*"Monsters exist, but they are too few in numbers
to be truly dangerous. More dangerous are...the functionaries
ready to believe and act without asking questions."*

~Primo Levi

Lincoln spotted me by the window and walked over and patted me on the shoulder.

"How are you, Tommy?" he asked, his voice sounding surprisingly tired.

"Okay," I said, stifling another urge to erupt into a coughing fit.

"I'm sorry," he said, apologetic. "I didn't realize the dirt and dust would travel that far, I should have given you more time to get down the tunnel."

The mention of the tunnel caused me to make a furtive glance around the room for evidence of the opening. To my surprise, I saw no such evidence. Lincoln evidently saw the question in my eyes.

"The tunnel is not here, it is across the street," Lincoln said as he stood aside and beckoned the man behind him to come forward. "Thomas, this is Riggs Guffey. He owns this townhouse. We are in his basement."

Riggs Guffey extended his hand and I grasped it and shook. There was little doubt that this man was an Impal, my hand was frigid. The odd thing was that he didn't seem to have the same silvery sheen as the other Impals. Of course the lighting in this cellar was not ideal but Mr. Guffey almost seemed, well … I think normal is a relative term. Mr. Guffey looked like me. He looked like a flesher.

"Why don't you …?" I began but did not know how to finish.

Mr. Guffey raised one eyebrow, causing his bald head to wrinkle precariously. He put his hands on his narrow, blue jeaned hips and cocked his head to one side. He looked to be in his late 50s or early 60s, about my size and build. He wore a very hip Atari t-shirt over stooped shoulders and a sunken chest.

"Why don't I look like an Impal?" he finished for me.

I nodded my head stupidly, a few vestigial particles of dirt slid into my eyes, causing me to blink stupidly as well.

"Well, first of all, I am a recent convert, so to speak. What is the government calling us … RDIs?"

He shrugged, then continued.

"Well, anyway, I became this way just a few days ago. Talk about an out-of-body experience, oye!"

I didn't know whether to smile or not at his dry attempt at humor, but when I saw his smirky grin, I managed one of my own.

"I'm still upstairs, if you get my drift. Three days … it's a good thing us Impals can't smell too good, oye!"

He was still half-smirking and half-grinning, but all I could manage was something between a smile and a grimace. I couldn't help but think of Miss Chenowith passing away in her home. What if I had not been there to call it in? Well, that was stupid, she and Shasta would not have been taken away if I had not called it in. Part of me wanted to blame Mollie for turning them in. She probably had, considering recent events. But, even after her treachery; I don't think I can convince myself of that 100-percent. There was still too much room for doubt, and I wasn't going to be going back and asking our devious ex-host to confirm or deny. Not that I would believe anything she had to say.

Mr. Guffey had at least been smart enough not to let anyone know of his demise. But still, none of that explained why he looks different from other Impals.

"Back to your question. Why don't I look like an Impal?" he said as he stuck his hand in his pocket. I thought this was an odd gesture in itself because I had never seen an Impal put anything in his pocket, Seth included.

He withdrew his hand and held out a tightly-closed fist to me. I indulged him and stuck my hand out under his, palm up. I felt three metallic objects drop into my hand. Before my brain could register what they were, Mr. Guffey had begun to emanate the same ethereal glow as the other Impals in the room. I looked with dumb incredulity at what rested in my palm: three Duracell AA batteries.

"Does that help?" he said with a satisfied smile.

I stared at the batteries like they were some strange alien artifact.

"Batteries?" was all I could manage. "How?"

"Dunno," he said, "just figured it out by pure happenstance. I hadn't tried the TV since this whole thing started, didn't know it was out. I went to the drawer in the kitchen to get a fresh set of AAs for my remote and happened to notice the change on my hand. I looked in the hallway mirror, and wouldn't you know it? I looked normal again."

"How?" I blurted.

"Like I said, I don't know. I'm an accountant, not a scientist. Isn't it enough to know that it does work? A quick trip down to Walgreens," he said jerking his thumb over his shoulder, "and we can get all of us out of here inconspicuously." He glanced at Lincoln and frowned. "Well, the ones who aren't famous and have a little more modern attire, anyhow."

The dad side of me leapt for joy at the prospect of getting Seth out and about, not to mention taking him to the Air and Space Museum, or possibly even having a normal life—whatever normal may be now. The protective parent side of me called for caution. Could a battery be harmful to Seth? I had no answer for that question, but Mr. Guffey seemed to return to a "normal" Impal when he handed me the batteries.

I smiled and handed the batteries back.

"Incredible," I said.

"Indeed," Mr. Guffey said as he placed the batteries back in his pocket. The glow immediately faded like someone turning back a dimmer switch. A moment later he could have passed for just another one of the thousands of fleshers bustling about outside.

"Mr. Guffey spotted us last night when we came out of the tunnel in the basement across the street," Lincoln said.

"Saw the creepy glow coming through the basement windows," Mr. Guffey added. "Knew something was up and knew it had something to do with Impals."

"I'm glad he did," Lincoln said, stoic. "It's only a matter of time before the military finds out where the other end is. I don't think Mollie even knew that, thank God," he said, shaking his head dejectedly.

I wondered about Mollie's motives, not to mention her morality. Maybe it was just senility, but that concern was secondary to the point of where we were and what we would do next. What had happened, happened, and there was nothing we could do to change it.

Mr. Guffey came across the street last night with as many batteries as he could carry and led each and every Impal to the safety of his own basement. He then helped Lincoln and a couple of other battery-laden men carry me across.

"We only saw one cop," Mr. Guffey cackled, and then rotated his hand back and forth like a beauty contestant waving at admirers, "and he waved at me!"

I did appreciate Mr. Guffey's dry sense of humor, however morbid it tended to be. I guess if you didn't have a sense of humor in times like this, one could go completely insane. I wondered if insanity made any discrimination between Impals and fleshers. I thought it probably didn't, but I didn't care to test that hypothesis. My thoughts floated back to Jackson. I tried to push the image out of my head of the poor dog lying helplessly under tons of dirt, restrained for eternity with his iron collar. I think insanity would be a foregone conclusion in that scenario, whether man or beast, flesher or Impal.

"No, he was captured by the military," I told myself. He was probably doing tricks on some military base as we speak. I wasn't sure I believed that, but that was the story I was telling Seth. It was the only thing I could think of that wouldn't be too upsetting and yet not insult his intelligence. He is a smart kid.

The military did show up later that afternoon at the abandoned townhouse across the street. After at least 30 minutes of searching the basement and upstairs, they fanned out and began combing every alley and drainage ditch in a wide radius. I watched from the corner window of the cellar with Mr. Guffey as he nervously clutched a half-dozen AAAs he robbed from his ceiling fan remote. A fiery block of ice slid into my gut as I caught a glimpse of General Garrison pacing furiously up the street.

My heart leapt into my throat when we heard a loud knocking at the front door. This was accompanied by a muffled shout.

"Military, open up!"

To my surprise and relief, the soldiers gave up and went on their way after a couple of minutes of no response. I guess we hadn't reached the point yet where the military was indiscriminately kicking in doors. But I had no doubt that if they knew we were in the basement they would knock it off its hinges with no hesitation. I sat down on a nearby wooden crate, General Garrison's and Mollie's faces swimming in my head. Why? Why was he so hell bent? Did he actually believe he was doing the right thing or did he just get his kicks from doing this? Why had Mollie done this, especially to her own friend, Esther?

I remembered my psychology professor telling the class one time that men are not inherently evil, they just have misplaced values sometimes. Even some of the most heinous acts committed in the history of man, the perpetrators believed they were on the side of right. I guess some people are just born with a broken moral compass. It still pisses me off, though.

The Impals in the basement had huddled in the far corners, out of view of the windows. Some had immersed themselves in the brick wall. I'm sure the military knew that Impals are capable of passing through solid objects if they so desired and they would be difficult to find if they didn't want to be found. That is probably why the search was little more than a perfunctory inspection of the surrounding area. That, and the fact that it would be a PR disaster for the military to shake down homes and businesses just blocks from the White House.

I watched as the military vehicles started leaving one by one. The last three were large trucks with a canvas cover on the back, similar to the ones I had seen on the interstate. My heart sank as the last truck passed just a few feet from my vantage point. I saw the frightened face of Esther Baldwin peering out the open flap in the canvas, her hands bound in front of her like a common criminal.

My heart filled with rage when I saw this pitiful sight. The injustice, the brutality, not to mention the betrayal, was more than I could stand. I didn't know Esther Baldwin well at all, we had barely exchanged a few sentences in our brief acquaintance, but she was innocent. If she had been guilty of anything, it was being a long-time companion to an old woman, a woman whose moral capacity seemed to have withered over the years and now was as feeble as her arthritic hands and brittle legs. Maybe she thought she was doing the right thing, but … I just can't see how.

Strangely enough, as I watched the truck pull away, I saw a sight that made me feel a little better and at the same time caused my anger to soar. Sitting in Esther's lap, tongue lolling with excitement, was Jackson. I had told Seth earlier that morning that Jackson was gone and made up the story of him being a performing dog on the base. At least I only felt like half a liar now; the military did have him, but I had no clue as to what they were going to do with him. I could feel my ears turning red with fury when I thought of Seth's dejected little face and deluge of silvery tears when I told him the news of his friend's disappearance. My anger was cooled both literally and figuratively when I felt an ice-cold hand on my shoulder. I turned and looked into the somber face of Abraham Lincoln.

"I didn't know," he said. "I was there a few days and I never would have guessed. It seemed too good to be true, a refuge for Impals with a kind host. I guess I let hope get in the way of common sense. I'm sorry, Tommy."

"We would have come whether or not you were there," I said. "You have nothing to be sorry for."

He shook his head emphatically.

"People looked to me for reassurance, and I trusted her. I'm so sorry."

I took a deep breath and looked over Lincoln's shoulder. Seth and Patrick were playing together like they didn't have a care in the world. They had found a couple of discarded brooms and were playing out the epic lightsaber battle between Anakin Skywalker and Obi Wan Kenobi. To my surprise, Seth had subrogated the role of Anakin to Patrick.

A child's resilience can teach us a great lesson about letting go and moving on. They do it so easily; it is a fine art that most adults have forgotten over time. It is no wonder that kids don't have high blood pressure and ulcers. I decided at that moment to put Mollie out of my head, to move on, and to focus on our time together. I would learn from our experiences, to be sure, but I wouldn't dwell on them.

I didn't respond to Lincoln's second apology but instead changed the subject completely.

"So, was this building here when you were president?" I asked.

He blinked at me like I had just asked him to describe nuclear physics.

"Well ... yes, yes it was," he said, and proceeded to tell me an anecdote about a time he and Mary Todd had lunch on a bench just outside the basement window.

The next couple of weeks were interesting and, to say the least, uncomfortable. We stayed in the basement for obvious reasons, but none so obvious as when you stuck your head out of the basement door and into the kitchen. Mr. Guffey had been dead for several days when we first arrived, and the upstairs smelled like, well ... there really is no odor to compare it to, but I can honestly say it is one that is hard to forget. The odor was as horrific to the nose as I'm sure the remains of Mr. Guffey would have been to the eyes. I don't know for sure, because I never looked.

Since I was the only one who could walk around in public sans batteries, I made several trips to a number of neighborhood drugstores and convenience stores. Mr. Guffey had brought most of his wardrobe downstairs before the smell started to permeate everything, so I thankfully had a few changes of clothes. I couldn't have very well wandered about the streets with my mud-sullied clothes from the tunnel.

My mission was to collect as many different kinds or air fresheners and batteries as I could without being conspicuous. I accumulated several cans of Lysol and various other brands of smell-good products, along with enough batteries to power the space shuttle. The main thing I learned from this ordeal was the one thing that smells worse than a corpse is a Lysol, Glade, Renuzit, forest pine car freshener corpse. I know it is a disgusting thought, but that is the reality that we find ourselves faced with at the moment.

The moldy basement was like a rose garden compared to the rest of the house, so that is where I spent my home time. It wasn't that bad; at least I could play with Seth and his new friend, Patrick. I don't think it was really fair, but somehow I always got cast in the role of Darth Vader. You really have to be on your guard when two kids who barely come up to your waist are wielding broom-handle lightsabers. Fortunately for me, that was not all we played. An old checkerboard and a dusty deck of playing cards also provided hours of quality entertainment.

Patrick was starting to take to me as if I was the father he didn't have. I say "didn't" because the subject of his parents has yielded nothing. Every time I asked, he gave me a shrug and halfhearted smile, then clammed up, which is unusual considering the kid would talk my ear off otherwise. I don't know if they are living, Impals, or moved on. Dead just doesn't seem to have the same meaning anymore, at least not in the traditional sense. I think I was starting to realize that death has never really existed; there is no death, only transition. The evidence is all around me.

I was curious to know about Patrick's parents but that was a subject with which I would have to be patient. I couldn't do anything at the moment, anyway, other than to be his surrogate dad, and that is the role I would play for the little guy. If they were still around, I could imagine what they were going through right now. I could picture it vividly because all I had to do was think how I would feel about losing Seth.

As we played our games in the cellar of the ancient townhouse, some of the Impals ventured out cautiously, batteries in hand, or in pocket, as the case may be. They wisely never strayed more than a couple of blocks. I was encouraged from their reports that no one seemed to pay them any attention, including several police officers and military personnel. The Impals that made the transition prior to 1950 required a little more discretion, however. Due to their eternally antiquated wardrobe, they were forced to relegate their city walks to nighttime tours, avoiding the curious that might question why someone was dressed like they were in an episode of *The*

Untouchables, or worse yet, an episode of *Little House on the Prairie.* Sure they could have gone to a clothing store and gotten clothes to wear over their permanent Impal clothing, but clothing took a lot of effort for an Impal to keep on. My understanding is that it is much more difficult than squenching. It also wasn't worth the risk of having an eager clothing store clerk make contact with their skin, which would have been an instant giveaway.

Putting the clothing issue aside, what did all this mean? It meant that I might yet be able to keep my promise to Seth. We may be able to walk in the door of the Air and Space Museum just like any other father and son that the government deemed to be "normal." I was excited and had a sense of purpose again for the first time in a while. Things were going to work out. Things were going to be okay. At least that is what I thought until the next morning, when I woke up and Seth and Patrick were gone.

CHAPTER 30
ACROSS THE MALL

*"I am determined to live without illusions.
I want to look at reality straight. Without hiding."*

~Hanif Kureishi

I shot up off my cot when I realized the absence of the two boys, my heart hammering. I had been having the stupid dream again, the one that had been thankfully absent from my sleep since the storm began—the one where Seth disappears.

I calmed momentarily when my rational brain woke up and realized that they must be off playing somewhere. But, my rational brain was soon overruled when I conducted a search of the cellar and realized they were not there.

Surprisingly, no one had seen them leave. I almost kicked over one of the squench buckets—there were no animals in the cellar—as I bolted for the stairs. Taking them two at a time, I recklessly flung myself through the kitchen door and straight through the torso of

Abraham Lincoln. I let out a cry of shock as I fell back against the china cabinet, which fortunately had solid wood doors, not glass. Lincoln looked at me with an uncharacteristic expression of shock and horror. I had the wind knocked out of me, so he spoke first as he gingerly rubbed his abdomen where I had made my rude entrance.

"Are you okay, Tommy? What's wrong?" he asked with a disconcerted look at the open cellar door, which was gently tapping against the wall.

"Seth is gone!" I rasped as I pulled myself up and headed for the front door. I had barely taken two steps when I felt a cold hand on my arm.

"I'm here, Daddy," a familiar voice said.

I looked down to see Patrick beaming up at me, a silver spoon clutched in his other hand.

"Where's Seth?" I blurted.

Patrick gave me a sad frown and pointed to the other side of the kitchen. There sat Seth stuffing his mouth with a large spoonful of Chockit Berries, as he calls them. He beamed at me from across the green wooden table, his cheeks swollen like a hoarding hamster with his favorite cereal.

"Seth, where ... how ... I was worried," I stammered, hardly noticing the ever-prevalent odor that still permeated the upstairs of the house.

Impals seemed to have a very poor, if any, sense of smell. Eating a large bowl of cereal would have been the last thing I would attempt because I would have done my own version of squenching all over the antique tile floor. But the smell was the last thing on my mind right now.

I walked over and hugged my boy and kissed him on the forehead. "I was worried, son."

"I'm afraid that's my fault, Tommy," Lincoln said. "He asked for cereal and we didn't have his particular brand, so I ... went to the market around the corner."

"Like that?" I asked incredulously, pointing at Lincoln's clothing. Had he given us away, all for the want of Chockit Berries?

He straightened up with a look of righteous indignation on his face and grasped his lapels, running his hands up and down along the length.

"I can assure you, sir, that this was a very stylish wardrobe in my day, very stylish indeed."

I didn't mean any disrespect; my worry had gotten the better part of my brain for a few minutes. Thankfully, I saw the mischievous twinkle return to Lincoln's eye. He pointed to a coat rack in the corner where a long beige trench coat hung from one of the arms.

"As it turns out, Mr. Guffey's brother and I are about the same size, and he left his coat here last month," he said as he walked over and patted the pocket of the coat. "A pocketful of batteries didn't hurt either."

"No one recognized you?" I asked.

"I got some funny looks and some laughs, but I don't think anyone knew I was an Impal."

I shook my head in exasperation and sat down at the table beside Seth. I patted his cold little head while he shoveled the last remaining spoonful of chocolaty goodness into his mouth. I felt a cold tug on my other hand. I looked down to see Patrick smiling at me with anticipation. I patted him on the head and winked, then turned my attention back to Seth. I guess Patrick was expecting a little more, because he skulked across the room and sat down under the coat rack. A look of weary dejection melted his face into a pitiful frown. I was about to call him back when Seth spoke.

"Can we go to the moozem today, Daddy?" he asked.

I smiled and winked, then turned back to look at Patrick. He was gone.

"Where …?" I asked Lincoln as I pointed at the coat rack.

"He went back downstairs," Lincoln said then shrugged. "He didn't look too happy."

I started to get up and go after him when Seth spoke again.

"P-l-l-l-e-e-e-a-a-a-s-e, Daddy," he begged.

I looked at Lincoln.

"What do you think?" I asked. "Do you think it is safe?"

Lincoln motioned for me to follow him into the hallway. I did so, but not before soaking a kitchen rag in lemon juice and placing it over my nose and mouth; the smell was much, much worse out there. When we were reasonably out of earshot of Seth, he spoke.

"My honest opinion, Tommy? I don't think it will ever be completely safe for Impals. It's only a matter of time before they get wise to the battery trick, and then where will we be?"

"I don't think they have, though. I think we would have heard something about it on the radio."

The truth was there was very little news on the radio anymore. What there was had been filtered into government fluff pieces. The press was no longer free, just free of dissent. A chill ran down my spine when I thought of how all this had happened in such a short time.

Lincoln put his fist to his mouth and laughed; not a mirthful laugh, but one of restrained and somehow polite mockery. I guess that was the politician in him.

"Please tell me you don't believe that," he pleaded. "If they have discovered it, do you honestly think they would announce it to the public? That would certainly put a dent in their ability to round us up if they said they knew. For all we know, they might even have some high-fangled machine that detects Impals with batteries."

I shook my head and shrugged.

"You're right, of course," I said, casting a furtive glance over my shoulder at Seth, who had just prepared another heaping bowl of cereal. "So we just sit here and do nothing?"

Lincoln shook his head and smiled.

"Now, that wouldn't be living would it?" he said with a wink.

"You think we should go?" I asked.

"Tommy, life is always dangerous and full of risks, but those risks are what make life worth living." He waved his hand dismissively. "I know, I know … Impals aren't living life in the traditional sense, but the concept is the same."

I looked at him for a long moment. He returned my gaze with a serene smile.

"If I don't go now I may never be able to," I said. "This is what we came for, this is what I promised." I took a deep breath and finished. "We'll go today."

Lincoln said nothing but just smiled and patted me on the shoulder then went back down in the cellar. That was the last conversation we would have before Seth and I left for the museum. I was filled with excitement because it looked like I would finally be able to keep a promise to my son.

We left as a threesome a little after 10 A.M. It didn't take much coaxing to get Patrick to brighten up when I told him where we were going. There was no need for a change in wardrobe since both of the boys had fairly modern and hip clothing.

They each stuffed their pockets with a fistful of batteries. My heart both swelled and sank at the same time. Seth looked exactly like I remembered him before the accident. Not that much had changed other than the silvery glow was gone. It was not even a change in attitude. It was more like a reinforcement that I had my son, a reminder of what I had lost and then found again.

We stepped out the door and then turned left toward the Washington Monument, its tip barely visible above the surrounding buildings. Seth pointed excitedly when he spotted it looming over the top of a brownstone hotel and Patrick gave him an acknowledging smile. The walk to the mall only took five minutes, but in that time Seth said enough to fill a book—a thick one. He pointed out every historical site we came across and then gave a brief synopsis of the historical importance. I knew he was smart for his age, but geez. He could have probably made a good tour guide.

He asked to climb on my shoulders to get a better look at a

monument of someone on horseback across the street. At first I was hesitant because I knew Seth had a tendency to relax on occasion and, well … start sinking.

"Seth, stay steady and stay up, understand?" I said.

"Yes!" he said and smiled reassuringly.

I lifted him up and set him on my shoulders. He bounced excitedly a few times, causing his butt to sink between my shoulder blades, but that stopped when I squeezed on his calves.

"Seth, up and steady," I reminded him.

He instantly settled in, resting his hands on my cheeks. Luckily it was a warm day or that would have been very uncomfortable.

When we reached the Mall, I was dumbstruck with awe. It was a sight I could never get used to, no matter how many times I have visited the capital city. The sprawling expanse with the enormous Capitol building on one end, the gargantuan tower that is the Washington Monument in the center, and the impressive Lincoln Memorial on the opposite end were breathtaking sights to behold, but it was different today.

The lavender skies with the yellowish clouds were an eerie backdrop to the manmade beauty of the city. It was hard to describe, but it seemed to magnify everything, making the already impressive seem absolutely fantastic. Having been cooped up in a cellar for days caused me to forget about the weirdness of the phenomenon, but in a way it was good. If the skies were lavender and yellow and the nights looked like ultraviolet light on a black-light painting, then that meant Seth was still here. That being said, I think I could get used to it.

We had just come around the corner of the American History Museum when Seth spotted the goal to our quest across the way.

"There it is, Daddy!" he shouted.

I felt a cold hand on my side and looked down to see Patrick looking up at me with a hopeful expression, but once again, Seth drew my attention.

"Let me down! Let me down!" he shrieked with rabid, kid-like anticipation.

Fearing Seth's excitement would send him sinking all the way to my navel, I carefully lifted him off my shoulders and placed him on the ground. He was like a windup toy with one purpose in mind when he hit the ground with his feet churning. I laughed when I thought of the Energizer bunny, because Seth was running on batteries, in a manner of speaking, even though they were Duracell.

"Whoa, buddy!" I said as I grabbed his hand, which quickly sank through mine as he pulled away. "Seth!" I barked, probably a little too loudly, drawing the stares of several pedestrians. The last thing we needed was to draw attention to ourselves. To my relief he stopped and turned around.

"Sorry," he said.

I knelt down so I could look him in the eye.

"Remember, buddy, we have to be calm, we have to be smart, and then we can have fun."

"I've been good," Patrick mumbled.

Before I could acknowledge his comment, my heart leapt into my throat at a shrill noise behind us. I turned to see a police car flanked by two motorcycle cops. Trailing the police officers was a convoy of dark SUVs and a couple of limousines with fluttering flags adorning each side of the hoods. It was a motorcade of VIPs or dignitaries, maybe even the president himself. We couldn't tell for sure because a crowd swarmed in front of us to get a better look, obstructing our view.

We had gotten this far without drawing much attention to ourselves, so I decided not to press our luck. With the crowd's attention now drawn to the motorcade, I grabbed the boys' hands and led them across the grass toward the Air and Space Museum on the opposite side. We passed a carousel, which of course Seth begged to ride until I reminded him that our objective was just right across the street.

We crossed the street and went up the stairs; I think I was almost as excited as Seth as I could see some of the historic planes hanging from the ceiling through the large glass windows. When I looked back down, the wind drained right out of me as my heart sank. I had forgotten about security.

On any normal occasion, it would have been no big deal—just empty your pockets of anything metal and step through the detectors. Only these weren't normal circumstances. The one thing that Seth and Patrick had that was metal was the one thing they needed to keep their cover: the batteries.

CHAPTER 31
THE PLAN

"Nothing is more imminent than the impossible . . .
what we must always foresee is the unforeseen."

~Victor Hugo, "Les Miserables"

I grabbed the boys by the hands and led them as discreetly as I could to a bench not too far from the entrance. Patrick was still pulling, trying to get through the door, just as I felt his hand start to slip through mine I reached out and forcibly grabbed his other arm and directed him to the bench. The movement was regrettable. While it was impossible for me to hurt him physically, Impals' feelings are every bit as fragile as any flesher. He looked up at me with shocked surprise, making me feel like the biggest scumbag on the planet.

"I'm sorry," I said in a low apologetic voice. My sudden violent motion had drawn the ire of several bystanders as they looked at me like I *was* the biggest jerk on the planet. "We can't go in now; the batteries will set off the metal detectors."

His hurt and confused expression slowly faded into one of comprehension. Seth climbed in my lap and looked at me with a seriousness that seemed beyond his years, even though his comment was not.

"We can just take them out of our pocket and put them in that little bowl," he said.

I smiled and hugged him, but when I looked at Patrick, who was maybe a year or two older than Seth, he was shaking his head like that was the stupidest thing he had ever heard.

"You can't, dummy!" he said. "If you get rid of the batteries they can tell what you are!"

I reprimanded Patrick for his name-calling, but then quickly pointed out that he was absolutely right. I don't think he heard my validation of his remark because he sat down on a rock wall near the bench with a scowl on his face.

I racked my brains for several moments while Seth fidgeted impatiently on my lap. Patrick sat with a sullen expression, gazing blankly at the carousel across the street as happy children waved to proud, doting parents each time they completed another lap on their colorful steeds.

I guess I could say that I was vaguely aware of Patrick's unhappiness, but that would not be entirely accurate. The truth is I relegated it to the back of my mind as I pondered our dilemma. We had come too far and overcome too much to be stopped by something like batteries and a metal detector. I was trying hard to be a good father but in the process I was not being a very good surrogate father. Had I not learned anything?

The tunnel vision I had self-imposed before in the name of *financial security for my family* blinded me to the bigger picture of what was really important, what was more important than any monetary reward my absence from their lives could have provided. It seemed that I had pulled the old blinders out again, dusted them off, and renamed them *the mission to make my time with Seth worthwhile.*

Hadn't it already been worthwhile? Whether we made it in the museum or not, I would not have traded my last few weeks with Seth for anything. I don't think Seth would have, either. Sure, he would have been disappointed for a while if we couldn't go in, but he would have gotten over it. I guess I couldn't bear the thought of breaking another promise to him, not now … not like this.

My single-minded obsession eventually provided a viable yet dangerous solution. Seth and Patrick may look completely normal now with a pocketful of batteries, but they were still Impals, and that meant they could still pass through solid objects—objects like a museum wall or a window. The problem is that they would have to do it without being seen. That was a huge problem in a place with a lot of people and a lot of security. I had to think … where is the best place to accomplish this? A moment later the answer dawned on me.

My last visit here had been on a business trip when Seth was just four-years-old. I had an afternoon off and was glassy-eyed from a full morning of meetings, so I decided to get out and get some fresh air. I walked up the mall from the hotel and visited the Air and Space Museum. I am not sure why I chose this museum from all the other possible destinations in the capital city, maybe it was because I had watched the movie *Apollo 13* the previous night in my hotel room and I had space on my mind. I had a nice visit, and just as I was preparing to leave, a thunderstorm hit. Having no umbrella and no raincoat, I decided to wait it out in the museum.

After 30 minutes of steady downpour with no letting up in sight, I broke one of my rules that I had vowed I would not do again: I ate fast food. No, I didn't walk to one; as convenience would have it, there was a large McDonalds attached to the museum

This particular restaurant was most unorthodox for a typical McDonald's; it was solid glass from floor to ceiling. It provided an impressive view of the surrounding buildings through the rain streaked glass ceiling. On one side of the restaurant there were rows of tables along the glass windows, windows that ran right up to the sidewalk on the back of the building. On the surface that wouldn't sound like anything noteworthy except for the fact that the tables obstructed lower three feet of the window. I knew this because I had been startled to see a young couple sitting against the outside glass and making out when I sat down with my Big Mac and Coke. It was nearly impossible for someone inside to see a person sitting outside the window or, perhaps, a child crawling through it.

The outside of the window was the rub because it had a clear and unobstructed view from the street. Someone, especially a wanted someone could easily be spotted from outside. But, assuming the place hadn't been remodeled since my last visit and we timed it carefully, this could work.

With exhilaration of newfound hope, I jumped up and grabbed Seth and Patrick by their hands and led them to the sidewalk. Both boys were resistant at first until I sat them down on a bench a good distance from the hustle and bustle of the entrance.

"I thought we were going to the moozem, Daddy," Seth said in a pitifully sad voice. Patrick didn't say anything; he just looked at me with a mixture of sadness and curiosity.

I explained to both boys my plan in detail, making sure they understood every single aspect, emphasizing the consequences of what could happen if we got caught.

"You mean they would take me away?" Seth asked.

Patrick still did not speak, instead he alternated his gaze between me and Seth for a moment, then smirked and stared at the ground.

I guess I had been operating under the assumption that Seth was fully aware of what was going on. He is a smart kid, and even though I had not come right out and told him he was in danger of being rounded up like a wanted criminal, I assumed that laying low in the back of the SUV with Jackson, narrowly escaping the police after his kidnapping and carjacking, fleeing down an old tunnel with the military in pursuit, hiding in a basement for days, and then having to use batteries to go out in public incognito, well … I assumed he had taken the hint. Kids are trusting and optimistic as a general rule, a little too much at times. It ripped my heart out as I watched his innocence wash away as the truth sank in. He looked at me with terrified eyes.

Tears dropped from Seth's cheeks and then turned to silvery streaks in midair before disappearing without a trace into the sidewalk. Like any good father would, I reached out and pulled Seth tight, taking care not to squeeze too hard, which could give us away to an observant bystander. This did not help Patrick's sullen attitude. He looked at us as if I were a dancing hippopotamus in a tutu, and then he started walking slowly up the street, staring down at his shoes.

We caught up to Patrick before he made it to the end of the block. He didn't look at me but reluctantly took my hand as we made a right turn and around the glass McDonald's attached to the east side of the museum. I could see dozens of people dining on fast food goodness along with a large number of kids running about. It was getting close to lunchtime and the place was packed; this was not going to be easy to do without being spotted.

We made it to the next corner a minute later and made another right turn. A few moments later, we were at a large courtyard area that separated the McDonald's from the sidewalk. The courtyard spanned the length of the restaurant up until a few feet before it connected with the actual museum. It was sparsely populated by small round flower beds, a number of stone benches, and a few trash receptacles. Most of the benches were full of weary tourists and one was occupied by a sleeping homeless man. I did a double-take at the man because there was something unusual about him. Was he...? I didn't have time to ask the question, because before I could fully form the thought, it was answered for me.

A loud screeching of tires behind me made me jump with surprise and when I turned around and saw the police officers piling out of their DC Metro cruisers, I knew what was going on. I grabbed Seth and Patrick, turning them away from the scene and directing their focus to the other side of the courtyard. I believe I was successful in diverting Seth's attention but not Patrick. He watched with fervent curiosity as the hapless man, who was actually a hapless Impal, was cuffed with iron around his neck and wrists, then savagely tossed into the back of the lead police cruiser. I was shocked at what happened next.

A smattering of applause rang out from a good number of the bystanders. Not everyone clapped, though. Several people had looks of disgust on their faces, like me, but it was enough to give me a moment of pause, which quickly turned into a moment of rage. I felt like breaking every single one of their hands. What the hell did they mean by applauding such barbaric behavior? Surely the government had not been this effective with anti-Impal propaganda in such a short period of time.

I guess if you repeat a lie long enough, people will eventually start to believe it. If a person had no Impal acquaintances then really they had no idea what to believe and no choice but to believe the government. Why not believe that Impals are devious, want to take over, and will very shortly cause a population problem? After all, the moniker of ghost or spirit has carried a negative connotation for centuries.

I had not felt this vulnerable on our entire journey as I felt at this exact moment. I was asking two young boys to pull together and potentially reveal themselves to a group of people who obviously despised them, all to go and look at a bunch of old airplanes. Was I crazy? No, I just loved my son too much to disappoint him again. I had to keep my promise. There was no other option.

A pair of Army trucks rumbled by on the street, probably full of Impals, but I did not look. I was determined to have nothing shake my resolve as I led the boys over to a bench, less than a foot from the glass window of McDonald's. I sat them down and began to give them instructions, putting our fate in the hands of two young boys who wouldn't even be old enough to vote if they combined their ages. When I had finished, I stood up and patted both of their heads reassuringly, gave them a wink and the most confident smile I could muster, and then set out for the main entrance on the other side of the building. I looked over my shoulder as I rounded the corner of the restaurant; both boys were still sitting on the bench as I had instructed and swinging their legs with nervous excitement. They passed from view as I made the turn and I focused myself on the task at hand, picking up the pace a little as I headed for the entrance.

A few minutes later, I was in the line for security check. As far as I could tell, I had no more metal on me than the zipper on Mr. Guffey's borrowed slacks. I passed through the metal detector flanked by intimidating security people with solid black uniforms brandishing a museum patch on the right breast, which depicted the Kitty Hawk and the space shuttle. I made it through with not so much as a beep.

I felt a strong tinge of worry when I saw one of the security people looking at me conspicuously, a large black woman with short bobbed hair and a rigid stone face. After a few moments she smirked, shook her head, and turned her attention back to the door. I assumed she was looking at my white ankles exposed by my loaner britches, which were about two inches too short and just slightly snug in the waist. Yes, I looked like a dork. Especially with the brown bowling shirt, but with the millions of people that came through here each year, I was sure they had probably seen worse.

Not wanting to leave Seth and Patrick alone any longer than I had to, I quickly rushed to the gift shop to carry out the next objective of my plan: I bought batteries. I figured about six AAs apiece would suffice; I didn't know how to judge a battery's life expectancy with an Impal anymore than I could explain what was going on with the phenomenon. Sometimes you just have to wing it and hope for the best.

I made my way across the museum as casually and covertly as I could. Until I was passing the Apollo 11 capsule, it didn't sink in how much I had been sweating. The cool, sterile air pumping from the vents high above is common in most museums and something that I appreciate under normal circumstances, but not today. When I passed under the behemoth vent, I felt like 100 Impals had touched me all at the same time. My chest under my saturated shirt, my pasty arms and face not to mention the back of my neck all screamed with shock as the frigid air engulfed me. It was not an overly warm day, but my nervous perspiration made me look like I had just come in from the desert. A young couple passed by, pushing matching strollers, one with an infant and the other with a toddler. The man paused to look at me.

"Are you all right?" he asked, genuine concern in his voice.

"Yes," I replied as I wiped sweat beads from my brow and the end of my nose. My heart thundered in my chest as another security guard passed, looking at me suspiciously. "I just ran here from the Lincoln Memorial to catch up with my wife and son," I lied. It must have been a convincing lie because he nodded his head and smiled then continued on with his wife.

The security guard was not as convinced of my benevolence. He continued to look at me for several moments after the couple walked on. I suppose I would have stared at me as well in all my sweat-saturated, high-water pants dorkiness. I stood out and that was not good. As I sat down on a nearby bench to try and collect myself, I stupidly wondered if that would be considered as some sort of illegal profiling. My self-indulgence into politically incorrect humor did little to calm my nerves. The only thing that would do that is time, no ... that's not true. The only thing that would do that is to get Seth and Patrick safely back to Mr. Guffey's. When I felt that I had reasonably reduced my perspiration from a downpour to a drizzle, I stood up and set out for the large golden arches on the opposite side of the exhibit hall.

As luck would have it, we were now on the backside of the lunch hour so there were only a few people in line. They were scattered among the five lines that were open, so fortunately there was one completely devoid of patrons. As I walked up to place my order, a pimple-faced, redheaded teenager smiled broadly from behind a set of glasses that looked like a pair of Coke bottle bottoms. He didn't look at me judgmentally, but instead just happily took my order. I guess the young man was not a hypocrite, because his awkward appearance probably trumped my own.

I ordered my old standby, a Big Mac and chocolate shake; I didn't feel very hungry, but that was not the point. If I went to the table without an order it might draw attention. In the two minutes it took to get my food, I tried to discreetly look at the window where Seth and Patrick should be waiting. It was a good 30 yards away and I didn't see them, which caused me a twinge of worry, but that was also a good thing if they were following instructions, staying low and inconspicuous.

I set my gift store bag containing the batteries on my tray and casually walked toward the window where the boys should be waiting. I paused when I saw an attractive young woman sitting about ten feet away from the planned point of entry for the boys. She had a preschool age girl who was contentedly munching on fries as she examined her happy meal toy, which looked like a horse with a rainbow-colored mane. The woman was bottle feeding an infant while she took intermittent sips of her soft drink. I hoped they would get up and leave soon, because she had a clear line of sight to where the boys would be coming in. I slowly approached the table and sat down, peering carefully over the table as I sat. My heart both lifted and dropped at the same time. Seth was there waiting patiently, just as I had instructed. When he saw me through the glass his face lit up with excitement. The problem was that Patrick was nowhere to be seen.

Seth had been good and patient and followed my instructions, but when he saw me, caution fled his brain. I had not given him the signal or even had a chance to get the batteries out of their package and ready to hand off to him. He dropped his batteries on the concrete of the courtyard where they slowly started rolling toward the street.

Seth dropped to his knees and slowly pushed his now luminescent body through the glass. A few moments later he was hunkered under the table with his hand outstretched for a battery refill.

I quickly tore at the package and popped it open, sending batteries scattering across the table and dropping with loud clicks into the floor. Seth scooped them up and stuffed them in his pocket. The silvery glow faded, restoring his flesher appearance. I started to breathe a sigh of relief as Seth climbed out from under the table and took a seat across from me. My breath was cut short when I looked at the woman. She was staring at us with a look of bewilderment frozen on her delicate features. The drizzle of sweat turned back into a downpour as my guts twisted with panic. She was going to scream or report us or something, and that would be the end—the end of our journey, and the end of my gift of borrowed time with my son.

CHAPTER 32
JOURNEY'S END

"Words have no power to impress the mind w
ithout the exquisite horror of their reality."

~Edgar Allan Poe

To my surprise, the woman did none of the above. She continued to look at me with the same expression for a few moments and then looked at Seth. He smiled at her with his infectious grin then reached over and took a sip of my milkshake. The only thought that penetrated my numb brain was that his casual sip would require squenching later. I also realized at that moment that I needed to perform my own brand of squenching as well. I had too much coffee before we left that morning. It's amazing what insignificant thoughts our brains sometimes highlight for us under extreme stress.

Her fear started to slowly melt from her face as a pleasant smile formed. The reaction by her daughter to Seth's sudden appearance helped her relax a little. The little girl had not seen Seth until he had been out from under the table for a few moments, but when she noticed him sitting there she crinkled her nose and protested.

"Eeeeeew, a boy," she said as she turned in her seat to face away from Seth to where there was absolutely no chance that they could make accidental eye contact. The woman leaned over and whispered a few scolding words to the pretentious tot, then looked at me.

"Sorry," she said in a whisper.

I smiled and lightly waved my hand to indicate no problem.

"*Is he your son?*" she mouthed more than she spoke.

I nodded my head and smiled.

"He's a cutie," she said, a little more audibly this time.

"Thank you," I said, and then looked searchingly at her. Was she just trying to play it cool until she could blow the whistle on us?

She gave me an understanding smile and leaned toward me as much as the infant in her arms would allow.

"My husband died last week. I am here to talk to our Congressman about what is going on. It is very unfair." A pair of tears slid off her cheeks and splashed delicately on the side of the baby bottle.

"The military took him?"

"Yes, based on that stupid Executive Order," she said between sniffles. "Members in Congress are fighting it but I don't know if it will do much good. Too many people believe what they are being told. Aaron was … *is* a good man. He is not a threat to anyone." She looked at Seth and then back to me, tapping the skin on her forearm.

"How?" she asked.

I held up the torn battery package and then placed it in my burger bag.

She gaped at me incredulously for a minute then her lip started to quiver. She bit her lip and mumbled in a distant voice.

"That easy. If only I had known, Aaron might still be with us."

I looked at her sympathetically. I could definitely understand her pain. But while I felt sorry for her, I also had my own problems to consider. Seth and I were finally here, but I knew we needed to move because I didn't know if the batteries would last forever or just a few hours. We needed to take our tour and get back to safety as soon as possible. I also had another issue to worry about: where was Patrick?

"Mrs....?" I asked.

She smiled sheepishly.

"Cower," she said. "Andrea Cower."

"Mrs. Cower, it's very nice to meet you. I'm Thomas Pendleton."

She nodded her head and smiled.

"Seth and I really need to get going, we came a long way to get here, and I'm afraid we may not have a lot of time. It was a pleasure to meet you, and I wish you luck with your Congressman. Hopefully, this will get better soon." I didn't really believe the latter, not after everything I had seen, but one must always have hope.

She smiled and extended her baby-free hand. I took it and shook.

"Good luck to you, Mr. Pendleton. Please stay safe and protect your boy," she said.

I nodded and took Seth by the hand and led him toward the door leading back into the museum. When we were out of sight of Mrs. Cower and her small family, I picked out a secluded, vacant table and led Seth there and we sat down across from each other.

"Seth, where is Patrick?" I asked.

He shrugged.

"He said he was bored and was going to go back home." He frowned. "He said he didn't want to look at a bunch of stupid old airplanes."

"What did you tell him, Seth?"

"I said they had rockets and spaceships, too."

"No, what did you tell him when he said he was going home?"

He shrugged and said, "I told him he was being stupid and that *we* would have fun without him."

I winced as Seth spoke the words. I knew Patrick was feeling left out and was desperate for my attention since he had no parents, at least none that we knew of. I had intended on trying to make it up to him once we were in the museum, but now that was not to be. I felt sorry for the little guy, I truly did. I hoped he made it back to Mr. Guffey's safely, and I probably should go after him, but I couldn't put Seth at risk to do that. Patrick knew where to go for safety and Seth and I were finally here. Maybe it was selfish, but I wasn't going to let a kid I barely knew upset that. The problem was that I did feel responsible and I did feel guilty. Like it or not, it was going to affect my mood the rest of the day.

"Okay." I stood up. "Let's go have fun," I said as I took Seth by the hand.

We walked into the museum hand in hand with little notice from the security personnel. I guess I looked a little more normal with a happy and excited kid in tow. Seth happily skipped inside and made a beeline for the first exhibit we saw, a large-scale replica of Skylab. Once he had perused the inner rooms of the large simulation, I strongly urged that we should take a restroom break. As I mentioned earlier, I had drank too much coffee that morning and now my bladder seemed to be stretched to its limit. The cold air in the museum didn't help matters, either. I also knew that in the course of my conversation with Mrs. Cower, Seth had taken several more sips of my chocolate shake. I guided Seth into a stall where he could squench privately while I took care of my business.

We had the best time over the next hour. We decided to go upstairs first and then work our way down. Seth was as bright-eyed and happy as I had seen him in a long time. As I watched him go from exhibit to exhibit with sheer joy and ecstasy etched in his small face, my eyes welled up with tears of regret. Why had I put this off for so long? He was not just excited about seeing the cool airplanes and space stuff; his occasional looks of glowing admiration were all the confirmation I needed that he was happy to be here with me. He was happy to be here with his daddy.

We were just about to leave an exhibit containing moon rocks and meteorites when we heard a loud commotion downstairs. The continuous droning noise of a buzzer echoed through the museum. I peered over the railing overlooking the downstairs where we had an unobstructed view of the front door. My suspicion was confirmed when I saw the red light on top of one of the walk through metal detectors, someone had set it off. My first thought was that someone must have forgotten their Coke money or their keys, or perhaps it was a smoker who had forgotten and left his lighter in his pocket. Those theories were quickly dashed when I saw a group of no less than six security guards sprinting madly in our direction from below.

My heart jumped into my throat because I had the disturbing notion that they were coming for us, but if that were the case, why was the metal detector going off? That idea was replaced with a cold hard truth as I looked below me and saw the subject of their pursuit. My heart sank down from my throat and slid into my gut like a block of ice. Fear and regret filled me like a poison when the certainty of what was happening had sunk in. The guards were pursuing Patrick, who had evidentially bolted through the metal detector. My first thought was to hide, but that thought had come too late because Patrick had spotted me and was heading for the stairs.

I took Seth by the hand and started to walk toward the stairs on the opposite side of the museum, but it was no use because everyone in the museum had stopped to look as I heard Patrick pointing in my direction and yelling.

"Daddy, wait!" he screamed frantically as he bounded up the stairs.

I found that we had but one option. Running away would not be effective because I was reasonably certain we would have been stopped and questioned before we made it out of the museum. No, with attention now focused in our direction, plus a crazed Impal kid bearing down on us, we had no choice but to stay put and hope for the best. Hope was not on our side today.

The logic of children has always escaped my comprehension, possibly because there is rarely any actual logic to it, only a kid's view of how the world operates. What they desperately want to be the truth often becomes logical facts in their minds. I understood what Patrick was trying to accomplish, as horrible as it may be, but that didn't make the situation any better. I was filled with a bizarre mix of shock, rage, terror, and pity that had me frozen in place, unable to react, unable to stop it.

When Patrick reached us, he turned on Seth with venomous fury, knocking him to the ground.

"Get away from him, Impal!" Patrick shouted.

I started to move toward them, but it was too late. Patrick had voided Seth's pocket of the batteries and they went rolling across the floor and under the railing, dropping with loud metallic clangs as they hit an airplane a couple of stories below.

Patrick sat up triumphantly and turned to look at me with a huge smile as if seeking approval and praise for what he had just done. I felt like I was moving in slow motion as I fell to my knees and clambered toward them. Patrick's full attention was now fixed on me as his smile grew bigger, splitting his freckled face from ear to ear. His attention diverted, he did not notice Seth's shimmering hand moving toward his pocket until it was too late. Seth scooped the batteries out of Patrick's pocket and, in one fluid motion, flung them past the railing, pelting the same airplane again.

Patrick turned on Seth furiously and they both started to roll about like a large glowing ball as they scuffled. I moved to break them up but just as I grabbed Seth's arm, I felt two pairs of strong hands grab me by each arm and pull me backward. I landed squarely on my back, expelling every ounce of air from my lungs. As I gasped and tried to roll myself over to get up, I heard a sound that filled me with terror, the loud clanking of iron.

I pushed myself up, still sucking desperately for a breath, but in some ways I wish I hadn't. I saw the sight that had filled my nightmares ever since I saw that first Impal girl in the Army truck. Patrick and Seth had iron collars around their necks and were being pulled rudely to their feet. Patrick looked stunned while Seth wailed inconsolably; silvery tears disappeared through the carpet just in front of his Spiderman tennis shoes. What the hell had I done?

With every ounce of strength I had left, I lunged forward trying to take Seth in my arms, trying to hug him, to console him, to tell him everything would be okay, that Daddy would make it better, to tell him that I love him ... but that was not to be. Before I could scarcely move I felt a blinding white pain on the back of my head, and everything went black.

Seth was left alone.

CHAPTER 33
THE SHREDDER

*"Genocide is an attempt to exterminate a people,
not to alter their behavior."*

~ Jack Schwartz

I didn't see how Hell could be any worse than what I had endured. I had been shut away in a hole that seemed every bit as dark and joyless as the void in my heart, a void that refused me sleep, refused me an appetite, and refused me happiness. How could I be happy when Seth was gone and I had no idea where he was or what they were doing to him? My head had healed rather quickly after my incarceration, but my soul was damaged beyond repair. After all, this was my fault. I could have kept him safe, kept him hidden, but as Lincoln said, *"What kind of life would that be?"* I didn't know the answer to that, but I did know that we would probably still be together, and to me that seems like a pretty damn good life.

My first inclination was to blame Patrick, but really how could

I? I mean he was just a kid, a kid with no parents and a desperate desire to have that connection again. I could tell by the brief look I had at his face shortly after the iron collar had been slapped on that he realized he had made a mistake, but it was too late.

I did some really stupid things as a kid, like trying to get Cindy Carmichael to like me. We were both five-years-old at the time, and for some reason I got the idea that the best way to get her attention was to dump a bucket of minnows over her head. That didn't have the desired effect, and I probably had an expression on my face similar to Patrick's after Cindy brained me with the aluminum minnow pail before marching home to tell her folks. No, I couldn't exactly blame Patrick, but having no one to blame for the situation did not make me feel better, so I blamed myself.

I have had a long time to think about what happened that day in the museum. I haven't seen the sun since then and my watch was confiscated, but, judging by the frequency of my room service, I would guess that it has been at least a month. Room service in this case is a tray filled with what seemed to be grisly leftovers shoved through an opening in the bottom of the iron door separating me from freedom. There were no windows in the room except for one small one near the top of the door which looked out into a placid white hallway. The only items in the room were a worn out old cot, a toilet, a sink, and a tiny table with two small chairs. The table was so small that two grown men could not have sat across from each other with their elbows on the edge of the table and not touched. I could be anywhere, but no one was talking, not even my usual cordial visitor.

I had received just two visitors since I had been imprisoned, not counting the faceless person or persons that shove my food through the door. The first was General Ott Garrison himself. He came under the guise of collecting information, but I think it was more of an attempt to gloat since we had eluded him so embarrassingly when we escaped through the tunnel. He acted as if he did not recognize me, but I could see the look in his eye, a look of hateful recognition. He didn't divulge any information, and I did not give any since he would not answer my one simple question as to what they had done with Seth. That's all I said to the man, and I don't care to say any more.

My usual cordial visitor did not start coming until a few days after General Garrison's first visit, but he has been coming about every couple of days since then. He would never give me his name, requesting that I refer to him simply as Sarge. He was a middle-aged man, maybe late thirties or early forties. His normally brown hair was cut in a typical military buzz, and his pale blue eyes exuded trust. He always wore standard Army camo with no name and no rank insignia. He was a very nice man, and always listened with polite interest to my stories about Seth and our trip to Washington.

We had visited about four times in the past month and on his last visit he had promised to check on Seth. He showed up a day earlier than expected with urgent news. He didn't relay the same calm and collection as he had on his visits before; he seemed very troubled.

"What is it?" I asked him as he sat down at my tiny table with his hands folded before him as if in prayer.

"It's ready," he said so distantly, as if his voice were coming from a faraway crypt.

"What's ready?" I asked. I didn't like the tone of the conversation, and it began to feel like icy fingers were massaging my spine.

He blinked as if he had just awakened from a trance. He looked at me for several long moments before he spoke.

"The—the Tesla gate," he said with the same haunted voice.

"Tesla gate? What is that?" I asked, starting to worry.

He blinked at me then took a deep breath, sidestepping my question, at least for the moment.

"Mr. Pendleton, I have two kids, two girls. They are the whole world to me. I'm sure you understand."

I nodded. That was the one thing he had said so far that I did understand. I understood it very painfully.

"I would do anything to protect them … *anything*," he said.

He stood up and walked to the door, staring blankly through the small porthole. He rubbed his nose and I could have sworn I heard a faint sob from the man.

"My grandfather is in one of these detention centers in Arizona. He passed away when I was just nine-years-old. I never got to see him after this phenomenon started, not till he was rounded up and chained in a room like a criminal."

He let out a small bark of a laugh that sounded more like a wounded animal than anything remotely humorous.

"He told me he loved me, can you believe that? He told me he loved me even though I was a part of the people that had done this to him. Can you believe that?"

"Yes, I can," I said. "He's your granddad."

"Do you think your son would still tell you that, Mr. Pendleton?"

I looked him square in his eyes, which I could now see were swollen with tears, and answered without hesitation.

"Absolutely."

He looked at me searchingly then slowly started to nod his head.

"I hope you get that chance, Mr. Pendleton, because I know where Seth is."

"Where?" I asked with every muscle in my body, including my heart, taut with anticipation.

"You are in a military detention center in Quantico, Virginia," he said, then pointed at the wall by my cot. "Seth is about 150 yards that way."

I turned stupidly as if I expected to see him standing there smiling his goofy kid smile, but all I saw was the dull gray wall of my cell.

"Chained?" I asked as my stomach knotted.

Sarge nodded and swallowed hard.

"Yes, but not for long."

When I first heard this statement, my first thought was he would be released soon, or at least unchained. The optimist in me jumped for joy, but Sarge's tone didn't suggest a celebration was in order, actually quite the opposite.

"What do you mean?" I asked.

He sat on my cot and put his chin on his knuckles.

"Rounding up Impals and locking them up was only going to work for so long, they knew that. That's why they have been testing this—this Tesla gate. Some of the less sensitive among us have nicknamed it 'The Shredder.'" It sounded like the last word caused Sarge a lot of pain to utter.

I wasn't 100-percent sure why, but the name seemed to cause sharp ice to slide down my throat and into my belly. I could feel fear and worry starting to gnaw at me like a nest of hungry rats.

"What is the Tesla gate?" I asked.

He looked at me stony-faced for several moments before he answered.

"It's supposed to get rid of Impals, puts them back where they belong."

"How does it do that?" I asked.

Sarge shrugged.

"I'm not a scientist, but as near as I can figure, it switches their energy signature back to the way it was before the phenomenon started. Puts them back in the dimension or realm or other level, whatever the hell you wanna call it … it puts them back where they were, or should be."

"Have you seen them test it?" I asked, the fear and worry taking bigger bites of my soul with each passing second.

He nodded.

"I have."

"Did it work?" I prodded.

Sarge shrugged and then stared at the floor for several long moments. I think he started to cry again, but that was the least of my concerns. I only wanted one thing—Seth.

"I don't know for sure, they disappeared and didn't come back.

We couldn't detect any sign of them afterwards."

"How do you know it didn't kill them?"

He blinked at me and started to state the obvious, that they were already dead, when the meaning sunk in; he stared at his hands. Could a soul be destroyed? I didn't think so, but before this phenomenon started I didn't think ghosts existed.

"I-I don't, I guess it's possible," he said rubbing a fist under his nose. "Oh, Jesus, we have to move and move today. Oh God, oh Jesus ..." he repeated over and over again.

I agreed, we needed to move today because if they were about to start feeding Impals into the Tesla gate, or the shredder, Seth didn't have much time. Even if this damned machine did exactly what they claim it does, the best case scenario is that Seth would be back where he was, alone in a world that is invisible to me. If there was any chance at all, I had to act and act fast. I tried to push my fear and worry firmly down and concentrate on what Sarge and I could do. As it turned out, it was quite a bit considering his clearance and access. It was hard for me to trust anyone in the military, but I realized I had little choice if I wanted to save Seth. Besides, after a month of consideration I already had my own plan in mind—a plan that would require Sarge's help, but not his knowledge or consent. There was only one thing I could do to help Seth and Sarge was providing me with the means to do it.

In less than 30 minutes, I had a camo uniform that fit fairly well considering my slight paunch. He also showed up with some items that were necessary but made me very uncomfortable: a couple of handguns and half-dozen grenades. I had done target practice with my dad when I was a kid, but it had been years since I had handled a gun. I don't even hunt. The grenades made me the most uncomfortable, and he handed the lot of them to me.

"You are going to need these for your part of the plan. Put them in your pockets and keep them there until you are ready to use them," he said like I was a new recruit, which in a sense I was.

I complied and put one in each of my utility pockets, handling them like an egg that could shatter from the slightest pressure.

Sarge explained the plan in detail, showing me a map of where the shredder was located in a nearby hangar and where the Impal detention area was in relation to it. I paid attention somewhat; I had other plans in mind, but I did not tell him. I had other plans in mind because his was just too risky and had too limited options. I had been thinking about this since I woke up in this God-forsaken place. I was convinced that my approach would be the appropriate one; I just needed the opportunity. Thankfully, Sarge was giving me that opportunity.

I was supposed to approach the building containing the shredder through a back door that was unguarded. When I got inside, I was to release the deadly contents in my pockets at the damned machine, thus accomplishing two objectives – to destroy it and to create a distraction so Sarge could free Seth.

He turned to me once he had looked out the door to make sure the coast was clear.

I grabbed him on the upper arm. This was all happening so fast and I had too many questions.

"Why are you helping me?" I asked.

"We don't have time," he protested.

I didn't back down. I looked at him sternly, demanding an answer.

"Because I'm a parent and I would do anything for my kids."

I nodded my head in agreement but refused to break eye contact; I knew there was something he wasn't telling me.

He sighed and shook his head slowly. "I have a lot to amend for," he said.

I stared at him, waiting for an answer.

"My name is not Sarge, and I am not a sergeant. You should know that before we go through with this. My name is Cecil. Major Cecil Garrison."

When I heard the last name I looked at him with narrowed eyes.

He saw my expression and turned three shades of red before he replied.

"Yes, General Ott Garrison is my father, but please don't hold that against me. We haven't seen eye to eye on several things for a number of years."

The shock of discovering who I had been talking to all these weeks left me speechless for several moments, but like a slowly erupting volcano, I felt the anger well up in me and then explode into a fiery accusation.

"You've been pumping me for information to take back to him, haven't you?"

He looked at me with sincere hurt etched in his face, enough so that I immediately felt guilty for hurling the allegation. He shook his head and turned back to the door.

"I understand why you would think that, but trust me, it is not true. All I want to do is help Seth and you and all Impals."

As angry as I was, I realized that I had two choices. I could trust him and seize this opportunity, or I could continue to sit in my cell and do nothing. When I looked at it that way, there was really only one choice.

"Okay," I said.

Without another word, we walked out the door and turned to the right down the hall. I don't know if it was always like this or Major Garrison had cleared the floor, but there was no one in sight.

The revelation of the identity of my cordial visitor did not change what I had resolved in my mind after weeks of pondering. If anything, it strengthened my resolve. I had to deviate from Garrison's plan; I really must. I had no choice. I had to do what was best for Seth. I had convinced myself it was the right thing to do.

I found my way outside and it didn't take long to locate the building. It was a huge hangar about 100 yards away. Major Garrison wished me luck and headed down a path through a grove of oak trees to our left. I watched him disappear around a brick building in the distance.

I took a deep breath and headed toward the hangar to carry out my amended plan. I was scared as hell, but I would do anything for Seth. I started out walking at a good pace, my heart hammering against my ribs liked a caged bird. I took special care not to jostle my cargo until it was time. Unfortunately, that time was closer than I realized.

Just as I cleared the group of trees, I saw a sight that made my heart stop. There was a large paved tarmac in front of the hangar, probably at least a quarter of a mile long, full of Impals all lined up in straight lines with their necks and hands bound with iron. They were being marched slowly toward the hangar. It was happening already.

I couldn't see Seth or Major Garrison anywhere, but that did not deter me. As disturbing as this sight was, it actually made my plan so much easier. I started in a sprint toward the hangar, yelling at the top of my lungs. I pulled a grenade out and waved it crazily in the air. I had no intention of pulling the pin, what was the use? There were probably other "shredders" elsewhere.

I had gotten about ten yards from the hangar when it felt like two huge fists punched me in the back. I sprawled forward, and then got to my feet to continue my stampede, but something was wrong, or maybe a better word is something was right. Something had definitely changed. I looked in my hand that had been carrying the grenade: the grenade was gone. But even though I had planned this, knew what must be done, it was still a shock as much as it was a relief. The hand holding the grenade was devoid of any weapon, but it glowed with the same ethereal light as Seth and all the other Impals I had encountered. It was actually a pleasant feeling, nothing hurt and I felt more alive I think than I ever have. I looked down and saw my lifeless body, blood pooling from two large gunshot holes in my back. There was no doubt what I was now. You know, I thought I would have regrets, but strangely enough I didn't.

I felt oddly at peace even as the soldiers slapped the iron around my neck and wrists then dragged me rudely toward the large group of Impals a short distance away. Yes, it was very uncomfortable, but I was able to shut it out with the peace of knowing that I had done what I had to do. I couldn't stop what was happening, not even with Major Garrison's help. I could have blown up the machine, but another one would have been brought in eventually with more security, and they would still carry out their plans of 'relocating' Impals. I would have just prolonged the inevitable. It may sound crazy, possibly even horrific to most, but I had achieved my objective. The only real objective I could see that would help my son. I thought briefly about Father Wilson's visit. I had not committed suicide any more than a soldier does when he is killed in battle. I had accomplished the same result but I was still awake.

The soldiers started to march me to the back of the line, which must have been a good half-mile long with only a foot of separation between each Impal. It was truly incredible; the scope of this terrible undertaking and that just increased the horror of it that much more. We had made it maybe 50 yards from the back of the massive line when we were met by Major Garrison. He was leading Seth on an iron leash like a dog, but at least he was being gentle.

I had gotten close enough to see Seth's exhausted face light up at the sight of me when an MP jeep screeched to a halt and two officers got out and threw Major Garrison to the ground. I heard a sickening crack as his nose met the tarmac. He was handcuffed then jerked to his feet. His face was blood-soaked due to his shattered nose, but he stood and looked at me for a few moments with a great look of satisfaction on his face. I think he would have saluted me if he had been able to. The moment didn't last long because he was quickly marched to the jeep and shoved viciously in the back. He made a single plea as one of the officers started to lead Seth away from me.

"For God's sake, that's his father! For the love of God, let them be together now!"

His words came out distorted and suppressed, due to copious amounts of blood in his throat and a broken nasal cavity, but the sheer earnestness and command left little doubt of what he was asking. The soldier leading Seth away turned and looked at the two soldiers escorting me. He shrugged and nodded his head for me to follow. I was rudely thrust forward and the lead soldier took both of our chains and led us to the far side of the line where we were placed like cattle going to slaughter.

I guess Major Garrison had been an honorable man after all, at least a lot more so than his father. I said a silent prayer for him, but then I turned my attention back to Seth and that's where it would remain until we entered the hangar and on to relocation or ... permanent death? I didn't know but I firmly pushed that thought aside because it would do me no good to dwell on it, not now.

It is truly amazing being an Impal. There are no physical infirmities to speak of. My back has not been completely pain-free for years. The iron was uncomfortable, and I guess that is to be expected since it is the only known substance that can restrain an Impal. I think the best thing is that this is the first time since our adventure started that Seth has felt normal to me. No icy touches, no arms or feet going through me; it was like he felt before ... well, when Ann was still here. I cried a few silvery tears of mixed joy and sadness when I squeezed Seth tight and when I thought of my absent wife. Would I possibly see her again ... waiting on the other side of the Tesla gate?

We were at the hangar door before we knew it. It seemed like it had only been a few minutes, but in actuality it had probably been an hour. The shredder was not hard to identify. It was a large arched opening in the middle of the room, about 20 feet high. The cold steel construction seemed almost symbolic of its cold purpose. Electrical arcs flicked like lightning between the two sides of the arch, making the opening seem like it was filled with bluish snow from a dead TV channel. I had the stupid thought of wondering if TV signals were working again, but that thought quickly disappeared as I saw a group of five Impals goaded through the arch.

Electricity arced momentarily on their iron constraints and then with a loud clang, the iron hit the ground and the Impals were gone. A metal grate in the floor opened to collect the discarded restraints and then closed back, ready to accept its next victims. It made me think of the trap door on a gallows.

I held Seth's face close to me so he couldn't watch. I talked to him about everything I could think of, told him how much I loved him, and we were going to take another trip. I felt like the same misleading jerk that I had been before, with all the promises I had made but never kept. We weren't going on a trip, but what else could I tell him? What happened next shocked me into silence. Seth may be naïve about some things, but he is also very perceptive. He reached over and squeezed my neck, kissed me on the cheek, and whispered in my ear.

"It's okay, Daddy, I love you, too. Thank you for taking me to the moozem."

At that moment I felt a gentle tap in my back from one of the soldiers. I turned and looked to see him staring at me with a sallow expression.

"It's time," he said in a voice barely audible above the crackle and hum of the Tesla gate.

I grasped Seth more tightly and slowly stepped forward. I didn't look at it but kept my eyes firmly focused on Seth. The hum and buzz grew louder and louder with each step. I started to feel a tingling sensation in my side closest to the arch like a part of me was slowly dissolving. It didn't hurt, but it was not enjoyable either. I closed my eyes, hugged Seth as tightly as I could, and stepped into the arch.

My plan had worked because I knew it was impossible to rescue Seth and for one man to stop what was happening. The very least I could do was to make sure that Seth was never alone again. Besides, I just don't think I could live without him again. It *was* the only foolproof plan. Whatever fate lay before us, we would be together – father and son.

ACKNOWLEDGMENTS

I would like to express my gratitude to the people who have supported and encouraged me over the years; to all those who provided support, talked things over, read, wrote, told me when my writing stunk, and also told me when it soared. These people are listed in no particular order; they have each had a significant hand in my development and without them this book would have not been possible.

I want to thank my wife, Aimee, who supported and endured me in spite of all the time it took me away from her. It has been a long and difficult journey for us.

I would like to thank my parents, Jerry and Kaye Mimms, for believing in me and encouraging me to follow my dreams, also for instilling in me a love of literature and reading.

I would like to thank my sons, Tyler and Luke, for giving me authentic insight to the father-son relationship, which is the heart of this book.

I would like to thank my fellow writer and good friend Marie D. Jones for all of her support and guidance; she is a truly generous and selfless person.

I would like to thank my fourth grade teacher, Marilyn Larson. A refrigerator box converted into a magical wardrobe served as the entrance to the reading area in our classroom and my imagination.

Special thanks to my agent, Italia Gandolfo, for seeing the potential in my writing and giving me my first 'yes,' which every aspiring writer hopes for.

Another special thanks to my publisher, Premier Digital Publishing, for giving me a chance. And thank you to my editor, Ann McKinley.

Last and not least: I beg forgiveness of all those who have been with me over the course of the years and whose names I have failed to mention.

ABOUT THE AUTHOR

John D. Mimms is a business owner, paranormal researcher, and author. Mimms served as the technical director for the Arkansas Paranormal and Anomalous Studies Team (ARPAST). During his four-year tenure with the organization, he helped supervise over one hundred investigations and wrote more than sixteen technical articles. One of his articles, titled "A Christmas Carol Debunked," was read live on Parazona Radio by Paul Bradford of Ghost Hunters International fame. Mimms also wrote the ARPAST technical training manual, which is a comprehensive guide on equipment usage, investigation protocol, and scientific theory for paranormal research.

In 2009, Mimms decided to couple his knowledge of paranormal phenomena with his lifelong love of literary fiction. Among his titles are *The Great Keep, Death Theory,* and *The Lemonade Girl.* He is currently working on book two of the Tesla Gate trilogy.

OPEN ROAD
INTEGRATED MEDIA

Open Road Integrated Media is a digital publisher and multimedia content company. Open Road creates connections between authors and their audiences by marketing its ebooks through a new proprietary online platform, which uses premium video content and social media.

PROPERTY OF
KENAI COMMUNITY LIBRARY

CPSIA information can be obtained at www.ICGtesting.com
Printed in the USA
LVOW11s2242070914

402929LV00003B/234/P